Sex and Other C

David Nobbs was born in Kent. After army, then tried his hand at journalism and advertising before becoming a writer. A distinguished novelist and comedy writer, he lives near Harrogate with his wife Susan.

Praise for David Nobbs

'He got where he is today by being very funny over a very long period of time' *Observer*

'He perfectly encapsulates the British sense of humour in all its many guises. Nobbs has a matchless ear for the rich absurdities of human life . . . His love of finding "comedy in the little things of life" is positively inspiring' *Daily Telegraph*

'A funny and moving exploration of the impact of our physicality on who we are' *Time Out*

'Playwright, comedy scriptwriter, and author of some of the finest humorous novels of recent years, David Nobbs has extended his range yet again, showing he can be just as funny writing about real events . . . Read all his novels you can lay your hands on, then read this book for a rare glimpse at the roots of comic inspiration' *Sunday Express*

'Like all the best comic novels, mixes sadness with laughter to great effect' *Independent*

'A bold novel . . . told with humour and courage' *Daily Mail*

'A highly readable and strangely affecting comedy of embarrassment, resentment, grief and love' *Sunday Times*

'One of the most noisily funny books I have ever read' Michael Palin

'Wry, gentle and funny autobiography' *The Times*

'Cleverly, deftly written and wonderfully funny' *Financial Times*

Also by David Nobbs

Sex and Other Changes

David Nobbs

arrow books

Published by Arrow Books in 2005

5 7 9 10 8 6 4

Copyright © David Nobbs 2004

First published in the United Kingdom in 2004 by William Heinemann

Arrow Books
The Random House Group Limited
20 Vauxhall Bridge Road, London SW1V 2SA

Random House Australia (Pty) Limited
20 Alfred Street, Milsons Point, Sydney, New South Wales 2061, Australia

Random House New Zealand Limited
18 Poland Road, Glenfield,
Auckland 10, New Zealand

Random House South Africa (Pty) Limited
Isle of Houghton, Corner of Boundary Road & Carse O'Gowrie,
Houghton 2198, South Africa

The Random House Group Limited Reg. No. 954009
www.randomhouse.co.uk

A CIP catalogue record for this book is available from the British Library

Papers used by Random House are natural, recyclable products made from
wood grown in sustainable forests. The manufacturing processes conform
to the environmental regulations of the country of origin

Typeset in Ehrhardt by SX Composing DTP, Rayleigh, Essex
Printed and bound in Great Britain by
Antony Rowe Ltd, Chippenham, Wiltshire

ISBN 9780099421658

For Susan

Acknowledgements

I cannot emphasise too strongly that this book is an entertainment and not a documentary. However, I have tried to get the facts about sex changes right, and in this connection I am greatly indebted to Dr D.H. Montgomery, MB ChB (Otago) FRANZCPsych FRCPsych, Consultant Psychiatrist, who worked for many years at the Gender Identity Clinic of Charing Cross Hospital. Any errors are due to my misinterpretation and not to his misinformation. (I must point out that my psychiatrist and my Gender Identity Clinic are totally fictional.)

I am also grateful to Roz Kaveney, who read the manuscript from the point of view of a transsexual and made several suggestions which I found very helpful.

I must also thank Geoffrey Lean and the *Independent on Sunday* for giving me permission to quote the article on sex changes among whelks which he wrote as Environment Correspondent of the paper in 1998.

I also owe a great debt to my agents, Jonathan Clowes and Ann Evans, and to my publisher and editor, Susan Sandon, for their trenchant but extremely constructive criticisms of my first draft.

Contents

1 Two Different Uses for Trees

People were shocked when it all happened. Afterwards, though, they claimed that they hadn't been surprised. That is so very Throdnall. The town's main products are railway carriages and hindsight.

'I always thought there was something *not quite right* about that marriage,' commented an osteopath's wife in the Warwick Bar of the Cornucopia Hotel in Brindley Street.

Where does the story of Nick and Alison Divot begin? In the womb, Alison would say, but we won't go back that far. Too much speculation and not enough action.

In childhood, then? Certainly Alison felt that her childhood was deeply significant. Her mum had told her, so many times, oh so many times till she was sick of it, how, when she was two, at tea, at Granny Huddersfield's, she had said, 'Why haven't I got a willy like the other boys?' How everyone had laughed. 'I wish I was a boy' became fourth in her top twenty childhood sayings, behind, 'Mummy, I'm bored', 'My tummy hurts' and 'Are we nearly there?'

Marge had never seen anything particularly significant in that remark at Granny Huddersfield's. She wouldn't have told the story if she had. Even Alison didn't realise its full significance. 'I wish I was a boy.' Well, a child has many wishes, a child has many heartaches and disappointments and learns to live with them, and Alison never said, 'I'm going to be a boy when I grow up.'

They weren't well off. Her father, Bernie, was a guard on the railways, and they lived on the wrong side of the tracks in the South Yorkshire town of Thurmarsh. Marge 'did' for a couple of families on the posher side of the town. She cycled to work.

They had two daughters. Alison was the elder by two years, and ruled Jen with a rod of iron. Alison was brighter than Jen. Jen was prettier than Alison. All the motives for civil war were there.

Jen was blonde, gorgeous, delicate, fluffy, self-righteous and devious, with the attention span of a hyper-active newt. Alison was dark, intense, passionate, tough, rough, gruff, hot-tempered, straightforward and an utter tomboy. Her greatest pleasure in life was hitting Jen. When her mother rebuked her, she retorted indignantly, 'But, Mum, that's what sisters are for.'

Alison believed herself to be utterly charmless. Tall, gawky, awkward, she was all of these, but no, she was not charmless. She loved the theatre, appeared in all the school plays. Her charm was in the passion in her eyes as she brought other people to life. Of course she was often cast in the male parts, to her mother's fury. 'Why couldn't Andrea Houseman have played Richard the Third? She's got a hump already.' Her charm was in the toss of her head as she climbed the scratty trees that lined the River Rundle. Her charm was in her honesty.

How lucky that her mother didn't 'do' for the Divots, in genteel, middle-class Upcot Avenue. How could Nick have fallen for his charlady's daughter?

Nick was an only child. His father, like Alison's, was in transport, but his transport was the stuff of Bernie's dreams. Daniel Divot was a purser on the cruise ships. Barbara Divot hated the sea. Nick was a mother's boy.

Nick and Alison saw each other once, actually, when they were both aged eight. It was a lovely summer's day. An artist had dotted the sky with just the right number of puffy white clouds. There was no breeze at all in the Divot garden, and just a faint zephyr up on the top of the sycamore that Alison had climbed. She had trespassed into the garden of the house next to the Divots. Nobody in Thurmarsh was better than Alison Kettlewell at climbing trees. She stood right at the top, like an overgrown stork, holding on with one hand. She was Queen Boadicea. She scanned the horizon for enemy troops. Nothing. The only person she could see was a thin, sandy-haired child in the next door garden, who was doing something very earnest and very boring with a book. She gave a great cheery holler and saw the child jump.

Nick was just about to press an oak leaf into a notebook when the holler startled him. He looked up and saw Alison. His eyes widened in amazement. He waved. To his horror she waved back so vigorously that she almost fell, clutched the top branch, and swung on it so violently that it seemed it must break. He was terrified that she would fall and he would have to do something. She wasn't frightened at all. Gradually, she regained her equilibrium, but not before he had broken out in a fine sweat.

A homing pigeon, en route from Hyde Park to Featherstone, flew past Alison. She reached as if to grab it, and gave a blood-curdling yell. Startled, it shat itself. A white stream descended into the Divot garden and fell plop all over the cover of Nick's notebook, on which he had written, in a careful childish hand, blissfully unaware of his spelling mistake, 'Thurmarsh and Evnirons – Summer 1964'.

The pigeon flew on, unaware of the tenuous initial link it had provided for the unusual love story of Nick and Alison.

Nick spent much of his childhood reading. His mother thought that he was literary, but he read because he preferred other people's lives to his own. His favourite book was *Tess of the D'Urbervilles*. He was drawn to its miseries like a gambler to the tables. He read it eleven times. His mother disapproved; she wanted him to read different books, she found his obsession unhealthy, so he had to read it in secret, which added to its appeal.

'Nick,' she said one day, 'I hope you aren't reading *Tess* again.'

'Of course I'm not,' he lied.

'You should find a real girl to be friends with.'

He looked at her in astonishment. How could somebody as experienced as a grown-up get something as wrong as that?

He had the sense not to tell her that he didn't keep reading the book because he loved Tess, that he read it because he was Tess.

He always used his father's postcards as bookmarks. 'I was so sad you weren't beside me as we steamed into the heart of Venice. Your trip to Filey sounded fun.'

It's hardly surprising that he was a late developer. One speech day, when he was sixteen . . . 'I'll be with you in spirit, old son. I'll think of you as I hunt out a little trinket for your mother in the souks' . . . as he was walking towards the hall with his embarrassingly overdressed mother, they overheard a boy say, 'Nick's so retarded he thinks Wanking is a town in China.' He met his mother's eye and blushed. 'I always was bad at geography,' he said. He had no idea whether she'd understood. He had no idea about anything, really.

Three weeks later, in the last week of term, he met Alison properly.

A fine summer's evening in Thurmarsh. In the cricket pavilion there was a meeting of the Thurmarsh Grammar School Bisexual Humanist Society, to debate the rather ambitious proposition 'Is unselfishness impossible?'

Nick's friend Prentice, a thickset, plump youth with a round face, had urged him to join. As they'd approached the pavilion for the first time, Nick had said, 'What am I doing here? Why are you bringing me here?'

'I want you to speak,' said Prentice. 'I want you to take part. I want to draw you out of yourself.'

'Why?'

'Because I'm your friend. Incidentally, it's about time you called me by my Christian name.'

'What is your Christian name?'

'Prentice.'

'Well, it'll be just the same as calling you by your surname.'

'It won't. I'll know. Will you do it, Nick?'

'All right then . . . Prentice.'

'Thank you.'

There were usually fewer than twenty people at these meetings. Nick had hated the first one, which had been on the subject 'Can tests on animals be justified?' He had been frightened that he would dare to speak. He had been trying to force himself to speak. He had only just failed – several times. It had been terrifying.

Gradually, however, through 'Should smoking be banned?', 'Does Socialism kill initiative?', 'Is philosophy a waste of time?' and 'Is marriage before sex too risky?' he had bravely come to terms with the fact that he would never dare to speak, and there was no need for him to dare to speak, and he had begun to enjoy sitting there anonymously in the pavilion with its faint unthreatening aroma of the stale sweat of generations of jockstraps.

Sometimes he would allow himself to dream that he was at the girls' school, that after the debate he would wander off with Prentice and they would . . . well, he could never bring himself to use the actual words even to himself. He had to be so careful, he thought, not to reveal any hint of this to Prentice, or he might lose the only friend he had.

On this occasion, however, Nick didn't have time to dream. He was entirely taken up with Alison. She spoke fluently, confidently, loudly, as if to a vast crowd that only she could see. She insisted that unselfishess was possible. True, she hadn't met any of it in her life, and none of it among her friends, but she gave examples of her own unselfishness as proof of the absurdity of the proposition.

Her speech did not go down well. Later speakers offered other motives for her apparently unselfish actions. Nick didn't care. It wasn't what she said that impressed him. It was how she said it. It was what she was.

He felt that she was speaking directly to him. He recognised that her confidence was bluster. He realised that her conceit was grown out of self–disgust. He knew that she was as lonely as he was, that she was as awkward with herself as he was with himself, that they were soul–mates. It wasn't love. It wasn't even sexual attraction. It was compatibility at first sight.

After she had spoken, he began to plan what he would say to her after the meeting: 'You were magnificent', 'You can inspire me to total unselfishness', 'I thought you were marvellous about the shortcomings of the rest of the world', 'I do totally agree about the awfulness of humanity', 'Your cynicism is excessive. I will prove it by being as unselfish as you', 'Would you like a milk shake?', 'Where have you been all my life?', 'Where have I been all your life?', 'Would you like to come and see my pressed ferns?', 'Have you read *Tess of the D'Urbervilles*?', 'My dad could get us on a Mediterranean cruise if you're interested', 'I don't suppose you'd fancy coming to my friend's father's camp site near Filey?' All were tried, weighed up, placed in a constantly varying order of possibility.

And then the meeting was over, and she strode out contemptuously, and he had to struggle past Prentice's thick legs and by the time he got out she was already striding away across the outfield of the cricket ground. A low sun made her shadow immensely thin and long.

Nick ran after her but, even though no match was in progress, he couldn't bring himself to walk on the outfield. He scurried round the boundary.

'Hey!' he cried.

She stopped and turned. At that time she was at least three inches taller than he was. He felt over-awed. All his opening gambits, so carefully rated from one to twelve, flew away. He could think of nothing to say. He approached her slowly. She stood there, mercilessly. In the nets, a ball thudded into a batsman's box. Behind them some wag had arranged the scoreboard to read 'Home Team 1176 for 2. Last man 617.'

His mouth was dry. His tongue was sticking to the side of his cheek. He found it almost impossible to speak at all.

He only spoke three words, and it's ironic to realise, with the hindsight for which Throdnall is so famous, that his statement, so apparently simple, was actually something in which he had no confidence, something which he didn't believe to be entirely true even then.

'Hello,' he said. 'I'm Nick.'

2 A Damper

Nick's mother was a snob. 'You'd think he was Captain of the *Queen Mary*, not a piddling purser on a crummy cruise line,' was the comment of her chiropodist. She wasn't liked in the shops. She thought that shopkeepers feared her. 'They see me coming,' she said proudly, 'and they cringe.' They did see her coming, but they didn't cringe. The greengrocer gave her the oranges that had been on the shelves too long and would soon go bad.

She was not the ideal mother for a boy who had the natural inclination to be a mother's boy.

Nick loved his father's postcards. 'You would have adored the Malacca Straits, old son.' His father seemed like a hell of a fellow, on deck, seeing the world. In Thurmarsh, on leave, he seemed smaller, less real. His shore leave always came in term-time. 'Holidays are synonymous with our peak periods, my boy.'

One day, just after his father had gone back to the ship, Nick asked his mother, 'Do you think Dad likes me?'

'Of course he does,' she said. 'He loves you.'

'Then why does he never invite me on the ship? Surely he could wangle a cruise?'

'He doesn't want you to see his other life,' hissed his mother through gritted teeth. She raised her hand to her neck in horror at what she had said. Her neck went red. She swept out of the room, slamming the door.

Everything in Nick's life propelled him towards Alison.

It would have been impossible to have invited his mother to Garibaldi Terrace, or to have taken Bernie and Marge to Upcot

Avenue. Nick and Alison's relationship grew in secret, and secrecy is heady stuff.

During their last year at school they went to several films and several concerts together. He preferred the films, she preferred the concerts. Sometimes they went to pubs. She liked pubs, he didn't. Eventually he did get to meet Bernie and Marge. Occasionally they went to the pub with Bernie, and even more occasionally with Bernie and Marge. Nick liked that. He felt more comfortable in the pub then. He felt he had his camouflage on. He dealt with the class divide by mocking it. 'Got your cloth cap, Bernie?', 'Ferrets locked up, Bernie?' Alison held her breath, but Nick had realised that Bernie found every joke funny as long as he featured in it, and the routine made Nick begin to feel, for the first time, that one distant day he might become a man of the world.

He no longer welcomed his father's cards. His father wrote, on his eighteenth birthday card, 'How I wish you were here to share the incredible views of Istanbul from the incomparable Bosporus, old son. What a shame this is such an important year of study for you.'

He tore the card into twenty-seven pieces – his best yet. He felt that if he'd controlled his anger he could have topped thirty.

Nick and Alison didn't have access to any place where they could make love without tension. To do it in Garibaldi Terrace would seem like a betrayal of trust. To do it in Upcot Avenue would be like suspending weightlessness on the moon. Neither of them minded this at all, though each pretended to.

The first time they spent a night in bed together was in Prentice's father's static caravan near Filey. They'd gone over there for a party. Prentice had said it was fancy dress. They'd gone as Helen of Troy and Achilles. Alison was used to dressing up and made a convincingly warrior-like Achilles. Nick was extremely shy and self-conscious about the whole thing. Somehow his unease made him disturbingly attractive as Helen. At the time they thought it all a great joke. Later, much later, looking back on it, they wondered how they could have been so naïve.

They only thought it a great joke until they arrived at the party to find that no one else was in fancy dress, not even Prentice.

'You are a bastard, Prentice,' said Alison.

'That's true,' said Prentice.

Nick and Alison got so drunk in their embarrassment that when they got to bed they fell asleep straightaway, and in the morning they were so hungover that they made straight for the toilets. Alison held Nick by the shoulders while he retched into the bowl. He found that extraordinary. He didn't think many women would have done that.

Would Nick and Alison ever have made love to each other, would they ever have married each other, if the driver of a white van hadn't fallen asleep at the wheel just two days after Daniel Divot had arrived home on shore leave?

It's impossible to know. The driver *did* fall asleep, Nick's parents *were* killed instantly, he *was* all alone in the world.

Oh he had uncles and aunts, and a granny with dementia near Knebworth, and cousins, but they were never close.

One of his uncles made all the funeral arrangements. Nick drifted through the nightmare, rudderless, steered by Alison. On the morning of the funeral she dressed him. In the church she held his arm and led him to and from his seat. At the funeral tea she held him when she thought he was going to faint. That night she fucked him for the first time.

They had woken up that morning as friends, chums, a bit more than platonic but a lot less than sexual. During that one day Alison became his father, his mother and his lover.

Where did they make love? Friends in Throdnall would find this difficult to believe, but it was on the back lawn of his parents' house, just beside the tool shed, under the stars, on a groundsheet (Nick was subject to chills of the kidneys as a young man). Mock ye not, though. Grief is a great aphrodisiac, and Nick was a fine and fervent lover that night, for all his inexperience. He turned his sorrow into love, and poured it into Alison.

The following week, Nick passed his driving test first time, to everyone's astonishment, and the week after that, heady with excitement and independence, he set off on what he called *La Grande Route de Sympathie*, or *Der Grossmitzgefuhlstrasse*. In other words, he drove round rural England in an elderly Ford Anglia which he was only just capable of controlling, and spent two nights at each of five different outposts of Divots. He returned with a multitude of vague offers of future support, but had met no great warmth. 'Divots tend to be good people, but they take some getting to know,' his Aunt Jessica warned him. Long before the end of his little trip, the excitement was a thing of the past, and independence seemed a lonely game. He proposed to Alison on the day of his return, and she accepted him. They were both eighteen.

The wedding was a quiet little affair. The loss of both Nick's parents forced it to be so.

He risked a break with his family by not inviting any of them. As he wrote to his Uncle Stanley, the unofficial leader of the tribe, 'If we invite anyone we have to invite everyone. We can't afford to invite everyone, so we're not inviting anyone. We hope you'll all understand.'

He relied on Uncle Stanley to pass the message round. He half hoped that somebody might say, 'Don't worry. I'll pay', but nobody did.

So Bernie and Marge were there, and a smattering of Thurmarsh friends, and Prentice, and Jen, and the registrar of course, and the photographer, and that was about it.

The men wore suits. Prentice, the best man, already showing intimations of obesity, told Nick, 'You look better in a suit than any eighteen-year-old should. You look as if you were made for suits.'

'Thank you.'

'It wasn't meant to be a compliment.'

Alison wore pink in the knowledge that she needed help to look feminine, but her dress was simple in view of the recent tragedy and of her temperament. Jen looked tactlessly gorgeous in virginal white, which Alison thought inappropriate and inaccurate. Anyone who had seen them on the steps of the register office would have assumed Jen to be the bride.

Marge, with Alison's permission, wore the dress in which she had got married to Bernie twenty-three years before. She could still get into it, but only just. Bernie, awkward in his shiny best suit, had tears in his eyes when he saw it.

'You still look a picture, love,' he said, 'and I don't mean no Picasso neither.'

'I hope so,' said Marge. 'I daresay it looks old-fashioned, but we have to put on a show for them. It'd all seem so straggly else.'

'Straggly?'

'Forlorn. They're marrying under a cloud. We've got to pull all the stops out.'

'Oh aye. We've got to pull all the stops out.'

So there was champagne at the reception, which was held in a small private room at the Midland Hotel, where they were watched over by photographs of railway engines from the golden age of steam, and there was a slap-up, sit-down breakfast of lobster, steak and Black Forest gâteau, washed down with lashings of Mateus Rosé. Nobody could say they weren't well done by.

Prentice made a short speech, full of tasteless references to the activities of the wedding night, references so oblique that luckily nobody understood them. Then he read out the telegrams. There were three.

' "Good luck – Uncle Stanley, Auntie Flo and all the Divots",' read Prentice.

'Very nice,' said Marge.

' "Don't do anything I wouldn't do. That leaves you quite a lot – Len Pickup",' read Prentice.

There was laughter, but not much.

' "Wish you could be sitting here beside me in heaven, old son – Dad",' read Prentice.

There was a stunned silence. Nick went white. His mouth opened but no sound came. He swooned. Alison grabbed his face before it crashed on to the table, and lowered it gently. He soon came round. Sweat poured off him.

Prentice sat with no expression whatever on his jowly face.

After the meal the drink flowed. Bernie went on to pints – 'I can't be doing wi' fancy drinks, me' – and the other men followed suit. Nick felt obliged to join in, though he hated pints. He just couldn't find room for all that liquid. And as the drink flowed, people moved around, and tongues were loosened.

'I hope it isn't an omen,' said Jen to Alison.

'You hope what isn't an omen?'

'That stupid telegram.'

'You hope it isn't an omen of what?'

'I don't know. Nothing.'

'You hope it isn't an omen of nothing. Well, that's brilliant.'

'You know what I mean.'

'Yes, I do know what you mean. You hope I'm not going to be happy.'

'That's a dreadful thing to say.'

Jen ran from the room in tears. Alison had to go to the Ladies' room to calm her and bring her back.

In the Ladies', Alison kissed Jen and said, 'Oh, Jen. I'm sorry. I'm sorry for all the things I've done to you. I've been horrid.'

'I deserved it,' said Jen. 'I resented you because you're clever.'

'I resented you because you're beautiful. You're so beautiful, Jen.'

They hugged each other and kissed each other and began to help each other repair their ruined make-up.

*

'Who's Len Pickup when he's at home?' asked Marge.

'He never is at home,' said Nick. 'He's a womaniser. He kept calling and trying to do odd jobs when Dad was at sea. He used to bring his tool box. It was enormous.'

'Did he get anywhere?' asked Bernie.

'Now then, Bernie,' warned Marge.

'With his tool box,' said Bernie. 'I'm talking about his tool box.'

'Nowhere,' said Nick. 'He mended a few fuses, but it'd be easier to get into Fort Knox than into my mum.' He blushed scarlet. 'Oh hell,' he said. 'I didn't mean . . . that wasn't . . . I . . . Oh Mum! I'm sorry.'

Marge leant across and kissed him, warmly, left her cheek on his for a moment. He was astounded. Nobody in his family had ever kissed him as warmly as that.

'I must go and see if those girls are all right,' she said.

Marge put her head round the door of the Ladies' and saw her two daughters standing at the washbasins and chatting and laughing like . . . like loving sisters.

'Come in, Mum,' said Alison. 'We were chatting about the hotels in Cyprus and that awful dirty old man on the beach.'

Marge entered. How typically British, she thought. We sit in silence on trains till three minutes before the terminus, when we begin to speak and discover that all the people we've been avoiding are extremely interesting. Alison and Jen had begun to talk properly for the first time two hours before Alison went off to lead a new life.

'It's nice in here,' said Marge.

'Go and tell the boys to come and join us, Jen,' said Alison.

While Marge was out of the room, Bernie approached Prentice.

'Why did you do it?' he asked.

'Joke,' explained Prentice. 'I'm training to be a comedian.'

'It wasn't funny,' said Bernie.

'No, I'm quite pleased about that, actually. A comedian has to overcome his fear of failure. I'm quite pleased with how I handled myself.'

'Not a thought for Nick's feelings, then.'

'We can't afford to consider the feelings of our audience. We're lost if we do.'

'Well, I thought it was very offensive, Prentice.'

'Probably. But then we're here to expand our boundaries.'

'I'd have expanded your boundaries if there hadn't been ladies present. I'd have punched you in the face if this wasn't a three-star RAC hotel.'

'Well, good, I got a reaction, then. It's indifference I dread,' said Prentice complacently.

Alison approached her mother and led her over to the window, which afforded a view over the railway line and the signalbox to the messy canal and river beyond. An Inter-City train was pulling out towards Sheffield.

'Mum,' she said. 'We don't want you to feel any of that losing a daughter nonsense. Our home will be your home always.'

'That's very nice of you, Alison,' said Marge, 'but you've got to put Nick first now, you know.'

'I've discussed it with Nick. He's in complete agreement.'

'Oh, it's been passed *nem. con.*, has it? That's nice.'

'What?'

'You sound like a management committee, not a young couple. It's very nice of you, but it's your wedding day, and you're emotional. Don't make rash promises.'

When Alison had moved off, Bernie sidled over to Marge. He touched her bottom briefly, put his arm round her waist, and looked out at the fading day.

'Well?' he said.

'What do you mean – "Well"? Well what?'

'Well, do you think it's gone well?'

'Well there've been almost more tears than at the funeral, but, weddings, that's par for the course.'

'It's all so quick.'

'Oh, I know. They're so young.'

'I know.'

'They know so little.'

'I know.'

'We know too much.'

'I know. I mean, he's very nice . . . *very* nice . . .'

'He is very nice. He's a triumph of the individual over the environment.'

'You what?'

'I read in the *Reader's Digest* – are people more shaped by their environment or their heredity? But there's no warmth in his family, and yet *he* has warmth. Where does it come from? Not from his environment *or* his heredity. From him. It comes from him. There is nowhere else.'

'I see what you mean. Oh aye. He's a triumph of the individual over the environment when you look at it that road. It's just . . . we . . , well . . . I think there's summat a bit . . . a bit odd about it all.'

'Odd?'

'Not quite right.'

'Oh dear. Not quite right in what way?'

'I don't know. It's just a feeling. Summat not quite right.'

'Oh dear. About him?'

'No, not really.'

'About Alison?'

'No, not really. About . . . them. Him and her together. I hope I'm wrong.'

'I'm sure you are.'

'I expect I am. It's probably that telegram. It's cast a damper.'

3 A Revelation in a Popular Store

On her thirteenth wedding anniversary, Alison had a blinding revelation. It didn't occur on the road to Damascus, but in Marks and Spencer's, in Throdnall, in the menswear department.

When she got home, she sat at the dining table and wrote to her sister in Sydney.

> 33, Orchard View Close
> Throdnall
> Warwickshire TL2 5XJ

Dearest Jen,

I had a revelation this morning, in Marks and Sparks of all places. I decided I needed some shirts, and I walked into the menswear department, and started looking at the shirts, and suddenly I thought, 'No, Alison. Wrong!' I'd forgotten, in a dreamy, confused moment, that I was a woman. I just stood there, stunned, among all the dully displayed rows of trousers and jackets (Throdnall isn't Milan). And I thought, 'Alison, this is ridiculous. You've read about those sex change operations. You can have one. You don't have to be a woman for ever. You can do something about it.'

A great excitement swept over me. You remember how fearless I used to be? My spirit's been rather ground out of me by matrimony and motherhood – but it's still there.

An assistant approached me and said, 'Can I help you, madam?', which was a little miracle in itself in Throdnall, and I said, 'Not with what I need, no,' and went over to the women's department and bought some sensible blouses for my new job. I start work on Monday as Personal Assistant (do you have that title in Australia?) to the MD of Throdnall Carriage Works, and I've been getting nervous. Me, nervous? How far I've sunk!

Now, of course, with the prospect of a far greater change, I don't feel nervous about my job at all. The old Alison is back – ironically, she's back because she's realised that she doesn't have to be Alison for ever!

I can hear you thinking, 'I know she was always a bit of a tomboy, but sex change?? Why?? What's she referring to when she says, "I can do something about it"? About what?'

About my situation, Jen. About my agony. About all the things that I have never mentioned in any of my letters, which have been minor masterpieces of evasion.

I know that this will all come as an enormous shock to you, Jen, and to Bruce . . .

She paused to allow herself a little smile, in which affection was mingled with contempt. It was somehow symbolic of Jen's lack of originality – she had never had an original thought in her life, as far as Alison knew – that the Australian she had married should be called Bruce.

. . . but I hope in the end you'll quite like the idea of having a brother!

Don't be alarmed, Jen. Nothing's going to happen in a hurry. I'm going to need to do an awful lot of research. I couldn't possibly do it till Emma and Graham are a lot older. I rather doubt if I could do it while Mum's alive. (She's looking older suddenly, and thinner, which worries me, but you know what she's like, she won't go to the doctor, she says, 'They've enough on their plate without worrying about me', which is ridiculous.) So, please, Jen, you must promise not to mention a word of this in your letters to Mum and Dad.

I've had a dreadful recurring dream, Jen, all my life as long as I can remember. I dream that I'm in the womb, assuming that I'm going to be born a boy. Sometimes I wake up at that point and am absolutely mortified when I remember I'm a woman. I reach down to say a friendly good morning to my prick, and there isn't one! Other times the dream goes further and I am going through the process of being born – horrid, messy, what a shock – and everyone looks at me and screams, even Mum screams. That's so terrible, Jen, I wake crawling with sweat. Sometimes it takes me hours to forget Mum's screams.

I know how proud you always were of your breasts. I'm ashamed of mine. I hate them. I think of them as aliens, sometimes I've felt I could chop them off with a kitchen knife, I've felt frightened to be in the house on my own for fear I'll do myself a dreadful injury. I know that sounds mad, but my incarceration in a female body *has* been driving me mad.

Somehow I don't think I'll ever feel as desperate as that again. The knowledge that there is an escape, that one day I can change, I can become me at last, is amazing.

Now that I'm into confession mode I may as well tell you that all is not well with our marriage. Hardly surprising, really, under the circumstances. I mean on the surface we seem pretty happy, I suppose – I don't think the kids suspect anything – but we haven't made love since I got pregnant with Gray. Things tailed away quite a bit after Em, actually. I think Nick blames himself. Sometimes he goes to bed early and pretends to be asleep when I go up, sometimes he works late in his study, invents work, I think, or reads – he's so much more of a reader than I am – and creeps up late so as not to wake me, and *I* pretend to be asleep. It's a farce. I long to tell him that I don't mind, that I don't want sex with a man any more, that I hate the submissive gesture of opening my legs, that it's all right with me that we don't have sex, but I can't. Not till I pluck up the courage, one day, to tell him that I'm going to become a man. I can just imagine his face.

How silly we were to spend so much of our youth fighting. Life's difficult enough without putting obstacles between us. Jen, darling, I miss you so much, I no longer feel remotely jealous of your beauty. I'm so proud of you, I need you, please write back a proper letter, please let's be close as we never really were, and have no secrets from each other ever again.

I do hope you and Bruce are well, also of course Craig and Kelly.

Your loving sister (but not for ever!)

Alison

Just as she was beginning to address the envelope – she found it difficult to think of Jen as Mrs J. Hackenburger – she heard the back door slam.

She went through to the kitchen and gave Em a hug. Em at ten was going through a really sweet phase.

'Love you, Mum,' said Em.

Three innocent words. Two of them warmed her heart. The third stuck a dagger into it. Mum. It came as a shock after all she'd been writing.

She made herself a cup of coffee while Em piled two scones with butter and Marmite.

'Your hand's shaking, Mum.'

'It is, isn't it? Did you learn anything interesting at school today?'

'Not really. Why's your hand shaking, Mum?'

'I must have been thinking about rather frightening things.'

'What frightening things?'

'Oh, things from a long way away, Em. Wars and things.'

'Oh. I don't think there should be wars, Mum.'

'Nor do I, Em.'

'If we can see that, why can't everybody? Are they stupid?'

'No. I'm afraid there are some wicked people in this world of ours, Em.'

'I know. Sandra Copeland, for one. She pulled my hair again today, the cow.'

Alison smiled. It was a weary smile. She realised, looking at Em in all her innocence, what a long time it would be before she could begin her sex change. She felt sad, but calmer than she had felt for a long time.

She went back into the dining room, sat at the table, picked up her letter to Jen, read it with the speed-reading techniques she'd learnt at a course in Luton, sighed, stood up, fetched a box of matches, lit a candle (she'd make the table really pretty, this evening, for their first anniversary dinner in the house) and held the candle to the letter. When it had all been reduced to ashes, she swept it carefully into the Habitat waste-paper basket, seated herself at the table again, sipped her instant coffee, grimaced, and began to write another letter.

33, Orchard View Close
Throdnall
Warwickshire TL2 5XJ

Dear Jen,

This has to be hurried as it's our wedding anniversary. I'm making Dover Sole, Nick's favourite. I start my new job next week, went to Marks and Sparks today and bought some blouses. Very sober and sedate. Not me at all. I've been appointed PA to a man called Clive Beresford. He's the big wheel behind Throdnall Carriage Works. It's quite a job to have landed and a big increase in pay. He asked me if I was going to have any more children. I said, 'No, we've one of each and they're fine and we're happy with that,' and he said, 'Excellent. Keep taking the precautions,' and I said, 'I will!'

I must say we are lucky. Em is lovely and Gray is very bright.

She didn't think Jen was clever enough to deduce from that that Gray wasn't at all lovely, and they weren't sure if Em was bright.

Things are going very well at the hotel. Nick was very bucked this week. The local rag called it 'The jewel in the Throdnall crown'. The manager has to retire next month, he'll be sixty-five, and Nick has high hopes of promotion. We'll see.

Sorry this is so brief. Where does all the time go?

Lots of love from us all to you all.

Alison (and Nick, of course)

Jen didn't send letters, just cards and an odious round robin at Christmas. 'Craig is the best outside half Mr McWilliams has ever seen at seven years old. We gave Kelly a violin for her fourth birthday. Mrs Carstairs says you can't hold a prodigy back.'

She dreaded the day when Craig and Kelly would turn up on their gap years with their gap teeth and their outdoor smiles and their irritating suntans and their bloody violins and rugby balls.

Well, she'd have a shock for them. She'd be their Uncle Alan.

She tried to make the table look stylish with flowers and candles, although she knew that on the rare occasions when he cooked Nick did that sort of thing much better.

The room still looked bare, without any pictures on the walls, and that scratty sub-Laura Ashley wallpaper would have to go, and it was a pity there still weren't any curtains to draw, but never mind, they'd make their own atmosphere.

Nick brought roses, lovely roses, kissed her on the cheek, said, 'Nice day?', and she found it so difficult to resist replying, 'Not bad. Bought some blouses. Decided to change sex. You?', but all she said was, 'Quiet. How about you?'

'Not bad. Brian remembered it was our anniversary and asked me what we were doing. I said, "We're eating in the best restaurant in Throdnall." '

This was so untypical of Nick that it fooled Alison for the moment, and she said, 'Oh. You should have told me. I've gone and got fish.'

'Idiot,' he said affectionately. 'That's what I meant. Your cooking makes it the best restaurant in Throdnall.'

'Oh. Well, thank you.'

'Not that there's much opposition in Throdnall.'

'Oh. Terrific. I thought you meant it.'

'I did. Oh, darling, I did. I didn't mean that your cooking isn't worth a compliment. I meant that the way I put it wasn't exactly a compliment since there's nowhere good to eat in Throdnall.'

'Oh Nick.'

'What?'

'You have a wonderful way of spoiling the nice things you try to do.'

'Oh. Terrific.'

'Oh, don't worry. It's one of the things I like about you.'

'I see.'

'Were they selling the flowers off cheap because they were closing?'

'No! They weren't. I'd have told you if they had been.'

'See what I mean!'

Em went to bed as good as gold, and said, 'Have a lovely anniversary dinner, Mum, Dad,' and they spent a few happy minutes with her. You have to cherish the moments when your children are sweet, they won't last for ever.

Gray was demanding. Just one more story. How can I get to sleep? I'm not tired. It's not a crime not to be tired, is it? Little bugger, master of the double negative already, and he knew they were longing to get him to sleep. Six years old, and already you couldn't fool him.

At last peace reigned. Nick took a sherry into the lounge, and Alison cooked the sole. Everything else was ready in the hostess trolley. She was glad Nick wasn't in the kitchen. She could enjoy her massive new secret. She knew that when she was with him she would begin to feel uneasy at having to keep it secret.

She hated the kitchen with its hideous cheap units with shiny blue doors, but it was because of things like that that they'd got the house cheap. As she cooked she was planning the changes she would make. She would pour into their new home all the frustration she felt at having no artistic outlet. Should she have tried the stage? 'Why didn't you, Mum?' Em had asked when she'd talked about her school plays. She didn't like to say, 'Because I always got the male parts, so as a pro I'd have got no parts.'

Everything came back to gender all the time.

The sole was done to a turn. The Pouilly-Fuissé was delicious.

What a job she had to keep her exciting news to herself.

Nick went slightly pink and she realised that he was going to say something important.

'I've an interview at Head Office next Tuesday.'

'Oh!!'

'Brian says he's recommended very strongly that they give it to me.'

'Is that good news or bad news?'

'That's the trouble, I don't know; but I mean I did run the hotel for a week when Brian had flu, and I think I steered a pretty good course between the Scylla of Authoritarianism and the Charybdis of Laissez-Faire.'

'I hope you won't put it like that to Head Office,' said Alison drily.

'Why? I thought it was rather good.'

'Oh, Nick, you're so unworldly. They won't share your knowledge of Greek mythology. They'll think you're talking about Cilla Black and some band they've never heard of.'

'If I do get made manager, and with your new job, it's going to be quite a time of change.'

Oh Nick, thought Alison. Don't give me cues like that. She had to grit her teeth to remain silent. Then she thought, Why should I remain silent?

'I went to Marks and Sparks today,' she said.

'And?'

'I . . . bought some blouses.'

'Ah.'

'Sober and subtle.'

'Good.'

She let out a deep sigh very slowly, so that he wouldn't notice. The moment of danger had passed.

They settled down with a celebratory Armagnac at either side of the log-effect fire. He buried his nose in a book. Opposite him, in the Parker Knoll, she studied interior design ideas.

The sitting room was still bleak too. They had not yet fully occupied their new home. They only had one painting, of dahlias, by his Aunt Jessica. It had been a house-warming present. There were ghastly little lantern lights on the walls, reminiscent of a pub with a Tudor theme. They'd have to go.

'Do you mind if I go on up?' she asked, shortly after eleven o'clock.

'Not at all,' he said. 'Do you mind if I try and finish my book?'

'Of course not,' she said. How polite they were, she thought with a grimace, for their anniversary. 'What are you reading?'

'*Tess of the D'Urbervilles*. I really want to know how it ends. Spins a good yarn, Hardy.' Well, she didn't know that he'd read it eleven times before he was sixteen.

She went upstairs with a silent yelp of relief, stripped off, washed between the hated breasts, washed around the loathsome crutch, crept into bed and dreamt of manhood.

She was only vaguely disturbed when he slid carefully in beside her. She dropped off again almost immediately, but it was an uneasy sleep, and in the morning she realised that she must have been dreaming at a very shallow level, because she seemed to recall that he had been sobbing his heart out there beside her, and that must have been imagination.

4 Unlucky Molluscs

'Alison?'

There was something in Nick's tone that made Alison's heart beat much faster. She straightened up from the dishwasher. They'd had vegetarian moussaka. Em was going through a veggie phase, and there was no reason why Alison should cook a separate meal for her, so quite often they all had a veggie meal. Gray moaned . . . well, he moaned for Warwickshire . . . but there was never anything left on his plate.

'Yes, Nick?'

'Could we . . . go through and have a chat?'

What could he be on about? He sounded ominously serious.

'Let me finish the dishwasher and get a coffee. Do you want a coffee?'

'No, no.' He waved the question away as intolerably trivial, then realised that sounded rude, so he added, 'No. No thanks. Sorry.'

He went through, and she finished loading in her own good time. Whatever Nick's crisis was, it could wait. It was his fault she was taking so long. He knew her back was stiff, but he never offered to do the dishwasher. 'I don't like this new one. It's badly designed,' he'd said. 'I just can't get the hang of the top shelf.' Excuses excuses.

Em was out with her boyfriend as usual, this one seemed serious. Gray was surfing the net as usual, that was serious, they'd lose him to the world if they weren't careful. Bernie was sitting in the granny flat with poor old Marge as usual. Everything was as usual, except Nick's tone of voice.

She made the coffee and took it through, handed Nick his, put hers on the garden bird coaster on the smallest table from the nest of tables, and sat in the Parker Knoll. It was well past its sit-by date, but they were reluctant to let it go; they'd had it at Cranbourne Gardens and at Eckersley Crescent.

This scene would be etched in Alison's memory for a very long time. Their cool, cream sitting room looked so placid. The log-effect fire was burning merrily. There were four pictures now, Aunt Jessica's dahlias having been joined by three more originals, which made it pretty stylish for Throdnall. One was a bold, bright Scottish landscape by John Morrison Lowry, who signed his name Jolomo. Another was a windswept picture of Bernie's beloved Dales by Richard Bolton. The fourth was a Hungarian landscape by Ferenc Gulyas, Nick's assistant manager. It was too tortured for a sitting room, but he had come round with it as a surprise present for their twentieth anniversary, and he might come round again, so they felt they had to hang it.

'I've something to read to you, old girl,' said Nick.

Alison hated that phrase. She was only thirty-nine, for God's sake, and soon she would begin the process of ceasing to be a girl. She knew that it was a reflection, probably unconscious, of something his father used to say, but oh Lord it was patronising, it was so slippers and leather patches on the elbows, so oldest member of the public school common room, so coated with the dust of a blessedly forgotten England.

He picked up a broadsheet, cleared his throat, and began to read.

' "Hope for sex change whelks".'

She gawped at him. She felt that she must have looked like a mullet that has got stranded on the North York Moors. Her first thought was that he had discovered that she was planning a sex change; maybe he had found one of the books that she had borrowed from the library. She'd thought they were safe enough in the dark cupboard behind the flour and the bicarbonate of soda – he never baked – but he must have discovered them.

' "Spare a thought for the sex-change dog whelks",' he read.
' "Tomorrow will decide their fate." '

'How long have you known?' she asked.

'Known?' he said. 'I don't quite know what you mean. About the whelks? Only since last week when I read about them and, I don't know, I thought maybe if I introduced the subject via whelks, because this isn't at all easy for me, Alison, and I know it's not going to be easy for you, that it might make it a little easier. I think you can guess what I'm driving at. Don't make it too difficult for me, Alison.'

Fury followed her amazement. It hadn't taken her long to realise that he was telling her that *he* was planning to change sex. She just couldn't believe it. Her mind was in a whirl. She felt outraged that he could have so little understanding of what she had been thinking, so little knowledge of her. She was damned if she'd make this easy for him.

'Go on,' she said grimly.

'Go on?'

'About those poor whelks.'

He didn't want to go on. The whelks had served their purpose, or rather they had failed to serve their purpose. They hadn't made things easier. He wanted to get it all over and done with.

'Read on,' she commanded. 'It's interesting.'

' "Representatives of the world's governments are meeting to decide whether to ban a chemical used to coat the bottoms of ships which is causing female dog whelks to grow penises, thus endangering the species. The chemical is also building up in other sea life and has been found in people who eat fish." '

'I'll never go to the Throdnall Whaler again.'

'Alison! Take this seriously! Please!'

'I *am* taking it seriously, Nick. I'm devastated for those poor whelks. Go on. You can't stop now. I'm riveted.'

What could he do?

' "Dog whelks, which mainly live on beaches between the high and low tide marks, have long been one of Britain's commonest seaside creatures. But they have disappeared from large areas because of their bizarre transformation.

' "Scientists collecting whelks discovered to their surprise that they could only find male ones. Close inspection revealed that half were females who had unaccountably grown penises.

' "The scientists suspected that tributyltin, the anti-fouling paint most widely used on the hulls of boats and ships, was to blame. Sure enough, when they painted the shells of unfortunate females with the chemical, penises sprouted and grew to alarming lengths.

' "The sex change females cannot mate, and die painfully if they do before the transformation as their new penises block the ovary ducts where their eggs go on growing inside them until they explode." '

Alison stood up.

'This is terrible,' she said.

He realised that it was. He'd only intended to use the first paragraph. As he read on, he realised that it was an utterly disastrous introduction to the advantages of having a sex change.

She went to the window, which afforded an excellent view of number thirty-eight opposite, its mock-Tudor frontage glowing in the sad sodium light of an autumn evening in Throdnall. She noticed that the window frames needed painting. She wondered if the Parkers were over-stretching themselves financially. Anything to give her emotions a breathing space as they fought to respond to this extraordinary development.

She would not make things easy for him. She decided to pretend deep outrage on behalf of the whelks, and, to be fair to her, although she couldn't be described as a whelk lover, she did feel sorry for the poor bemused molluscs.

She turned away from the window at last.

'Those poor whelks,' she said.

'For God's sake shut up about the whelks,' he said. Yes, he knew it was ridiculous. She didn't need to say, 'Well, you started it.' Her angry look said it for her. 'As far as I'm concerned, the whelks can go fuck themselves.'

They were both amazed to hear Nick use the f-word. Normally he hated it. He regarded its constant repetition as evidence of extreme paucity of imagination. The kitchen staff mocked him for it, though not to his face.

'Fuck themselves? That's the only thing the wretched sods can do, you callous bastard!' yelled Alison. She poured out her anger on him, her anger at being upstaged, her fury that he had got in first, her frustration that her intentions had been trumped. She approached him and for a moment he thought that she was going to hit him. He flinched.

'Those poor creatures – forced to live their lives on beaches between the high and low tide marks while we're swanning off to Majorca – the scientists discover the paint is destroying their sex lives, so what do they do? Ban the paint? No! They paint more whelks. Bastards!'

He had rarely seen Alison so angry, and all about whelks!

'They have to be cruel to some whelks in the short term in order to be kind to other whelks in the long term,' he said. He knew that he was sounding more absurd by the minute. He felt that they might go on and on arguing about whelks for ever.

She moved away. He swallowed. He'd have to abandon whelks and start all over again.

And at that moment Bernie shuffled in. His white designer stubble looked ridiculous at seventy-seven. There was an egg stain on the front of his shirt.

'I'm not interrupting, am I?' he asked, and didn't wait for an answer. (Typical, thought Nick. He never waits for an answer. God, he drives me mad. I must remind myself to remain aware of other people when I grow old.) 'Only she wants a cuppa, and we're out of tea-bags.'

They had facilities in the granny flat, but he ran out of things deliberately, so as to have an excuse for company.

'Only Doctor Rodgerson said to her, "Marjorie, you should get as much liquid running through you as you can. Flush those insides out." I'm hoping the *Nine O'Clock News*'ll send her to sleep. Last night John Major was defending the morality of the government, bless him, and she dropped off nicely.'

Alison went into the new kitchen. It was a friendly affair with free-standing wooden units. It had been designed by her and built by 'Cuisines de Throdnall'. It was attractive and user friendly, if a little phonily rural, matching the name of their road.

Bernie shuffled through behind her. He didn't raise his feet properly any more. Nick followed him.

'Nights are pulling in,' said Bernie.

'That's extremely observant of you, Bernie,' said Nick.

Neither Alison nor Nick could believe that Nick had said that. Alison looked at him in horror. He met her look and shook his head slightly in wonderment at his own insensitivity.

They needn't have worried. Nick's sarcasm washed over Bernie.

'Well, they are,' he said. 'I hate the autumn, me. Sod the glory of the Fall in New England. It's all damp, decay and death in Old Warwickshire.'

He had never accepted moving from Yorkshire and blamed Nick and Alison for living in Warwickshire; that was the thanks they got for providing Bernie and Marge with a home.

'Gray in his room?' said Bernie. 'That boy spends too much time on his own.'

'Thanks, Bernie,' said Nick, 'but he is only fourteen.'

'Sorry I spoke,' said Bernie. 'Em out? That girl goes out too much. She's never in.'

'Have you ever thought of writing a book about how to be a good parent?' asked Nick.

'Sorry I spoke.'

Alison said nothing during these exchanges, just touched her dad lightly, affectionately, a gesture of solidarity: she and he against the monster, Nick, the sarcasm addict.

At last Bernie shuffled off with his tray of tea and the swish swish of his slippers. Alison and Nick returned to the lounge, which she called the sitting room. He had to do it quickly this time.

'I'm going to change sex, Alison,' he said.

Because he did it so quickly it came out all wrong. It sounded far too casual, as if he'd said, 'I think I'll pop up to the Coach for a pint' (not that he ever did).

'I know,' she said drily. 'I did pick up the point about those whelks.'

'I have to,' he said. 'I'm a woman trapped in a man's body. I can't stand it any more. I hate myself as I am, Alison. I bloody hate myself.'

To her fury, Alison felt tears springing to her eyes. They couldn't be. She didn't do tears. Even when she fell from a tree she had never cried. You couldn't climb trees if you cried when you fell off.

She'd known that there was hatred in Nick. She'd thought some of it was for Throdnall and for his job and for his failure to go to university, but she had begun to think that some of it at least had recently been for her.

She couldn't stop the tears. They overwhelmed her. She cried as someone would cry who hasn't cried for years. For the last seven years she had planned her sex change and kept her vast secret. Now this had happened. It was too much.

He hugged her, held her tight. It was natural that she should cry, and she might have forgiven herself for it eventually. What she could never forgive herself for was what she said.

'I thought it was *me* you hated.'

Oh the odiousness for her of his discovery of her weakness. She'd have been angry, after saying that, even if he hadn't spoken the four worst words he could possibly have chosen to comfort her.

'There there, old girl,' he said.

She broke away as if stung, and hit him, hit him hard, a stinging slap on the cheek.

Women really are the most extraordinary creatures, he thought. How strange it is that I'm desperate to become one.

5 The Dog-Leg Ninth

The moment he'd left the room she tried to think about those poor whelks. Anything to take her mind off the crashing of her dream.

She still hadn't grasped what the hope was that could have justified that headline, 'Hope For Sex Change Whelks'. She felt, in an obscure way, that if she could concentrate on the whelks' hopes, it might help to give her hope.

Ah! The hope was, apparently, that the paint which caused the sex change might be banned from the bottom of boats. Good. She hoped so. Fervently, she hoped so.

The good news about the whelks didn't cheer her up as much as she had hoped. She had to get out of the house. There was a tightness across her head, which was throbbing. She understood, for the first time, just what it must feel like to be claustrophobic.

She went up to the master bedroom, which felt cold and starved of sex. She changed into a pair of jeans, a sweater and a thick anorak. Autumn nights in Throdnall could be sneaky.

He was in the kitchen, sipping a mug of cocoa. When he saw her he ran his hand across his cheek where she had slapped him. She knew that he had no idea that he was doing it.

'I'm popping out,' she said.

'Out?' he repeated incredulously.

'Out.'

'It's gone ten.'

'I need to clear my head, Nick. I've had a shock. You must realise that.'

'Yes, but it's not safe.'

'This is Throdnall, not New York.'

'Nowhere's safe these days.'

'Nobody's going to attack me, Nick.'

'I don't want you to go.'

'I don't want you to change sex, which I'd have thought was a bit more important than a nocturnal walk.'

She opened the back door and drank in the air greedily.

She walked down Orchard View Close and turned right into Badger Glade Rise, where no badger had risen from a glade since it had been built. Nature had been swept away, and commemorated in the street names to make the area sound attractive. Nobody would buy the houses if the addresses were Bovis Home Prospect and Bungalow Tedium Drive. How ingeniously our world fools itself, thought Alison with healthy contempt.

At the end of Badger Glade Rise she turned left into Spinney View, where there had been no view of . . . well, you get the idea.

At the end of Spinney View stood the Coach, trim with hanging baskets, cheery with subdued lighting, humming with idle talk, throttled by parked cars.

She walked towards it. She was gagging for a pint. What? 'Gagging for a pint'? She was a mother of two. Mothers of two don't gag for pints.

She hesitated. Dare she go in? If she was a man . . . when she was a man . . . oh God, would she ever be a man after tonight? . . . she would walk in, cheerfully order a pint, sit in a cosy corner, chew a peaceful and wide-ranging cud, take her glass back and say, 'Goodnight.'

'Goodnight, Alan.'

Alan!

If she went in now, people would turn and stare. They would speculate. 'Had a bit of a bust up with the old man, do you think?', 'A pint! Good Lord!', 'Looks tense. Something's wrong', 'Not too bad a looker. I suppose a fuck's out of the question.'

No, she wouldn't go in.

Oh Alison Heather Divot, née Kettlewell (39), of no fixed gender, has your youthful bravery descended into this?

But it wasn't for lack of courage that she wouldn't go in . . . Oh, Alison, is this what you've become – the Queen of the Double Negatives, the 'Is Unselfishness Impossible?' girl? . . . It was because there was no point in going in. Since she would get no peace, her visit would not avail her.

She retraced her steps down Spinney View, continued into Elm Copse Crescent, and went down the ginnel to the back end of the golf course. She saw no other human beings, and all the while her mind was racing.

Should she have told Nick straightaway that she was planning a sex change? Had she wasted her best opportunity? Had she already condemned herself to silence and long suffering?

But what could she have said? How could she have put it without sounding pathetic? She couldn't have said, 'Hang on a minute, I thought of it first.' She didn't even know if she had thought of it first. She had no idea how long his great plan had been festering in secret. She couldn't have said, 'Well I'm changing sex too. Shall we toss to see who goes first?' She couldn't even have said, 'Good Lord! So am I, but after you.'

Once your thunder is stolen it's ineffectual to raise a storm. There was no way in which she could have responded to Nick's pre-emptive strike with dignity.

Besides, she knew that she would never be able to begin the process while her mum was alive, and her mum was in remission, they all knew that.

So, actually, once the shock had died down, nothing need really be changed.

She had to put her plans on hold and help Nick with his. It was the only rational course, the only decent course, the only dignified course. She would hurry home and . . .

Would she hell as like? Let him sweat. Let him pay for his pre-emptive strike. Let him pay for his monstrous, typically male . . . no, she didn't believe that, that was stereotypical sex war propaganda . . . let him pay for his monstrous, typically Nickish, painfully Divotish failure to even consider what was going on in her mind. She strode on, she would walk on and on until dawn. He would send out search parties. She would be found in a ditch suffering from hypothermia, hypotension and hyperbole, he would be mortified, he would begin to appreciate her and . . .

No. That was so unfair. She stopped by the woods that lined the left-hand side of the dog-leg ninth. She had taken an eight there only last month. A quadruple bogey. 'I had a quadruple bogey last week too,' Gray had said. 'It was in my left nostril.' Why did boys have to be so disgusting? Why hadn't she been allowed to be disgusting?

It all came back to gender. Round and round it went. Back it came.

No, she must hurry home and enter a world of irony that only she would understand. She, so desperate to become a man, would have to play the part of the little woman, the supportive wife. She'd done it for twenty years, what did one or two more matter? 'Home, James, and don't spare the horses,' as her dear old dad said.

So why was she shinning up a hornbeam, in the light of a waning moon and the sodium half-light that surrounded the polluting town? Up up and up with all the old certainty of youth, footholds where none other could have seen them, up up and up.

Closing time in the Coach. Slamming of car doors far away in the stillness of the night. The sex call of a diesel train as it approached a level crossing. Up up and up. You're a big girl now, Alison. Will the topmost branches hold your weight?

She gave a great yell, a yell to freeze the blood of weasels, part anger, part defiance, part glory in the power of her lungs. Up it went, her great yell, up, up and up, towards the Milky Way, so sadly dim in the light from the town.

Oh what an actor she would have made, with her voice, if she'd been born a man.

'Friends, Romans, countrymen, lend me your ears,' she cried over the dark, deserted golf course. 'I come to bury Caesar, not to praise him.'

What a Mark Antony she would have made.

'The evil that men do lives after them.'

Maybe I will be Mark Antony yet, when it's all over. I could join the Throdnall Players, find out if I really can be any good.

'The good is oft interred with their bones.'

Her as Mark Antony opposite Nick as Cleopatra. Now there was a thought. Her mood was swinging like the branch of the hornbeam as she sought to balance it. She gave a tomboy's whoop, a teenage war cry. Somewhere to the right, over beyond the par five fourteenth, a sex-starved vixen replied to her. She laughed, the branch snapped with a crack like a rifle shot, and vixens ran for cover. She was falling, mother of two, PA to the MD, hurtling towards a broken leg, well-paid job up the spout, irresponsible mother, so childish. She clung, slithered, tore her hand, scratched her arm, jammed her feet, flung her arms round a branch like a desperate lover. She was safe. Bruised, cut, shocked, but safe.

She dropped to the ground and limped up the fairway towards the green. She felt suddenly weary. She lowered herself gingerly on to the grass and lay on her back, looking up at the stars, there on the ninth green. Her hands were stinging. Her toes were bruised. Her shoulder was aching. She had behaved ridiculously.

The grass was sodden with dew, but she wouldn't catch cold, she was tough. She alarmed herself by thinking how peaceful it would be to die here.

That wouldn't do. She leapt to her feet. It began to rain, a deluge of fine rain, she was soaked. It stopped as suddenly as it had begun, and then it came again, a wall of rain driven on the wind.

What wind? There was no wind.

She realised that she was standing in the path of the sprinklers.

She wanted to hide her cuts and scratches and bruises from him. She didn't want him to know that she'd been climbing trees like an irresponsible child.

How best to hide them from him? Sadly, by undressing in front of him in the chilly master bedroom in the same way that she did every night.

He didn't notice a thing.

They lay side by side, so close, so far away. He slid his right hand across, and clasped her left hand. She didn't respond, but she didn't take her hand away.

'Oh, Alison,' he whispered, although all the rest of the family were fast asleep, 'I don't expect you can even begin to imagine what it's like to feel trapped in the wrong body.'

For God's sake! The patronising beast! The infuriatingly complacent tub of lard. Could she bring herself to support him?

'I can probably imagine it more than you think.' Dangerous, Alison. Either tell him or don't. No hinting. You must forgo the delicious temptation, the glorious linguistic tension of the knife-edge. 'What I mean is, I am actually quite imaginative.'

Alison realised now why Nick hadn't wanted sex any more than she had. She remembered that party at the Billinghursts, only last month. They'd been tired and had left early. Someone had said, 'Can't wait to get home and get at it, eh?' They were like that in Throdnall. They'd looked at each other rather shiftily, rather shame-facedly, and thought, Thank goodness we'll be old by the time the government starts to publish league tables for copulation.

It was almost as if he'd read her thoughts – well, they did sometimes seem to be able to, that was the pity of it, that was the great waste of it.

'This is why . . . I find this very hard to talk about, Alison . . .' He squeezed her hand. 'This is why I . . . haven't wanted sex for so long. I hate my prick, Alison.'

'You're hurting my hand, Nick.'

'Sorry. I hate it. Bloody upstart.'

Hardly the most suitable phrase, thought Alison drily.

'I hate my testicles. I hate the hairs on my chest.'

What – all five?

The carriage clock in the dining room struck two.

'I absolutely loathe shaving.'

Yet you do it every day, for the sake of your self-esteem, although you could get away with doing it every other day, to be honest.

'I think I've felt inadequate every day of my life, Alison. For years I've thought it was because I was inadequate as a human being. Then I realised that it was because I was inadequate as a man. It didn't solve anything, but it was a huge relief.'

All this in whispers.

A late reveller drove past the house much too fast. The council were planning speed bumps to cut out that kind of thing.

'How long have you . . . you know?'

'Alison, I don't think I should tell you that.'

'Don't you think it's about time we stopped having secrets?' Oh ha ha, Alison. Very funny.

'You remember the night Gray was conceived?'

How could I forget? No, Nick, don't go into that. Please. Please!

'Yes.'

'The last time we . . . as it happens.'

'Yes.'

'You were so . . . so incredibly loving. I . . .'

'You were pretty good that night, actually.'

'Yes, but . . . no.'

'Oh, Nick, you can't stop now.'

'To . . . er . . . to . . . er . . . in order to . . . er . . .'

'Climax? Come?'

'Yes. I pretended you were a man and I was a woman, Alison. That's why I was under you.'

'You shouldn't have told me that.'

She withdrew her hand. She didn't want to, but she found that she couldn't not. Queen of the Double Negatives again.

'Oh, Alison, what a mess.'

'There was, wasn't there?'

'Alison! Don't be frivolous.'

'Don't you think we have to be if we're to survive, Nick? This is all too serious to be taken seriously.'

'On that note, Alison, maybe we should try and get some sleep. We'll be wrecked in the morning otherwise, and tomorrow we'll have to tell the family.'

'Oh God.'

'Yes.'

'One last question, Nick. When did you actually decide to do something about it?'

'Gradually, I suppose. It isn't something that strikes you in a blinding revelation.'

It is if you go to Marks and Spencer's. Oh it is tempting to say that. So tempting. Resist, Alison. Resist.

'Have I . . . has what I've said sort of given you an understanding of how terrible this has all been for me?'

Yes and no, Nick. No, because words can't. Yes, because I know that my words to you wouldn't be . . . won't be . . . any more convincing. Words can only take you so far.

'I suppose I have a grudging understanding, Nick.'

She wanted to be more generous, but couldn't. He'd given her such a shock and, which was almost worse, he had no idea that he had.

'Good. Night night, Alison.'

'Night night, Nick.'

The carriage clock in the dining room struck three. They slept. So close, so far away.

6 Thank You for Your Support

Alison was loading the dishwasher, Nick was sipping a glass of Chianti, sip sip sip. His delicate sipping irritated her. She looked across the kitchen table at him. With his soft fine hair, halfway between sandy and blond, and his finely flared, almost equine nostrils, he'd make a more than passable woman, damn him.

Suddenly Em stormed in, a whirlwind. She'd promised to be back by eight-thirty but it wasn't even eight o'clock. They stared at her in surprise.

'Men are such bastards,' she said, and she stormed off to her room for a good cry.

So young, and so little left to learn, thought Alison. She smiled to herself, grimly. Her desire to become a man wasn't based on admiration, it was simply a need to correct a monumental mistake. She felt so sorry for Em. Sometimes she looked quite pretty in a rather heavy sort of way, but that evening, in her anger and pain, she looked swollen and almost ugly.

'God, I'm tired,' said Nick.

'I kept you awake last night. I'm sorry.'

'It doesn't matter – and it isn't just that. There was a crisis in the kitchens today. Emrys threw a large wobbly.'

Emrys was a commis chef at the hotel. He was Welsh.

'I must say I feel . . .' She wanted to say 'knackered'. Such a nice masculine word. It didn't seem appropriate, now, to use masculine words like that. '. . . pretty exhausted myself.'

She wanted to switch the Ceefax on to see how Spurs were doing. They had a midweek match. But that would infuriate Nick. He hated football. Besides, if they were losing it would only depress her further.

Nick had asked the family to assemble in the lounge at half past eight 'for an announcement'. How absurdly theatrical. Alison knew that it was silly of her to hate calling it the lounge, but she couldn't help it. The fact that they had a lounge, not a drawing room, was like a symbol of how far her life had fallen short of what it might have been.

She plonked herself into the Parker Knoll, because she knew that he liked it. She wasn't usually petty, but she was still simmering with resentment.

Bernie was the first to arrive, irritatingly on the dot as always.

'She's dropped off nicely,' he said. 'The International Monetary Fund did the trick.' A thought struck him. 'Oh. Did you want me to bring her through? I didn't think. Is she supposed to hear your famous announcement?'

Alison looked at Nick, forcing him to take the responsibility of answering.

'Er . . . no,' he said. 'You can . . . er . . . relay the news to her tomorrow, Bernie. Let her sleep. After all . . .'

He stopped abruptly, to Alison's intense relief. She had feared that he'd been on the verge of saying something dreadful, like 'After all, she won't be around to see it, so it hardly matters.'

Em arrived soon afterwards, red eyes almost concealed. Alison's heart bled for her. She'd been very fond of Sam, and it would take months for her to realise that she was well out of it.

'Ah. Em. Splendid,' said Nick, oblivious to her red eyes. 'Go and drag Gray out, there's a good girl.'

'I wouldn't even if you hadn't used that ridiculous, patronising and utterly inaccurate description,' said Em. She had taken to using as many long words as possible, for fear that they'd think that in becoming a journalist she was dumbing down. They'd wanted her to go to university; she might not be the brightest but she could have scraped in to one of the lesser ones if the Collinsons' boy could. She could have done 'media studies' or 'golf course management' or 'PR' or 'forestry technology' or something unacademic. But no, she'd wanted to go straight into 'the media', which sounded rather an ambitious phrase when applied to the *Throdnall Advertiser*. 'He can drag himself from his self-imposed isolation.'

'I'll go,' said Alison.

'I've asked Em to do it,' said Nick.

'And she's refused,' said Alison, 'and family discipline is not what tonight is about.'

Nick knew that he had to give way. He was only too aware that he had no natural authority. It was quite a problem at the hotel. Even Ferenc had more natural authority than him. Ferenc could tell the chambermaids, quite quietly, to make less noise in the corridors when the customers were asleep (they weren't guests any more, they were customers, there had been an edict from Head Office) while Nick had to shout, so the customers were woken by a shrill cry of 'Cut that bloody racket out. There are people still asleep.'

'OK, thanks, Alison,' he said irritably.

Gray came down from his room very grumpily. He hated being interrupted. People told them that he'd grow out of it.

They all sat down. Nick looked across towards Alison, begging her to help by starting the ball rolling, but she wasn't having any of that. This was his show. She would offer no help.

He stood up.

'Er . . .' he began, 'erm . . . do you all know what a transsexual is?'

Gray and Em looked stunned. Bernie seemed utterly oblivious to the significance of the question. Alison wondered if his mind was beginning to go, or if it was just worry about Marge.

'Feller what dresses in frocks and knickers,' he said. 'We had one in our bowls team. Friday afternoons, as good as anyone in the South Yorkshire League. Saturday evenings, minces off to this club in Wakefield. Vince Brodley.'

'No, Bernie, that's a transvestite. A transsexual is someone who's been born the wrong sex and . . . er . . . lives as the opposite sex and . . . er . . . sometimes even undergoes medical and surgical procedures to . . . er . . . alter their . . . er . . . external sexual . . . er . . . characteristics . . . has what's known as "the operation".'

'Bloody hell,' said Gray.

Nick looked across at Alison again, for strength. She hadn't any to give. She was imagining herself making that speech – a little less hesitantly, she hoped, but probably not.

'I . . . er . . .' he resumed. 'I . . . er . . . intend to go through that process. Intend to . . . er . . . alter my external sexual . . . er . . . characteristics . . . have what's known as "the operation".'

'Bloody hell,' said Gray. He had a limited vocabulary.

'It'll kill her,' said Bernie. 'The shock'll kill her.'

'Marge doesn't need to know,' said Nick.

Alison flinched.

'I think she might notice, don't you?' said Bernie. 'She may be ill, she isn't ga-ga.'

'It's going to be a long process, Bernie. It doesn't happen overnight.'

'Are you saying she hasn't got long to go? She isn't dying, Nick. She's in remission.'

'I know,' said Nick. 'Of course she isn't dying. She's in remission and we're all delighted. I'm just saying she'll be able to be introduced to my change very gradually over the years. Of course she isn't dying. We all know that.'

Alison wished Nick hadn't repeated his assurance that Marge wasn't dying. It sounded hollow. But that's Nick for you, she thought. If he saw a pudding on the other side of the street he'd cross the road to over-egg it.

Bernie must have noticed, because he hit out, which wasn't like him.

'I always thought there was summat wrong wi' you,' he said. 'Summat not quite right. I said to Marge, "Marge," I said, "there's summat not quite right about that boy our Alison's marrying." '

Alison hadn't intended to support Nick even in the smallest way that night, but Bernie's attitude struck deep at her sexual political beliefs, and forced her to react.

'Yes, thank you, Dad,' she said. 'Most helpful. Nick isn't a freak.

They reckon about one in thirty thousand people are transsexuals.'

The moment she'd said it, Alison realised her mistake. How could she have known that, if she hadn't been researching the subject? She felt that she'd given herself away. She blushed.

'Unusual,' she continued hastily, 'but not a freak. Brave too. I will support him to the hilt.'

She was making the speech she would have liked Nick to have made to her. She hoped that he'd come over and give her a kiss, or at least a hug, some physical recognition of her support and of the enormous self-sacrifice which he didn't know she was making.

He did at least acknowledge her support, but not in words that she could welcome.

'Well said, old girl,' he said.

'I'm sorry, but I don't think it's well said,' said Em. 'I think he's being incredibly selfish. He isn't thinking of any of us. He's cocooned in his own emotional universe. But why should I be surprised? He's a man.'

'Yes, but I'm going to put that right, Em,' said Nick.

'Well I won't welcome you to the club,' said Em, and she stomped out, slamming the door.

'It makes my flesh crawl,' said Gray. He shuddered. 'Excuse me. Gotta split. I'm halfway through a chess match against the third best schoolboy in the Falkland Isles, and I'm winning.' He walked to the door and turned to speak. 'It does. It makes my flesh crawl. I feel . . .' He searched for some impressive description. Even at this tense moment Nick and Alison longed, as they always longed, to hear him say something impressive, clever, imaginative, poetic. '. . . all goose-pimply all over.'

'It'll kill her,' said Bernie, and he slunk back off to watch Marge sleep.

Nick looked across at Alison and gave a weary half-smile.

'Thank you for your support,' he said. 'I shall always wear it.'

Oh God, Nick, you're a pain, thought Alison. The sooner you become a woman, the better.

7 The Die is Cast

Nick went to bed, after he'd told them all, feeling that he'd climbed a mountain. He awoke feeling that he'd barely reached base camp. The whole terrifying enormity of it swept over him in wave after wave of panic.

He could hardly eat a thing at breakfast.

'Gray?' he said, as Gray pulled bits of his shirt out over his trousers so as to look cool as he waited for the school bus in Badger Glade Rise. 'Gray? About last night. Keep it under your hat, eh?'

Why did he use such a silly phrase?

'You don't think I'd tell anybody, do you?' said Gray. 'I'd be laughed out of town.'

Em swept through. She was dressed in combat gear and defiantly unfeminine in every respect, aggressive in her denial of being interested in men in the aftermath of the Sam fiasco (as Nick realised later. At the time he thought, So that's how they dress on the *Advertiser*.).

'Em,' he said, 'not a word about . . . you know.'

'But Dad,' she moaned. 'It's my first ever scoop. "Leading Throdnall Hotelier in Sex Change Shock." '

'Em, don't you dare! You can have the story, of course, but in the right way at the right time.'

She was out of the door before he'd finished. She was in 'Real Journalists Are Always In A Rush' mode.

As he drove to work, Nick reflected on the events of the previous evening. He had plenty of time for reflection. They were installing speed humps throughout Badger Glade Rise, and there were two sets of temporary traffic lights. He was caught by them both.

On the whole he thought the family had taken it pretty well. Gray had been quite cool about it really, but then he was so determined to be cool about everything that you never knew what he was thinking.

Em might become quite proud of him in the end. She'd find that he wasn't quite as boringly middle-class as she thought. She'd done a work experience at Throdnall General and had been delighted to discover entries on several forms saying 'NFT'. 'Surely all these people can't be working for the National Film Theatre?' she'd asked. Everybody had laughed. 'No, it means "normal for Throdnall",' somebody had explained. Em had the maturity to tell the story even though the laugh was against her.

Ever since then she'd delighted in using the phrase, 'Oh, Dad, you're so bloody NFT.' Well now she could never say he was NFT again. (The work experience put her right off the whole idea of medicine, incidentally.)

Poor old Bernie. Nick had almost let slip that they knew that Marge was sinking. His aim in life was simply to protect her. His quiet love was wonderful to behold. Nick would have liked to have waited till she'd gone, but who knew how long that would be, and time wasn't on his side. His next birthday would be the big four-oh.

At last he got into Clarion Road. The traffic ran freely for a while before coming to a complete halt outside the cake factory. Fancy living at the side of that, with its permanent, sickly smell of sponge and hot jam. He thought about how wonderful Alison was. He'd hardly been able to believe his ears when she'd come out with that statistic about transsexuals. She must have been looking the subject up during the day. Maybe they had a library at the carriage works, and in amongst all the books about rolling stock she'd come across one about sex changes and had pored through it, eager to understand what he was letting himself in for and to find arguments to support him. What a woman! He hoped Mr Beresford realised how lucky he was. Alison was the ideal PA for him. In her work clothes she looked very presentable but not in any way sexy, so there was no risk of Mr Beresford fancying her and his wife perceiving her as a threat.

They were moving again. He lowered all the windows, to get rid of the sweet tooth-rotting smell from the cake factory.

When he got to work he'd make an appointment to see Doctor Rodgerson. He would feel easier doing that from the office than from his house.

He turned left into Brindley Street and then right into the narrow alley that led to the hotel car park. The glass in the roof of the covered car park was tinted, and unwashed, so that the light in there was always an unhealthy yellow.

He entered the hotel from the back. That way he could see the reception desk through a pair of glass doors before anyone there could see him. He stopped short of the doors and had a sneaky look. There were three guests . . . sorry, customers . . . waiting, and only one member of staff to deal with them. Bad! He hurried through the door and approached the desk. He heard one of the customers say, loudly, 'Am I invisible or what?'

He went up to the man and said, 'Can I help you, sir? I'm the manager.'

'Ah!' said the man. 'Can you see me?'

'Certainly, sir,' said Nick. 'In my office straightaway, if you like.'

'No, no,' he said. 'You miss my drift. Can you see me? Am I visible?'

'Of course you are, sir.'

'I exist, do I? I am an extant being?'

'Well of course you are, sir.'

'Well will you tell that fucking cow on your reception desk that I am?'

Ferenc, Ferenc, wherefore art thou at this hour?

He should have said, 'Sir, I am extremely sorry if the quality of our reception service has not met the standards you expect of the

Cornucopia. However, the fault lies not with the one person on duty but with the fact that she has been left on her own, so I would be grateful if you were not insulting to her, and I will deal with you straightaway myself, sir.'

He should not have said, 'No, I will not, sir. None of my staff are copulating farm animals and if you can't be polite I don't want you in my hotel, so I couldn't give a damn how long you wait.'

No doubt he'd be in trouble over that. Hardly consistent with the Cornucopia Code of Conduct. Nor would Head Office be thrilled if he gave as his explanation, 'I was feeling tense about my sex change.'

On his way to his office he passed a notice board which stated 'General Manager – Mr Nick Divot'. Not for long, he thought with relief. 'Duty Manager – Mr Ferenc Gulyas'. He wondered what Ferenc would have to say about it. They went back a long way, Ferenc and he. A *long* way.

He felt nervous as he phoned the surgery. Now that was ridiculous. He wasn't even going to tell them what he was phoning about.

He would have to wait until the following Tuesday to see Doctor Rodgerson. 'Unless it's an emergency.'

'Er . . . no, it's not an emergency.'

Doctor Humphries could have seen him that morning, but he didn't want to see Doctor Humphries, nobody did, which was why he could have seen him that morning. He couldn't say to Doctor Humphries, face to face, 'I'm going to change sex.' It would be hard enough even with Doctor Rodgerson.

The very thought of changing sex made him want to pee. He hurried to the urinals. The cleaning roster hadn't been signed since 8.12 and it was seven minutes to ten. Oh God. He was running a slack ship.

How he hated standing up to pee. He loathed urinals, the sodden yellowing fag ends, the ineffective blocks of disinfectant, the shared expulsion of urine. Sometimes people even spoke to him. One man had actually commented only the other day, 'This is where the big nobs hang out.' He'd had to laugh, it was said by a big nob, the Mayor of Throdnall.

All this would change. Everything would change.

As he sat in the surgery he grew very nervous. He was tempted to give the whole thing up, just go up to the desk and say, 'I feel better. I'm going home. Sorry.' He didn't, of course. He'd spent nearly forty years in the wrong body. He wasn't going to give up now. But, oh God, if every stage was going to be as daunting as this . . .

Doctor Rodgerson was running late, because he was thorough. Nick was surrounded by coughs and sneezes. By the time he left he'd probably have double pneumonia.

He tried to concentrate on the magazines. 'Give the marrow a chance,' he read, and 'The Walsall nobody knows' and ' "Why don't we understand apostrophe's any more?" asks Bethany Sizewell.' No use. Even those gems didn't interest him. Sorry, Bethany.

A revolting child was crying. An ugly girl was coughing. He hated surgeries. He started on a bridge problem and as he did so he thought, Oh God, I'll have to transfer to the ladies' team. He began to get into the problem. He thought it must be a question of ruffing three times in the long trump hand. Suddenly he didn't want his name to be called just yet.

'Nicholas Divot.'

He didn't like hearing his name. He found it faintly ridiculous. He almost said, 'Yes. Sorry.' He came from a long line of Yorkshire Divots, which made him sound like mass carelessness on a northern golf course.

His heart was hammering as he walked towards Doctor Rodgerson's surgery. This was the beginning.

'Good morning, Nick.'

'Morning, doctor.'

'What can I do for you?'

'Er . . . I want to change sex. I want to become a woman. I want "the operation".'

'But . . .'

Doctor Rodgerson stopped. He didn't need to say any more. Nick could have finished several sentences for him. But this is Throdnall. But you're manager of the Cornucopia Hotel. But I've sat opposite you at the Collinsons' dinner table.

'You're serious about this, I presume,' he said. 'You've thought it through.'

'Oh yes. I've thought it through.'

'Well you're very brave, Nick,' he said. 'Very brave.' He sounded quite casual. He could almost have been discussing wine as he said, 'I haven't had a case of this before.' He was thumbing through a book. 'I . . . yes, here we are. Yes, this is a bit beyond my scope, Nick. What I think I have to do now is refer you to a gender identity clinic.'

He asked a few questions and then he stood up and held out his hand.

'Good luck, Nick,' he said. 'It's going to be a long haul, I suspect.'

They shook hands. Was it Nick's imagination, or did Doctor Rodgerson almost flinch at the touch of his skin? His expression was disturbingly brave. Was it the tiniest harbinger of what he might have to face?

He had to leave early for his appointment at the gender identity clinic. Alison made him a cooked breakfast. He managed most of it, though he drew the line at the black pudding. Such a masculine thing.

She drove him to the station. They felt that he might not be fit to drive, his concentration might lapse, and, besides, he'd always been wimpish about car parks. Alison found spaces. He didn't.

He'd got stuff from the library, and he re-read this on the train. He wanted to give a good account of himself.

He didn't get a taxi from the station, because he hadn't the courage to say, 'Gender identity clinic, please, guv.' He walked the streets of the big city, anonymous in the crowds, a tiny insignificant ant but also a very important person beginning a huge drama. As he got near he began to feel nervous, and when he saw the sign 'Gender Identity Clinic' on the discreet bland concrete building he panicked and walked straight past. Ridiculous! Nobody he knew could possibly see him here. He forced himself to turn back and enter the clinic proudly, with his head held high.

'Mr Divot to see Doctor Langridge,' he said, and the receptionist gave him a friendly but not inquisitive smile (very professional, far too good for the Cornucopia; surely if a heart beat under that blouse she must be curious about the kind of patients who went to the clinic?) and invited him to sit down.

He couldn't find a magazine with a bridge problem. He began to read an article with the absurd title of 'Our Changing Attitudes to Faces. Has the ear had its day?'

Ears were not his problem.

'Mr Divot?'

Doctor E.F. Langridge, MB ChB FRCPsych FRANZCPsych had a very pleasant, gentle voice. He almost made Nick's surname sound acceptable.

'Yes,' he replied.

No problem so far! Interview going well!

Doctor Langridge wasn't tall, and he was quite broad, but he didn't look fat, it was all muscle. Nick thought he'd probably played rugger in his youth.

He shook Nick's hand. Well, it would be more accurate to say that he crushed Nick's hand. Nick's eyes watered. Was the handshake a test of his masculinity? How much did he have to read into everything?

Doctor Langridge's office was like his voice, not his handshake. They sat, not facing each other across a desk but in leather armchairs. The walls were painted in restful pastel colours. They looked as if the clinic had employed a colour psychology stress reduction consultant.

There were a few preliminaries about coffee and travel, and then Doctor Langridge changed gear, but gently, and said, 'Tell me a bit about yourself, and your feelings about your gender.'

'I feel like a woman trapped in a man's body.'

Doctor Langridge frowned.

'I hear that phrase a lot,' he said. 'They all use it. They've got it from the newspapers.'

'Well, it's hard to put it any other way.'

'Try.'

'I . . . er . . . I feel humiliated by not feeling right about my . . . maleness.'

Doctor Langridge waited patiently. Nick could just hear the muffled roar of the heavy city traffic. It emphasised the silence rather than disturbing it.

'I . . .' This was so difficult. 'I . . . just don't feel right about myself and I never have, not for one single day. I feel a fraud as a man. I feel I'm playing a part and playing it badly.'

'Yes. Good. This is all rather generalised, Mr Divot. I have to assess your suitability for this very serious, lengthy and expensive process, which is to all intents and purposes irreversible.' He laid great emphasis on that last word. 'I have to assess your needs, the depth of your suffering, the depth of your understanding of what you are proposing to let yourself in for. It'll be difficult for me to accept you if you can't illustrate your condition a little more specifically than that.'

This was all a great surprise to Nick. It hadn't crossed his mind that he might be rejected.

'You see, Mr Divot, people get books from the library – some even buy them – and read up all about it to impress me.'

'Really? Do they really?'

'What I want is some insight into you, Mr Divot.'

'Right. Well, I . . . there are an awful lot of male activities that I just don't enjoy.'

'Such as?'

'I can't stand football. My wife loves it, but I just find it so . . . so crude. I feel uneasy in pubs. I feel I don't belong. I like to sip white wine, not gulp great draughts of beer. Oh, and there are all sorts of little things. Too silly to mention really.'

'Let me be the judge of that.'

'I'm not fascinated by the contents of my nose. I don't save up wind so as to fart in the bath. I would never pee in a hotel washbasin.'

'Other men do?'

'And boast about it. And they love crapping so much that they take their favourite books in with them so they can make the fun last a bit longer. And I hate smutty stories. I hear them all over the hotel – roars of harsh male laughter at some cruel or dirty joke. I can't think of any sound less humorous than the group laughter of English men. As a man I am an outcast, Doctor Langridge.'

'I see. Thank you.'

Nick was actually beginning to enjoy himself. It was rather nice to be forced to talk about oneself.

'I hate my hairiness. Not that I am particularly hairy, but I long to have smooth legs. When I look in the mirror and see my private parts I just think, What are they doing, dangling there? They look absurd.'

'Why do you feel you are as you are?'

Nick was beginning to realise that the softness of Doctor Langridge's voice wasn't natural, it was his style, his professional method. His questions were snakes encircling Nick's body.

'I don't know.' Feeble! 'Maybe I was just born that way.' Pathetic! 'Maybe it's because I was very close to my mother and my father was away a lot. He was a purser with a cruise line. They both died in a car crash when I was eighteen.'

'Absent father, tactile mother, facile explanation?'

'Absolutely!' This took him by surprise, Nick could see. One up for me, he thought. 'And my mother was not tactile. That could be the problem! But, no, I don't really believe my parents caused it. I believe it began before my birth. I think I was simply born the wrong gender. An accident of nature. I was always a bit of a cissy. I played with dolls. Well, I'm sorry, but I did. I can't pretend I didn't.'

'I said nothing.'

'No, but you make me feel as if I'm doling out clichés.'

'Clichés become clichés because they are repeated, Mr Divot, and the reason why they are repeated is that they happen frequently because they are true. Don't distort the truth by being frightened of clichés.'

'Right. Well, I also collected newts. I pressed wild flowers and ferns. The first time my wife saw me, when I was eight, she actually thought I was a girl. I thought she was a boy, incidentally.'

'And that doesn't mean she plans to change sex.'

'No!'

They smiled at the thought.

'Ever dress in women's clothes?'

'No. Innocent of that cliché.'

'Good.'

'Oh, except, damn it, we once went to a party in fancy dress. I went as Helen of Troy, Alison went as Achilles, but that was just for a joke. No, actually I always hated dressing up. Ugh!'

Muffled though it was, they could hear a siren out there in the real world. Police, fire brigade, ambulance, there are sirens all the time in cities these days. 'The real world.' The thought struck him as strange. Was this not real? Why could he never quite see himself as real?

'I don't have to go on the National Health,' he said. 'We both work, and I have quite a nice little nest egg from the sale of my parents' house.'

Doctor Langridge didn't like that. Nick had put the Divot foot in it. No surprise there, then.

'You seem to think if you grease my palm I'll whip you in, whip off your manhood and whip you out,' said Doctor Langridge slightly frostily, his integrity impugned as Nick now realised. 'You haven't come to some shady backstreet operator. We have strict procedures, criticised by some as too strict and causing unnecessary hardship to our patients. I will have to decide if you're suitable. I'll seek a second opinion, you'll receive counselling and regular assessments, and if we find you're suitable you'll undergo a lengthy spell of hormone treatment.'

'I see. I must say I thought it would all be much more straightforward, and I know that you have a more than 90 per cent success and satisfaction rate.'

'You've read the subject up pretty well. Yes, we have, but there are three points to note about that. One – the follow-up period is pretty short as the process is in its infancy. Two – patients are reluctant to admit to themselves, let alone to anyone else, that they wish they hadn't had the op on which they'd pinned such hopes. And three – our careful procedures are the main cause of that satisfaction rate.'

He leant forward. He was balancing his notebook on his lap. Nick noticed how large his knees were. He wondered if he'd find him attractive when he was a woman. Doctor Langridge noticed the look and raised his eyebrows.

'Yes? You were thinking?' he demanded.

'I was wondering – this is embarrassing – I was wondering if I'd find you attractive when I'm a woman.'

'I see,' said Doctor Langridge. 'And? Will you?'

'No.'

'Ah.'

'It's too dangerous. Doctor–patient relationship. Too danger-ous for you.'

'Nothing I can project imaginatively leads me to believe that I would be fighting any irresponsible unprofessional desires in your case,' said Doctor Langridge drily. 'We guarantee womanhood. We do *not* guarantee beauty.'

Doctor Langridge smiled for the second time.

'At the end of a thorough process of psychology and counselling,' he continued, 'I would hope that we would be in a position to allow you to start your Real Life Test.'

Nick knew about that, of course, but he'd hoped that it was all exaggerated, that it could be circumvented, that he could be fast-tracked to femininity.

'You will have to live as a woman in society for two years before your operation.'

Two years! Two years turning up at the Cornucopia dressed as a woman, but not a woman. And then he began to think of Head Office. They weren't going to stand for it, were they? Not the Cornucopia way. Clashes with our Corporate Code. He could imagine it, and in imagining it and being terrified by the prospect, he failed to listen to Doctor Langridge.

'I'm sorry,' he admitted. 'I wandered a bit there. I was thinking, the Real Life Test, it could be a bit of a problem.'

'Are you getting cold feet?'

'Very much so, but I don't intend to pull out. I haven't any choice, you see.'

Doctor Langridge nodded. That seemed to please him.

'Your wife will have to sign a letter agreeing to your hormone treatment and witnessed by a solicitor. She'll be told that you'll experience loss of sexual drive . . .'

'Not much to lose.'

'Ah. Loss of the capacity for penile erection.'

'Ditto.'

'Ah. And side effects that may include depression, deep vein thrombosis, liver damage and, conceivably, death.'

Doctor Langridge smiled for the third time, and more broadly than before. The effect was very disconcerting.

'I'm prepared to take that risk,' said Nick rather pompously. 'The dangers don't sound much worse than the list given out with the average packet of pills.'

'But is your wife prepared to take that risk?' asked Doctor Langridge.

'I hope so,' said Nick. 'I believe so. She's a truly wonderful woman.'

'Excellent.' Doctor Langridge's voice, while still soft, became grave, ominously so, like a newsreader beginning a new and tragic subject after something amusing. 'Now, the operation itself. You are going to have to be prepared to experience great pain and be laid up for a considerable period.'

'Talking of periods . . .'

'No. No womb. No ovaries. We can give you what we call a new vagina, or neo-vagina, but not childbirth.'

'A new vagina, but no new labour.'

Doctor Langridge didn't smile at that. He didn't look remotely like smiling.

'I welcome humour if it helps relieve the tension,' he said.

He took Nick through the details of the operation. They were gruesome. Nick gripped the arms of his chair as fiercely as he did when having root canal work done at the dentist's. He feared that he might pass out. There were droplets of sweat on his forehead, and his hair grew lank with perspiration.

'There are two things I must emphasise in conclusion,' said Doctor Langridge. 'There are those who will say that you can never truly be a woman, because you have male chromosomes and we cannot give you female chromosomes.'

'What do you think about that?'

'I think that one can use words to argue any point that one fancies. I think it all depends ultimately on you. I am only the conduit for your ambitions. You will have a vagina and, we hope, a mini-clitoris. You will pee sitting down. You won't even need to think about your chromosomes if you don't want to. It really is entirely up to you.'

'And the second thing?'

'One last reminder – which I cannot make too emphatic – that the whole process is going to involve a great deal of pain,' said Doctor Langridge. 'Are you truly prepared to undergo this pain?'

Nick swallowed. He had to summon up all the Divot grit, that bottom line that stopped the Divots from giving in, however wimpish they might seem.

'I am prepared.'

He asked if Nick had any other questions. Well, there was one he just had to ask.

'Will I . . . that is . . . how will my sexual feelings be? How much . . . er . . . sexual feeling will I . . . well . . . feel . . . sexually?'

'That one's impossible to call,' said Doctor Langridge. 'Intercourse could – perhaps should – be possible, though there is no written guarantee! In a few cases pain and bleeding render it . . . er . . . less than pleasant. Some people do tell us that they have experienced orgasm. Others most certainly do not. Nervous systems vary enormously.' He paused, and looked at Nick very solemnly, even sternly. 'Do you still wish to proceed at this stage?'

Nick paused before replying, not out of doubt but from a desire to emphasise his certainty.

'Oh yes,' he said.

The die had been cast.

8 Her Indoors

It was one of the longest days of Alison's life, the day Nick went to the gender identity clinic.

It should have been her. She tried not to be angry, but it was beyond her. She was simmering with rage. It should have been her.

She made him a cooked breakfast, grimly. He didn't even notice that she was grim, which made her feel even more grim. He was locked into his excitement. It should have been her excitement.

She gave him a whacking great piece of black pudding, throbbing with calories, gristled with fat, gross, masculine. She hoped it would spoil his breakfast as he skirted around it.

He was in such a state that she didn't even let him drive to the station. She suspected that he thought she did it out of love, and in a way she did. She had become very fond of both their cars.

She dreaded work. She dreaded the thought of Mr Beresford. As she turned into Sir Nigel Gresley Boulevard and saw the great, unlovely bulk of the carriage works ahead of her, she found herself longing to go home, and before she knew it she had done an enjoyably illegal U-turn and was being hooted at by a white van so filthy she could barely read the words 'The Throdnall Aquarium – Leaders in Garden Ponds'.

The driver of the van speeded up and came alongside her little Peugeot – Sir Nigel Gresley Boulevard was dual carriageway in both directions. His eyes were blazing.

'You aren't fit to be on the road, little lady,' he said.

Wrong! she thought. I am no little lady. I am a man trapped in a woman's body. You've picked on the wrong one here, little yobbo.

'How suitable that the driver should himself be an example of pond life,' she said.

His eyes glittered with aggression. Why were the English so aggressive?

'I've a good mind to report you,' he shouted.

'I doubt that,' she said. 'You don't seem to me to have a good mind for anything.'

'Oh fuck off,' he shouted.

'Case proven,' she shrieked triumphantly.

He flashed two nicotine-stained fingers at her and sped off. She saw that at the back of his van someone had written in the thick grime, 'I bet you wish your wife was as dirty as this van' and suddenly all her anger left her and she laughed inwardly at the thought of the little runt driving around all day, oblivious.

She pulled in to the side. She was breathing very hard. She had been so angry that she might have had a stroke. When she'd calmed down she drove carefully home, parked the precious Peugeot and phoned Mr Beresford to say she had a migraine, that she'd tried to get to work, got as far as the Boulevard (in case someone had seen her) and had suddenly felt that she couldn't make it. He was sympathetic. After all, she hardly ever took days off, and, besides, she knew that he rather fancied her, even though he was too much of a gentleman to show it.

The moment she'd made her phone call she knew that she'd made a big mistake. The house was so silent. Gray was at school, Em was at work, Marge was sleeping and Bernie was watching her sleeping. She had never known number thirty-three so silent. It clanged with silence.

She was trapped. She couldn't turn up at work and say, 'False alarm. I find I haven't got a migraine after all.'

She was alone with her emotions. She went to the front door and fetched the mail. Yet another offer of reduced car insurance. Yet another letter from Tom Champagne of the *Reader's Digest*. And a questionnaire from the Royal Mail. Would you describe your postman as 'neatly dressed', 'reasonably dressed', 'averagely dressed', 'untidily dressed' or 'badly dressed'? Is he 'very friendly', 'fairly friendly', 'averagely friendly', 'rather unfriendly' or 'very unfriendly'? Is he 'very polite', 'fairly polite' . . . well, you get the style.

She filled in that he was untidily dressed, very friendly, extremely impolite, any other comments? 'Yes, he has twice exposed himself to me in the front garden, in a very friendly, very impolite manner. He has also kicked the cat and broken three elves and a heron.'

She left the completed questionnaire on the kitchen table, in the hope that Nick would read it that evening and deduce how desperate she was.

There was nothing for it after that but to clean the house from top to bottom, except for the granny flat. Mrs Pritchard did that once a week, and that was disruption enough for Marge.

Alison was feeling an emotion that was strange to her and repugnant. She was feeling self-pity. She told herself not to be so ridiculous, but she couldn't help it. It should have been her. She hoovered with savage feminist resentment, forcing the horrid little machine across the hateful carpets. She really did hate carpets sometimes. God, how she longed to have cool Spanish tiles and elegant rugs, not these coffee-stained, wine-splashed, asthma-inducing housing estates for carpet mites.

'Nick, I hate you,' she said later as she lifted his odious photograph of the management team at the Cornucopia, all teeth and trousers, to dust round it.

She dusted round their wedding photograph. If they had known what was in store . . . ! She dusted round the photographs of Em and Gray at various stages in their little lives. Her eyes filled with tears. This was intolerable. It was becoming a habit.

She picked up the wedding photograph again and stared at it and knew that all her efforts to hate Nick had failed.

She loved him, damn it. She admired him. She'd have

described him as a wimp, if the word hadn't had connotations of strength that he didn't possess, and now here he was showing courage and determination and imagination. She knew better than anyone how much of all those things a sex change took.

She had always tried to be fair and just, and she realised now just how unfair she had been to Nick in blaming him for his monstrous self-absorption. That was simply the nature of consciousness. Hadn't she been exactly the same, planning her every move, unaware of the great journey he was making in his head?

She felt sick with nerves at the thought of him at the clinic. Oh, Nick, if we could only start the day again and I could say nice things at the station. Supposing he's killed in a train crash.

Don't even think like that, Alison.

She went to the kitchen, made herself an instant coffee, put a quarter of a spoonful of honey in it though normally she didn't sweeten it.

Bernie drifted in, in his braces and frayed shirt, and coughed shyly. It was the little cough he used before he asked a favour.

'Of course you can, Dad,' she said.

'I haven't said owt yet,' he said. He hung on to his Yorkshire dialect in this foreign place.

'Whatever you want you can have, Dad,' she said. 'You're my dad.'

He frowned. He didn't like her making it as easy as that.

'Seeing you're here today,' he began, and the thought struck him for the first time. 'Why are you here today?'

'The works are being fumigated. Legionnaires' disease.'

'Oh. We had that in a chimney in Wath-on-Dearne. Archie Millington's dad who wasn't really his dad died of it.' He coughed again. 'Seeing as you're here, I thought . . . it was Marge's idea like . . . I thought . . . 'cos Tommy Pilbeam and one or two others play doms in t'Coach on a Thursday dinnertime, and seeing as you're here, Marge thought . . . she's a saint, that woman . . . "I don't like you stuck here with me all day," she said. "It's not right." Just for an hour like.'

'Of course I don't mind,' she said, answering the question he hadn't quite dared to ask – was she really so difficult to approach? 'Be as long as you like, but you aren't going like that.'

'Aren't I?'

'Look at yourself, Dad. You look like a scruffy old man. Smarten yourself up. Imagine there's a young barmaid there.'

'There *is* a young barmaid there.'

Suddenly he looked about two inches taller and when he went to say goodbye he was that smart, you could have thought he was going to a wedding, not just for a few hands of fives and threes, which he'd taught the locals who had never played it, and a couple of pints of mild and bitter, which was a very popular drink in Throdnall.

She kissed him and he looked very surprised and said, 'What's up wi' you?'

She waved goodbye as if he was going to the North Pole, and then she sat with her mum for an hour or so. The granny flat was foetid with heat and old age, but it was strangely peaceful. Marge hadn't the energy to resent dying.

After that she set to in the kitchen, making one of her soups. The whole kitchen came to life when she cooked. Suddenly it didn't seem sad and sterile and suburban any more. People should cook more, she thought, then their houses would buzz and smell nice; they'd be happier.

She remembered the questionnaire and realised that she no longer wanted Nick to read it and realise how desperate she had been.

She went to the table, to throw it in the bin, but it had gone. The freepost envelope had gone too.

Could Bernie have taken it and posted it? Surely not? He never raised a finger to help. He certainly never used his initiative.

She heard him shuffling up the drive. She opened the door. He stood there looking foolishly surprised, with his key held towards the keyhole that was no longer there.

'Service with a smile,' he said.

'Dad?' she said. 'Did you post a questionnaire that was on the kitchen table?'

'Aye, I did,' he said. 'I saw it were completed like and I remembered what you said t'other day: I never raise a finger to help, I haven't shown any initiative around the house since the day I moved in.'

'Did I say that?'

'You've been in a funny mood lately, and I thought, "Hey up, our Bernie, this is your chance to show her. So I popped it in t'envelope, and posted it in t'box in Badger Glade Rise. Did I do wrong?'

Yes, Dad, you've probably caused utter mayhem at the sorting office.

'No, Dad, of course you didn't.'

She kissed him.

'Hey up!' he said. 'Twice in one day. What's happened to the woman? She's going all continental on us.'

She got to the station twenty minutes early. She stood on the platform. A lazy wind had sprung up. There was litter between the lines, and a child's yellow breakdown van, and a pear squashed by a train. The wrong kind of pear?

His train was going to be seventeen minutes late – reasonable going for the Throdnall line. Her 50p parking ticket was valid for forty minutes. If it over-ran because the train was late, and she was fined, she'd challenge it in the courts, she'd refuse to pay the fine, she'd go to prison if need be, no, she wouldn't, that was stupid.

She felt very nervous. She didn't remember when she had felt so nervous. She wasn't a nervous woman.

Supposing he'd decided he wouldn't go through with it. How disappointed he'd be. Supposing he'd been rejected as unsuitable. She felt so anxious for him and for herself. It wouldn't be a good omen for her if he was turned down.

By the time the train arrived it was twenty-two minutes late. She stood by the footbridge, looking both ways for him as Throdnall Man in his many forms strode by. Some strong, some weak, grey, tired, sagging, skins as lifeless as their briefcases. And there he was, her man, well, her partner, her . . . her Nick. He looked so frail, but not grey at all, he looked golden, her golden girl. It was just a flash, and then it was gone. She kissed him soberly, carefully, Throdnall-ly, not wanting to seem too emotional, not sure how emotional he was feeling.

'How did it go?'

'All right.'

So British.

'Only all right?'

'Well, pretty well, really. On the whole. I suppose. Well, very well, I suppose, really.'

So Throdnall.

'I mean nothing was said, nothing was actually said, perhaps nothing is said on these occasions, but it sort of seems by implication as though it's been tacitly agreed that I've begun the process. The doctor was OK. He has very large knees, but he was OK. God, though, it isn't half going to be a long-drawn-out process. Years.'

Her heart sank. Years for him, and she hadn't even started!

'Oh they gave me a letter you'll have to sign, if you're prepared to.'

He handed it to her, and she stood and read it, there on the platform.

I understand that my husband has requested that you recommend to his GP that he receive female hormones and possibly an anti-male hormone drug.

I understand that some of the effects of these substances on my husband may be loss of sexual drive, loss of the capacity for penile erection, breast growth, feminizing contours of the hips, and an accelerated course towards more feminization and possibly sex change surgery, including removal of the male genitalia and creation of female genitalia. There may also be side effects such as damage to the liver and increases in cholesterol and levels of fat in the blood. Depression may result, especially with the anti-male hormone drug. An additional complication of female hormone treatment is the possibility of deep vein thrombosis (blood clot in a vein or blood vessel) that could result in a medical emergency and possibly death. The chances of this occurring are increased if my husband smokes.

With this information I nevertheless grant you full permission to notify my husband's GP that my husband may be given female hormones at this time and anti-male hormone drugs in the future, should this be considered to be indicated by his psychiatrist and requested by my husband at that time.

My signature to this letter is being witnessed by a solicitor and by my husband.

They gazed at each other, there on the platform. They were all alone. The train had gone, the passengers had gone, even the porters had gone. They both felt over-awed by the letter's tone, and by the immensity of the tasks that lay ahead. It all seemed almost too much when expressed in such official language.

'Aren't you scared?' she asked.

'Of course I am,' he said.

She kissed him on the cheek, then put her arms round him.

'I think you're very brave,' she said.

He looked at her in astonishment. She saw him realise that the astonishment was tactless. She watched him try to hide it. She laughed.

'What's so funny?' he asked.

'You are,' she said.

9 Kiss and Make-Up

They were very worried about how Bernie would take it, now that the moment had come at last.

'I'll have a little chat with him,' said Nick.

Alison went pale. She knew his little chats.

'Well, be tactful,' she said. 'I know your little chats.'

Nick was indignant.

'Oh, come on,' he said. 'This is all myth. A family joke, if you like. I think I'm actually rather a sensitive and considerate human being. That's why I'm suggesting taking him to the pub, to be on his home ground, as it were, not mine. Tact.'

They didn't go to the Coach, where Bernie knew people, but to the Rose and Crown, where the landlord had had a quadruple charisma bypass, and privacy was guaranteed.

Nick bought a pint of mild and bitter for Bernie, and a gin and tonic for himself. Bernie said the beer was undrinkable, but drank it; they discussed Clinton's re-election ('They like a man with lead in his pencil', 'That's your considered political reaction, is it, Bernie?'); and football, which was difficult with Nick knowing nothing about it (why should he care about people who earned in a week what he got in a year?); and then he plunged in.

'Bernie,' he said, 'you know I said I was going to have the . . . er . . . that sex change business. Become a woman.'

'Oh aye,' said Bernie. 'It's not summat that slips your mind. Still on, is it? I didn't see owt happening. I thought mebbe you'd changed your mind.'

Nick couldn't be bothered to tell him about all the second opinions and consultations and analysis sessions and hormone treatments and painful bouts of electrolysis that he'd had. He was

70

a little hurt, actually, that Bernie hadn't noticed the admittedly slight but definitely detectable 'feminizing of the hips', the softening of the voice and skin, the fact that he was only shaving about once a week now. For Nick these were great victories, but all he said was, 'No. I haven't changed my mind. I . . . er . . . I need to begin what's called my Real Life Test now. Dress as a woman. Go to work as a woman. I just wanted to . . . well . . . run it past you . . . hope that you . . . er . . . at this time . . . because it's a difficult time for you . . . hope that you . . . that I . . . won't upset you.'

He really didn't think that he could have put it much more delicately than that. Tact? It was positively oozing out of him.

'I couldn't give a sod now she's gone,' said Bernie. 'Couldn't give a sod. You can have a face transplant and a nose job and such like and call yourself Barbra Streisand for all I care.'

Nick took that as getting the green light.

He tried to buy Bernie another pint, and that offended him.

'I'm not a bloody pauper,' he said.

There's no winning with some people, thought Nick. He did manage to buy a packet of pork scratchings, but that gesture went sour on him. Bernie lost a filling on one of them.

'It's the bloody dentists what come round and sell the pubs pork scratchings,' Bernie said. 'They're fiendish bloody things.'

'You didn't have to eat them,' Nick pointed out.

'You bought them for me. There's such a thing as manners in my book.'

There was no pleasing him, the way he was feeling, and Nick sympathised. They played a couple of rather desultory games of dominoes and that didn't go down too well either.

'You're a bad sport, you,' said Bernie.

'What? Bad sport? It doesn't worry me a bit, losing.'

'Exactly. So there's no fun in hammering you. No point at all.'

Nick didn't mind all this, but when they got home Bernie couldn't wait to tell Alison. 'He bought me pork scratchings.

They've buggered me second left incisor,' and she gave Nick a look which said, unmistakably, 'You and your little chats!'

And then she screamed, 'My God! Look at the Axminster! Who had that on his shoe?' (It was the carpet when she dirtied it, the Axminster when Nick did.)

It was Nick, of course. It always was. He suspected that dogs lay in wait until they heard him coming and then slunk forward and shat all over the pavements in front of him because they knew he didn't like them, as a result of which he liked them a whole lot less.

They drove into town on the Saturday morning. Nick hated shopping at the best of times, and this was the worst of times. He had to buy a complete wardrobe of women's clothes. He'd been putting it off and putting it off and now he could put it off no longer. He made for Castlegate Long Stay (there hadn't been a gate for ninety years, there hadn't been a castle for three hundred, if Throdnall saw anything old it shuddered and pulled it down, goodness knew how they had the cheek to put up those new signs 'Throdnall – Historic Market Town').

'Use your reserved space, for goodness sake,' said Alison.

'No. That's my work space. If I'm not working, I don't use it.'

'Oh for goodness sake. Who's going to know? Is somebody going to ring Head Office? I mean, it's yours, it's there, nobody else can use it, it's ridiculous.'

'There's a principle.'

'Oh for goodness sake.'

'Well I'm not using it today, anyway. I'll never live it down if Ferenc sees me coming back piled with bras and knickers.'

'He'll see you wearing bras and knickers on Monday.'

'That's different. I'll be prepared. I'll do it with dignity.'

They walked to the High Street from Castlegate Long Stay. There were crowds of the most horribly dressed people. Throdnall isn't Paris, not by a long chalk. In fact it's the World Capital of Leggings. The sky was the colour of old men's skins, and there were the faintest specks of rain on the prowling wind. Winter was coming. Nick felt very depressed. This should have been his first brave step towards womanhood, and he was hating it.

'We could try Next first,' said Alison, 'and Dorothy Perkins next.'

'I can't do it,' he said. 'I can't go through with it. It's too horrendous.'

She squeezed his arm.

'You must!' she said. He found her fervour strange. 'You must! You've set your heart on it.'

'Oh, I wasn't talking about the sex change,' he said. 'I was talking about shopping in Throdnall. I just can't do it here. I'll see people I know.'

'You'll see people you know when you go to work.'

'I know, but then I'll have to face them. I don't have to now.'

They decided to shop in Stratford. It upset Nick to leave several hours of a parking ticket unused, it went against the grain, but there was nothing else for it. Stratford is full of tourists, so nobody they knew would be seen dead there, and, as Alison pointed out, Shakespeare made cross-dressing very respectable. (In his plays. As far as we know he didn't visit Anne Hathaway in twinset and pearls.)

There were some great challenges ahead, but Nick was beginning to realise that it was the little things that were going to be the hardest. He found that he just couldn't go into shops and say, 'Good morning. I am going to have a sex change and before that I have to live in society as a woman for two years, so I need a complete wardrobe suitable for working as General Manageress of a leading hotel in Throdnall, plus assorted leisure wear for a middle-class lady of forty with a wide range of cultural and sporting interests, including golf and bridge.'

He knew that if he had been able to say all that, he would have mounted the first hurdle with ease, but if he could mount hurdles with ease he wouldn't have been Nicholas Divot Esquire.

What he actually said, amazing Alison even more than the assistant, was 'I want some clothes for my sister. She can't get out as she's severely agoraphobic.'

Oh God. A great new adventure, one man's heroic journey into womanhood, and they were straight into farce. Nick had never been at ease with shop assistants. In Austin Reed in London an assistant had once said to him, apropos of collar size, 'Are we fifteen?' and he had said, rather wittily he'd thought, 'I wish I was', and the man had flattened him by saying, without a flicker of amusement, 'Sir is a wag.' In Dobson's, Throdnall's own family department store, long gone, an assistant not only measured his inside leg, but stroked it, and Nick couldn't say anything: the assistant knew his mother, she went in every Thursday lunchtime for a cheese omelette and a glass of sauvignon blanc.

There was no stopping the agoraphobic sister, once she'd been invented. When Alison said, 'She'll need a full outfit for work', the assistant said, 'Will she be able to go to work if she's agoraphobic?', and Nick had to improvise with 'No, but luckily her work comes to her. She's a consultant', and Alison said, teasing him with just a touch of irritation at his stupidity and weakness, 'But we do hope to persuade her to go out, don't we, darling, and if she's got nicer clothes that she feels good in she might find it easier.'

Then the assistant said, 'What size is your sister?', and Nick had to say, 'Er . . . much the same size as me, funnily enough. Quite tall, flat-chested, slim hips, big feet.'

He really did think that Alison was going to giggle. He went red and began to perspire. Oh God, if this went on he'd make the clothes sweaty as he tried them on.

He tried a fairly sober skirt suit and the assistant said, 'Oh, yes, sir. It's . . . her to a tee.'

He almost confessed. Wanted to. Couldn't.

They bought a few oddments – bras and knickers and tights and a handbag, and as she packed them the assistant said, 'Funnily enough I have a cousin who's claustrophobic. It's a small world, isn't it?', and Nick said, 'I hope it isn't if she's claustrophobic. It certainly is if you're agoraphobic.'

He couldn't wait to get out into the street. The air smelt so soft and sweet. He didn't know if he'd ever smelt air as sweet as on that November day in Stratford.

They took their purchases back to the car and went for a reviving coffee in Ye Olde Falstaffe Coffee Shoppe.

Alison gave him a warning frown as he said to the waitress, 'I'll have ye olde toastede tea-cakey, pleasy.'

'Nick,' she said very seriously, after the waitress had scurried off with some relief.

'That's an ominously serious tone,' he said.

'Well I'm being serious,' she said. 'I think you just have to start telling them the truth. That sister of yours is grotesque. You have to jump your first great hurdle. You have to think of yourself as Nicola. You are Nicola now. You're wearing men's clothes because you're odd. This afternoon you are going to begin to cease to be odd. You are Nicola, not Nick or Nicholas. Concentrate on that.'

'Right. I am no longer sick Nick who gets on your wick. Ah, waitress, I am not Nicholas and I am definitely not knickerless. I am knickerful Nicola.'

The waitress gave them their coffee and toasted tea cake as rapidly as she could, and beetled to the safety of the kitchen.

'Don't be so silly, Nicola,' said Alison severely.

'I can't help it. This is frightening.'

'It won't be frightening once you've faced it.'

It helped that the clouds had been blown away, and it was a gusty but sunny afternoon, mild and soft with just a hint of invigorating crispness.

Nick – he couldn't see himself as Nicola yet, not in his Nick clothes – barged into the first women's clothes shop he saw, he didn't even know which one it was.

'Good afternoon,' he said. 'I'm going to have a . . .' He swallowed. '. . . a sex change.' There! He'd said it. What a relief. 'Before I have the operation I will have to live as a woman for two years. I need quite a lot of clothes.'

'I'll take your measurements, sir,' said the assistant calmly.

While she went for a tape-measure, Alison said in a low voice, 'You see. No problem. She didn't bat an eyelid.'

'What does that mean?' asked Nick. 'How do you bat an eyelid? Have you ever seen anyone batting an eyelid? Have you ever heard anyone say, "Oh look. There's a man over there batting an eyelid"?'

Alison was happy to let him waffle on. She realised that in his nervous, self-conscious state he needed the outlet.

By half past five he was the proud possessor of bras, panties, underskirts, blouses, tights (not stockings – he wasn't going to titillate men with glimpses of his marble thighs), smart jackets, skirts, medium-heeled shoes for work, low-heeled shoes for home, outdoor coats, scarves, woolly gloves (couldn't find any other sort to fit – large male hands – problem), handkerchiefs, high-heeled boots, low-heeled boots, ankle-length skirts, twinsets, cardigans, skirt suits and an evening outfit with evening bag.

'Why do I need an evening outfit?' he had asked.

'For evenings. When we go out.'

'Out? Where will we go?'

'Well, the Collinsons'.'

'They'll drop us when this comes out.'

'The golf club dinner.'

'Oh God. I can't go to the golf club dinner.'

'I'll support you to the hilt, Nicola, but I am not going to become a hermit. Real Life Test, not skulking in corners.'

He bought an evening outfit.

As they staggered back to the car with their purchases, Nick said, 'Well at least that's over.'

'Till the spring,' said Alison.

'What?'

'Till the spring fashions come out. You'll need light clothes. Fine cottons and silks for summer. And there'll be new styles. New colours. Summer colours. And next winter these colours that you've just bought won't be *the* colours any more. There'll be new winter colours. Mauve's tipped for a dramatic come-back.'

'My God,' he said. 'I don't know if I can afford to become a woman.'

'And you always thought I was extravagant,' said Alison.

They got home just in time for his appointment with Karen. Karen was Alison's hairdresser at 'A Cut Above' (Throdnall's Premier Hair Stylists) and she'd agreed to come and do his hair at home, partly to save him embarrassment and partly for security reasons. (They didn't want the story breaking before Em got her exclusive, which would give her CV such a boost when she applied to the Nationals.) Karen did a very good job, using Nick's slight natural curls to create a soft, wavy look. He'd let his hair grow longer than he'd liked over the last weeks, at Alison's suggestion, even though towards the end he'd begun to feel very uncomfortable and unmanagerial and positively un-Cornucopian. But he saw why now. Cut in a bob with a side parting, and falling over the face to one side, it softened his features enormously. It made him look quite feminine, it really did.

He woke up feeling extremely excited, sexy even. To his horror, with an insensitivity that shocked him to the core, his prick had one of those semi-erections that even he got very occasionally, first thing in the morning. He gave it a little smack, and said, silently, 'Get down, you insensitive fool. Oh well, I suppose I'd better forgive you. After all, your days are numbered, you sad little person.'

Alison felt the movement as he smacked it and said, 'What's up?' and he said, 'I thought I'd been bitten.' He wanted to take her

77

in his arms, but then it might have led to a very rare bout of sexuality and to say that this would have been mistimed would be an understatement. Anyway, the shock of this thought shrivelled his rebuked organ back into its habitual insignificance.

He lay there for a minute or two, more than somewhat shocked. He soon rationalised it, of course. He was feeling sexy because at last he was going to live as a woman, but since the only organs that he had that were capable of expressing sexuality were male, he was forced to express his feminine sexuality through a masculine mechanism. It wasn't shocking at all. It was complex and absurd, but it was also a perfect affirmation of why he had to become a woman – to free himself from this complexity and absurdity.

He dressed in his new jeans and a lemony blouse, and they went down to breakfast.

'My God,' said Bernie.

'Yes, Dad, very helpful,' said Alison.

Gray took one look, said, 'Is it any wonder I'm twisted?' and took his coffee and toast back to his room.

Em burst in, had a black coffee and a bun standing up, said, 'Gotta split, ciao' and didn't even comment on how Nicola looked. Giorgio was arriving from Modena that day. She'd met him in Venice and had been into everything Italian ever since.

Suddenly she'd bought lovely clothes that made her look elegant, but she got very grumpy if they mentioned it; it embarrassed her to look lovely, she only did it for Giorgio. In the last few weeks they'd all eaten a lot of pasta, for Giorgio, and drunk a lot of chianti, for Giorgio.

Alison suggested that they have a dummy make-up run after breakfast. Nick couldn't wait. This was it! His transformation was beginning. It was the first day in the existence of Nicola Divot.

He no longer needed to pretend. Never again. Yesterday in Stratford had been a nightmare. Today in number thirty-three was a dream come true.

He tried hard that day to prove that his fabled insensitivity was

78

a myth. Alison and he had spent more than twenty years together. He couldn't let her see how eager he was to become a woman, how eager he was, therefore, in essence, to cease to be her husband. 'Can't I read the papers first?' he asked. Luckily Alison wouldn't have it.

They went up to the en suite. First, of course, he had to shave. He took his blouse off. He didn't want to get shaving cream on it. Alison was touched by the sight of his bra. It was poignant that he had so little to put in it. Maybe with the continuing hormone treatment, and the psychological impetus of living as a woman – she didn't know.

While he shaved, she laid out the make-up products she had bought. She had chosen Estée Lauder as the right look for Nicola, who gawped at them. 'What?' he said. 'All those?'

'Now you're going to find out why I'm always late,' Alison joked. He was so tense. She longed to put him at his ease.

A wave of excitement shuddered through Nicola. I feel like a little boy in a . . . he thought. No, what am I thinking? . . . a little *girl* in a sweet shop. He had to take a very deep, slow breath to stop himself hyperventilating. He clung to the washbasin. He was frightened of passing out. Alison was very concerned.

'Are you all right?' she asked.

'Fine,' he said bravely. 'Just fine.'

She took him gently and carefully through the process: showed him how to smooth moisturiser over his face and neck, how to apply foundation liquid – she thought he might prefer that to cream – over his face, finishing well under the chin, how to brush face powder over the entire area. His face began to look more feminine. It was an eerie moment for Alison. She began to see the man she loved . . . yes, loved, she might no longer have been his lover, nor he hers . . . but, yes, loved . . . she began to see him disappear before her eyes. She began to see the woman he would become. She didn't know what she thought about it. She tried not to think about it. She had a job to do.

She showed him . . . her? . . . the intricacies of applying eye-shadow, deeper on the outer upper eyelid, and into the socket, and a lighter shade on the inner upper lid, finishing the eyes with a highlighter on the brow bone. Her eyes did look more feminine, they were a very pale blue, it was a very intense moment, there in the en suite, separated from the rest of the world by frosted glass. She wanted to give her a quick kiss, but she couldn't without ruining the very make-up she was teaching her to apply.

She showed her how to brush any surplus powder off the eyebrows, how to apply two coats of mascara to the lashes, how to brush the blusher on to the cheek and up towards the outer area of the eye, how to apply a lip-liner and then the lipstick. Not half bad. A good, thorough job. Anyone could see he'd been meant to be a woman.

Alison turned away and rushed to the bedroom, and lay on the bed, on his side of the bed, and sobbed. She didn't really know why, that was the silly thing. For her lost husband? Images of their early days when they seemed almost normal flashed through her mind – the honeymoon in Crete, a midnight swim in Cornwall, the birth of Emma – he'd been there to witness it even though he'd been terrified and it hadn't yet become compulsory for the man to be present – Gray's birth. Oh God. Poor disappeared Nick, how devastated he'd be if he ever found out Gray wasn't his. She cried because she so regretted her sole affair – it stood out in the calmness of their lives like a grain silo among oast houses. Yes, she cried for Nick and she cried for Nicola and she cried for herself and she cried for the world. She had come to crying late in life and, maybe for that reason, she seemed to have no control over it.

Nicola went into the bedroom and put her arms round Alison, and she had a sudden dread that Nicola would say, 'There there, old girl', but she didn't. Maybe that would go, now that he was being a woman.

They sat on the edge of the bed, Alison and her . . . well, her ex-husband who was still her husband . . . arms round each other.

Alison's sobs ceased, and she blew her nose angrily. She had always found mucus humiliating.

'I know that this is very difficult for you,' said Nicola, 'but I want you to know how much I appreciate how very understanding you've been . . . on the whole.'

Nick might be Nicola but that 'on the whole' was so very Nick. Alison half-smiled through the last of her tears.

Nicola led her back to the en suite, and watched as she washed her face and repaired her make-up.

'A refresher course already,' said Alison.

They went downstairs. Nicola wanted to settle down to read the Sunday papers; he'd always liked to read the travel sections and dream. He would cut bits out, although they never went to any of the places he so carefully filed away. But Alison wouldn't let her read the papers yet. There were so many simple things still to learn – how to walk, how to sit down, how to sit in a chair, how to stand up. She tried to inject a bit of feminine elegance into his clunking masculine gait, tried to get him to sit with her legs together, guarding her honour, rather than knees apart like some elderly spinster aunt, with no honour worth guarding, revealing yards of flannelette knickers.

'You've got quite fetching underwear,' she said. 'Sit like that and Ferenc'll start getting ideas.'

She wished she hadn't said that about Ferenc.

Bernie wandered in to see if lunch was ready and Alison realised she'd forgotten all about lunch. She told him it'd be late. 'Maybe I ought to dress as a woman, maybe I'd get some service,' he grumbled.

She started to make the lunch and took Bernie a cup of tea. He was poring through old photographs of his life with Marge. She didn't know if it was the best thing for him to be doing, but it seemed to console him.

'I'm not telling her about Nick,' he said. 'It'd only upset her.'

He saw Alison's look of surprise, which she couldn't quite hide.

'I talk to her sometimes when no one's around what might cart me off to the funny farm,' he explained. ' "Hello, Marge, love," I'll say. "I'm just feeding t'ducks and such like, like what we used to." Silly, i'n't it?'

'It isn't silly at all, Dad.' She went up and kissed him and said, 'Dinner won't be long. We aren't having a roast, what with everything.'

It was a strange Sunday lunch. They had omelettes, with oven chips and salad. The wind howled. Nicola tried to eat with delicacy and femininity. Bernie shivered and said, 'I hate the winter, me. The other seasons I can cope with like, but winter, the bastard gets into my bones.'

'Is your omelette all right?' Alison asked.

'Very nice, thank you,' he said.

She wished that just occasionally he'd say something was nice without having to be prompted. He's becoming very ungracious, is my poor old dad, she thought.

And Gray! They got the usual 'My God!' when he saw Nicola in her full make-up. 'Is it any wonder,' he asked rhetorically, 'that I'm a psychological wreck, with a dad like that?', and it did cross Alison's mind for a moment that maybe it would actually help him if he knew that Nicola wasn't his dad. He bolted his food and said, ''Scuse me', which was in itself a big advance in manners, 'Gotta split. I'm playing chess against a friend from Prague and it's almost Czech-mate. Czech-mate, get it? Oh, laugh, will you? That was a witticism. I'm becoming civilised.'

In the afternoon Alison relented and let Nicola read the papers. She cut out an article about the attractions of Split. When was she ever going to go to Split?

The wind howled and whistled, but silence ruled in number thirty-three. Bernie re-arranged his memories in his stifling room. Gray played chess in five continents. Nicola ploughed resolutely through the *Sunday Times*. Alison read a book. That was what their family was like. A commune of loners. A gathering of hermits.

Em returned just before supper. Her face was ashen, and she'd been crying.

'Didn't he come?' asked her mother.

'He bloody did,' she said. 'We've had the most terrible row, Mum. It wasn't like what it was in Italy.' She rushed through, did a double take, looked at Nicola, said, 'Oh my God,' and hurried to her bedroom.

It sounded serious. Alison wondered if it was over with Giorgio, then, as she began to make supper, she realised that it was. She could faintly hear the buzz of an electric razor, and thought it might be Gray shaving, although she didn't think he'd started and he certainly didn't need to, but then he rushed in, and he couldn't wait to tell them in an excited whisper, 'Em's shaving her armpits.'

'Don't you dare make any comment whatsoever about it to her,' said Nicola sternly.

'As if I would, Dad,' said Gray. 'What do you think I am – a freak? Can't have two freaks in one family.'

Just you wait, Gray, thought Alison drily. You're going to get a shock.

10 The Manageress

They set the alarm for six-thirty. There was an awful moment when Nicola couldn't remember why. Then there was an even worse moment when she did.

She knew that if she ate breakfast after she'd got ready, she'd spill something on her smart, dark brown skirt suit, and almost certainly ruin her make-up, so she tried to snatch a bit of breakfast straightaway, but it was no use, she couldn't even get a quarter of a slice of toast down.

She had a shower and cleaned her teeth and then she called for Alison, who stood by her side while she tried to do her make-up without assistance. Alison had to prompt her a couple of times, but on the whole she didn't do too badly. Then she did her hair, which wasn't difficult; Karen had done a great job and it was behaving itself well.

Beyond the frosted glass the night gave up its darkness grudgingly. It was going to be one of those Throdnall days that never get properly light. This suited her mood perfectly. She'd never kidded herself that today would feel like the beginning of a great journey, a giant first step to womanhood, but she hadn't realised just how tense she would be, just how much courage it would take to walk into the Cornucopia Hotel as Ms Nicola Divot.

With her suit she wore brown shoes, an apricot blouse, and a pearl necklace with pearl earrings (the jewellery lent by Alison, bless her). She wobbled precariously to the garage in her medium-high-heeled shoes.

She reversed very carefully out of the garage. She didn't feel in full control. She realised that she should perhaps have worn flat shoes for driving, and changed into the others at the hotel. She couldn't be bothered now. If she didn't get straight off, she might panic. She felt as if she was going to break into a sweat. That was all she needed! A grotesque general manageress with BO. She needed to breathe. She stopped the car, lowered the window and gulped in air, but it wasn't cold enough. It had turned disgustingly mild overnight and the air was damp and soupy.

Pull yourself together, Nicola. You chose to do this. You didn't have to.

She closed the window and reversed into Orchard View Close. When she got to Badger Glade Rise she didn't turn right, she turned left into Coppice Vale to avoid the road works.

She turned left again into Meadow Prospect, intending to turn right into Owl Hoot Lane, which was a good cut-through to the Kenilworth Road. In her anxiety, however, she forgot that there were new traffic calming measures there too (they didn't calm her!). About ten yards into Owl Hoot Lane they'd narrowed the road so that two cars couldn't pass. She turned too fast and had to screech to a halt to avoid a head-on collision with a red Honda. The young man in it glared at her, and she realised that he wouldn't reverse. Why should he, to be fair? It was her fault.

She tried to back up, but in her state she couldn't find reverse and the gears crunched horribly. She began to have to fight off another bout of sweating. She became very conscious of her tights. At last she managed to move. The Honda pulled forward, the young man lowered his window and shouted, 'Bloody women drivers!'

She wanted to cheer. Well, why not? She lowered her window, leant out and gave a massive 'Hurrah!' The Honda driver was so taken aback that he lost control and crashed into the new island in the middle of Meadow Prospect, demolishing it on its first day. She sped off down Owl Hoot Lane as fast as the Subaru could carry her.

The traffic was very heavy in the Kenilworth Road. That didn't worry her unduly. Half of her wanted to get there quickly and get it over with. The other half welcomed any excuse for delay. She noticed that the tattoo parlour had closed down, which seemed incomprehensible in view of the bodily habits of the majority of the townsfolk. It was hard to imagine a greater example of incompetence in business than running a failed tattoo parlour in Throdnall.

One of the windows of the pet shop was boarded up. An extremely fat girl in unwise leggings was unlocking the door of the hairdressing salon, Maison Doreen, and, good Lord, there was Mr Parker from number thirty-seven opposite, unloading boxes from his elderly Volvo (it did look as if they were overstretched) into the new herb and spice shop, Piccalilli Circus. Not a good location, the Parkers struck her as naïve, how long would that little dream survive?

Some bright spark had blacked out the letter O on the sign outside the County Library.

The right turn into Brindley Street took for ever. The filter system was very badly set, about two cars at a time got through.

She drove past the hotel and turned left into the narrow alley to the hotel car park. She pulled into her reserved space – General Manager – and looked in the mirror to check her make-up. She didn't really know what she was looking for, but she knew that no self-respecting woman would get out of her car in a car park without checking her make-up first. She didn't like what she saw. In that light she looked like a gargoyle with jaundice.

'Come on, Nicola. This is it,' she said out loud.

She could have slunk in straight from the car park, but she decided that on this occasion, for the sake of her self-respect, she would boldly climb the front steps.

She walked carefully down the alley from the car park to the street, past the frosted glass windows of the ground floor toilets, and walked even more carefully along the pavement. She was frightened of catching her heel in one of the many cracks and crevices, ravines and hollows that made Brindley Street's pavements resemble the surface of the moon.

The Cornucopia Hotel had been an old coaching inn, called the White Hart. It was one of only two old buildings left in Brindley Street. The other one was a sex shop. Above the steps, atop the entrance canopy, there still sat a rather splendid, if now completely irrelevant, white hart. It was probably a listed animal which couldn't be pulled down. Two storeys had been added to the top of the building, ruining its Georgian proportions.

Nicola sighed deeply as she went in. This really wasn't easy.

The moment she entered the hotel she could always see the whole picture. Nothing escaped her. It was obvious that morning that there was a bit of a hoo-ha at the reception desk. Sandra was a tough nut as befitted a retired lady footballer who played centre half for Throdnall Amazons, but she was looking a bit frazzled as she faced a very determined businessman.

Nicola hurried over, glad of the excuse for some kind of immediate action.

'Morning, Sandra,' she said.

Sandra's mouth fell open in astonishment.

'Mr Divot?' she asked.

'Ms Divot,' said Nicola, and she turned to the businessman, whose face was florid. 'Can I help you? I'm the Manager.'

'I booked a superior room. My room has not been superior. There must have been some mistake.'

There had been no mistake. None of their rooms were superior. It was absurd of Cornucopia to classify the rooms as Standard and Superior. Slightly Below Standard and Very Below Standard would have been more honest.

'Have you sent for the Duty Manager, Sandra?' asked Nicola.

'Er . . .' Sandra hurriedly stopped gawping at her. 'Not yet, Mr . . . er . . . Ms . . . er . . . no.'

'Right. Well I'll deal with it. Who is Duty Manager today, by the way?'

'Mr Gulyas.'

'Fine. Will you tell Mr Gulyas I'll see him in my office in

twenty minutes? Now, sir, may I ask you why you didn't complain last night?'

'I didn't have time. I arrived late, and had to go straight to a function in the Assembly Rooms. The Heart of England Financial Directors' Dinner Dance. I dumped my stuff, barely glanced at my room, jumped into my penguin suit and buggered off.'

Most people didn't complain about their rooms for the simple reason that they weren't paying, but Nicola could see why a financial director would want value for money.

'Which room were you in, sir?'

'Two three two.'

'Right . . . er . . . Mr . . . er . . . ?'

'Wilmer.'

'Right, Mr Wilmer, let's go and have a look at your room, shall we?'

They shuddered up to the second floor in the painfully slow lift. A small advertisement asked, 'Why not give our Kenilworth Brasserie a visit?' Nicola could think of eleven reasons.

'The word Cornucopia suggests "plenty",' said Mr Wilmer.

And there is plenty – plenty to complain about, thought Nicola. She looked at the second floor corridor through Mr Wilmer's eyes – carpet, threadbare and dirt-coloured (had been beige), lifeless prints of Warwickshire scenes, lighting just too dim, piles of dirty sheets at intervals. Only splashes of colour, only objects with any style – fire extinguisher and fire bucket.

They entered room two three two.

'Limp pillows,' said Mr Wilmer. 'A damp stain on the ceiling. Cracked paint on the radiator. Cheap curtains that don't quite meet. Tiny mites beneath the glass in the print of Old Throdnall. A tomato stain on page ninety-three of the Gideon Bible.'

He led her into the bathroom.

'A chip in the enamel of the washbasin. A brown stain in the bath. Two loose floor tiles. Pubic hairs in the shower.'

The first morning of my brave new life and I'm bending down to examine other people's pubic hairs, thought Nicola. She stood up gingerly, anxious not to snag her tights.

'I'm very sorry about the pubic hairs,' she said. 'Heads will roll. The Gideon Bible will be replaced. With regard to the other matters, we are, I must admit, awaiting refurbishment.'

She didn't tell him that they were fifth on the list, behind the Coventry Cornucopia, the Haverfordwest Cornucopia, the York Cornucopia and the Crawley Cornucopia.

'Is this one of your superior rooms?' demanded Mr Wilmer.

'Yes, it is,' she said, 'though I must admit it's not one of our best.'

She was lying. It was one of their best.

'My wife has left me,' he said.

I'm not surprised, thought Nicola.

'I'm so sorry,' she said.

'I'm not,' he said. 'I half thought I might pull, to be honest.'

You? No chance.

'How could I bring a woman back to a room like this?'

Nicola didn't point out that he had claimed not to have noticed how bad the room was the previous evening, so he wouldn't have known that he couldn't bring a woman back.

Mr Wilmer picked up the little folder on the desk and read out loud, 'Mr Nick Divot and his staff welcome you to the Cornucopia and will do all they can to make your stay a pleasurable one.' (Damn! That should have been changed to Ms Nicola Divot, get Ferenc on to it.)

'Pleasurable, my arse,' said Mr Wilmer.

The unworthy thought flashed through Nicola's mind that even when she was a fully-fledged woman she would find nothing pleasurable about Mr Wilmer's arse. But the customer was right, even if he was a complete tosser, and Nicola's first decision as a woman was the degrading one of offering Mr Wilmer a fifty per cent reduction in his bill.

On a more positive note, he hadn't appeared to find anything odd in her appearance as a woman.

He hadn't attempted to pull, though.

Ferenc had a soft little knock, but he was only playing at being diffident.

'Come in.' Nicola tried to make her voice sound soft and feminine. It had never exactly been deep and masculine, and she thought the hormone treatment was having a gradual effect.

Ferenc slid in as if on castors, shut the door gently behind him and raised his eyebrows in a way that, frankly, was just a trifle supercilious. Don't waste my time. Tell me what your little game is, said Ferenc's eyebrows.

Damn it, she wouldn't!

'Do sit down, Ferenc,' she said.

Ferenc settled himself elegantly into the chair on the other side of her excessively neat desk. Ferenc, it couldn't be denied, had style – a rare quality in Throdnall. He'd had it as a waiter – he'd stood out in the Pizza Hut in Plockwell, which was where Nick first saw him. He'd been fresh out of Budapest and could serenade a woman with a menu as if it was a gypsy violin. If he'd had a violin he'd have caused mass orgasms. There'd been trouble with a customer, he'd got into doubtful company and left. When he next came across him, Nick had just been appointed Manager at the Cornucopia, Ferenc was married and less wild, and Nick had given him a job as a waiter. Only eight years later, and already he was Assistant Manager. Nicola didn't resent it, but she was well aware that he might rise to heights that she couldn't aspire to. It wouldn't surprise her if one day he opened Throdnall's very first Hungarian restaurant.

What she found difficult in her relationship with him was to establish any power over him. He had more natural authority than she did, and they both knew it. Today was different, though. Today she had something to tell him, and as long as she refused to tell him she had power over him.

'Ferenc,' she said, 'I need to talk to all the staff. I . . . er . . . I have something important to tell them.'

'I see.'

Good! She had forced him into the English habit of saying the opposite of what he meant. Clearly he didn't see and didn't know quite how to ask her.

'Er . . . ?' he began.

'I'll leave you to arrange things,' she said. 'Obviously I can't speak to the whole staff at once – the hotel still needs to function in its usual smooth, efficient way.'

She smiled slightly, just enough to let him know that she knew what a crap-hole it was. It crossed her mind that this was something that she could never have acknowledged as a man, and just for a moment she felt quite light-headed.

She began to wonder about Ferenc's sexuality. He was quite small, lithe, with a mobile face. She'd never given his sexuality a thought before, but she found herself considering whether he might be bisexual. He had a reputation as a ladies' man, but that might be a smokescreen.

Was she interested because she was going to be a woman, she wondered. Would she end up saying to him, 'Take me, Ferenc'?

No, because he wouldn't.

She realised that while she had been musing he'd been speaking, and she had no idea what he'd said. That wouldn't do. That wasn't masterful (should that be 'mistressful' now, or was that politically incorrect? Personful? Concentrate!)

'Sorry,' she said. 'What did you say?'

'I asked you – I should think it's a question anyone would feel that they must ask – why you are wearing ladies' clothes?'

'Good question. Very good question. So I'd like you to divide the staff into two in such a way that while one lot hear me speak the other lot will be able to keep the place ticking over. I'll . . . er . . . the Aston Suite's free today, isn't it?'

'Yes.'

'I'll use the Aston Suite. One lot at eleven, the other at eleven-thirty. I'd like you to be there as well, Ferenc, for one of those times.'

She smiled, quite mistressfully. It was a good moment and she was determined to enjoy it. She sat back in her chair behind her neat desk and crossed her legs luxuriously. She had completely forgotten that she had balls and a prick and as she crossed her legs they got badly squashed inside her tights. It was excruciating.

'Are you all right?' he asked.

'Never better, Ferenc,' she gasped. 'In the pink.'

The worst of the pain passed and she stood up very carefully, and tried to move her legs in such a way that her genitalia would cease to stick together and would rediscover their separate identities. In vain! There was nowhere for them to go. Her surprising feeling of well-being ebbed away. She found the prospect of carrying her male private parts around in her knickers for two whole years deeply depressing.

'Are you sure you're all right?'

'Yes. Yes. I was just wondering if my skirt was straight.'

'Er . . . yes . . . yes. Pretty straight.'

'It's difficult when you're not used to it.' She smiled. 'I'll get used to it.'

His eyes widened slightly.

'Don't tell me you're going in for a sex change,' he said.

She supposed that it was inevitable that he would guess – there weren't that many possible explanations – but it added to her sudden feeling of flatness. It rather took the gilt off her gingerbread. Nick had always felt that he was a man destined to have the gilt taken off his gingerbread, and now it looked as if things might not be very different for Nicola.

It was to be expected, on this dramatic morning and with all the hormones that were coursing through her body, that Nicola should experience mood swings. As she stepped on to the raised platform at the end of the Aston Suite she no longer felt flat. Yes, she was nervous. Yes, she realised that she must cut a rather absurd figure. (Not *that* absurd, though. She had looked at herself in the mirror in the Ladies', and thought that on the whole she really wasn't too bad; she could have imagined fancying her if she had been a man, which of course she had been, so probably she wasn't a bad judge.) But above all she felt – perhaps for the first time in her life – that she was interesting. She sensed a crackling tension in her audience, not the usual 'Oh God it's him again', but 'What's going on?'

She felt a surge of great joy. Her liberation had begun.

The room had been arranged in lecture mode, with rows of chairs facing her. It was far from full, and her audience had gathered themselves into little clusters – kitchen staff and waiters at the back where they could giggle and whisper – receptionists, office staff and management at the front, looking serious and corporate – a gaggle of chambermaids to the left, huddling together for comfort in this formal set-up – a couple of porters to the right – one of the barmen all on his own to the left.

Behind and beside her audience there were photographs of various Aston Villa stars of the past. She had learnt their names. Charlie Athersmith (who once took an umbrella on to the pitch), Pongo Waring, Ron Saunders, Charlie Aitken, Peter McParland. She'd never in her heart of hearts given a damn about them, but now she had a fanciful feeling that even they were interested, they looked interested, especially Pongo Waring, and her heart warmed to them.

She launched straight into it.

'You'll all be wondering why I'm dressed as a woman,' she said, and then she explained about the operation, the Real Life Test, etcetera. There were one or two sniggers. She saw Emrys, the Welsh commis chef, murmuring something that was only too obviously obscene to Paulo, the Portuguese sommelier, whose gammy leg made it so difficult for him to cut an adequately authoritative figure as he bore down on customers with the dismal wine list. She saw the chef, Leonard Balby, turn and hiss at Emrys for silence. There was a snake's venom in that hiss. Nick had always given thanks when each week went by without a drowned body in the potage du jour.

'Snigger if you must,' she said, and all sniggering stopped abruptly. 'I hope I don't look too grotesque, but I have no illusions that, even with the hormone treatment, I will ever be another Marilyn Monroe. I don't mind a few laughs, we're all human, but please remember at all times to preserve the dignity of the hotel.'

The dignity of the hotel! Even as she said it she realised how OTT it sounded, but nobody smiled – not outwardly, anyway.

'I will be known as Ms Nicola Divot. Please would you adjust the board in the foyer, Naomi?'

Naomi nodded. She was from New Zealand. She was attractive in a sturdy, outdoor way. What on earth was she doing in Throdnall?

'Why am I doing this?' Nicola asked rhetorically. 'Because I have never been happy with my gender. All my life I have been uncomfortable. I have never felt a real man.'

'I have,' whispered Tracey too loudly. Nick would have glared. Nicola had to resist the temptation to give her a smile as one woman to another.

'I come now to a very serious point,' she continued. 'Head Office doesn't yet know, and I'd like to have time to show them that the efficiency of the hotel is unimpaired before they summon me. I ask, therefore, for complete silence about this. That is the loyalty I demand. I do suggest that if I go you may get somebody much less easy to work with. So, please, no idle gossip. I don't want the local press finding out about it just yet. Even my own daughter, who works for them, is sworn to silence.'

At the end of the talk she asked if there were any questions.

'Yes,' said Iris from the office. 'This is probably a silly question, but which toilets will you use?'

'It isn't a silly question at all,' she said. 'I'm dressed as a woman, but I am still technically a man. I believe that to comply with the law of the land I ought to continue to use the Gents', but in order not to look out of place I intend to use the Ladies' from now on. I trust none of you will grass on me, and if I forget myself at first and use the Gents', somebody remind me, please.'

'How please should we address you?' asked Paulo.

'That's another good question. You already address me in different ways, so . . . er . . . if you've called me "sir" it'll become "ma'm", I suppose. Nick will become Nicola, and Mr Divot becomes Ms Divot.'

The new young porter went a bit red and began to speak. He didn't look more than sixteen. He had a Black Country accent as thick as soot, and his skin was an eruption of spots. It was brave of him to contribute.

'I want to say something, Ms,' he began. 'It's . . . er . . . well it's not exactly a question exactly like, but what it is is . . . I've had the . . . you know, been told like . . . I suppose I shouldn't be saying this, I'll get into trouble like . . . been told that you're . . . you know . . . like a bit of a wimp like.'

There was a gasp. Ferenc turned and glared at the other porter, the long, thin one with the big nose with the drip on the end of it every time he went out to get luggage. Clearly Ferenc thought he was the one to have said that Nick had been a wimp. Nicola missed nothing on this morning of high awareness.

'No, please, carry on,' said Nicola.

'Well, I don't think you are a wimp like. I don't know what anybody else thinks, but I think what you're doing, I think it shows a lot of . . . er . . .'

'Balls,' interrupted Leonard Balby. He was from Goole.

Nicola was furious with Leonard, but she knew that she mustn't show it, she would have to ride with the laugh.

'Yes, I still have those,' she said, and she could see that one or two of the girls thought that surprisingly risqué of her.

'No, well, yes,' continued the young porter with the spots. 'I mean it takes guts like to do it and guts like to face us, and I just want to say, "Ms . . . good luck like." '

Nicola was moved, and she sensed that the lad wasn't the only person in the room to feel some admiration for her.

'Thank you,' she said, and she realised that her voice was going to crack. Oh God. How un-British. She could feel tears welling in her eyes; if she was as emotional as this on the first day what would she be like as a fully-fledged woman? She couldn't bear to break down in front of her staff. Desperately she plunged into Cornucopia-speak. 'And I think it illustrates something important about the Cornucopia Code of Conduct. We are all a family – the Cornucopia family. Every one of us is valuable – even invaluable.' In the Code of Conduct booklet it actually said, 'Never forget that in every Cornucopia inn every member of staff is inn-valuable.' 'Everyone is a member of the team,' continued Nicola, 'but also a valued individual. How fitting, how quintessentially Cornucopian, that I, your General Manager, should receive support and praise from the newest member of our team.' Nicola felt that she was making something rather wonderful out of it – a truly beautiful corporate moment. 'Thank you very much indeed, Mike.'

'My name's Mark,' said the young porter.

Ferenc smirked. Nicola could imagine Alison, if she'd been there, cringing.

It was clear that while some things were going to change now that she was no longer Nick – she would feel like smiling at cheeky chambermaids instead of glaring – others would remain the same.

She would still not be able to manage beautiful moments without spoiling them.

11 Broken Nuts

Alison felt sick in the stomach as she shepherded the Peugeot through the rush hour traffic. The sky was dark and lifeless. A bus had broken down just before the Colton roundabout, on which the flowers were sponsored by Rentokil. There is something deeply depressing about a broken-down bus. All that power nullified.

But the bus wasn't the cause of her feeling sick. The cause was four-fold:

1) She felt so anxious for Nicola. She knew how difficult things would be for her on her first day.
2) She felt so anxious, by extension, for herself, and for the day when she would first drive up Sir Nigel Gresley Boulevard in men's clothes.
3) She felt very nervous about telling Mr Beresford about Nicola's sex change. Mr Beresford wasn't an easy man to talk to about anything, let alone a sex change.
4) She had received a very disturbing letter from Customer Services at the Royal Mail. Would she arrange a meeting to discuss her serious allegations against her postman?

She was tempted to do another illegal U-turn in Sir Nigel Gresley Boulevard – there was something about Mr Beresford, some indefinable hint of darkness, which made him difficult to be with, however immaculate his behaviour – but she had to face him. She couldn't get into the habit of inventing migraines.

She showed her car pass at the gate, even though it was Leroy and they went back years.

She always felt so tiny, sliding along the edge of the great carriage sheds in her little car. At the end of the sheds she turned right and crossed the railway lines that came out of them and snaked through the industrial estate to the main line. Round the back, she parked against the brick wall of the Administration Block. A notice on the wall above her parking space proudly announced to the world, 'Personal Assistant to Mr Beresford'. She'd have preferred it if it had just said, 'Mrs Divot'. She took the form of words as a reminder that she wasn't indispensable.

Mr Beresford was in. She could see his Daimler. Damn. She was only a minute or two late but he was a stickler for punctuality.

She climbed the creaky stairs and walked along the corridor that ran the length of the block, affording a view over the canal to the out-of-town shopping centre with its phoney Greek pillars, its B & Q and its Toys Я Us.

Halfway along the corridor there was a door, and beyond it the corridor was carpeted. She had entered first class.

The carpet had been decorated with white circles which held the letters TcW, the uninspiring logo of Throdnall Carriage Works. In the early days Carriage Works had been spelt as one word, but that had given an even less inspiring logo, so it had been changed.

The corridor ended at the door to Mr Beresford's office. Her office was just before that, on the right. It was much smaller than Mr Beresford's. That didn't worry her, but it was somewhat galling that it was exactly the same size as Connie's next door, and Connie was only PA – well, glorified secretary really – to Mr Beresford's second-in-command, the aptly-named Mr Bland.

She sometimes tried to think, 'Millions are starving in Africa, forget the size of your office and pray for an end to famine.' She didn't often pray – she didn't believe in God, she only prayed very occasionally as security in case she was wrong – but when she did pray she prayed for an end to famine in Africa *and* a larger office.

'Mrs A. Divot'. One day that sign would say 'Mr A. Divot'. She felt exhausted just at the thought of the long journey she had to make, just to lose an ess.

She entered her office and, as she began to take her coat off, she looked down through her internal window on to the great sheds where the carriages rotated slowly and were added to by extremely complicated machines. She saw that strange, repetitive world and didn't ever enter it. She was of it and not of it.

Before she'd finished taking her coat off, Mr Beresford was through the adjoining door and saying, 'Ah! Mrs Divot! You're here!', which was Beresfordese for 'Three minutes late again.'

'Yes. Park Road was very congested.'

He gave a thin smile. That's why we should leave home five minutes earlier, isn't it? shouted his thin smile.

'If you have a moment, Mrs Divot.' Beresfordese for 'Come into my office instantly.'

She had a moment. She went into his office instantly.

'Nice weekend?' The interest was perfunctory.

'Very nice.'

'Do anything interesting?'

Bought a complete set of women's clothes for my husband. Showed him how to use make-up, did a dummy run in the en suite, showed him how to walk and sit as a woman.

'No, not really.'

'Fine. Fine. Good. Excellent.' He handed her a sheet of names. 'Late payers. Send them all a very stiff warning.'

'Right.'

'How's your husband?' Perfunctory!

'She's very well, thank you.'

'Good. Good. Excellent. Get on to . . . what? "She"?'

'Yes, Mr Beresford. My husband has begun the process of having a sex change.'

'Shit!!'

She had hardly ever heard him swear.

'Well, no,' she said. 'I'm actually being . . .'

'What? No, no. No, no. I was meaning this email. Mercia First Southern have found broken nuts on two carriage wheels. Two different carriages. That's all I need. That is all I need.'

He went to the internal window and looked down into the sheds, as if he thought he might be able to spot some broken nuts.

'I'm sorry.'

'Yes. Yes. Nasty. Very awkward. Sex change? Good God!'

He sounded really disgusted. Suddenly, amazingly, through the external windows, they saw the sun burst through a gap in the thick clouds, and a single shaft of sunlight lit up the canal behind them. No sunlight ever penetrated into the carriage sheds.

'I'm so sorry, Alison,' he said.

He'd never called her Alison before. She'd often suspected that he wanted to, but he was a bit of a stickler for the proprieties, was Mr Beresford.

The sun went in again behind its black duvet. It had given a brief glimpse of what the day might have been like. Now it seemed darker and more depressing than ever.

'Get on to Mercia First Southern, will you, Mrs Divot?' said Mr Beresford, and she had a strange feeling that the clouds had also closed in on her name, and she would never be sunny Alison again to Mr Beresford. 'Get the numbers of the two carriages off them.'

'Certainly, Mr Beresford.'

'Oh, what a thing.'

She had to be very alert, to work out when he was talking about Nicola's sex change and when he was talking about railway carriages.

'Well actually, Mr Beresford, I don't really mind. I understand.'

'What? But the man's turning into a freak.'

'No. No! That's exactly what he isn't turning into, Mr Beresford. He feels that he's *been* a freak. He says that every time someone changes sex, there's one less freak in the world.'

'Sorry. I can't agree with you. If the good Lord had meant him to be a woman he'd have made him a woman. So when is he having the operation?' A dreadful thought struck Mr Beresford. 'I hope you won't be wanting time off.'

'No, Mr Beresford.' For mine, yes, but not for his. God, imagine his face when I tell him about mine. 'And it won't be for a couple of years. He has to live in society as a woman for two years.'

'Good God! That is completely over the top! That is ridiculous!'

'Well, actually, I can see the point, Mr Beresford.'

'What? Oh, no. No, no. No, I was reading down this email. They want us to recall every carriage. Every carriage, for goodness sake! That would be disastrous. Disastrous from a financial perspective. Disastrous from a public confidence perspective. Disastrous logistically. Just plain disastrous. Right, get those carriage numbers and then get on to Balshaw and see if they're from the same batch.'

She went back to her office. She couldn't concentrate on anything until she'd sorted out this business with the Royal Mail. She phoned Mr Gamble from Customer Services.

'Now this complaint,' said Mr Gamble. 'It is, as you'll realise, extremely serious. Do you think it would stand up in a tribunal?'

'No, it wouldn't, Mr Gamble,' she said, 'and neither would I. I made it all up.'

'You made it up? Why should you do a thing like that?'

'I was in a mood. I have problems at home.'

'I have problems at home,' said Mr Gamble. 'We all have problems at home, that's what homes are for, but we don't all go around making up answers to questionnaires.'

'It made me angry. I thought the whole concept so stupid. "Would you say your postman was averagely smart?" What nonsense.'

'It was my idea, my personal initiative,' said Mr Gamble tartly.

'I'm sorry.' Oh heavens, Mr Beresford was peering through the glass door at her. He loathed private phone calls. He seemed to be able to sniff them out. 'I don't want to offend you, Mr Gamble, but I just think people with busy lives haven't the time for such things. I filled it in stupidly to make myself feel better. My father posted it by mistake. I hadn't any intention of sending it.'

'I don't believe you. I believe something happened to make you change your mind. Has your postman threatened you?'

'No! If I'd been serious, would I have written all that stuff about elves and herons? Do you really think I have elves and herons in my garden?'

'Why, what's wrong with elves and herons?'

In her anxiety, with Mr Beresford still watching her, Alison failed to read the danger signals.

'Nothing,' she said, 'except that they're the most ghastly form of sentimental bad taste.'

'I have five elves and two herons.'

'I'm really sorry, Mr Gamble. I had no intention of offending you.'

He was coming in! Beresford! Oh God.

'Look,' she said. 'I have to go now. It was all nonsense and I want you to ignore it.'

Mr Beresford raised his great bushy eyebrows.

'It isn't quite as simple as that, Mrs Divot,' said Mr Gamble. 'Your complaint tallies closely with two others.'

'What?? About our postman?'

Mr Beresford was capable of raising his eyebrows more than she had suspected. In the world of eyebrow-raising, he was a giant.

'I'm not at liberty to comment on that, Mrs Divot. Replies are given in strict confidence.'

'Mr Gamble, I meant nothing of what I said and I didn't mean to post it. I am making no allegations whatsoever and will write to you to confirm that. So far as I am concerned our postman is wonderful and I can't believe he would ever expose himself to anybody. Now I must go.' She put the phone down and met Mr

Beresford's eyes. 'Problems with our postman,' she said.

'So I gathered.'

'I'm sorry to phone in office hours but I had to clear my mind before I dealt with our more pressing matters.'

'More pressing, Mrs Divot? You really think our little business more important than your postman? I'm honoured. I'm flattered. I'm touched. When you've rung Mercia First Southern and Balshaw and sorted out any problems you may have with flashing milkmen, perhaps you'd run up a draft reply to Mercia First Southern arguing against their ridiculous over-reaction. Do you think you could spare me the time for that?'

The heaviness of his sarcasm, the bushiness of his eyebrows, the flashing of his eyes, it was disturbing to think that only ten minutes ago he had called her Alison.

'I'll get it done straightaway, Mr Beresford.'

'Good.'

He went back to the connecting door to his office, then turned and gave a twisted smile.

'He won't hold his job with Cornucopia,' he said. 'I've played golf with Sir Terence Manningham.'

And he left her to pick the bones out of that.

The *Throdnall Advertiser* leaked the story straightaway. 'Leading Throdnall Hotelier in Sex Change Shock.'

And there, near the bottom:

> Mr Divot is married with two children. Neighbours said today that they found it hard to believe. "They're such a lovely family, they seem so normal," said Edith Percival (73), a retired schoolteacher. "We've never had any trouble with them. I could understand it if it was 'riff-raff'."

Mr Divot's wife Alison (40) is personal assistant to Mr Clive Beresford, Managing Director of the besieged Throdnall Carriage Works.

Em was absolutely furious about the article. 'You promised me an exclusive,' she said. 'You promised! Bloody Mick Perkins getting a front page lead about *my* dad. I'm a laughing stock. Pipped to the post with a story about my own family. I'll never live it down. You promised, Dad, and I believed you. I thought I could trust you now you're becoming a woman. I should have realised you're still a man.'

Nicola protested till she was blue in the face that the leak hadn't come from her.

'Well it was stupid of you anyway to think it wouldn't come out,' said Em. 'All the people who go to your stupid hotel – God knows why – it was bound to come out. I feel such a fool. I feel humiliated.'

Mr Beresford was no less furious.

'I don't like it,' he said. 'I don't like being associated with it. And what do they mean – "besieged"? Have they got wind of the broken nuts? Have you said anything?'

'Mr Beresford!' she said indignantly. 'I am reliability personified. I embody the spirit of confidentiality. You said so yourself.'

'I know,' he said. 'I know. I'm sorry. I can't think straight. But what *do* they mean – "besieged"?'

What could she say? She couldn't say, 'Well, Mr Beresford, I think it's pretty well-known locally that the carriage works are going through a bad time.' It was the great unspoken fact, which could never be acknowledged.

'Well I don't want it happening again,' he said. 'Right . . .'

Cold winds had set in from the east, and Alison could feel a chill of fear gnawing away at her insides. Nicola had been summoned to head office. If she lost her job with Cornucopia, how could she possibly find another one? She would have to come clean about her condition. The voice might have softened, but there'd be no mistaking those large hands.

'Did you get that?'

'I'm sorry, Mr Beresford, I . . .'

'Pull yourself together, Mrs Divot. I cannot have a Personal Assistant whose mind wanders.'

'I'm so sorry, Mr Beresford.'

'These are some notes I've made on safety of rolling stock. Things I should say when I face the Strategic Rail Authority. Knock them into shape, please, and type them up for me.'

'Yes, Mr Beresford. Sorry, Mr Beresford.'

She was dismissed. She went to the door. She couldn't believe how often she was having to apologise to Mr Beresford. She wasn't an apologiser. Nick had always been the apologiser in the family. She was forthright, uncompromising Alison. What had happened to her?

'Mrs Divot?'

She turned, and saw that he was giving her a rather intense look. She wouldn't have gone so far as to say that his face softened. She wasn't sure if his face was physically capable of softening. But . . . there was a certain . . . almost warmth . . . in his eyes. She wondered if he was going to say something personal – hoped that he would, yet dreaded it.

'You've become virtually indispensable to me, Mrs Divot,' he said. 'I don't know what I'd do if I had to manage without you.'

A threat wrapped in a compliment with the delicacy of spicy meat wrapped in cabbage leaves on a stall in down-town Bangkok. Or was it a compliment wrapped in a threat?

She returned to her office and tried to make sense of his notes, but the words danced before her eyes. Nicola would lose her job. She would lose her job. They'd lose their house. The family would disintegrate. Well, get on with the work, then. Fight for your job.

Rail travel remains the safest form of travel in every continent and every country in the developed and developing such anxiety about our future that I can't sleep, can't eat. No, Alison, stick to the notes, forget your puny little life. The record of carriage makers in railway history is well-nigh unblemished. In two hundred and forty-six railway accidents analysed by the Penfold Rail Safety Research Group only five contained any element of failure of component parts of me long for the sex change, parts of me are beginning to wonder if the sacrifice is going to be too much, the risk too . . . No! Concentrate. Concentrate, Alison. Component parts of carriages. Checking procedures are . . .

She began to manage to give her mind to the job. She'd finished by twenty to five. The last angry defiance of the sun was still tingeing the sky a livid pink behind Toys Я Us. She could sense that outside their centrally heated sauna the world was fiercely cold. She handed the typed-up notes to Mr Beresford. He read them through very quickly, he could grasp a document within seconds.

'Yes. Fine. Good. Good. Ah, you've split up the statistics a bit. Good. Effective. Excellent. Well done, Mrs Divot. Mrs Divot?' This in a different tone, again she sensed the approach of something personal.

'Yes?'

'What do you do about sleeping arrangements?'

'I beg your pardon?'

'You and your "husband". Do you sleep in separate rooms now? I'm sorry, you think that too personal?'

'No, I'm . . . er . . . I'm just astounded, Mr Beresford. You've never . . . you never ask me things like that.'

'I couldn't help thinking about . . . your predicament. I mean if your husband is living as a woman, then in essence, if you were sharing a double bed you would be two women in one bed, you would be . . . lesbians!' He spat the word out.

'Oh no,' she said. 'Not that I have any objection to lesbianism between consenting adults . . .' She wasn't going to be cowed by his prejudice, 'but, no, we . . . I . . . we . . . there is no physical relationship between us, there hasn't been for some time.' She didn't want to be telling him all this, but she refused to be coy with him, and looked him full in the face. 'We do share a bed, we haven't said anything about that being odd, we just take it as a fact. We have no alternative, we haven't a spare room with the two children and my father living with us. It's something we, I suppose, since we can't do anything about it, just don't mention.'

'Mrs Beresford and I have slept in separate beds for thirteen years.'

She didn't think she really wanted to know that. Why had he told her? Was it a hint? Was he paving the way for an approach? Oh God, that would make things difficult; it would be harder than ever to tell him.

Oh Lord, he was going to speak again. What now?

'Yes,' he said, 'I think armed with this little lot I shall face the Strategic Rail Authority with confidence. Thank you, Mrs Divot.'

Alison had never felt so exhausted at the end of a day's work, and it wasn't exactly an evening of sweetness and light at home. Nicola was very touchy because she was nervous about her impending interview with Head Office. Em was still depressed over Giorgio and still furious about the article in the *Advertiser*. Gray chose that evening of all evenings to announce that he'd been surfing the net for male to female sex changes that had gone wrong, and had come up with a minister in Minnesota who had died of heart failure during the operation, a chiropodist in Ecuador who had suffered a mental breakdown after his body rejected his vagina, and a financial consultant in Kuala Lumpur who had returned to work after an apparently successful operation, only to bleed to death during a seminar on company pensions.

'Terrific,' said Nicola. 'Thank you for that, Gray. You've made my evening.'

And then Bernie came in very upset and said, 'I've just been to the loo in Garibaldi Terrace.'

'What do you mean?' asked Nicola.

'I know what Dad means,' said Alison. 'It's obvious. He went where the loo would have been in Garibaldi Terrace because he got confused.'

'That's right,' said Bernie. 'I were snoozing. I woke up. I said to her, "I'll just pop to t'loo", and I went there and it were the broom cupboard.'

'I hope you didn't pee on the brooms,' said Gray.

'Gray!' shouted Nicola edgily. 'That's no way to speak to your grandfather.'

'No, but what I mean is, me mind's beginning to go,' said Bernie.

'Your mind isn't beginning to go,' said Alison, putting her arm round him. 'I never heard such nonsense.'

'Of course it isn't,' said Nicola. 'Why, I myself went to the Gents' in the hotel the other day by mistake. Force of habit.'

'Aye,' said Bernie. 'That's different, is that. Force of habit, I can understand that in your case, Nick.'

'Nicola.'

'You what?'

'I'm calling myself Nicola now, Bernie. I did tell you.'

'You see. Me mind's going.'

'Your mind is *not* going, Dad,' said Alison. 'You'd been asleep and you woke up and your mind played a trick . . . a wish-fulfilment if you like. You wanted to be back in Garibaldi Terrace. You wanted Mum to still be alive.'

'Oh aye. I wanted that right enough.'

Alison was last to bed as usual, because she had to clear everything away and switch off all the lights.

She was so desperately tired, too tired to sleep. She knew that

Nicola, lying beside her, was pretending to be asleep. She thought of all the long hours that he had spent like that, over the years, never knowing that she didn't feel let down, that she had dreaded their inappropriate sexual fumblings just as much as he had. She suspected that they both imagined that everyone else in the street was doing it fifteen times a night, followed by a quickie on the breakfast table.

As she lay there, she wished that she had understood, years ago, why they didn't want sex with each other. She would never have embarked on her little affair if she had.

And it had been a little affair. Just three times she had gone to bed with her 'lover'. He was an attractive and persuasive man, and she had felt lonely and pleased to be wanted, so pleased to be wanted. Three agonies of hope and despair and fulfilment and disgust. It was on the third occasion, as he thrashed around like an elephant in Chester Zoo, that she had suddenly wished that she was a man and he a woman. God, what a shock. And that had been the time that she had conceived! One in the eye for those sentimental fools who said that you had to be in the right mood to conceive. That had been the day when she had understood that her childhood regret at not being a boy was the central fact of her existence. And nine months later she had given birth to Gray. What a secret to carry to the grave.

She had sensed that she was pregnant almost immediately. She couldn't be certain, but she couldn't risk it, so she'd had to get Nick to make love to her very shortly after that. With the compliments she paid him the night it happened, the fervency with which she told him how much she loved and admired him, success was sudden and joyous. Gray was born eight months and seven days later, and Nick never worked it out sufficiently accurately to suspect anything.

All this went through her mind in the long reaches of the endless night, as she lay next to Nicola, listening to her pretending to be asleep.

The carriage clock in the dining room struck three. Only three! They couldn't lie there like this all night, pretending to be asleep. It was farcical.

It's very hard, at three in the morning, to be up-beat, but Alison was nothing if not a fighter, and there in that bed in the middle of the long, slow night she forced herself back into a spirit of strength and resolve. Suddenly she knew that Mr Beresford would not defeat them, Cornucopia Hotels would not defeat them, Gray's warnings would not deflect them.

She longed to tell Nicola of her plans, but it was too soon – too soon to tell Bernie, she had to give him more time to grieve, and so she couldn't burden Nicola by telling her in secret.

She must offer some support, though, so she pretended to wake up, stirred, groaned, grunted, stretched, sighed. Moments later, Nicola began to pretend to wake up, groaned, stirred, stretched, sighed, grunted.

'Are you awake?' whispered Alison.

'Yes,' whispered Nicola. 'Just woke up. I was having a terrible dream.'

'Nicola?'

'Yes?'

'There are bound to be moments of doubt, but we mustn't let them defeat us.'

We! What a give-away! But Nicola didn't seem to have noticed.

Alison felt a great wave of love for Nicola. Instinctively, her fingers felt for her prick.

Nicola gasped.

'Alison!' she whispered. 'What are you doing? Please don't touch that. It's a dead thing, waiting to be removed.'

So much love to give, and no way of giving it. Hours later, the carriage clock struck four, and some time after that, eventually, they both fell asleep.

12 The Heavy Mob

Nicola presented herself at Cornucopia House, that inelegant glass box, that beacon of budget architecture, ten minutes early.

She was looking as smart as she knew how to be, not too blatantly feminine but not remotely masculine either. She'd chosen a grey pin-stripe trouser suit which she wore with a white blouse. Her shoes and handbag were black. She looked the essence of a well-groomed businesswoman. Alison had helped put the finishing touches to her make-up, and now, as she titivated in the Ladies', she felt that she really didn't look at all bad.

She sat in the ante-room to the Board Room, facing a large photograph of the Amsterdam Cornucopia, their first venture into Europe. She opened a copy of *Hotels and Hoteliers* and thumbed through the Situations Vacant.

> Manageress required for elegant sea-side hotel. Transsexuals preferred. The successful candidate must be requiring three months off for a major operation in the near future.

Some chance.

She hunted for a bridge column. There wasn't one. Pity. She felt starved of bridge. She hadn't yet dared go to the bridge club and tell them that she wanted to transfer to the ladies' team.

She tried to concentrate on an article entitled 'Tomorrow's Food?'

> Will the day come when hotel chains
> will cook their food centrally in
> powder form and send it to their
> individual hotels to be reconstituted?
> The savings could be enormous and
> Sebastian Snodgrass of the Instant
> Gourmet Group believes it could
> soon become a viable option.

She snapped the magazine shut. That sort of thing was only going to depress her. She recalled an astonishing word that Alison had used in bed the other night. She had said, 'We mustn't let them defeat us.' We! What an amazing word for her to use. What a woman. She was so involved in Nicola's sex change, so supportive of it, that she thought of it as a joint project. Nicola mustn't let her down.

A secretary, neat enough but rather shown up by Nicola's smartness, approached uncertainly.

Nicola stood up.

'I'm sorry,' said the secretary. 'I was looking for Mr Divot.'

'I am Mr Divot.'

The secretary hid her amazement most professionally. Nicola sympathised with her for her slight discomfiture. She should have been warned.

'Ah.'

'Quite.'

'This way.'

'Thank you.'

She opened the door of the Board Room and ushered Nicola in. She found herself in a large, long room dominated by a huge table, oblong with shallowly rounded ends. At one side of the table sat three men. At the other side, all the chairs had been removed except one.

Along the wall behind the men there was a huge picture

window. Along the opposite wall were paintings of leading Cornucopia hotels. The Throdnall was not among them.

'Good morning . . . er?' said the man in the middle.

'Ms Divot.'

'Do sit down, Ms Divot.'

Nicola sat down very carefully indeed. She was beginning to get more practised at not squashing her genitalia in her tights, but you couldn't be too careful.

She felt very isolated in her solitary chair. That, of course, was the idea.

There was silence as she arranged herself, and the silence continued after she was settled. It made her feel uneasy. That, of course, was the idea.

It is said that one's whole life flashes past one as one is drowning, and at that moment every aspect of the Throdnall Cornucopia flashed through Nicola's mind. She realised, to her amazement, that she loved that crappy old hotel. She loved the worn, stained carpets, the dusty chandeliers, the creaking, achingly slow lifts, Paulo's sad limp as he struggled across the barn-like restaurant with their over-priced wine list, the synchronised dome lifting to reveal the pitiful creations of Leonard Balby from Goole.

Behind the three men Nicola could see a great expanse of crisp blue sky criss-crossed by widening vapour trails. London's skyscrapers were glinting in bright sunlight.

'Ms Divot,' began the man in the middle, a large, crumpled man with a paunch and a double chin. 'I am Sir Terence Manningham, Chairman of Cornucopia Hotels. On my right is Mr Jeremy Barnstorm, OBE, Managing Director.' He indicated a neat, dapper man with an elegant suit, an expensive haircut and a well-groomed smile. 'On my left is Mr Brian Jukes, Personnel Officer.' He pointed towards a tall, untidy man wearing a lurid tie and an expression of anxiety.

Nicola felt an absurd pride. They had brought the heavy mob in for her.

'We have a board meeting this afternoon, so I'm afraid you've got the heavy mob,' said Sir Terence Manningham. He switched on a smile, but only in order to switch it off abruptly. 'We have been sent faxes of an article in the *Throdnall Advertiser*.' He invested deep contempt for local newspapers into those last two words. 'Do you have any comment?'

'Not really,' said Nicola, trying to make her voice sound soft and feminine. 'Pretty accurate on the whole.'

'Why didn't you inform us that you were planning a sex change?' asked Brian Jukes.

'I didn't think it relevant.'

'You didn't think it relevant,' said Jeremy Barnstorm, OBE in recognition of services to himself. 'It's hardly a minor detail.'

'Not to me, no, but I fail to see how it could affect my ability to do my job.'

'You fail to see how it could affect your ability to do your job!' Jeremy Barnstorm had come to hotels via steel, from where he had received a substantial settlement on his dismissal for poor results. He had gone to the steel industry from electricity, from where he had also received a substantial settlement on his dismissal for poor results. Clearly someone clever enough to receive repeated payments for failing must be the ideal man to run Cornucopia Hotels, especially as he was completely ignorant of hotels and would therefore come unencumbered by ideas. Nicola had to admit to a feeling of disappointment that, on the evidence of this interview, the brilliant man's technique of repeating everything she said seemed rather basic.

She thought of saying, 'Yes, I do. I fail to see how it could affect my ability to do my job', but then she thought that if nobody moved the conversation on the interview might go on for ever.

'Yes, I do,' she said. 'After all, I'm still the same person with the same brain, the same principles and the same experience. I must point out that I am not so much turning into a woman as accepting that I should always have been one and ironing out a few minor details.'

'Ironing out a few minor details,' said Jeremy Barnstorm, OBE for services to repeating things. 'That sounds a bit of an understatement for a sex change.'

'Yes, I like understatement. I'm very British.'

Nicola thought, afterwards, that she was being guided by her feminine intuition, the intuition that had so influenced her in deciding to become a woman. She hadn't intended to adopt so bold an attitude. She'd had no tactical plans as she entered the room.

'You wouldn't deny, I presume, that your sex change might affect how you're perceived?' asked Brian Jukes.

'Absolutely not,' she said, 'but that's other people's problem, not mine. I would also point out that in the nature of my work I don't have a great deal of day-to-day contact with the general public. They meet our waiters, our head waiter, our sommelier, our porters, our receptionists, our bar staff, but not me. If a manager does his or her job well enough, he or she is invisible.'

'Well now,' said Sir Terence Manningham, 'in considering whether you are one Divot that needs to be replaced – huh! . . .'

'Ha ha ha ha,' laughed Jeremy Barnstorm.

'Her her her her,' laughed Brian Jukes.

Oh God, thought Nicola. You'd think these people in these positions would be bright enough to realise that an adult has heard every possible joke about his name several hundred times at least. But she smiled, thinking as she smiled how callous it was of Sir Terence to joke about her possible dismissal in front of her.

'. . . we have to consider the publicity angle,' continued Sir Terence complacently. 'Publicity of this kind . . .' He waved the fax. '. . . is not helpful. This sort of thing could lose you the Rotary. Bit of a disaster, I would have thought, in Throdnall, if you lost the Rotary Club.'

'If publicity worries you,' said Nicola, 'I hope you'll reflect on the kind of publicity you might receive from the sexual equality lobby in these politically correct times if you sacked me almost immediately after I'd decided to become a woman.'

Think her naïve if you must (and when she looked back with hindsight she was astounded by her naïvety), but she hadn't even thought of this line of approach. It only occurred to her as she listened to Sir Terence.

She knew she'd scored a bull's-eye immediately. She realised afterwards that they probably thought she was issuing an unspoken threat. (She would have hated to have sued. She despised the culture of litigation. She didn't like lawyers and she liked their fees even less.)

All three men stared at her in silence for a moment, then exchanged looks for a moment, then went into a huddle for a moment, then whispered to each other for a moment. Then they nodded in unison, withdrew from the huddle in unison, and looked across the table at Nicola in unison.

'We believe that it is only fair, within the Cornucopia Code of Conduct,' said Sir Terence Manningham, and the other two men nodded in unison, 'to give you a chance to prove what you have claimed today, viz – that your . . . er . . . transsexuality . . . that is, I believe, the term . . . will have no adverse effect upon the Throdnall Cornucopia. Thank you, Ms Divot.'

'Thank *you*.'

13 Close Encounters of the Throdnall Kind

On the first Saturday after Nicola had 'come out', Alison went to their lawyers and instituted proceedings for divorce, on the grounds that Nicola had rendered them incompatible by changing sex. She had told Nicola that she was going to do it, and Nicola hadn't objected. It was inevitable.

She hadn't told Nicola that one day she would be changing sex and would want to be free to pursue a new life.

She knew that it was what she wanted, but she still didn't enjoy the visit to the solicitors. It was a sad moment.

Just after seeing them, she met Jane Collinson in the Saturday Market. This being Throdnall, there was no longer a market in the Saturday Market on a Saturday.

Jane looked embarrassed and said, 'Oh, I'm so glad I've run into you, Alison. It saves phoning.'

'What's happened?' asked Alison innocently.

'I . . . we . . . I hope you'll understand, but . . . next Saturday's dinner party. We're not going to be able to invite you after all.'

'What?'

'Well . . . you know . . . and Andrew's very . . . how can I? . . . conservative with a small c, well as well as with a big one really . . . and . . . it'll all be couples and you coming together, both as women . . . well . . . it'd untidy the table.'

Alison's mind worked quickly when she was angry. She decided to avoid outright rudeness. Sweet sarcasm would be more stylish.

'Of course I understand, Jane dear,' she said. 'We've been good friends for . . . what is it? . . . must be the best part of ten years. I'd always help you if you were in trouble, you know that, so of course I'd hate to untidy your table.'

Jane Collinson reddened and said, 'I'm sorry, Alison, but you know how it is', before escaping into the doorway of the nearest shop, only to discover that it was Woolworth's, in which she wouldn't be seen dead, so she had to come rushing out again past Alison in ever deepening embarrassment.

Nicola was upset when Alison told her the story.

'Look what I've landed you in,' she said.

'Don't even think like that,' said Alison.

Early in the new year, almost two months after Nicola had 'come out', there came an event that she dreaded but refused to avoid. It was the first round of the Ladies' Knock-out, the Palmerston Cup, at Throdnall Bridge Club.

There was considerable opposition, within the club, to her participation in the event, but, since nothing could be found in the rules that actually prohibited such a thing, it was decided to allow her to take part 'in the spirit of fair play and tolerance for which the club has always been noted'.

But who could she partner? It would have been easier, everyone felt, if she had partnered Alison, but Alison always played in the Palmerston Cup with Ann Pilkington, who was very easily slighted – she had no confidence, no woman could have any confidence if she was married to Philip Pilkington, so Alison felt that she couldn't let Ann down.

The solution was to pair Nicola with Hilda Neff. Hilda Neff was a dragon. Nobody wanted to play with her. It was an unspoken rule in the club that nobody should be forced to partner Hilda Neff two years in succession. She was running out of suitable partners and, faced with the stark choice of playing with Nicola or with nobody, she narrowly chose Nicola.

Nicola didn't enjoy the evening. She had a bit of a cold, which made her voice sound deeper and more masculine just when the hormones were really kicking in and softening it. Hilda Neff frowned every time she sniffed or blew her nose, so she took to visiting the lavatory to blow her nose between hands.

Throdnall Bridge Club saw itself as a fortress of morality surrounded by swamps of decadence. There were no unisex toilets. A proposal to make the toilets unisex had been rejected by the committee as 'giving out the wrong signal to our members'.

It might have been fine for Nicola to use the Ladies' in the hotel, but two lawyers, three wives of lawyers and four barrack-room lawyers were playing that night, and Nicola felt obliged to use the Gents' each time. This was very convenient, as there were no men present, but it incurred resentment because there was sometimes quite a queue for the Ladies'. 'I was in a no-win situation,' she said to Alison after the event.

Hilda Neff didn't make one piece of small talk to her all evening, but she clearly wanted to win very badly. Nicola realised that she desperately wanted to lose. She had made her stand, but she couldn't have faced playing in the second round, so she bid two absurd grand slams, both of which failed dismally, to ensure that they did lose.

Hilda Neff never spoke to her again.

Shortly after that, Nicola faced similar difficulties at the Golf Club. It was her second visit since the article in the *Advertiser*. On each occasion she had played a competitive eighteen holes with Alison, winning once and losing once. On each occasion she had used the men's locker room, believing that it would embarrass the ladies (except for Jennifer Griffin, of course, whom nothing could embarrass) if she used the ladies' locker room, complete as she still was with prick and testicles.

On each occasion they had gone into the nineteenth hole for a drink afterwards. Arnold Willink had said, 'Good on you, Nicola', rather spoiling it by adding, 'I said to Phyllis, "I'd never have thought he'd have the bottle"', but nobody else referred to the matter at all. The avoidance of it was like a constant shriek. One or two people snubbed them, others avoided them out of embarrassment, some clung to safe avenues of conversation, so that by the time they went home they felt qualified to become weather forecasters.

They were just finishing their second and last drink after their second eighteen holes when the PP entered, strode to their table and said, 'Word in your ear if you don't mind, Mr Divot.'

'I see no one of that name here,' said Nicola bravely. Alison felt that she had already shown more courage than she had ever shown as Nick.

'You know what I mean,' said the PP.

'Yes,' said Nicola. 'I shall be there, don't you worry, wing commander.'

Wing Commander Miles Forrester, Secretary of Throdnall Golf Club, known throughout the club as the PP, which stood for Pompous Prat, examined Nicola's use of his rank for traces of sarcasm, wasn't sure if he could find any, nodded, said 'Ten minutes?', didn't wait for an answer, and retired from the bar.

'Oh dear,' said Nicola to Alison. 'Crunch time.'

She presented herself at the Secretary's Office ten minutes late.

'Do sit down,' said the PP.

Nicola sat down carefully and glanced round the PP's room. The walls were covered in photographs and there were several framed photographs on his desk. All of them were of the PP. There were so many of him in front of aeroplanes that Nicola suspected that he had never actually held a flying job in his career.

'You have entered the men's competition and the ladies' competition,' said the PP. 'That's what we used to describe in the RAF as hedging your bets.'

First reference to the RAF! The PP would have been mortified if he'd known that people regularly had unhedged bets on how often he would refer to the service in a given time.

'Well yes,' said Nicola. 'I wasn't sure which one I should enter, so I entered both, awaiting your expert ruling.'

The PP failed to examine Nicola's remark for traces of sarcasm, and nodded modestly.

'Thank you,' he said. He scratched his wig as he regularly did while summoning up his authority. It wasn't a bad wig, but, since everybody knew it was a wig, Nicola failed to see how it could make him feel better about his baldness. 'The answer, I'm afraid, is neither. You cannot play in the ladies' competition because you are not technically a lady. Which tees would you play off? I think the ladies' tees would give you a most unfair advantage. None of the ladies would be happy to accept that. But how can one person in the ladies' competitions play off the men's tees? Surely you must see how impossible it is for you to play in the ladies' competitions.'

'So what will happen when I've had the operation and am a woman?'

'Shall we cross that horse when we come to it?' The PP had a disconcerting habit of muddling his metaphors.

'All right,' said Nicola, 'I accept that I can't play in the ladies' competitions, but why can't I play in the men's?'

'Because you are claiming to live as a woman,' said the PP. 'You have decided to give up your status as a man. I couldn't allow you to be untrue to your status as a man. I couldn't allow you to be untrue to your principles.' He smiled. His self-satisfaction erupted. 'You have consigned yourself to a golfing limbo. Golf-wise, Nick . . . Nicola . . . you are temporarily stranded in no-man's-land.'

'I think you mean no-woman's-land,' said Nicola.

'You are more than welcome, of course, to continue to use the club's facilities.'

'And you are more than happy to accept my subscription,' said Nicola, 'while not allowing me to participate fully in the club's activities.'

'You are welcome to resign any time you wish,' said the PP. 'I learnt in the RAF how important it is to run a happy ship.'

Even the PP looked slightly unhappy about that mixed metaphor.

These humiliations, little though each one might be, made Nicola's social life very wearing. She was in no-man's-land, and she was in no-woman's-land. The exhilaration of being able to live as a woman faded, as exhilaration does. She was still happier than she had been as a man, yet she longed not to *live* as a woman but to *be* a woman. How she yearned for the thing she dreaded – the surgeon's knife. She counted the days like a national serviceman longing for demob.

Life is short, Nicola, she told herself. Do not wish your life away. Relish these two years. Enjoy Alison's amazing support. Take comfort from your pleasant, desirable home. Enjoy the growing up of Gray, for all that ninety-seven per cent of it takes place in the privacy of his room. Take pride in how much prettier Em is looking, now that she has met François, even if the gamine, Parisian-waif look that she is adopting sits uneasily on her slightly heavy frame. Enjoy your family.

In the first three months after Nicola 'came out', the bedrooms of the Cornucopia Hotel averaged an occupancy rate of 67 per cent. In the Kenilworth Brasserie, 23.2 per cent of the tables were occupied, on average, at lunchtime, and 36 per cent in the evenings. The Warwick Bar served an average of twenty-two meals a day, compared to its theoretical maximum of a hundred and twenty.

Be proud of these improvements, Nicola. Do not long for your time in the hotel to pass, she thought.

Nicola felt that it was churlish of Head Office not to make any comment, modest though the increase in business was. She knew that at least some of it was the result of her sex change. People were curious to catch a glimpse of her. Businessmen wanted to see whether her legs were muscular or elegantly slim, and just how much or how little she had in the bust department. It was a shock to her to realise just how much of a sex object a woman was, but she had put herself into the public domain and she must live with it. Truth to tell, she was just a little excited to be an object of interest. She had never been an object of interest before.

Sometimes, though, it was thoroughly unpleasant. She could never be sure that she wouldn't be taunted, in the shops or the streets, by someone who suspected. One day a man lurched out of the betting shop in front of her and shouted, 'Show us your prick, sweetheart.' She could never be certain who knew and who didn't. A man she'd nodded to several times over the years stood back in the newsagent's and said savagely, 'I can wait. Serve the perv.' It happened rarely, but the threat was ever-present. On days when she felt weak she had to force herself to venture into the town. She became self-conscious about her large hands, tried to hide them, but you couldn't sign credit cards with your hands in your pockets.

On the staff front, things went on much as before. She found Paulo a little more difficult, a little less respectful, and she summoned him to her office.

'Are you not respectful to women in Portugal?' she asked him.

'But of course we are,' he said. 'We are a romantic race.'

'I don't want you to be romantic,' said Nicola, 'but a bit of respect wouldn't come amiss.'

She didn't have any trouble with him after that.

Emrys, the Welsh commis chef, asked for an interview, at which he requested that there should always be a Welsh speciality on the menu. He suggested a rotation of Glamorgan sausages, and cawl, and of bara brith and butter pudding.

'I'm sorry, Emrys,' said Nicola, 'but I don't have the authority to change the menu. It's dictated by Head Office policy.'

'You have Warwickshire specialities.'

'Yes, but this is Warwickshire. You know as well as I do that the Cornucopia menu is standard with one local dish and one chef's signature dish. In any case, nobody ever orders the Warwickshire specials.'

'No, because they're not genuine, see,' protested Emrys. 'Who ever heard of Leamington Force Meat Balls? Who ever heard of Edgbaston Pie? Mine are genuine, see. I think there'd be a call for them among the Welsh expat community.'

'Is there a Welsh expat community in Throdnall?'

'There's Councillor Watkins.'

'I agree he's overweight but he hardly amounts to a community. And he never eats in the hotel.'

'Maybe he would if there were Welsh specialities!'

'Look, I appreciate your initiative and your patriotism, but rules are rules.'

Emrys leant across the desk, short, stocky, with his dark eyes glittering fanatically.

'I want to be head chef,' he announced.

'We have a head chef, Emrys.'

'That long streak of Yorkshire piss. That miserable . . .'

'Emrys, please don't talk about my staff like that.'

'. . . plodding journeyman. There's no love of food in his blood. No passion. He's . . .'

'Emrys, please!'

'He's a manager, not a chef.'

'Emrys, I run this hotel, not you.'

She tried to stare Emrys out, and it worked!

'My quarrel's not with you,' he said.

'Look, Emrys,' she suggested, 'if you're ambitious, perhaps you should go back to Wales.'

'I can't. My wife hates Wales. The kids have settled at school. Settled, do you see? What can I do? The kids come first in my book. I'm trapped, Ms Divot. Trapped.'

'What can I say, Emrys? Leonard isn't a young man. He won't be with us for ever. Continuity is highly valued in the Cornucopia Code of Conduct. Be patient. Your reward will come if you behave yourself. *If* you behave yourself. So lay off Leonard. There's no room for hatred in my kitchens. And don't think, Emrys, that I'll be a pushover just because I've become a woman.'

'I don't think any of us think that,' said Emrys, and he couldn't quite hide the surprise in his voice.

Two days later, Leonard Balby asked for an interview, plonked himself opposite Nicola and looked across her desk at her with an expression that would have curdled mayonnaise.

'Has that Welsh windbag asked for Welsh specialities on the menu?' he asked.

Nicola tried to remain calm.

'My interviews with my staff are completely confidential, Leonard.'

'I knew it! Bloody Welsh windbag.'

'Please don't refer to a colleague in that way, Leonard.'

'Colleague? Bloody Welsh toerag.'

'Leonard!'

'T'other day – last Tuesday – no, I tell a lie, Wednesday, 'cos Warwickshire speciality were Coventry Tart – he were cooking gammon chops, he were looking vacantly into space, I said, "Hey, Taffy, what's up wi' you?" He said, "Our menu's boring. I was just thinking about the fricassee of rabbit with leeks my nan used to make." I said, "Emrys, the man has ordered gammon chop, we can't say to him, 'Sorry. We'd rather you had fricassee of rabbit with leeks like Emrys's nan used to make.' So, Emrys," I said, "get real and . . ." May I swear in front of you, ma'am?'

'Of course. I want the truth, Leonard.'

'I said, "and fuck off about your fucking fricassee".'

Nicola wanted to laugh. She knew that as Nick she would have been very uptight about the f-word. As Nicola she just wanted to laugh at poor Leonard. She couldn't find it in her to hate him.

'He doesn't respect me like what he should,' said Leonard Balby. 'He has a look in his eye, contemptuous like. I want him gone. I want rid, ma'am. That kitchen isn't big enough for the both of us.'

Nicola no longer found Leonard funny. This was intolerable, and she hadn't liked that 'ma'am'. There had been sarcastic undertones.

She met her head chef's eye and didn't flinch. She was a little frightened of him, and her heart was racing, but she was brave enough not to show it. Compared to the process of changing sex the problem of Leonard Balby paled into insignificance. She realised that she had become at least a slightly stronger person than she had been.

'Who do you think you are?' she asked. 'Wyatt Earp? Gordon Ramsay? Please don't tell me what I should do with my staff. You are always free to resign – if you believe that at the age of fifty-six you will be able to land a comparable post.'

'I'll take this further,' he said. 'I'll complain to Head Office. Don't think I don't have the courage of my convictions.'

He had handed it to her on a plate, so much so that she almost didn't want to take it. It hardly seemed ladylike.

'I would remind you,' she said, 'that Head Office are unaware that your *convictions* are for GBH, drunkenness and driving while uninsured.'

Leonard Balby's mouth opened and closed twice, but no further sound emerged from it.

On the whole Nicola was pleased with the way she had handled her first staff crisis as a woman, but she didn't kid herself that she had solved the problem, and when she saw the billboard, her blood ran cold.

It was the Saturday after the interview with Leonard. She was driving home from the wine merchant's (she refused to take advantage of the preferential terms she could get on Cornucopia wine; she didn't think there was anything drinkable on their list) and there it was outside a newsagent's on Clarion Road.

Chef Drowned In Canal

Her heart thumped. Her head thudded. Her brakes screeched. Which of them was it? She hoped it wasn't Emrys, because of his children, but if it was Leonard, Emrys would be imprisoned for life anyway.

She ran to the newsagent's, practically grabbed the paper, hunted through it, couldn't read for panic.

At last she found it.

When she read that the chef of a burger bar in Birmingham had fallen into the Coventry Canal on his drunken stag night, and drowned on the eve of his wedding, she felt an overwhelming flood of relief.

A wasted life. A distraught bride. Devastated parents. A flood of relief.

Man, woman. Nick, Nicola. We can escape from some things, thought Nicola, but we can never escape from the self-centred nature of our puny little lives.

14 Alison Makes Her Move

It was about six months after Nicola had 'come out' when Alison realised that her father had recovered from Marge's death as much as he ever would. He might live for many years. The time had come for her to make her move.

She had waited so long that she felt more nervous than she had when she had first resolved to do it. She had waited so long that it almost seemed as if waiting was her natural activity.

Having seen how rigorous the examination of Nick had been before he had been accepted, she decided that she would consult the doctors before she took her family into her confidence.

As she sat in the surgery she thought of Nick sitting there at the beginning of his journey.

Doctor Rodgerson was running late. Good doctors always run late, because they take an interest. Bad doctors, unlike bad trains, always run on time.

She tried to interest herself in dreary articles in elderly magazines. She pictured Nick reading similar articles all that time ago. 'Hedges can be sexy,' she read without interest. 'The Walsall Nobody Knows' failed to grab her imagination. She greeted 'Bridlington – the new Dubrovnik' with bored disbelief. She couldn't concentrate.

She tried a bridge column, but suddenly had an image of herself in the men's team, playing against Nicola. What a sensation that was going to be.

'Alison Divot.'

She strode into Doctor Rodgerson's surgery.

'Good morning, Alison.'

'Good morning, doctor.'

'I've missed seeing you round the dinner table.'

'You could always invite us. Then you'd see us. But of course it would untidy your table. There ought to be signs on the roads approaching town. "Throdnall Welcomes Tidy Tables".'

Doctor Rodgerson was disconcerted. Alison's directness often disconcerted people.

'How's . . . er . . . your . . . er . . . your hu . . . your wi . . . er . . . Nick . . . ola . . . doing?'

'Very well, thank you, doctor. I'm surprised she hasn't kept in touch to tell you. We shouldn't consider you only when we need you. I hope I won't do that.'

'Quite. Absolutely. Good. What? What do you mean?'

'After my sex change.'

'What?! You too?'

'Yes. Sorry.'

Doctor Rodgerson lowered his voice dramatically.

'You *are* serious, are you? It isn't April the First, is it?'

'It isn't April the First. No, I'm afraid I'm serious.'

'I have to ask you, Alison: did you get the idea from Nick . . . ola? Is this some kind of copy-cat thing?'

'*No!*'

'All right. All right. I didn't mean to be offensive. One has to ask, Alison, if only to eliminate it.'

'Yes, of course – I'm sorry – and why are we suddenly speaking in such low voices?'

'Well we don't want this to come out, do we? It'll cause a sensation, both of you doing it.'

'You think so?'

'Of course. People are fascinated by sexual deviation.'

'I wouldn't describe it as sexual deviation.'

'No, no. No, no. Oh, no, no. No. I know. Quite. But people will. The world can be very small-minded, especially in Throdnall. We need to proceed carefully. The first step is to send you to Langridge at the gender identity clinic.'

As she drove to the station car park Alison thought of that day when she'd driven Nick to the station. There was nobody to drive her.

As she sat in Doctor Langridge's waiting room, trying to get interested in an article entitled, 'We Were All Marsupials Once. Doctor Eunice Barrage Knocks A Hole Through Darwinism', her mobile suddenly rang in her pocket, startling the living daylights out of her and vibrating her breasts like jelly on dinner plates in a force eight in the Bay of Biscay.

'Hi,' said Nicola. 'It's me.'

This amused Alison on two counts. As Nick he had hated it when people said, 'It's me.' 'A phone call is always from "me",' he would say. 'All it means is, "Hello, I am the person speaking to you on the telephone." It's a philosophical impossibility for it not to be "me".' And he'd never said 'Hi.' He loathed 'Hi'. 'What's wrong with good old dignified "hello"?' he would ask.

Now, after just a few months, he was becoming a thoroughly modern miss.

All this flashed through her mind in seconds, along with her dismay that Nicola had rung her here. She didn't want the news to break accidentally. She would have to lie.

'Where are you?'

'At work. Why?'

'Well I rang you at work. They said you were off with a migraine.'

'I say "at work". I'm just driving to work. I tried to get to work and then the migraine came on and I went home, but then it began to wear off again so I've forced myself to go in. We've a lot on.'

'You shouldn't use your mobile in the car. It's dangerous.'

'Well you shouldn't have rung me.'

'I didn't know you were in the car!' Nicola sounded irritated. 'What did you ring me for?'

'To say I was sorry you had a migraine.'

'But you didn't know I had a migraine when you rang the office.'

'No, but they told me.'

'So why did you ring the office? On the off-chance that I might have a migraine and you could be sorry about it?' She had never had a migraine. All her migraines had been fictional.

'Of course not. Actually, to be honest, I just suddenly felt that I wanted to hear your voice, and I rang on impulse.'

'Oh, Nicola.'

Doctor Langridge emerged from his office.

'Mrs Divot?'

'I have to go now, Nicola. I've seen a policeman.'

She rang off hastily, and stood up.

'A policeman?' enquired Doctor Langridge.

'It was my husband. I didn't want her to know I'm coming to see you yet.'

'Yes, of course.' He said this drily, meaning, 'Well, this is a situation, isn't it?'

He shook her hand. His handshake was like a rock crusher, she expected her bones to shatter, but his voice was pleasant and reassuring.

He led her into his office. They sat in leather armchairs, which squeaked like nervous gerbils. The room was almost aggressively neutral, a place of overwhelming calm. Doctor Langridge made her feel calm.

'Well, this is extraordinary, Mrs Divot,' he said. 'Quite extraordinary.'

'I suppose so. Sorry.'

'No, no. Don't be sorry. I'm not sure if I should say this, Mrs Divot, but professionally this is . . . rather intriguing. A privilege. Your husband is doing terribly well. She really is. Terribly well. Now, tell me how *you* feel about your gender.'

'I feel like a man trapped in a woman's body.' He frowned. She had known he would. 'Well I know it sounds like a cliché, but I can't find any way of expressing it better.'

'Did you . . . this question may irritate you, but I have to ask it. Did you get the idea of changing sex from your husband? Is there . . . a competitive element in this? A copy-cat element?'

'No, there is not, Doctor Langridge,' she said indignantly. 'I do not copy. I'm not the pathetic little woman who gets ideas from her hubby. I'd intended to do it. I couldn't do it while my mother was alive. He got in first – the story of the man–woman relationship throughout the ages.'

'So, is there a political element in your desire?'

'Doctor Langridge, I am expecting to go through great difficulties and great pain. Do you think that politics, especially sexual politics, which is what I assume you mean, could ever be worth enduring that?'

'I have to ask these questions, Mrs Divot. It's my job. I'm delighted to be able to eliminate these irrelevances, believe me. I have my problems too, Mrs Divot. I receive considerable professional flak. Many people dispute the validity of what I do. Many people believe that we are exploiting vulnerable people for our own professional and financial ends. I have to be as thorough as the wind and as pure as the driven snow. I have to be 110 per cent certain that we are doing the right thing for you. If we find out, after the operation, that it wasn't right, it's too late.'

'Yes. I know. I'm sorry.'

He asked her a lot of questions about her childhood, her puberty, her adolescence, her adulthood. She found it quite comforting, surrounded by those carefully restful walls, to talk about herself. She understood why people had psycho-analysis, though she was profoundly sceptical of whether they should, since the unhappy are usually too self-absorbed and she couldn't see how such people could be helped by being encouraged to talk about themselves. Anyway, she told him all about her youth as a tomboy, and how people who didn't know her sometimes said, 'Isn't he a lovely little boy?', to her mum's fury.

'I always preferred boys to girls. Mum thought it was because I was over-sexed. I never told her it was because I felt like them, not because I fancied them. I think I knew instinctively that she might find that an even more dangerous thought than sex. I think I knew that this was my naughty secret which must never be revealed.'

She told him about being sent home from school for swearing, about her hatred of netball and lacrosse, about the day an uncle from London took her to White Hart Lane and she saw Spurs beat Wolves and felt that she belonged there in that vast aggressive mass of maleness, so that she was hooked into a lifetime of completely avoidable misery season after season.

She told him, just slightly shyly, how strange she had found the act of copulation, in particular the element of submission. She had never grown to love it and had been grateful when it disappeared from their lives quite naturally. She told him that she had found the sight of an erect penis absurd rather than stimulating, how a schoolfriend's parents had grown an asparagus bed and one May she had seen the asparagus coming up like rows of erect penises, how she hadn't much liked asparagus since, let alone . . . she let him finish the sentence in his mind. She was, after all, still a woman. She couldn't be too indelicate.

However much we tell, we never tell everything. Nobody does.

She didn't tell him – it would have seemed like a betrayal of Nick – that her dear husband's penis had not been vast, as she had discovered from the only other man she had ever slept with, although she supposed that it was possible that Hungarians had unusually large penises, and Nick's was normal. She had never seen any league tables of international penile dimensions, though in this age of tables and lists it was inconceivable that one didn't exist somewhere.

Doctor E.F. Langridge MB ChB FRCPsych FRANZCPsych nodded, even looked on the verge of smiling once or twice. Outside, far away, Alison could hear a siren. It emphasised the calm in the room, rather than disturbing it.

'You'll know from your husband's experiences what a lengthy

process you're putting yourself forward for,' said Doctor Langridge. 'On the whole the problems are greater for women wanting to become men than for men wanting to become women.'

'Surprise surprise.'

'It seems odd to see feminism raising its ugly head . . .' He frowned at his inappropriate choice of phrase. '. . . from a woman on the verge of abandoning womanhood.'

'I'm not abandoning it because we get a raw deal. I'm abandoning it because I have to because I am not a woman.'

'Well anyway there is one part of the process that women find easier than men, and that is the Real Life Test.'

'Well I suppose women wear trousers and shirts quite naturally, while men don't wear skirts and dresses.'

'True.'

'There's a great tradition in theatre of laughing at men in drag, but not at women dressed as men. In pantomime the comic is a man dressed as a woman, the hero is a woman dressed as a man.'

How she'd suffered, taking the children to pantomimes in Throdnall. They featured 'B' List or even 'C' List celebrities and they were tacky.

'You've thought about all this quite a lot,' said Doctor Langridge.

'A great deal. A very great deal.'

'During the period of your Real Life Test you will be given testosterone by injection. Your voice will deepen. You will develop facial and bodily hair. You will become more muscular. Now I really must talk you through the operation, or rather, operations. I'm afraid that for women there are several.'

'I might have guessed.'

'Mrs Divot, this is due to God or evolution or a combination of the two and not prejudice or cruelty on the part of the medical profession.'

'I know. I'm sorry.'

Her throat was dry. She sipped the water so thoughtfully provided.

'I'm merely pointing out what you'll have to go through without any guarantee of a happy future at the end of it.'

'I can guarantee an unhappy future if I don't go through with it, so what have I to lose?'

'Several parts of your body for a start. Now, I . . . I must ask a very important question. Do you want to have a penis?'

'Well . . . er . . . yes, I . . . I would like one, please, if . . . er . . . if there's one going. I mean, surely . . . er . . . to become a man . . . er . . . without one would be a very incomplete process?'

'Let's not fool ourselves, Mrs Divot. This is going to be an incomplete process whether or not you have a penis. You will not have testes. You will still have female chromosomes. Now I need to ask you a question that will surprise you because you won't have thought about such a choice. What is the thing that you most want from your penis – sexual gratification or urination?'

'Goodness, what a question.' She took another sip of water. It began to feel very hot in that screamingly quiet room. Sometimes she found it difficult to think silently. This was one of those times. She had to articulate her thought processes as she was thinking them, in order to think them. 'Well, I mean, one would have to say that sex is generally regarded as a far greater source of pleasure than peeing.'

'That is undoubtedly true.'

'On the other hand, you can live without sex, but you can't live without peeing.'

'That is undoubtedly true, too.'

She couldn't believe that they were taking this conversation seriously, yet she realised that they had to, it was at the heart of the matter.

'Although if nobody used penises for sex the human race would have peed itself to extinction long ago.'

'True yet again.'

'Which doesn't help much, and yet I suppose it does, because . . .

because, do you know, I have to say, rather to my surprise, and rather to my disappointment, that the answer's urination.'

'I'm glad of that. I cannot guarantee you a satisfactory sex life as a man, but I can almost certainly promise that you'll be able to stand at a urinal with the best of them. Note that I say "almost certainly". In this dangerous area nothing, but nothing, comes with a guarantee. I really must point out that, while there are of course nerves in the clitoris, in its elongation into a penis there is no probability – not even, I would say, a possibility – of a capacity to have erections and/or orgasms.'

Doctor Langridge had not been speaking in a loud voice, but now he began to talk in little more than a whisper.

'I'm not a surgeon, but I'm now going to tell you what's involved in the operations that you will need.'

He went through the details of the mastectomy, hysterectomy and phalloplasty that Alison would need to undergo. His voice was calm and kind and methodical. It would have been impossible to have described the gruesome details less harshly, and Alison was a brave and determined woman who refused to flinch. Injections did not worry her, dentists did not alarm her, the sight of blood did not upset her, she watched operations in films without flinching. Yet by the time Doctor Langridge had finished his detailed account of the horrors that her body would have to endure, her knuckles were almost as white as Nick's had been in that very chair all those months ago.

When he had finished there was silence, a long silence. Alison could think of no suitable comment with which to break it. She waited patiently.

'So,' said Doctor Langridge at last, 'do you still want to go through with it?'

'My kids used to say, "I need an icecream," ' said Alison. 'I'd say, "No, you don't *need* an icecream. You *want* an icecream." It's the other way round with me. No, Doctor Langridge, I don't want these operations. I dread them. But I need them. Oh God, Doctor Langridge, how I need them.'

15 Bon Appetit

Alison and Nicola faced each other across the sitting room/
lounge, in a slightly combative way, although Nicola had no idea
why they were being combative. Alison stood with her back to the
log-effect fire and it crossed Nicola's mind that she looked a bit
like the squire in front of his hearth, but she still didn't twig.

'Special occasion?' she said. 'Dinner? What is all this?'

'I've something to announce. Something to tell you all. I'd like
to tell you first, now, before they all come through.'

Bernie was watching snooker in the granny flat, Gray was
officially doing his homework but was more likely to be surfing the
net, Em was packing in readiness for her visit to Paris to see
François. They had the room safely to themselves, as usual.

'Nicola? When you said you were going to change sex . . . oh
shall we sit down? This seems so confrontational, and there's
nothing confrontational about it.'

They sat down, Alison on the settee, leaving Nicola the Parker
Knoll.

'When you said you were going to change sex – and afterwards
when you began your Real Life Test – you said that I'd been very
understanding about it all.'

'Well I thought you were.'

'I was understanding because I understood because I knew all
about such things because I'd read all about such things. You must
be able to see what I'm driving at. Use your instinct. You're a
woman.'

Nicola gawped at her. It couldn't be. She . . . she didn't know
what to say. She was so shocked that she couldn't bring herself to
articulate the words.

'Yes,' said Alison. 'I was planning to become a man. I wasn't going to do it while Mum was alive, but I had definitely decided to do it. You pre-empted me.'

'Good Lord,' said Nicola. 'Good Lord. I never . . .'

'No. You were utterly wrapped up in your own journey. You didn't have room to spare a thought for me.'

'Oh, Alison, Alison. I'm so sorry.'

'Well now it's time for my journey.'

'What??' Nicola still hadn't realised that she actually intended to do it.

'I've seen Doctor Langridge. There's a long way to go, as you know, but I seem to have sort of been accepted. You'll have to sign a letter just like I did.'

Nicola could think of no articulate reply. She was shocked.

'You aren't shocked, are you, Nicola?'

'Of course I'm not.'

'You couldn't be. Even you couldn't be hypocritical enough to be shocked.'

'No. Quite. No, I . . .' Nicola was floundering. 'I . . . I'm not remotely shocked. I mean, not in the sense of "shocked". Surprised, yes. Astounded, yes. I mean . . . I just can't get over it. Both of us.'

'Come and sit beside me. Hold my hand.'

'What?'

'Is that too awful to ask? We are man and wife. Well, woman and wife.'

Nicola went over to the settee and held her hand. Alison gave her a sudden kiss on the cheek. Nicola didn't feel entirely comfortable about that.

'What about the family?' she asked. 'You have to think of them, Alison. You just can't do this to them.'

Alison leapt up from the settee. Their time together there had been brief.

'I don't believe I'm hearing this,' she said. 'I support you through thick and thin and then you tell me I can't do it.'

'Only because you're doing it second, and it'll be too much for them to take.'

'So if I'd got in first you'd have dropped the whole idea, would you, for the sake of the family?'

'Well . . .'

'You wouldn't have, would you?'

'We can't know, can we? It's hypothetical.'

'It's not hypothetical. It's hypocritical.'

'I'm thinking of them, Alison. It's nothing to do with me any more. And . . .' Nicola stopped abruptly.

'And?'

'Nothing.'

'No, go on. You can't stop now.'

'It's going to . . . no, it'll be all right, I expect.'

'What? What are you talking about?'

'No. It's all right.'

'No, sorry, I insist that you tell me what you're talking about.'

'Money. It's going to stretch our resources, but we can do it.'

'I don't believe what I'm hearing.'

'That's why I didn't want you to hear it. That's why I stopped.'

'So we can afford you doing it, but not me. Is that it? Terrific.'

'I didn't say that. I was just stating the obvious, that if we both do it privately, money will be tight. We'll manage, though. Just. We'll manage, Alison.'

Nicola didn't have a leg to stand on in these arguments, and she was honest enough to admit it to herself, if not to Alison.

If she didn't have a leg to stand on, they might as well sit down again. Nicola held Alison in her arms and gently pulled her down on to the settee. She didn't want to, but she didn't feel that she could do otherwise.

'I'm sorry,' she said. 'It's just that it's been such a shock. I mean, I can hardly believe it. It's such a coincidence.'

'I don't think so.'

'What?'

'Look back on those early days in Thurmarsh, Nicola. We were outcasts in a world of gender clichés. It was our sexual ambivalence that attracted us to each other in the first place.'

'So the thing that's attracted us to each other is what's driven us apart.'

'Yes.'

'Sad, really.'

'But a fact.'

Nicola squeezed Alison's hand. Alison squeezed hers. And that was that. No increase in intimacy beyond that was possible to them under the circumstances.

'I'll get dinner,' said Alison.

They ate in the dining room. For some reason everybody in the family complained when they ate in the dining room, but Alison didn't see the point of having one if you didn't use it. Nowadays lots of homes had through rooms and the dining area was just part of the lounge, and many homes didn't have a dining area at all. Alison found that quite awful. To her having meals together was the centrepiece of family life. She thought that our civilisation was hurtling towards its end, but she kept quiet about it.

She couldn't pretend that their dining room was exciting. It had the chill stamp of disuse upon it, like a roped-off parlour in a damp, stone-built stately home. It was quite small, and you couldn't have the coal-effect fire on full-blast or the person nearest to it roasted.

On the wall above the hostess trolley there was another Ferenc Gulyas – Lake Balaton, he said, although it looked suspiciously like Derwentwater to Alison.

She had done her best to create an atmosphere – lit some candles – dimmed the lights – drawn the curtains against the sodden Throdnall night.

Things passed off fairly peacefully during the French onion soup – Bernie slurped but Alison didn't comment, she didn't want to provoke – but Em and Gray began sniping during the coq au vin. Em had abandoned vegetarianism the moment Giorgio appeared on the scene. 'It's a battle we're never going to win,' she'd told them, sheepishly. 'I'm going to support free-range, natural, organic foods from now on. That's a battle we can win. It's fine being radical, but you have to have practical goals.'

Alison had caught Nicola's eye and she'd half-smiled. Before he'd begun his sex change process he'd have made some sarcastic comment about Em's opinionating, like 'Really? Hang on while I get some paper and make a note of that.' Not any more. She was becoming softer, less sarcastic, gentler. A nicer person.

'Lovely,' said Em of the coq au vin. 'Don't tell me you can't tell it's free-range and organic. I mean it tastes . . .'

'. . . happy,' interrupted Gray. 'It tastes very happy. Bit pissed off about being decapitated, but basically happy.'

'Do shut up, Gray,' said Em wearily.

'I was agreeing with you,' protested Gray insincerely.

'It's expensive, I know that,' said Bernie. 'I were with her when she bought it. She told me what it cost. "How much??" I said. I were flambergasted.' That would have been all right, but he went on to add, 'Fads are stupid.'

'Fads??' said Em, rising to the bait like a starving salmon. 'Stupid?? Oh. Caring about animals is stupid, is it? Caring about animals is faddish, is it?'

'Sorry I spoke,' said Bernie complacently.

Alison should have held her tongue, but she was tense, and she wasn't brilliant at holding her tongue, and she didn't.

'No you aren't,' she said. 'You're out to make trouble tonight. Snooker not going well?'

'Switched it off,' said Bernie. 'Couldn't bear it. Jimmy White's leading Stephen Hendry five–one.'

'I thought Jimmy White was the one you liked, Gramps,' said Em. She was trying to make amends. There was a good girl buried under all her nonsense.

'He is,' said Bernie. 'Marge loved him. I turned to her just now, at the end of the fourth frame, which Jimmy won on the black, and I smiled at her, and she wasn't there. That's one of the saddest things about losing somebody. You lose the pleasures you used to share.'

There was a silence at that.

'She's been gone months.' He could never bring himself to use the word 'dead'. He always had to soften it. 'Months. And I turned to her as if she was there. It's the first sign of Alzheimer's.'

'It isn't a sign of Alzheimer's, Bernie,' said Nicola. 'It's a sign of a great and wonderful love.' She seemed almost embarrassed by her emotion, emotion that she could never have shown as Nick.

'Mind you, to be fair,' said Bernie, 'she liked Stephen too. But she wanted to mother Stephen, but she'd have fancied a night on the tiles with Jimmy. Vulnerable, you see. What it is with women and sport, they fall for the vulnerable ones. Jimmy White, George Best, John McEnroe. They fall for the ones who wear their hearts on their sleeves.'

They rounded the meal off with tarte au citron. Em was only really happy with French food now that she was in love with François. The land of Em's lovers became paradise, and Alison went along with it for the sake of peace. A pall of garlic had hung over the house since François had come on the scene, but Bernie didn't like garlic, so on that important night Alison had chosen dishes that were French but had minimal garlic. Choosing menus had become a difficult balancing act.

At the end of the meal, Alison stood up.

'Coffee will be served in the sitting room,' she said, 'but before that I have an announcement to make.'

Behind her, the coal-effect fire glowed cheerfully.

'I have something important to tell you. There's no way of breaking it gradually. I'm going to change sex too. After tonight, you will please know me as Alan.'

They all just gawped. Shock united them as nothing else could.

The alarm call of a blackbird pinked loud in the silence of the dusk.

'I've lived too long,' said Bernie.

'What a story!' exclaimed Em.

Gray didn't say anything. He tried to stand up, swayed, swooned, and crashed to the ground in a faint.

16 A Taste of Fame

Alison hardly slept all night. Beside her, Nicola slept, woke, pretended to be asleep, fell asleep, stirred, grunted, and, just after four o'clock, said, 'I really am very sorry, sir', so she must have been dreaming about a customer at the Cornucopia.

Alison dropped off just once, only to be woken a few minutes later by an almighty clattering of bottles. An urban fox was rooting around in the black bags outside number thirty-eight. One of the Parkers, or maybe both, had a major drink problem. It wasn't surprising, really. Their house was up for sale. He said it was because the area was bad for her catarrh, but that was nonsense. They'd been declared bankrupt and they had to sell, and they had to keep it all secret from people they would never see again.

Alison told herself that her problem was nothing compared to the Parkers' difficulties, but that didn't help her sleep. Her mind was too busy.

She was thinking, of course, about the approaching morning, when she would face Mr Beresford for the first time dressed as a man. She tried not to be nervous about it. Damn it, she wasn't a nervous woman – but she defied any woman not to be nervous when facing Mr Beresford at such a moment.

Several very long months had passed since that evening when she had told the family, but she was thinking now of the years she still had to face, the two years of the Real Life Test, the three major operations, this vast journey to an uncertain destination. There was a temptation, just a little window of temptation, as dawn crept into the bedroom like a guilty husband, to give it up, quietly drop the whole thing, take all the clothes back to London.

It was a temptation that made her uneasy, even though she knew that she wouldn't give in to it.

It was absurd of her, as she listened to the magnificence of the dawn chorus, to wish to be a garden bird. How happy the birds seemed, but they weren't free from the fear of predators for one waking second of their brave little lives.

She thought about Em, sleeping . . . or not sleeping . . . on the other side of the wall.

She had taken Em to London to help her buy men's clothes. She hadn't dared buy them within a thirty mile radius of Throdnall, for fear that the story of the double sex change might break. That would have devastated Em. This time it had to be a scoop.

They'd gone by car because it would have been hard to carry a whole wardrobe of clothes on the train. They'd gone to Harvey Nicks and Harrods and Selfridges and Austin Reed and Jaeger. The hurt inflicted by Giorgio still ran deep, despite François, and Em saved her mother quite a lot of money by saying, 'It just isn't you, Mum' about anything by Armani or Cerruti.

They'd done themselves proud. They'd eaten in San Lorenzo in the hope of seeing somebody famous (they didn't, or, if they did, they didn't recognise them) and enjoyed the fusion cooking in a Pacific Rim restaurant. The Pacific Rim hadn't yet come to Throdnall, where the cooking was more confusion than fusion.

In their double room, after slightly too much wine, they had had a giggly girly chat long into the night.

The poignancy of that chat seared Alison's heart on that long, slow, Throdnall night. It was the first truly adult chat that mother and daughter had ever had, and it was the last that they ever would have.

'Did you enjoy that?' Alison had unwisely asked on their arrival home.

'Of course I did, Mum,' Em had said. 'My last ever weekend with my mum,' and she had walked into the house very quickly.

Alison wept silently for her daughter as the birds greeted the dawn.

Then she found herself leaping out of bed, without being aware that she had decided to do so. Her fears had gone. She owed it to Em to be happy about it, otherwise she would have inflicted grief to no purpose.

She pulled the curtains energetically. A charm of goldfinches flew from the cherry tree in the back garden, unaware that their collective name was the prettiest in the language, and almost as pretty as them.

She owed it to the birds to be as brave as they were. No. That was silly.

She owed it to herself.

Alan looked at herself in the . . . Alison looked at himself in the . . . Alan looked at himself in the mirror. That was it. You're Alan now, Alison, he told herself. No, you're Alan now, Alan. He couldn't tell Alison that he was Alan. There was no Alison to tell. There was no herself. He was Him Indoors. He had crossed his Rubicon. He smiled at the pretentiousness of the phrase.

He didn't like the look of his face. The sleepless night had taken its toll. He had great black bags under his eyes. Be quite a make-up job, that.

No. He was a man. Men didn't use make-up. Well, not in Throdnall, anyway.

Men didn't need make-up. A woman has bags under her eyes, it's a disaster, her looks are ruined. A man has bags under his eyes, he's been on the tiles, his face looks lived in, he's a hell of a fellow.

'Good morning, Alan,' said Alan to Alan in the mirror. 'Are you a hell of a fellow?'

Alan in the mirror smiled ruefully at Alan. 'Hardly, Alan,' he said. 'Not yet.'

He examined his upper lip. There had always been, in certain lights, the faintest trace of downy hairs, though one would have had to be very ungenerous, he felt, to have called it a moustache.

There were also . . . or was it wishful thinking? . . . the first faint hairs on his chin and cheeks.

He felt, with a little spurt of excitement, that there was just the faintest justification for shaving.

He opened his brand new shaving bowl, got his beautiful virgin brush from the cupboard – 'sorry, Brock' – brushed his hairs with hot water to soften them – ha ha! – gently covered his face in the luxurious cream, which was scented with sandalwood; nothing but the best for the novice shaver.

With infinite care he drew his disposable razor around the edges of his nose and lips, across his chin, down his cheeks, right to the bottom of his ears, so slowly, so carefully, so enjoyably. He felt so wonderfully masculine. It was a real shock, when he went down to breakfast in his smart dark suit and Pierre Balmain tie ('François would love it') to be greeted with 'Hi, Mum, where's the Weetabix been put?'

Gray was trying to be extremely cool about the whole thing, as he had done ever since his fainting fit. Fainting wasn't cool.

'Nice tie, Mum,' he said coolly.

Unfortunately, at fifteen he was not yet mature enough to maintain his cool. When Alan couldn't resist offering to drive him to school, he was horrified.

'Christ, no,' he said. 'Do us a favour, Mum.'

He felt tempted for just a moment to make another illegal U-turn in Sir Nigel Gresley Boulevard. No! Wrong! 'You are Alan Divot and you fear no man,' he told himself. 'You didn't when you were Alison. Why should you begin now?'

He turned left along the sheds, then right at the end. The Daimler was there. He glanced at the clock on the dashboard. Thank goodness, he wasn't late, but Mr Beresford would look at him as if he should have been as early as him.

He'd never been very interested in cars, but he found himself gazing longingly at the elderly Daimler, that old gentleman of a car, and wishing that he could have a vintage car, now that he was a man.

He walked along the bare corridor, then through the door into carpeted first class. He suspected that within a few minutes he would be being carpeted. He walked into his office. Mrs A. Divot. Have to get Andy the sign-writer to change that. He sat at his desk and began to open Mr Beresford's mail in the usual manner, calmly sorting it into four categories – urgent, non-urgent, I can deal with and bin – as if nothing whatsoever had happened.

Oh no. There was a nasty one about the faulty coupling incident on the Great South Central train, the notorious 6.22 from Godawfulming, as railway people now called it. You remember the incident, I'm sure. The last carriage of the 6.22 from Godalming – one of their carriages, of course – became detached from the rest of the train. A signalman failed to notice that the three-car train had become a two-car train – he couldn't really be blamed – and the last carriage had slid to a halt between Godawfulming and Haslemere. Ten minutes later, another train had narrowly avoided running into the back of the stranded carriage, only because the driver had been keeping a particularly sharp look-out because there had been reports of deer straying on the line. The wrong sort of deer, of course. He had pulled up extremely abruptly, causing an osteopath with prostate problems to fall while urinating and cut his head on the flushing lever, thus flushing the toilet and soaking his dinner jacket as his arm went down the bowl. He injured his back in the fall and had to miss the Osteopaths' Dinner, to which he had been travelling. Next day he had endured death by headline, a figure of fun in all the tabloids and indeed most of the broadsheets. There had been no other casualties, but it had all been further bad publicity for Throdnall Carriage Works, not to mention the threat of the recall of two hundred units for testing of the couplings. Now here was a letter from a potential customer, Northern Vision, threatening to withdraw from a proposed contract if additional safety checks were not introduced 'at no extra cost to ourselves'. Today of all days.

No. Think positive, Alan. Welcome the problem. It will take the spotlight off you and your problem. That was the way to look at it.

He marched into Mr Beresford's office.

'Morning, Mr Beresford. Nasty one here, I'm afraid. Northern Vision. They're seeking additional safety checks in the wake of Godawfulming.'

'Oh my God, are they? Let's see.'

Mr Beresford snatched the letter, began to read it, suddenly did a double take.

'What on earth? Jacket and tie?'

'Yes, I'm going to change sex too. I see they want these checks at no extra cost to themselves. Shall I just acknowledge and play for time?'

'Change sex?'

'Yes. I was planning it before my husband did it, so I had to put it off. I mean if the checks find that there is nothing faulty with our couplings we'll be in a stronger position.'

'If there *is* something wrong we'll be in a weaker position, Mrs . . . become a man, do you mean?'

'Yes, that's right. Have to change the name on my door to Mr A. Divot. Obviously anyone who wants to can call me Alan. I don't think we should allow ourselves to be too frightened by Northern Vision, Mr Beresford. I don't think their cash flow is particularly brilliant, and so . . .'

'Never mind Northern Vision's cash flow, Mrs Divot. I cannot have a man as my PA.'

He had a fierce look on that sullen, square face. His eyebrows needed trimming. Untrimmed, they were too chaotic to be effectively ferocious.

'I will still be the same person, Mr Beresford,' said Alan. 'Still someone whose judgement you have come to respect. Nothing against Connie, for instance, but I don't think you'd get the same – how can I put it? – "gravitas" in her advice. I realise, Mr Beresford, that the change won't be easy for you.' His unspoken addition, of course, was 'knowing that you've rather fancied me all these years'.

'I don't want to seem to be threatening you, Mr Beresford,' he continued. 'I'm really not. I'm just pointing out that in these days of political correctness there might be quite a stink about your sacking me on grounds of sex discrimination.'

Mr Beresford stared at him.

'That may have worked at Cornucopia Hotels,' he said. 'I'm made of sterner stuff.'

'I feel as if I know every little detail of how you tick, Mr Beresford,' said Alan. 'Every little detail. I can inform my successor of all sorts of little things, but it won't be the same.'

Mr Beresford went pale. All the colour went from his cheeks. Just for a moment he didn't look at all like the strong man Alan had come to know. Just for a moment he looked like a lost and sullen child.

'You have a point,' he said. 'I have to admit you have a point. I'll give it a try; see how things work out.'

Alan was happy to get out of Mr Beresford's office before he changed his mind. He stood for a moment at his internal window, looking down at the great length of the sheds, with carriages at different stages of creation. He went over what he had said. Why did it have such an effect? It was clear that Mr Beresford believed that he was threatening him. But what with? Later, much later, when it happened, he would think back over those words, and understand something of their significance. At the time he was happy just to accept his good fortune.

Mr Beresford came through the adjoining door into Alan's office. Alan turned away from the window. Their eyes met. Alan realised that he had no idea what Mr Beresford was thinking.

'Yes,' said Mr Beresford. 'Play Northern Vision for time. Let me see your letter when you've drafted it. Thank you, Mr Divot.'

*

That evening, they held a press conference and photo-shoot with Em – if you can call the efforts of the *Advertiser*'s overweight undertalented chief photographer by a term as impressive as 'photo-shoot'. He took hundreds of pictures. Photographers always do. They like people to think they're being thorough, but usually it's because they're too lazy to work out in advance what they want.

Nicola looked extremely feminine in a knee-length tan skirt that matched her high-heeled court shoes. Her blouse was a fetching feminine pink. When she crossed her legs nobody would have guessed that she had ever been a man. Alan felt that he played his part too, casual and relaxed in stone-coloured slacks, with an open-neck rust-coloured check shirt and an expression so relaxed and so masculine that he might have been posing for a pipe-tobacco ad.

Em had talked to them very seriously about publicity. Neither Nicola nor Alan had given it any real thought. It was a publicity mad world out there, full of people whose sole aim was to be famous. Television fed on it. They alone seemed not to want publicity, but to dread it.

'A story of a double sex change is bound to be widely covered,' she'd said. 'And you must expect distortion from the tabloids.'

Alan remembered how Marge used to examine behind her ears for things called mastoids, and how the word had seemed sinister and frightening. It occurred to him now that tabloids sounded like a form of disease. 'I keep breaking out in sensational allegations, doctor.' 'You've got a bad dose of tabloids.'

He realised that the reason why his mind was wandering was that he couldn't cope head-on with the nation's publicity machine. His own daughter berated him severely. 'Concentrate, Mum, for goodness sake,' she said. 'Look, my view is that if you try to hide it people will be fascinated and it'll run and run. Your only chance is to tell the world, tell them on your terms, tell them everything so that there's nothing else to tell, seem to be eager for publicity, seem to long for it. People will soon get tired of you.'

'Isn't that a high risk strategy?' Nicola had asked. 'The papers are full every day of the same mini-celebrities craving publicity and getting it.'

'Yes, but you won't crave it, so you won't go on seeking it, so you won't go on getting it.'

Nicola and Alan felt very proud of Em that evening and in the hectic days that followed. She became their publicity manager for the whole of their brief spurt of fame. Some parents are blind to their children's faults. That is sad. Others are blind to their children's virtues. That is sadder. Alan and Nicola tended to fall into the latter category. They were amazed when they saw any evidence of maturity in Em or Gray.

It felt strange to them both to be standing alongside each other, dressed the other way round, but they didn't discuss it. They were strangely shy with each other.

Em interviewed them both separately, then together. They found it difficult, but they must have done all right because the article that appeared under the supremely inelegant headline 'Throdnall Double Sex Change Shock Sensation' wasn't overly cringe-making. The editor, incidentally, loved the headline. He had once told his chief sub-editor, 'There are four words that I love to see in my headlines. They are, in order of importance, Throdnall, sex, shock and sensation.' This headline used all four of them, and in the right order too.

Em's predictions over publicity were pretty well right. They were plastered all over the national press for a day or two. They appeared on breakfast television, and did some radio interviews. Nicola rather lost her way on the first radio interview, and the interviewer said, 'Never mind, we can edit that out.' Then they went on Radio Throdnall and the interviewer said, 'I wouldn't have thought Throdnall would be a comfortable place to be a freak,' and Alan, always the more outspoken – well one can hardly say 'freaked out' under the circumstances – let's say he lost his rag.

'Listen, young man,' he said. 'The world is full of people who might be described as freaks – exhibitionists wearing drag in public, inhibitionists wearing drag in private, drag queens in the King's Road, drag kings in the Queen's Road, cross-dressers getting dressed down by cross partners, gender blenders going on gender benders in down-town Capetown and up-town Motown, Daisy, Daisy, give me your answer do, what shall we do on a bisexual made for two – and we are just two ordinary, decent people trying to find our identity in a respectable way, so don't speak to us like that if you don't mind, you cheeky, prejudiced, ignorant, pathetic young media whippersnapper,' and then there was silence, a stunned silence, and Alan said, 'Sorry about that. I lost my temper. You can edit it out, can't you?', and the interviewer said, 'Can I hell as like? We're still on the fucking air . . . oh shit!!'

17 Friends and Enemies

If you go to the window, just before the evening light begins to fade, and you stand there for more than an hour, looking out over your garden, you will never see the light fading, but in the end it will be dark.

Nicola and Alan's sex changes were rather like that. Ferenc never said, 'Good morning, Nicola. Your voice seems softer today.' No waiter at the Trattoria Positano ever said, 'That man's voice at table eight has just gone gruffer halfway through his cannelloni.' Gradually, though, Alan's voice deepened. Imperceptibly, Nicola's softened.

The only person to comment on these changes was Denise Ploughman at the bridge club. 'Have you got a cold, Alison?' she asked, and then she remembered, and blushed, and looked confused, and apologised. 'Sorry, Alan.'

'It's quite all right,' said Alan.

People didn't know what to talk to them about, and they received only one invitation all that long winter, and that was to speak, both of them, at the annual dinner of the Transvestite Crown Green Bowls Society – secretary, Bernie's old bowling colleague, Vince Brodley. They turned it down.

One evening at the table in the kitchen Nicola said of Alan's chicken curry, 'Very nice, Alan. As always.'

'Talking of "always",' said Alan. 'Why should it always be me who cooks?'

'Well, you're . . .' began Nicola, and found that there was nowhere for her sentence to go, '. . . the person who always cooks,' she finished lamely.

'I thought for one moment you were going to say "the woman",' said Alan.

'I was,' admitted Nicola.

'Well, you're the woman now. You should cook.'

'I don't believe what I'm hearing,' said Em. 'I don't want either of you to change sex, especially Mum – there are too many men in the world without women becoming them – but you really did have, I thought, a wonderful chance to deconstruct the bi-genderist ethos of a capitalist patriarchal sexual hegemony.' Like many people who aren't quite as original as they'd like to be, she sometimes took refuge in long words to endow her thoughts with meaning. 'So far as sexual politics are concerned, this family is in the Dark Ages. Correction. They aren't anything like enlightened enough for the Dark Ages. They're cave dwellers.'

'Nobody sat around in caves doing nothing and saying, "When will it be ready?"' said Gray.

Em looked at him in astonishment.

'Sixteen years!' she said. 'That's all we've had to wait for him to say something intelligent. Not bad. Cool!'

Gray blushed. He squirmed with embarrassment like an eel with an itchy back.

'Dad was outrageous all those years,' continued Em.

'So now *I* should sit around and say, "When will it be ready?"' said Alan.

'Absolutely not, Mum,' said Em. 'The one good thing about all this is that it's put a rocket up the arse of sexual stereotypicality. We have the woman sitting around doing nothing and saying, "When will it be ready?"'

'Which I have to say, Nicola, is not in the spirit of your Real Life Test,' said Alan. 'You are supposed to play the woman's role. Come on. Do the cooking. Start the dishwasher. Change the beds. Be a woman, or I'll snitch to Doctor Langridge.'

'And what are you going to do, Mum?' said Em.

'Sod all. I have to, for my Real Life Test. I take mine seriously.'

'Oh come on,' said Nicola. 'What sort of a man are you proposing to be?'

'The sort you were. Lazy, insensitive and selfish,' said Alan. 'What are we having for tea tomorrow, Nicola?'

'It's all beyond me,' said Bernie. 'I've lived too long.'

In bed that night, Nicola whispered, 'We're getting on each other's nerves. Do you think we should split?'

'You're only saying that because you think you'll have to do all the work,' whispered Alan. 'I was only joking about that. I think we should share the work equally.'

'What??'

'Surely you can't object to that.'

'I suppose not. My God. You mean . . . I cook every other night?'

'Yes.'

'Hell's bells.'

'Yes.'

'Is there much point in our staying together? We don't have sex.'

'You could have said that any time during the last fifteen years.'

'You're divorcing me. I should move out.'

'If you don't feel I can offer you any support, do. I just thought . . . this is very hard for both of us . . . we'll have to split up one day, of course, but for the sake of the kids the longer we're together the better. We can't do much separately till we've had our ops. Why don't we try to support each other as long as we can? We did love each other once, you know.'

Two cats began to wail at each other. If that didn't wake the rest of the family, nothing would, but Alan and Nicola continued in whispers.

'Yes. Yes. Well, all right,' whispered Nicola. 'But . . . do you really want me to do half the work around the house?'

'Yes. Yes, I do.'

'This is a shock, Alan.'

'Good.'

That winter seemed like an eternity. They tried to be patient, tried not to wish their lives away, but oh how it dragged.

They fell into the new routine, Alan more easily than Nicola. Equality. Task sharing. Burden sharing. It was utterly equitable, unlike life, but it seemed unfair to them both. Nicola had never had to work so hard at home, while Alan was still working far harder than Nicola had when she'd been a man. A winter of elaborate fairness and aching resentment!

By Christmas they had reached shaving equipoise: they were both shaving every ten days. By springtime Alan was shaving once a week, Nicola once a fortnight.

In March, unnoticed by either of them, came their bicipital equipoise. From that moment onward, did they but know it, Alan's biceps were the stronger. Another triumph for British hormones.

At last, spring came. The suburban street erupted with daffodils. There were carpets of tulips in the vandalised parks. Spring excited them, but it brought its own problems.

It brought The War of Jenkins' Plate at the golf club.

Jenkins' Plate was a competition for men, and Alan put his name down for it.

The invitation to the PP's office came swiftly.

'You can't play in the Plate,' said the PP, running his hand nervously through his wig. 'I'm sorry, but you just can't.'

'Why not?'

'Which tees would you play off?'

'The men's.'

'You aren't muscular enough.'

'I'm becoming more muscular by the day, and, in any case, who will I be handicapping but myself?'

'I'm glad you mentioned handicaps,' smirked the PP. 'The

whole handicap system is based on gender. I cannot just transfer your handicap willy-nilly from woman to man. That would be the road to anarchy.'

'I don't care how severely you handicap me. This isn't about winning. It's about taking part.'

'You cannot take part, Alison.'

'Alan. It's Alan, Miles.'

'Alan, then.' He made the concession as if it was a minor matter, ground yielded in order to regroup for the major battle to come. 'You cannot take part as a man. Your vagina disqualifies you.'

'Does it say anything about vaginas in the rules?'

'Of course it doesn't. The rules were framed when men were men and decent.'

'Well then, it's all a load of bollocks.'

'Thank you,' said Wing Commander Miles Forrester primly. 'You've reminded me of another cause for disqualification.'

'I don't suppose you had many friends in the RAF,' said Alan. He hadn't meant to say it. It had just been a thought, but it had slipped out, as his thoughts sometimes did.

The wing commander's eyes narrowed. There was real hatred in them.

'I don't think you'll find you have many friends in Throdnall Golf Club,' he said. 'Frankly, Alison . . . Alan . . . frankly, a lot of people around here think your behaviour . . . and Nick's . . . Nicola's . . . to be "a bit off".'

'"A bit off".' Strong words!

The sarcasm escaped him. Quite a lot escaped Miles Forrester.

'We have no intention of expelling you from the club,' said the PP, 'but between you, me and the gatepost, the sensible thing to do would be to move to another club.'

'I don't do sensible,' said Alan. 'And thank you for being so polite. I could have been expelled, but I've escaped with a wigging.'

It was very childish, but he couldn't regret it.

*

Spring also brought an embarrassing meeting with Jane Collinson. Well, it was embarrassing for her.

Alan was shopping in Asda, and he found himself in the queue behind Jane at the check-out. He peered into her trolley; other people's shopping trolleys fascinated him, they bought such dreadful things that he despaired for civilisation, and he rather enjoyed that.

Jane's trolley contained a very substantial joint of lamb and several large parsnips.

'Hello, Jane,' he said. 'Having a dinner party?'

Bull's-eye. Jane looked very embarrassed.

'Yes. Yes we are. Saturday.'

'Just a reminder, Jane. Now that we're both doing our Real Life Tests, we wouldn't untidy your table.'

'Ah. No. No. Quite. Yes. Absolutely. No.' Words tumbled out of Jane's mouth like bats from the roost. 'No . . . er . . . well no . . . Sometime perhaps, yes. Jolly good.' She lowered her voice. 'We've got the Mallenders. Very conventional. Easily shocked. But, yes, well . . . and how is . . . isn't it a cold spring?'

They were never going to be invited again. Thank God! How could they ever have been part of all that?

Alan agreed that it was a cold spring.

Spring brought Prentice.

He'd seen them on television and had been impressed by their courage and had realised how fond he was of his old school friend, the former Nick. He'd kept in touch with Christmas cards, but now he felt that he wanted more. He wanted to see them.

'We ought to have him to stay,' said Nicola.

'I have a feeling I didn't like him,' said Alan.

'Well he is my oldest friend,' said Nicola.

'Well, all right, then,' said Alan, 'but where can he sleep? We can't move Bernie or Em or Gray out.'

'Why not? It'll only be for a couple of days. Em could sleep on the Zed-bed.'

'Oh, it has to be Em who moves. You don't like her now you're a woman, do you? She's a rival.'

'That is ridiculous nonsense. I'm very close to Em. Closer than I can ever get to Gray, actually. It's as if . . . I don't know . . . well, anyway, my relationship with Gray just isn't as close.'

Alan hoped he wasn't blushing.

'Gray has exams and studies. He needs his computer. And Prentice would go into obscene chat rooms.'

'I'm sure he would. Why are we inviting this man?'

'He's my friend.'

'Some friend.'

'Your dad's too old to sleep on Zed-beds. We could at least ask Em.'

They did, and to their surprise she agreed. They'd forgotten what a good mood she could be in during the couple of weeks before her visits to Paris to see François.

Prentice arrived with a bottle of wine.

'I didn't bring flowers or chocolates or anything like that because I wouldn't have known which of you to give them to,' he explained.

He had grown decidedly obese, eighteen stone at least. His round face bubbled with chins.

'Emma has given up her room for you,' said Alan.

'Thank you, Emma,' said Prentice.

Alan thought that he could have been more fulsome.

They had a bottle of champagne before dinner. It wasn't often a friend came to stay.

Bernie joined them but chose a beer. It was a Kronenbourg.

'Even the bloody beer's French in this house,' he said.

'Em has a French boy friend,' explained Nicola.

'I see,' lied Prentice. 'Cheers. Spring in the air.'

He gave a little jump, managing to lift his huge frame at least an inch and a half off the ground.

'What?' said Alan.

'It was a joke,' said Prentice, gasping for breath like a beached whale after his exertions. 'It's spring, so I said, "Spring in the air". Double meaning. Riveting. I'm now holding a glass of champagne and your attention. Zeugma.'

'What?'

'It's a figure of speech, in which a word is used to modify or govern two or more words although appropriate to only one of them or making a different sense with each, for example, Mr Pickwick took his hat and his leave. Zeugma. Or was she married to Scott Fitzgerald?'

The family looked at Prentice with utter bemusement. It had dawned on them all that this was not going to be an easy visit.

Bernie latched on to the only thing that he had understood.

'I hate the spring, me,' he said. 'The man what came to read the meter said, "Aren't the leaves lovely and green?" I said, "Course they bloody are. They are every sodding year. What did you think they'd be this year – beige?" He gave me a funny look.'

'I'm not surprised,' said Alan.

'No, but what it is, you see, with the spring, all that rebirth, it's a bit of a bastard when you're waiting to die.'

Prentice laughed. His laughter was like gunshot. The family looked at him in horror.

Over an anxious dinner, Prentice announced that Ferenc Gulyas's painting of Lake Balaton was 'appealing or appalling, according to your spelling', but he did praise the food. He ate greedily. 'Oh, this is beautifully garlicky,' he said.

'Garlic?' said Bernie. 'I don't like garlic.'

'You've eaten it every day for the last year and a half,' said Nicola.

'Have I? Oh,' said Bernie.

'Em's French boy friend again,' said Gray.

'Ah!' exaggerated Prentice.

'Why are we drinking Italian wine?' asked Em.

'Prentice brought it,' hissed Nicola.

'Oh sorry. Sorry, Prentice, I don't drink Italian wine,' said Em. 'It tastes of bad experiences.'

'That's ridiculous,' said Nicola.

Alan just wanted Prentice to be gone. He hated his wet lips and the bits of white spittle at the edges of his mouth.

There was a lull in the conversation. Nicola became very aware of the faint hissing of the coal-effect fire, and the gurgling of the central heating and Prentice's stomach. It was as if the stomach and the radiator were holding a conversation in gurgles. She wanted to laugh.

'So what are you doing these days?' she asked Prentice.

'I'm a financial consultant.'

'Ah.'

There isn't much to say in response to 'I'm a financial consultant' except 'Ah'.

'I thought you were going to be a stand-up comedian.'

'That has to be my hobby at the moment. I haven't broken through yet.'

'What venues have you played?'

'The Comedy Store in Dumfries. Various pubs. The Cellar Café, Lowestoft. Nowhere *absolutely* top-notch yet. Oh, and . . . er . . . yes, rather interesting, the Allied Dunbar Christmas Party.'

'Good God! How did that go?' asked Nicola.

'Brilliant. I didn't get a single laugh. Well, I'd have given up in despair if I had, from those bastards.'

'Not your usual audience?' asked Alan with a politeness that he didn't feel.

'True, but I die a death with my usual audience too. Laughs are cheap. Laughs are easy.'

'Do you joke about being so fat?' asked Gray, and Bernie spluttered into his chilli. Prentice was on to his third helping. Nicola had just known he'd be a glutton for chilli, which was why she had made it, it being her turn.

'Gray! Please!' said Nicola.

But Prentice was not offended.

'No, Gray,' he answered. 'That would have been too obvious. I joke about being thin. The audience don't get it.'

There was another lull. Prentice squelched his chilli like a man walking through long, wet grass.

'I met a man yesterday who told me he had a pronounced limp,' he continued.

'Couldn't you see he had?' asked Gray.

'He was sitting down. I asked him how he pronounced it? He said, "Limp". I said, "But that's how everyone pronounces it."'

'That story was limp,' said Alan icily.

'Exactly,' said Prentice. 'My point precisely. Well done that man.'

Everyone was very tired that night and went to bed early, leaving Nicola alone with Prentice, a large whisky and several zeugmas.

'Bit of a thing you turning into a woman,' said Prentice. 'Bit of a thing. I find it rather exciting actually.'

'Oh?'

'Sexually.'

'Ah.'

'Come to bed with me. Christen those crisp sheets so thoughtfully provided.'

A thought occurred to Nicola and, however you spelt it, it was appalling, not appealing.

They hadn't asked Prentice how long he was staying.

Many and varied were the attempts to find out.

'Have you got any comedy engagements coming up in the near future?'

'No.'

'When are you due back at work?'

'Oh, not for a while. Got some holiday owing.'

Not even those great exploiters of the double negative, Alan and Nicola Divot, could successfully use the device to winkle out Prentice's intentions.

'Don't you find there's not a lot to do in Throdnall?'

'There isn't a lot to do anywhere. Hadn't you realised?'

After eight days, Prentice announced, 'I'm afraid I have to leave today.'

Such is the inherited pressure put on the English middle classes to show good manners that Nicola had to fight to stop herself saying, 'Are you sure?'

The only thing that stopped her was the fear that Alan, whose background was so much less middle-class, would have killed her.

When he'd gone, they danced round the dining room table, shouting, 'He's gone! He's gone!'

And there he was, looking in.

Alan opened the front door to him.

'Made some notes for my act,' said Prentice. 'Left them upstairs.'

Not a word was spoken about the scene in the dining room.

'I have to admit that the visit was not a huge success,' said Nicola over their evening meal in the kitchen. 'I do apologise for inviting him. Do you know, he even tried to get me to bed?'

'And me,' said Alan.

'What?'

'He said he hadn't yet managed to find a man attractive enough to have sex with, but he felt rather excited by the thought of a man who had once been a woman.'

'He's so twisted,' said Nicola. 'I don't expect he can get aroused by somebody straight and normal.'

'I think he can,' said Em.

'What?'

'He clambered on to the Zed-bed last night. Said he'd lost a heroic battle against temptation.'

'Oh, Emma! Oh, Em!'

'Oh don't worry, Mum. I dealt with him.'

'How?'

'I lost a heroic battle against kicking him in the goolies.'

'Oh my poor girl.'

'Don't worry, Mum. I don't mind. Look at it this way. If he hadn't, and I hadn't, he might still be here.'

'I feel left out,' said Gray.

Spring ripened into summer. By July Nicola had only two hairs on her chest. She was shaving once every three weeks. Alan was shaving every five days, and he had six hairs on his chest. There were severe thunderstorms on the seventh.

18 The Last Supper

Alan wanted it to be a really good family evening. Tomorrow night Nicola would be facing 'Nil By Mouth'. Next time she ate supper in this house she would be a fully fledged woman – or as fully fledged as she would ever be.

'Well this is nice,' said Nicola as Alan placed a succulent portion of chicken paprika in front of her. She didn't actually feel at all hungry, her stomach was churning, but she knew that she must eat, or Alan would be hurt. Much though Alan had come to irritate her through these tense times, she had to admit that he had attempted to be supportive. 'A nice family dinner.'

'Supper,' said Alan. 'A nice family supper.'

'What's the difference?'

'No starter. I didn't want it to seem too formal.'

Bernie burped and didn't apologise. He was definitely beginning to deteriorate.

'Thank you, Dad,' said Alan.

'What for?'

'Burping. Adding that casual touch. Making sure it isn't too formal.'

Nicola looked at Alan in amazement. Was he taking over her mantle of sarcasm now that he was going to become a man? He really was beginning to look quite manly, apart from that somewhat smaller but still embarrassingly prominent bosom.

'Your hair's changed colour, Em,' said Bernie.

Alan had wondered when anybody would comment on Em's hair. It was bright blonde. What other family could sit through the best part of a weekend and not mention a thing like that?

'Carl likes blondes,' said Em. They were beginning to get quite a few references to this Carl, and, although the lighting was dim, Alan thought she was blushing. 'I thought I'd try it for him.'

'What nationality is Carl?' asked Gray.

'He's American actually,' admitted Em. 'He thinks the senate will acquit Clinton.'

'I'm sure President Clinton will be very relieved to hear that,' said Bernie.

'Dad!' hissed Alan.

'Sorry I spoke,' grinned Bernie.

He's being wicked tonight, damn him, thought Alan.

'Oh God!' said Gray.

'What?' said Em.

'At last I'm allowed to drink a decent amount of wine, and all we're going to get is Californian,' said Gray.

It was fair comment. French wine had been banned since the François debacle.

'Stop sniping, you two,' said Alan firmly. 'It's your dad's last night.'

'You don't expect her to die under the surgeon's knife, do you?' said Gray, and Nicola smiled, but it was a false and frightened smile.

'I meant, her last night as your dad,' said Alan angrily.

'Well what will she be?' asked Gray. 'Not my mum. I can't have two mums.'

'All right,' shouted Alan. 'He'll still be your dad, but this is her last night as a man. Oh, do stop splitting hairs. I've worked hard to cook you a nice meal. Let's enjoy it.'

'I am enjoying it,' said Nicola. 'It's delicious. Can't eat much, my stomach's too tense, but it's lovely.'

It seemed ridiculous calling her a man or a dad that last night. Alan thought she looked really pretty. She was wearing a burgundy and pink ankle-length tweed skirt and a long-sleeved pink angora sweater, and now she had her own pearl necklace and earrings and no longer needed to borrow Alan's.

'I'm not splitting hairs, really,' said Gray. 'I mean, when I apply to join Pricewaterhouse I'll have to fill in a form. What am I going to say under "Father"? I'll never get a job.'

'I thought you were going to uni if your results are good enough,' said Nicola.

Alan was amazed to hear her say 'uni'. The old Nick despised such lazy shortenings.

'Same difference. I'll have to fill in forms.'

'I can't understand anybody wanting to be an accountant,' said Bernie.

'We all need accountants, Bernie,' said Nicola, suddenly the great appeaser.

'Oh aye,' said Bernie. 'I can understand folk ending up as accountants. Somebody has to, like, but to set off on life's great adventure wanting to be one, it's tragic.'

'Excellent, Dad. Very helpful indeed. I think we're all grateful for that nugget,' said Alan. Privately, he agreed, but it should never have been said and not that night of all nights. He was surprised Gray didn't explode.

'Sorry I spoke,' said Bernie.

Alan gritted his teeth. An old car clanked rustily as it swished over a speed hump too fast.

He cleared the plates. Em was the only one to help. He couldn't have expected Nicola to do it that night, but Gray and Bernie just sat there like statues. Then he brought in the lemon meringue pie and made the mistake of saying 'There you go' as he handed Em a slice. He didn't know why he said it. It was an expression that irritated him when other people used it. It slipped out due to tension, and proved a red rag to a dad.

'I hate that expression,' he said. 'It's stupid. It doe'n't mean owt.'

'Would you very much mind if I don't have any, Mum?' asked Em. 'Only I ought to be getting off. Carl sort of wants to see me.'

'I did hope we could have a family night tonight,' said Alan.

'Doing what?' mumbled Gray, through a mouthful of lemon meringue.

'Don't eat with your mouth full, Gray,' said Alan. It was obvious that he meant 'Don't *speak* with your mouth full', everybody knew that, but Gray being Gray had to make capital out of it. Well, accountants are good at making capital. When he'd finished his mouthful he took a pretend mouthful and chomped on it.

'What on earth are you doing?' asked Em.

Alan would have thought she'd have realised, but she was already miles away (probably in bed with Carl). 'He's not eating with his mouth full,' she explained wearily.

'So it's OK if I go, is it?' asked Em.

'Well I suppose so.' Alan knew that he couldn't stop her. 'But I thought we might play games or something.'

'Games?' said Gray incredulously. 'What games?'

'I don't know. Cards. Scrabble. Charades.'

'Charades???' said Gray with at least three question marks.

'Marge loved charades,' said Bernie.

'Right. That's out then,' said Alan. 'Cards?'

'I think I really have to go. *Really*,' said Em. 'Carl has a bit of an obsession about Sunday evenings. He thinks they're depressing, and watching TV is too negative. He thinks you need a more pro-active way of coping with the tensions of the approaching Monday, or you risk developing a work phobia.'

'Carl sounds a bundle of fun,' said Gray.

'Gray!' said Alan, but privately he sympathised with Gray's sarcasm. Also, he could see that Em was a bit frightened not to go out with Carl, and that didn't bode well for their relationship.

'Right, well, I'll be on my way, then,' said Em.

'You could have eaten your lemon meringue pie by now,' said Gray, 'or does Carl think you're *fat*?'

Alan supposed that he should have been glad that Gray was bright enough to have scored a bull's-eye, but he was livid. This was the family *at its worst*. They'd have Em going anorexic on them if they weren't careful.

Em glared at Gray, kissed her dad, said, 'You don't mind, do you, Dad?' and Nicola said, 'No, of course not', but Alan knew that she did. 'Love you, Dad. Bye, Mum, Gramps, see you later.'

'Why does she say "see you later"?' asked Bernie. 'We won't see her later. We'll be in bed before he's even finished giving her one.'

'Dad!' hissed Alan.

'Why does everybody say "see you later" all the time nowadays? What's going on?'

'I'm sorry you find existence so irritating, Dad,' said Alan.

Gray stood up.

'Thanks, Mum,' he said. 'Great nosh.' He knew Alan didn't like the word 'nosh', especially about his cooking. 'Er . . . look, I . . . er . . . family games, great idea, cool. Only thing is, got an appointment with some mates.'

'Going out?' asked Nicola, half hopefully.

'No! On the net. Throdnall bores me rigid. Britain bores me rigid. I'm a citizen of the world.'

'No, you aren't,' said Bernie. 'You're a citizen of your bed-room.'

Gray stomped to the door, flung it open, made to slam it behind him, thought better of it, tried to catch it before it banged, caught his fingers in it, gasped.

'Shit!' he said. 'Now see what you've made me do. Thank goodness it was my left hand.'

Neither Alan nor Nicola realised the significance of that until later.

Just after Gray had gone, the phone rang. Nicola went out to the hall, and while she was gone Alan poured them all another glass of the Zinfandel, and turned to Bernie.

'Why are you in such a bad mood, tonight of all nights, Dad?' he demanded.

'Because,' said Bernie. 'Because it *is* tonight of all nights.

Because she might not have popped her clogs if people like Nick – I can't call him Nicola, sorry, 'ti'n't in me – weren't wasting all the nation's resources on all this vanity.'

'You've understood nothing if you think it's vanity.'

'I don't care what it is, but these fellers, Alison, these fellers must be clever buggers if they can turn a man into a woman, and there'll have been research and I don't know what and such like, and it'll have cost millions, and the millions could have gone to curing cancer, and keeping my Marge alive.'

It was the first time Bernie had ever used the word 'cancer'. There wasn't any answer that Alan could give. He just reached out and took his dad's hand and held it. A huge breath of wind roared down the chimney, and they should have felt very cosy in their snug little dining room, but they didn't feel cosy at all. The lighting, which might have seemed atmospheric, looked merely dim now.

'It's political correctness gone mad,' said Bernie. 'It's sexism gone berserk. Everyone's bending over backwards not to offend women like. It's women, women, women. It's no surprise men want to become women. They can see which side their bread's buttered.'

Alan smiled to himself, wryly. He would have liked to have set his dad down in the middle of the world of sexual politics. He'd read all about it. Some of those experts thought that all transsexualism was caused by sex stereotyping by a patriarchal society. They would argue that Alan hated his female body because he'd been conditioned by men to do so, and they would argue that Nicola hated her male body because it was so much more desirable to be a woman. They had corkscrews instead of minds and could twist the facts round until the cork popped out and released a great stream of whatever it was they wanted to believe. None of it seemed to have any relevance to his individual life or to Nicola's individual life. Theory never was related to individual life.

That was his theory, anyway.

Bernie sat patiently beside him, waiting till he stopped thinking. Alan was a little distressed by the deadly cocktail of love and irritation that he felt for Bernie. He squeezed his hand, and this set him off again.

'What it is with grief, I reckon they've got it wrong. They say time heals. I don't know about that. It does and it doesn't like. You learn to live your life again, oh aye, course you do, but you miss your loved one more and more, you're forced to, because it's longer since you saw them. Them footballers always say, "It hasn't sunk in yet" and such like, and I think "By, you must be thick." Well, the fact that I'll never see my Marge again, never ever, it's still sinking in, Alison.'

It wasn't the moment to remind him that she was Alan.

And then Nicola returned from the hall, and Alan's intimate moment with his father was over.

'Andrew Collinson,' said Nicola. 'Rang to wish me luck.'

'That's rich, coming from him.'

'Well, be fair,' said Nicola. 'Jane might have been making it up about Andrew being the reason. I bet it was Jane all along.'

Bernie stood up, and said, 'Aye, well, you can't play games with three.'

'You can, Dad,' said Alan. 'You can play sergeant major.' It's a card game that can only be played by three. Bernie quite liked it usually.

'Aye, well,' he said, 'but if it's all the same with you I think I'll pop over to t'Coach like.'

'It's pouring out there, Dad.'

'Aye, but it's me legs.'

'Your legs?'

'Doctor Rodgerson said I'd lose the use of my legs if I didn't keep exercising them. Gangrene. They go rotten from the bottom up. I mean, fair play, it's no contest, is it, gangrene versus charades?'

'He's determined to go, Alan,' said Nicola. 'Let him.'

'Aye, but, what it is, like, Billy Hazledene's lonely, and you at least have each other,' said Bernie.

So Nicola and Alan were left on their own.

'I am sorry, Nicola,' said Alan. 'I really had hoped you'd spend tonight in the bosom of your family.'

Alan wished that he hadn't said 'bosom', and Nicola must have sensed what he was thinking – he really did believe that she was getting more intuitive as she approached full womanhood – because she said, 'Don't worry, Alan. I'm not sensitive about my appearance. There is a little detectable swelling; I hope it will accelerate once I've had the op, but I know that nobody is going to shout, "Hello! Dolly Parton's here" when I walk into the foyer of the Cornucopia.'

'Game of Scrabble?' suggested Alan. He was aware that it was a pretty creaky gear change, but Nicola didn't seem to notice.

'Why not?'

Alan went to get the board from the utility and Nicola fetched the card table from the porch – they'd always had a bit of a storage problem at number thirty-three – and they both heard extraordinary gasping noises coming from Gray's bedroom. Nicola rushed upstairs with Alan in hot pursuit. She didn't stop to knock.

Gray was lying on top of his bed, stark naked, breathing heavily, with an ecstatic grimace on his face and Alan's Tottenham Hotspur away shirt held round his genitals. He went bright red and glared at them.

'Don't you ever come into my bedroom without knocking again,' he said icily.

'And please don't borrow my shirt again without asking,' said Alan.

It was a far cry from the ideal evening that Alan had planned.

19 Visiting Time

Nicola realised that she had awoken from a deep sleep. She was staring at a complex pattern of cracks on a white surface.

It was a ceiling! Where was she? She moved her neck very very cautiously, because she had a dim feeling that she might have been in an accident.

She was in a small room, with white walls and one window which afforded a view only of sky, an incongruously placid sky of mackerel clouds and glimpses of blue.

It all came back to her. She was in hospital. She had had a sex change operation – or had she? She was truly Nicola at last – or was she?

Supposing something had gone wrong. Supposing she'd proved unsuitable.

She felt down, very nervously, to find out if she still had those hated protuberances – testicles and a penis.

Her hand touched only bandages. Well, that was promising . . . but not conclusive. Perhaps they had begun the operation and aborted it. (Horrid word. For 'aborted' read 'suspended'.)

She was attached to three drips. There were indicators attached to these drips. Promising . . . but not conclusive. Maybe she had lost a lot of blood and that was why they had suspended operations . . . suspended *the* operation . . . and that was why she was attached to three drips.

Had she had the operation or hadn't she?

There must be a bell. Where was the bell? Ah.

It seemed like minutes before anybody came. She felt so alone. She felt so trapped. Didn't they realise how people felt at moments like this? Fragile. Desperately vulnerable. Full of fear.

Ah. A nurse.

'Ah! You've come round.'

'Er . . . yes.'

A starched nurse. White frock, white tabard, red face – all starched.

'Nurse, have I . . . had the operation?'

'Well of course you have, Ms Divot.'

'Has it . . . er . . .?'

'Mr McWhinnie was very satisfied.'

Unlike you, nurse. You don't look as if you've ever been satisfied.

'Mr McWhinnie is an extremely good surgeon.'

Rebuked for her doubts, and at such a time. True insensitivity is an art. Only the really talented possess it. In love with Mr McWhinnie. Wouldn't look at her twice, starched little madam.

'So, I'm . . . I'm a woman.'

'I suppose so, Ms Divot.'

'Am I . . . er . . . doing all right, then?'

'You're as comfortable as can be expected,' she said. 'Oh!' she added. 'Your "wife" telephoned some while ago to say she'd been stuck in traffic but would be here soon.'

They were only the faintest of hints, the inverted commas that The Starchy One put round the word 'wife', but they were enough. She disapproved. Personal? Thought Nicola a freak? Political? Resented the waste of resources that should be used on diseases that she thought were real? Regarded this as cosmetic surgery, albeit of a private and very extreme kind?

Not your business, Nicola. Not your worry. It was a shame, though, not to have woken to a friendlier face.

She tried to move. Flames of pain burnt into her insides. Needles of pain thrust themselves into her veins. She gripped the side of the bed. Sweat poured off her. She was sweating down there beneath the bandages. Her new private parts – and after her conversation with The Starchy One she was almost convinced that she did indeed have new private parts – were beginning to itch. She longed to scratch them. She must scratch them. She couldn't scratch them.

And there was something more than all this, something even more disturbing than all this pain, something enormous, some consideration of vast importance just beyond the reach of her memory, some residue of worry from the anaesthetised night-mares of her unconscious subconscious earlier that day.

She closed her eyes, already weary of it all. She made a great effort to think of more pleasant things, of Alan arriving and smiling at her, of his basically kind if naturally rather severe face, as he stood there looking concerned and holding out a bunch of pink lilies. Alan loved lilies and he would choose pink for a girl; he wasn't brilliant at flowers and he would go for the obvious.

'Hello, Nicola.'

She opened her eyes and saw . . . not Alan holding pink lilies but twenty stone of blubber holding absolutely nothing.

'Prentice!'

'Hello, Nicola! Well, well! And how are we?'

'Singular. Please don't call me "we".'

'Sorry. I'm appearing at the Komedy Klub at midnight tonight . . .'

'That gives me a few hours, but I won't be up to it.'

'Don't be silly. I'm explaining why I'm here. I rang the gorgeous Alan, who used to be the even more gorgeous Alison, and he told me about your op, and I thought, "What a coincidence. The hospital's only a couple of miles away; I can go and cheer her up."'

'Thank you.'

'So I have.'

'Thank you.' It's too early. Too soon. I'm so tired. So tired. Please go. 'It's so good to see you.'

'Of course! Alan!'

Alan moved forward slowly, trying to hide the utter dismay on his face at the sight of Prentice, clutching his pink lilies as if he feared Prentice might steal them.

'Prentice!'

'I'm so glad you told me she was having the op today,' said Prentice.

Alan's eyes apologised to Nicola. He showed her the lilies.

'I've brought you some lilies,' he said. 'Pink for a girl.'

Oh God.

'They're lovely.'

He thrust them towards her nose. She sniffed dutifully. She wished they were doused in chloroform. She longed to sleep.

'They smell lovely.'

'Good. Well, how are you?'

'I don't know.'

'How do you feel?'

'Tired. Very very tired.'

Why didn't they say, 'Really? Well we'd better go, then, and leave you in peace' in perfect and thoughtful unison?

'It's no use being tired of life unless you can think of something to put in its place,' said Prentice.

'What?' asked Alan.

'It's a joke from my act. Em! The divine and sexy Em come to enchant us!'

Em didn't look divine or sexy or enchanting. She looked tired and worried and pale. It was one of her heavy days.

'Oh, no, Mum, you've brought pink lilies as well,' she said. 'Oh, Dad, how are you?'

She kissed Nicola very carefully.

Alan took the two lots of lilies out to get the nurse to put them into vases. Em peered at the drips and their attached indicators, but couldn't make any sense of them. Prentice stared at Em with naked lust.

'Carl had an interview, Dad,' said Em. 'Only round the corner really, so I thought I'd pop in. I can't stay long.'

Good! Good! Love you, Em, adore you actually, but . . . good! Good! Go! Take them with you!

'He's waiting in a pub round the corner.'

Em glared at Prentice as she said this.

'You could have brought him,' said Nicola.

'No. He can't take hospitals.'

'Oh dear.'

'Oh, not that he's a wimp or anything.' She was clearly very sensitive about Carl.

'He just chooses . . . to stay in the pub. Very sensible of him.' Nicola had been going to say, 'He just chooses only to confront those bits of existence that he likes' but she pulled back from the brink. She was just too exhausted to bother to be sarcastic.

'Anyway, it's hardly the best moment for you to meet him for the first time.'

'Absolutely not – but I'm glad *you* came,' said Nicola.

She reached out and clasped Em's hand.

'The only thing I find difficult is what to call you, Dad. "Dad" seems a bit absurd now. I can't call you "Mum". I can't call you "Other Mum" or "Mum Number Two". I suppose the best is Nicola, but that sounds a bit distant.'

'I think "Nicola" probably is the best,' said Nicola, drowsily. She closed her eyes. She didn't think she'd have lost her talent for pretending to be asleep.

Alan returned with two vases of pink lilies. 'You'd have thought I'd asked her to make a matchstick model of the Taj Mahal,' he said. 'Her body bristled with indignation. Ah, she's asleep.'

'I'll tell you what,' said Prentice. 'I am going to invite you two to see my act at the Komedy Klub. How does that strike you?'

'I have Carl waiting,' said Em.

'Bring him too. The more the merrier.'

'I'm not sure that Carl will appreciate your humour. He's American.'

What difference will that make? thought Nicola behind her closed eyes. Nobody appreciates your humour.

'Do you appear under a nom de plume?' asked Em.

'You don't *appear* under a nom de plume,' said Prentice scornfully. 'You write under a nom de plume. But, yes, I do have a stage name. It's Prentice Prentice.'

'But I thought that your real name was Prentice Prentice,' said Alan.

'It is, but on stage it's the other way round. Prentice becomes Prentice and Prentice becomes Prentice.'

'I don't understand.'

'It's a joke.'

'I'm not sure I'll appreciate your act either,' said Em.

'Well, maybe not. I think what you need to know is that it's not necessarily funny. Some acts aren't funny because they haven't reached the level of comedy. Mine isn't funny because it's gone through comedy to the beyond.'

Nicola tried not to listen, but she couldn't help it, and she couldn't help being irritated. Good God, she'd had major surgery of an incredibly delicate and painful nature, and they were talking as if she wasn't there.

'Thank you so much for ignoring me,' she said with a flash of the old Nick sarcasm. 'Very thoughtful, because I'm exhausted.'

'Oh, Dad, we thought you were asleep,' said Em.

'Let's go and get that curry,' said Prentice.

'What curry?' asked Alan.

'The curry you're all going to buy me in exchange for free tickets for my act,' said Prentice, 'and then we must go to my digs and get my dog.'

'You have a dog?'

'He comes on in my act, every time I say I'm barking mad.'

Nicola's eyes pleaded with Alan and Em. Go. Buy him a curry. Anything, but get him out of here.

The three of them moved towards the door. Oh, please,

please, don't stop, don't turn round, urged Nicola silently. Please!

Em stopped! She turned! She was coming towards the bed.

'I love you,' she said, bending down and kissing Nicola again. 'I'd love you whatever sex you were, because you're you.'

Then she was gone. They were all gone. She heard Prentice's diminishing voice.

'A word of warning about my dog. I'm not kind to him. His name is Spot, but the only name he answers to is Fuck Off. I'm sure he thinks he's Russian.'

She breathed a great sigh of . . .

He was back. He had returned, gasping for breath, heaving massively.

'Had to come back,' he said. 'Had to say "sorry".'

'What for?' asked Nicola, wearily and warily.

'You lying there, trapped, in agony, and the three of us discussing the wonderful evening we're going to have. Most inconsiderate.'

When Prentice had gone – and it was several minutes before she allowed herself to really believe that he had gone – Nicola thought about the words Em had spoken.

'I love you. I'd love you whatever sex you were, because you're you.'

It never ceased to surprise her that we humans, ridiculous creatures that we are, cry buckets when we're particularly happy. She was still crying when The Starchy One arrived to take her blood pressure. That stopped her tears in their tracks.

Nicola next awoke in the middle of the night. The anaesthetic seemed to have worn off.

So this was it. She was Nicola. But for two years she had pretended to be Nicola. What was more real about this?

She had a vagina – but she was still the me she had been before she'd had a vagina. She thought that she must have half expected to wake up and feel completely different. Impossible. She had the same brain.

It doesn't do to think about the brain. The brain wasn't designed to think about itself. You end up thinking that you're a series of chemical reactions, that there is no you, that you have no soul, that you cannot have anything that isn't scientifically describable. What was her soul? Was it different now?

There were moments that night when she wondered if it had all been a huge mistake. All that agony, all that courage, and here she still was.

To think that she had thought that when she woke up she'd feel exhilarated.

Slowly the night sky lightened. The pain kidded her that it had gone, and then came back as bad as before and all the more unbearable for the respite. He's a sneaky little chap, is pain.

She wanted to ring for the nurse, but she dreaded that it would be The Starchy One.

When at last a nurse came, joy of joys, she was different.

'Hello, Nicola,' she said cheerfully. 'I'm Pat.'

Nicola liked her immediately.

'Welcome to the wonderful world of womanhood,' she said.

Ah! thought Nicola inappropriately. That's what you get when you go private. Alliteration.

She was moved, though, and again she wanted to cry.

Pat washed her as much as she could. She was incredibly gentle, but Nicola was still cut by shards of pain.

'I wanted to spare you Mrs Mussolini,' whispered Pat. 'Don't tell her I call her that. It's our secret.'

Dear dear Pat. How you cheered Nicola up by giving her a shared secret. It made her feel human.

Mr McWhinnie breezed in at eleven.

'Well, Nicola, how are you feeling?' he asked in an urgent, low voice.

'Not so bad,' she said bravely.

'The operation was a complete success,' he said. 'I'm very pleased with the way it went. I took great care over you.'

'Thank you.'

'I don't need thanking – it's my job – but I do deserve, and need, proper answers. Come on. Nobody, after what you've had done to you, feels "not so bad". How are you really feeling?'

'Very, very sore. Moving is agony. Lying still is purgatory.'

'It will never be worse than it is now, and it will pass, but slowly, I'm afraid. How do you feel . . . psychologically?'

'Confused.'

He nodded sympathetically.

'Depressed.'

He nodded solemnly.

'Great sense of anti-climax.'

He nodded resignedly.

He was a versatile nodder.

'Doctor, I don't really feel . . . a woman. Am I a woman?'

'It's hardly the moment to debate the philosophy of it,' he said. 'You no longer have a penis or testes. You do not have female chromosomes. You do have a very nice vagina, though I say so as shouldn't. You even have a very passable attempt at a clitoris.'

'Thank you. Thank you very much.'

'My pleasure. I wouldn't specialise in this if I didn't believe it worked, Ms Divot, I can assure you. Relax. Help your body to heal itself and I believe that you will eventually feel good about it all. But you're going to have to be strong. This is only the beginning.'

'I thought it would be the end.'

'Every end necessitates another beginning. It never ends. It cannot end, except in death, and, we hope, not even then. That is the nature of life. You'll be just fine, Nicola. Just fine.'

The next day, when Alan came in, Nicola asked if they had gone to the Komedy Klub.

'We did, yes. We didn't know how to get out of it.'

'What was it like?'

'Awful. Three-quarters empty, and not one laugh from start to finish.'

'How did Prentice react?'

'Smiled broadly and said we'd been a wonderful audience. Oh, and he sent his love. Said he'd always liked you, but now you were a woman – wow!'

'Oh God.'

Gray telephoned to check that it would be all right for him to visit.

Nicola didn't really want to see him. The last time, he had been lying naked on top of his bed with a Tottenham Hotspur away shirt round his pudenda. This was something that she didn't feel well enough to comment on, but she wasn't sure if it would be possible to ignore it. She had only had the operation five days ago. She hadn't been allowed to get out of bed yet. She was weak.

She couldn't hurt him, though, and it had been very considerate of him to phone.

She prepared herself carefully for his visit, so that she would be able to cope. She sensed that the visit was hugely important for their relationship. It was too soon – too soon – but that was life, it wasn't a neatly packaged commodity.

She had been very moved by Em and she sensed that she was going to be very moved by Gray. I've been lucky in my children, she thought.

Her children! She felt surprised when she reflected that, despite her inadequacies as the male she never really was, she had managed to produce two children. Especially Gray. He was their little miracle, really. By that time their sex life was becoming very spasmodic, yet she vividly recalled the actual night when he was conceived as having been quite a passionate occasion. Alison had been exceptionally aroused and romantic and had said some wonderful things about him and her love for him, and they had risen to a rare joyous orgasm in a tide of words and compliments. Call me a sentimental fool if you must, she told herself in her hospital bed with the creased sheets and the crumbs, but I'm utterly convinced that it was that depth of positive emotion that enabled Alison to conceive.

She could see all this so much more clearly, now that she was no longer a man, as if she was looking down on it from the best seat in the house. She looked at Gray, on his one and only visit to the hospital, as if she had never seen him before. He took after his mother more than after her. In fact she could hardly see any of her in Gray at all. Perhaps, because of the level of emotion that his mother put into her love-making that night, in a sense Gray was more hers than hers, or, to put it another way, Nick had only been the conduit. Perhaps, though, it was an indication of a certain conceit in her that she'd never thought their gawky offspring to be very good-looking!

All this was flashing through her mind as they steered their way through the first shoals of their conversation. What did you have for lunch? What essays are you writing at the moment? How are Arsenal doing?

She shouldn't have asked that, partly because Gray was scornful of her pathetic attempts to show an interest in football, but mainly because it made it difficult for her not to refer to the affair of the Tottenham Hotspur shirt. (Alan had explained that Arsenal and Tottenham were intense rivals, and that Gray, a keen Arsenal supporter, had managed to enjoy sexual pleasure while also inferring that the hated Tottenham were wankers, a joke possibly cleverer and certainly funnier than anything Prentice had ever managed.)

Well, she would have to refer to it now.

'Er . . . Gray?' she said. 'I'm sorry I barged into your room without knocking.'

'It's something everyone does sometimes, Dad.'

'Well it's still wrong. I should have knocked.'

'I wasn't speaking about that, Dad.'

'Oh.'

'I feel ridiculous calling you Dad, Dad.'

'Em is just going to use Nicola.'

'That makes it sound as if you're not my dad.'

'I am your dad. You know I am. I know I am. We'll still know all that, even if you call me Nicola. I think you should try calling me Nicola.'

'I'll try, Dad. Oh, sorry. Er . . . Nicola?'

'Yes, Gray.'

'The world's full of horrible people who abuse other people in all sorts of disgusting ways.'

'Absolutely right, sadly.'

'What I was doing, you know, when you saw me, I wasn't hurting anybody but myself. I mean they call it self-abuse, don't they?'

'They do, yes.'

'Well . . .' He expelled a deep breath. Nicola could see that he was finding all this agonisingly embarrassing. '. . . I've been thinking. It's the same with you.'

'In what way, Gray?'

'You're only hurting yourself. Via the surgeon, I mean, but you know what I mean. Other people who are sexually . . .'

He ran out of acceptable words. Nicola prompted him.

'Odd? Deviant? Sick?'

'No! Well . . .' Nicola could see Gray's brain working overtime to find an acceptable word. He wasn't exactly what you'd call literate. '. . . unusual.' Not bad. 'Other people who are sexually unusual hurt other people. You only hurt yourself.'

'True.'

'So what I'm saying is, it doesn't upset me any more. I can live with it.'

'Good.'

'I can accept you fully as you are.'

'Good. I'm glad, Gray.' She felt that she sounded insincere. 'No, I mean it. I'm very glad, Gray.'

'Thanks. Nicola?'

'Yes, Gray.'

'Please promise not to come to speech day or anything like that, though.'

Bernie didn't go at all. Afterwards he told her, 'Hospitals! I would have come, but it's me chest.'

Nicola longed to call The Starchy One Mrs Mussolini to her face. She became terrified that she would give way to the delicious temptation.

She didn't, but she did give way to an almost uncontrollable urge to be confrontational.

'You don't like me, do you?' she asked.

Mrs Mussolini stared at her in astonishment.

'It doesn't come into it,' she said. 'I haven't even considered it.'

'You don't approve of "The Operation".'

She went even redder than normal. Nicola was pleased to see that. She'd got through to her.

'I suppose I don't, no.'

'How would you like it if you had a prick and balls?'

She was outraged, appalled, terrified, out of her depth.

'I . . . I couldn't have,' she spluttered. 'I am a woman.'

'Exactly,' said Nicola, 'and so am I, and always have been. So how do you think I've felt all these years?'

'If you're unhappy with my level of care,' said Mrs Mussolini, 'you should make a complaint. There are procedures.'

Nicola realised that Mrs Mussolini would have led a happier life if there were procedures for existing – preferably with an instructional booklet in five languages.

She realised something about herself too. She had come to expect too much from her transformation. The ending of confusion. The removal of trauma. The banishment of what was inappropriate. That was all she had a right to expect, and it was enough. It was everything.

*

Ferenc presented her with a vast Get Well card signed by every member of the staff. It was a surprise to her, in one or two cases, that they were prepared to put their names to such a message. It was a surprise to her, in one or two other cases, to find that they could write.

The sight of Ferenc made her uneasy. By this time she was walking up and down the ward – very gingerly, very slowly – and even sitting in the day room occasionally – but she happened to be in bed when he came, and she wished that she hadn't been, it made her feel rather defenceless.

'Now we all agree that you are not to worry,' said Ferenc. 'The hotel is in good hands.'

He knew that that was exactly what was worrying her.

'None of us want you to rush back,' he said, and then he tried to make it look as if he'd just realised that he'd said something tactless. 'Oh, that sounds awful, but you know what I mean. Your health is paramount, and we can cope. I'm sorry about that. My English, it is . . .'

Nicola finished his sentence for him. '. . . faultless and subtle.'

'I have some news that will cheer the cockles of your heart.'

'Good Lord. That good!'

'That good.' He smiled again. 'Takings last week were 2.7 per cent up.'

Nicola felt as if she'd been struck to the heart with a dagger.

'That's wonderful news,' she said. 'That'll certainly speed my recovery.'

'That's what we thought,' he said. 'How *is* your progress? Is there much pain?'

'A great deal,' she said, 'but gradually less, and I can cope. We Divots are made of stalwart stuff.'

'Now what else can I tell you? Oh yes. You remember Emrys, the Welsh commis chef?'

A tremor of fear passed through Nicola. What had happened to Emrys?

'How could I forget him? I've only been away ten days. Thrown another wobbly, has he?'

'Not at all. No wobbly.'

'Good. That's good.'

Pat came in to check her blood pressure.

'Ferenc, meet Pat, my helper and angel. Pat, this is Ferenc Gulyas, my assistant manager, currently holding the fort with distinction and aplomb.'

'Pleased to meet you, Mr Gulyas.'

Pat's second glance revealed that she found Ferenc interesting – what was it about him and women? – while he gave her a quick once-over, face, breasts, crutch, thighs, expertly concealed but not quite expertly enough for Nicola.

'Please call me Ferenc,' he said, which was Hungarian for 'I wouldn't say no if you offered me your body.' He turned back to Nicola. 'No, Nicola, no wobbly. He asked me if he could put a few Welsh specialities on the menu – just one each week, but rotating – Glamorgan sausages, cawl, cockle bisque, sea bass in laverbread sauce.'

'Oh he's asked me time and time again. I've explained that it's impossible till I'm as blue in the face as a bottle of Welsh water.'

'I've agreed to let him try it.'

Nicola met his eye and held it. She wasn't going to say anything more about this in front of Pat.

'That's funny,' said Pat. 'Your blood pressure's up.'

'That *is* funny,' she said. 'I can't think why that can be, can you, Ferenc?'

Ferenc shrugged. He could even make a shrug seem sexy. When Pat had gone, he said, 'You're upset. You think I have exceeded my powers.'

'Well, yes, frankly. I want to encourage Emrys, but there's no rhyme or reason for having Welsh specialities in Warwickshire.'

'Or Hungarian ones?'

'What??' Nicola's heart was beating much too fast. Thank goodness Pat wasn't there to monitor it. 'What have you done?'

'I shouldn't have mentioned it. I'm exciting you. That is bad.'

'What do you mean: "or Hungarian ones"? What have you done?'

'Just one Hungarian speciality each week,' gleamed Ferenc. 'That's all. This week, duck goulash.'

'*This week*! You haven't let the grass grow under your feet, have you?'

'We have a saying in Hungary: Don't wait till it rains before buying an umbrella.'

'We have a saying in England: When the cat's away the mice will play. No, I'm sorry, Ferenc, but I can't see duck goulash catching on in Throdnall.'

'Mr Summers thought it tasty. He's going to recommend it to his members for the next Rotary.'

She was being manoeuvred into an impossible position. She was going to appear petty and jealous, and all because . . . all because . . .

All because she was petty and jealous – and she mustn't be. She just mustn't be. She forced herself to calm down.

'Well, that's all wonderful,' she said, trying hard to sound sincere (always one of her problems, even when she was sincere, in fact possibly a greater problem when she was sincere than when she wasn't, and therefore not so much of a problem at the moment).

'You can of course cancel all these initiatives when you return.'

'I could, couldn't I? We'll see.'

She felt tired even at the thought of the battles that lay ahead. She forced herself to meet Ferenc's eyes – and it was strange, she felt a little trickle of energy returning, no, of *new* energy, of energy as a woman, as Nicola, as herself.

'Thank you, Ferenc,' she said. 'You've . . . you've been a help.'

That disconcerted him!

When he had gone she felt more tired than ever. It was all too soon. But, beneath the tiredness, she felt for the first time that she was truly happy as Nicola. No exultation. No excitement. Just a feeling of real contentment.

Then it dawned on her what the great consideration was that had been hanging just out of reach of her consciousness.

She was no longer in a Real Life Test. She had passed the test. Real Life itself beckoned. A new life beckoned. Now she would really be a woman. She wanted to meet new people. She wanted to reinvent herself.

She didn't want to live at number thirty-three any more. Alan had been wonderfully supportive, but she had stayed with him too long. All that was over. It was the past.

How on earth would she tell him?

20 Lost Innocence

Seeing my husband as a woman for the first time was a rather eerie experience, like having a decorator paint your house in his choice of colours while you're cruising the Norwegian fjords and coming back to find he'd done it in exactly the same shades as before. There was a feeling of anti-climax, mixed in with a little relief.

I was relieved of course, both for Nicola and my own future chances, that the operation had been a success. I was relieved, as well as disappointed, that the pale, strained, exhausted face that stared at me from the bed was so unchanged.

Nicola was so very, very tired that first time, and the dreadful Prentice was there – if he ever comes to Australia I'll warn you! – but I found that things didn't get much easier with succeeding visits. We didn't seem to have much to say to each other any more. Inspiration always seems to dry up in hospitals.

What worries me is that Nicola seems not to have thought about her future, whereas I've been thinking about it more and more. I think she truly believes that she'll be able to continue to live at number thirty-three. I don't think it's possible. Where would she sleep, for a start? We can't go on sharing a bed for ever. I should have told her to go at least a year ago, but I couldn't bring myself to do it. Her op was such a frightening business. But now that it's over, well, our life together is over. She is a new person. She needs new adventures, as, quite soon, I will too.

But how can I find the strength to tell her? Oh, Jen, I wish you were here to give me strength. I've had to be strong for so long that I think I'm exhausted. I wish we weren't separated by half a world.

When you're in hospital you get institutionalised and the world outside seems very far away. I didn't feel that while Nicola was in hospital I could tell her about the very sad incident with Dad.

It was Saturday morning, very bright, unseasonably mild, I was preparing food for the weekend, Em was out with Carl, Gray was in his room. Dad had popped down to the park, he loves the park, 'It's a very ordinary park, is Bradwell Park, but I don't know what I'd do without it. It's my life-line,' he said to me once, and I was chopping some red onions and watching two blue tits and a coal tit on the feeders, when the doorbell rang. In films, if it's going to be something horrid, people react with horror to the doorbell before they go to the door, as if their bells never rang except for things that were horrid, but this was real life and I didn't have a care in the world at just that moment. I thought it might be Jehovah's Witnesses or Mrs Willoughby wondering if I had any coriander, and there was Dad standing there with an *extremely* young policeman.

I recalled a comment Dad made the other week when Nicola said that she knew she was getting old because policemen were getting so much younger, and Dad said, 'Wait till you get to my age. Even Popes are getting younger', and I thought, 'Yes, he is getting old. He must have forgotten where he lives.' I felt a wave of compassion for him. He can be infuriating, but I love him, but anyway it wasn't that, and I suppose I should be grateful, but in a way it was worse, and of course I soon realised how silly it had been of me to think that he'd forgotten where he lives, because if he had he wouldn't have been able to lead the policeman to the house.

The policeman was pink-faced and perspiring with

embarrassment. He looked as if he was only just out of nappies.

'What's happened?' I asked, suddenly fearful.

'It's the mothers,' began the policeman. 'It's the mothers down at the park.'

'They've complained to the police about me,' said Dad. 'Bitches. They've ganged up and complained.'

'The mothers think . . . they don't like him watching their children in the playground,' said the very young policeman.

'I just like to sit on my bench and watch the kiddies playing,' said Dad. 'I like to hear their laughter. I like to hear their excited squeals on the swings. I lose myself there. I like to watch their healthy little bodies.'

I met the policeman's eyes. It was a pity Dad had mentioned their little bodies. It showed, of course, how totally innocent he was, but I wasn't confident that the policeman would be sophisticated enough to appreciate that.

'We have no reason whatsoever,' began the policeman slowly, quarrying the officialese out of his mind with a supreme effort, 'to believe that there is anything untoward in Mr . . .?'

'Kettlewell.'

'. . . anything untoward in Mr Kettlewell's relationship with, or attitude to, the said children. No reason whatsoever, Mrs . . .?'

'Divot.'

'Divot. However, a complaint has been made and we are bound to investigate said complaint. May I come in and ask you a few questions?'

I had to let him come in.

'I'm very sorry to do this when you're upset,' said the policeman. He seemed kind. I worried about his future in the force.

'Upset?' I said.

'I noticed that you'd been crying. We're trained to be observant.'

'I was peeling onions. Red onions. They're supposed to be milder but I think they're getting less mild. I was watching the birds on our feeders, as innocently as Dad was watching the children.'

The policeman asked for our names and the names of everyone living in the house, and I found myself worrying about whether I should tell him about Nicola, and I must have given myself away, because he said, 'Are you sure you've mentioned everybody?'

'Well there's my husband,' I said.

'Name?'

'Nicola Divot.'

'Nicola?'

'Yes. He's in hospital at this very moment, actually. She's just had the operation.'

'Ah! Is your husband manager at the Cornucopia?'

'That's right.'

'Oh yes, I've met h . . . her.'

He wrote it all down.

'His sex change has nothing to do with Dad, or sex. It's gender alignment really.'

'Oh, I know, but I have to do the paperwork. There's been a complaint of a potentially serious nature. Er . . .' He blushed. The incipient boil on his neck reddened. 'What is the name of Mr Kettlewell's doctor?'

Dad just sat there, slumped, staring glassily into space. I don't think he was even listening.

'Do I have to give that, if you believe Dad to be innocent?'

'If he's innocent you've nothing to fear.'

'Doctor Rodgerson.'

'Thank you. We will need to ask him one or two questions. Just a formality.' He turned to Dad and spoke in a loud, slow voice. 'Mr Kettlewell, have you ever been charged with any criminal offence?'

'Stealing a street lamp on Christmas Eve in Castleford in nineteen thirty-seven,' said Dad.

'Nothing wrong with your father's memory,' said the policeman. 'Thank you, Mr Kettlewell. I don't think you'll hear any more of this.'

'So that makes it all right, does it?' said Dad. I was pleased that he could be angry.

'Leave it, Dad,' I said. 'It's not the young man's fault.'

'Bitches!'

'Dad!'

'What it is, Mr Kettlewell,' said the policeman. 'They aren't bitches. They're just mums what's worried for their kiddies.'

I saw him to the door, stood at the porch with him. He'd used cheap after-shave, and his breath smelt of boiled sweets.

'The thing is,' he said, 'I don't think he should go down the park no more. I'd rather it was just done informal like. I don't want to have to issue an exclusion order.'

An exclusion order to keep our dad from the park! What is the world coming to?

Dad was staring glassily into space when I went back in. I offered him a beer.

'Oh, that'll really help, won't it?' he said. 'I'm banned from the playground. I'm a dirty old man if I smile at a kid. If I offer them sweets I'm in prison, a beer'll make a lot of difference, won't it?'

'Well don't have one then.'

'Well, no, I may as well.'

I got Dad a beer and returned to the onions, but now my tears were real. A starling went to the feeders, and the tits flew away. It was the way of the world.

'I like to hear the kids' laughter,' said Dad. 'I like to look at their smiles. I enjoy their joy. Seeing kids with their life ahead of them . . . well, it reconciles me to my life ending. I think that people like what them mothers think I am should have their goolies cut off very slowly with a blunt instrument and served to them lightly grilled. How the hell can they think I'm like that?'

I began to fry the onions though I'd lost all heart for the pork casserole (free-range, lived outside, we'd seen the farm they came from).

'I wish I'd died years ago,' said Dad. 'I called her in t'paper shop Marge again yesterday. Me mind's going.'

'Your mind isn't going, Dad,' I said. 'Look at the way you remembered that street light you nicked, which you never told us about. I didn't realise I was being brought up by a criminal.'

He didn't smile at my feeble joke. He was beyond jokes, where he was.

'Aye,' he said, 'but that just makes it worse. When your mind starts going, you remember things from far, far away. Me mum and dad took me to Brid for the day when I were six. I can still remember that t'bus had an advertisement for Smith Kenyon's Eucalyptus and Menthol Pastilles. You see! Alzheimer's.'

Oh, Jen, I haven't written as much as this since I had to do essays at school. I wrote such letters to you when we were younger, I poured out my heart, but I didn't send them. I didn't want to burden you. I was wrong. Burdens aren't nearly as bad as not being close. I feel so close to you as I write this.

Thank you for the photos. How big Craig is now and . . .

Alan didn't tell Gray or Em about Bernie being banned from the park, he couldn't bring himself to, but he did get very angry with Gray when the question of where Nicola would sleep came up, and Gray suggested putting Bernie in a home.

'Don't you ever dare say that again,' he said. It was unfair of him. He was angry because of the park incident, but Gray didn't know of the park incident, because he hadn't told him.

He got the kids together one evening before supper, and he said, 'Listen. Your father comes home next Tuesday. I don't think it's suitable for us to share a bed any more. Now I can't ask either of you to give up your room . . .' He paused. He had had a wild hope that one of them would offer, but neither of them did, and he couldn't really blame them.

'I can't,' said Gray. 'It's my existence. It's my link to the world.'

'Good idea to leave it then and start to *live* in the world,' said Em.

'I don't like your world. It has you in it,' said Gray.

'Children!' Alan shouted. Children! Gray was seventeen and Em was coming up to twenty-two. 'No, Gray, I couldn't ask you to leave your room. Not because of the Internet. Because of your A-Levels.'

Em said nothing. Well, she brought Carl home in her lunch-time occasionally. She thought Alan didn't know, but he had smelt sex and male feet in her room a couple of times when he'd checked it to see if it was clean enough for Mrs Pritchard to clean.

'No,' he said. 'I'm going to sleep on the Zed-bed in the sitting room.'

'You can't sleep in the lounge for ever, Mum,' said Em.

He didn't reply. He let it sink in. He didn't think they'd given a thought to the possibility that their father might not be there for ever.

On their journey back to Throdnall, as they slipped through the rolling Midlands countryside, through the trim villages and anonymous little towns, with the rain sparkling in the sunshine and a double rainbow in the west, Nicola was very quiet, obviously tense. One always feels very exposed on leaving hospital, and the immensity of what lay ahead was suddenly weighing on her. Alan drove very carefully. He didn't want to jolt her insides. This made it seem a bit like a funeral procession.

He told her the sad business about Bernie and how changed she'd find him. He was dispirited. He was defeated.

He took a deep breath.

'Have you given any thought to the sleeping arrangements?' he asked.

'What?'

'Well I don't think we can go on sharing a bed for ever.'

'No.'

'I'm going to sleep on the Zed-bed.'

'You can't do that.'

'What else do you suggest? You have to have a proper bed. You're recovering from a major operation.'

'I suppose so.'

'It wouldn't be fair on the kids. Not at this stage. They're too old.'

'I suppose so.'

'I might have to put Dad in a home one day, I'm not a heroine, but not yet, he isn't nearly ready, it'd kill him.'

'I suppose so.'

'Anyway that's the plan for the time being. You'll have the double bed.'

Nicola didn't reply. Alan wondered if the truth was dawning. Then, after a long delay, she said, 'Sorry. I should have thanked you. You're wonderful to me, Alan. I . . .'

She stopped. It did cross Alan's mind that she had been going to say 'I love you', and had realised how inappropriate it would have been.

She sighed as they passed the sign 'Throdnall – twinned with Verona.'

'Dreading being back in Throdnall?' asked Alan.

'We're hosting a twinning dinner. Dreading that. What *will* they think of our food? What on earth will they think of Throdnall?'

She walked back into the house very gingerly. It was slippery from the showers.

Alan had put flowers everywhere. The house was like a garden centre.

He'd made a succulent fish pie. They all loved his fish pie. It was comfort food, but not too bland. He used white wine and nutmeg and lots of pepper. It was the perfect thing to make, especially as Em had requested no garlic. 'Carl hates garlic on the breath. Well he hates it period.' Every reference to Carl diminished Alan's hopes for Em with him.

His fish pie was always so successful that it saddened him that night, in their candlelit dining room, with the coal-effect blazing and the Pouilly-Fumé flowing, to see how little enjoyment there was.

Gray bolted his food.

'I've got to rush,' he said. 'I've got a girl from Toronto in trouble.'

Alan's heart sank and rose all at the same time. Did he really mean . . . Could he really mean . . .? If he did, if he had, well of course Alan couldn't condone it, but to think that he might have got as far as that with a girl, it would make him reassuringly normal. But Toronto? It must be the Internet. Could you get girls in trouble on the Internet? Perhaps you met them on the Internet and then posted your sperm in a sealed container and she . . . wild thoughts! Why not just ask him? Hardly dared.

'In trouble?'

'Yeah. I've made a brilliant move with my bishop and I don't think there's any way she can escape now.'

Alan's heart sank and rose. He was glad nobody could see into his soul. The morality of his reactions was deeply questionable, but . . . mother first, moralist second.

Em bolted her food too. Carl ruled her with a rod of iron, but

Alan shouldn't have said, 'Does Carl have an obsession about Tuesday nights, by any chance?'

Bernie picked at his pie listlessly, despite which he ate quite a lot.

Nicola moved her food around on her plate like an anorexic model at a posh dinner party, but she didn't eat much, she was racked with tension. Alan's heart bled for her, and he knew that he couldn't talk to her about the future that night.

The apple crumble was no more of a triumph than the fish pie. Em forswore it altogether, hurtling off into down-town Throdnall. Gray rushed upstairs after the fish pie, made a move, rushed down, bolted his crumble, burped, apologised and rushed upstairs. Bernie just shovelled it in without any signs of pleasure or even consciousness. Nicola picked at it tensely.

After the meal Bernie went through and sat staring at the TV with the sound off, Gray fought a long and heroic battle against his Canadian conqueror, and Nicola said, 'I need to speak to you' in a hoarse voice.

'Aren't you tired?' asked Alan. 'Don't you want to go to bed?'

'Soon, yes, but we must talk.'

This was a surprise. He didn't clear away the pudding plates. They sat amid the wreckage of the meal, nursing the last of the Pouilly-Fumé.

'Alan, I'm sorry to be so blunt and to say it so soon, but . . . I don't think I can stay here.'

To say that Alan was astonished would be an understatement.

'I don't think it's fair on the kids to have a woman as their father. Alan, I think I'm going to have to leave you.'

The relief! Alan thought he was going to faint. Nicola reached across and held his hand. He was shaking.

'I've upset you,' she said. 'I've been too blunt. Oh, Alan, I . . . it's odd to be saying this, but I love you. I do, I do, but . . . it has to be over. Doesn't it?'

Alan found himself unable to make any reply.

'I'll go as soon as I feel fit. It's best. You're unconvinced. Honestly, Alan, I . . . I have to lead a new life. I . . . who knows . . . ?' She smiled bravely. '. . . I might even find myself a man.' She squeezed Alan's hand. 'Sorry. That was insensitive.'

Alan was surprised to find that he did think it insensitive. He didn't like the thought of her finding a man. It was a primaeval jealous twitch.

Alan looked after her brilliantly. Next morning he gave her her very favourite breakfast – two perfectly cooked boiled eggs and toast. She made no mention of the discussion of the previous night, but talked almost compulsively about all sorts of things, but particularly about boiled eggs.

'Nobody ever uses the boiled egg argument for the existence of God,' she said.

'What?'

'I'm not a believer. Sometimes I wish I was, but I can't, but if anything could persuade me it'd be boiled eggs.'

'What??'

'Well a chicken has no concept of cooking. It can't. It has no access to stoves of any kind. So how can it produce an egg, consisting of yolk and white, which cooks in such a way that the white goes solid while the yolk remains runny at the moment of perfection? The egg must be an invention of a benevolent deity.'

'I hate to be sceptical,' said Alan. 'I like your beneggolent God, but I can see why this argument has not caught on with clerics. Isn't it the truth that an egg just happens to be like that, and man has had to make the best of it, and so has accustomed himself to liking eggs with hard whites and runny yolks, because that is the only alternative to having no boiled eggs at all. If eggs happened to come out with hard yolks and runny whites, maybe we'd all be saying, "Yum yum. It's just how I like it." '

These were the sort of conversations they had in number thirty-three in those unreal days, as they avoided any further discussions of reality. Alan didn't sleep well on his Zed-bed. He developed bags under his eyes, and Mr Beresford kept asking him if he was all right. He had a job to concentrate on his work. He couldn't afford to make mistakes. They were weeks of stress. He longed for Nicola to go, and hated himself for it.

By the time Nicola had found a place to rent, on the other side of town, Alan was aching for the moment when she would leave, was counting the minutes, and had to resist helping her too much in case she would sense his eagerness to see her go. He had to rein in his enthusiasm as they sorted and packed her belongings, and curb his generosity when sharing out the accumulated possessions of so many years. He had to refrain from rushing out to stock her up with toilet paper and bleach, salt and pepper, marmalade and jam – all the little things that he thought she'd forget to buy because she'd been a man for so long.

Then, suddenly, he was watching her as she slipped out of the drive in the laden Subaru.

The moment she was out of sight he began to miss her.

What absurd creatures human beings are.

21 On Her Own

Nicola felt so very vulnerable as she embarked on the Great Trans-Throdnall Expedition. She had only been back at work for a week. She still wasn't remotely confident about her body. She still felt the occasional sharp pain in her nether regions. Mr McWhinnie was very pleased with her, though, and had explained that her body was still in the process of getting over a massive shock.

She was leaving the only true friend she had in the world – her wife Alan. She was forty-three years of age.

As she approached the end of Brindley Street, past the For Sale notice on the boarded-up Piccalilli Circus, she had to fight an urge to turn right and go to work. She did sometimes pop in on Saturdays. You can't ever leave your work entirely behind when you have the responsibilities of a General Manager.

Her first week back hadn't been as stressful as she had expected. She'd fought her real battle long ago when she'd walked in dressed as a woman. She returned to a warm welcome from some, resignation from others (literally in the case of a young porter whose mother had forbidden him to work under a freak) and indifference from most. The hotel had continued to function in her absence and it would continue to function in her presence. It was Divot-proof – at least at the low standards it was permitted to aspire towards.

Ferenc had introduced certain minor changes, and the Welsh and Hungarian specialities on the menu were proving surprisingly popular, given the conservative nature of the clientele. Nicola decided to pretend that this didn't annoy her. She even said nice things about Ferenc behind his back, though she couldn't bring herself to say them to his face. She didn't challenge any of his initiatives. She didn't yet have the energy.

All these thoughts were going through her mind as she led her two-vehicle convoy through the labyrinthine one-way system and up the gentle slope towards 'The Streets'. The second vehicle was the smaller of Bill Canning's two removal vans and contained her pitiful worldly possessions.

It's amazing how you can think of other things and still drive safely. She had no recollection of going round the new mini-roundabout at the end of Percy Road or of turning left into Mallet Street. She didn't remember passing the Shell Garage or the new doomed delicatessen, 'Mr Tasty', which wouldn't last even as long as Piccalilli Circus. (All delicatessens are doomed in Throdnall, even ones with sensible names. They open, there is early excitement, they struggle, they close.) She was thinking about the Cornucopia, about how she hadn't yet managed, on her return, to give a damn about it. Would she ever again?

'The Streets' are so called because all the roads are named after streets. It could only happen in Throdnall. The area could equally easily be known as 'The Roads', because all the streets are named after roads! Apparently, a man called Jasper Congreve, known as 'The Father of British Road Classification', once lived in a big house set back off what is now Avenue Crescent. He was instrumental (Throdnall believes, but this is very dubious, there are other strong candidates for the honour, if honour it be) in setting up the 'A' Road and 'B' Road classification system. Some half-wit in the Council's Highways Department thought that this incredibly exciting and radical achievement should be celebrated in perpetuity.

She drove along Street Lane, turned left into Lane Street (truly an inspired move in the Throdnall game of Confuse-A-Postman!) and then right into Lane Road, where she was now to live, just beyond the junction with Crescent Rise.

Flat Three, Eight, Lane Road, Throdnall. Not an address to

quicken the pulses. Not an address to inspire the poetic side of one's nature.

Number eight was a three-storey Victorian town house divided into six flats. Her new life, her exciting exploration of womanhood, would take place on the first floor. She had a high-ceilinged room furnished in Late Mean Landlord style, a small but high-ceilinged bedroom, and a bathroom so old it should have been listed.

As she looked at her bedroom her spirits sank. It looked such a lonely room, so bereft of warmth. How could she ever warm it? How could anyone ever warm it with her?

Old Bill, her removals man, was a former policeman so his nickname was regarded as witty. He moved very slowly, though not in a mysterious way, and as he lumbered down to the van to collect Nicola's sparse belongings, she looked at herself in the mirror in the unflatteringly brightly lit bathroom with the cracked basin. Was she remotely attractive? She had shaved that morning, but this was the first time for over a month and was largely symbolic, a full stop on her sentence as a man. There were signs that the continued hormone treatment and the removal of the hated male appendages, whether from a physical or a psychological effect, were continuing to turn her less and less male in appearance. But to find a man who was attracted to her, and to whom she was attracted, and to have the confidence as a woman to feel that she could give herself to him, those were massive steps – and then, should she manage to jump all those hurdles safely, there was still the bedroom. Could she ever bring a man to this tall, bleak bedroom? Or to any bedroom? Oh, the hurdles she faced.

To think that that very evening . . . but let us not anticipate . . .

She was forty-three, she didn't have a true friend in the world, she had an old car, old clothes, an old bathroom and a new or neo-vagina which she had dilated herself, as instructed, feeling about it rather as she would have felt about something that came flat-packed from Ikea. The prospect of its ever being dilated by anyone other than herself seemed remote, to say the least.

The loneliness that she felt that afternoon in her new rented flat, is it any wonder that that very evening . . . but no, let us not anticipate . . .

She made a cup of tea for Old Bill. She didn't want him to go. When he had gone there would be nobody.

She saw him out, went down the stairs with him, because that meant it would be at least a minute longer before she was alone. As she shut the communal front door, the door of flat one opened, and a man stood before her.

'Hello!' he enthused. He had a Christmas cake of a voice – rich, fruity, fortified by alcohol, and with an icing of sexuality. 'You must be the new tenant of flat three. How does the prospect of a little bevvy strike you?'

The prospect of a little bevvy struck Nicola much as the first sight of Samarkand would have struck a starving nomad with a sick camel. She could only think of one thing that she would prefer to a little bevvy, and that was a large bevvy.

'It's a bit early,' she heard herself say, much to her chagrin.

'Nonsense. If you don't drink early it'll be too late,' he said.

'Well if you insist,' she said. How very English. How terribly knees together. One day someone would say, 'No, I don't insist. Goodbye', and she'd deserve it.

But *he* didn't. 'I do. I do,' he said, and he led her into his flat, which was masculine, shabby and warm, and smelt of dog and urine and burning offal. 'Must switch the dog's meat off. I can't abide dog food in tins. Rex is too good for tins.'

Rex, a golden labrador, raised his head slowly, and seemed to nod.

He had a battered, rather blotchy face, and was almost bald. The man, not Rex. He was quite tall, and slightly round-shouldered, and looked as if he ought to have a moustache. She would have said that he was in his mid-fifties but found out later that he was forty-eight. Life had taken its toll. Life does.

There was nothing ugly about the man, though. He had a nice smile, which he flashed warmly as he said, 'Now. Liquid refreshment. G and T?'

'Please.'

'Ice and a slice?'

'Very nice.'

'G and T, ice and a slice, coming up. Have no fear. I'm Lance, by the way. I have the Lafayette Gallery, in Biscuit Passage.'

Good. Nicola had never been in there. There was a chance that they had never met. She didn't want Lance to know, just yet.

'I'm . . . I'm Nicola.'

She didn't add her surname. It sounded too formal. It might have struck a chord with something he'd read in the *Advertiser*. Nicola would do. Nicola was cosy. Nicola sounded fun. She could see it, on a little notice in the telephone box round the corner: Nicola, fun loving, gives French lessons. No. Stop.

'Pleased to meet you, Nicola. Think my luck may have changed. Am I to assume, from your little van, that there is no longer a Mr Nicola, if indeed there ever was? Though surely there must have been, you're a little cracker.'

She didn't say that there had indeed been a Mr Nicola, and it had been her.

'There you are, G and T, get your pretty lips round that.'

Well! Can you imagine? She knew that he was several sheets to the wind, but did she care on that bleak day?

Honesty compels me to record that Lance's G and T was not of classical proportions. It was all G and very little T.

At first he sat in one of his shabby old brown leather armchairs, from which he launched into a potted history of the disaster that was his life – his ex-wife, his estranged son, his ruthless bank manager, his business partner who had swindled him, his wine business that had been destroyed through sabotage that he could never prove. 'My life has been a chapter of accidents, but now I have an instinct, an instinct, Nicola, that my luck has changed.

You really are extraordinarily lovely. You're the quintessence of femininity.'

Already he could barely say 'quintessence of femininity', but she had to accept, with her history, that she might not find many men saying she was the quintessence of femininity until they were almost too drunk to say it.

When he brought her her second G with very little T, he of course took the opportunity to sit next to her on the sofa. She tried not to flinch as he put his nicotine-stained hand on her knee. She wasn't used to having men's hands on her knee. In fact it had only ever happened once, in Colchester, and he had been pretty firm with him. 'You're supposed to be giving me a short back and sides, not seducing me,' he had said. 'Any further nonsense and I'll have you drummed out of the National Union of Hairdressers.'

Well, now she was a woman and she ought to welcome a firm man's hand on her knee – or the firm hand of a man, rather. She forced herself to relax. Half an hour ago she had despaired of her looks and now she was the quintessence of femininity, it was better than her wildest dreams, and it was absurd to flinch. So she tried not to stiffen as he put his arm round her shoulders, and she tried to avoid his breath lest she sink into utter drunkenness. She tried not to drink her G and not much else too fast, but it was very pleasant, and she no longer felt sad and lonely and forty-three. This was a new and exciting life. It was lovely and cosy in the warm doggy masculine flat.

'You're an absolute cracker, Nicola,' he said. 'An absolute cracker. My faith in women had reached rock bottom, Nicola, thanks to my treatment by the cow.'

'The cow?'

'Forget the cow. I have. Bloody woman. Wish you hadn't mentioned her. She can't hurt me now. Rock bottom, Nicola, and when I say rock bottom, I mean rock bottom. And then you come along. It's almost as if you were sent. It's tempting to believe that you were sent. Another G and T?'

'No, please. Er . . . I mean . . . er . . . well yes, thank you, but less G and more T, please.'

'Absolutely. Moderation in . . . something or other.'

She thought of just leaving. She looked at Rex and his deep, affectionate eyes and she felt that they were imploring her to leave, but the battle between this warmth and her bleak, as yet unlived-in flat was no contest.

'T with very little G,' he announced, half collapsing at her side. 'You're a corker, Nicola, and in the morning I shall paint you.'

'You paint, then?' she deduced.

'I dabble and daub. I supplement my income. Running a gallery in Throdnall is not easy, Nicola. In fact it's difficult. The artistic colony is not extensive. Phyllis . . . Phyllis . . .'

'Philistinism?'

'Phyllis Perkins. That's it. Perkins. She said to me, "Lance, you'll be barking up the wrong tree, opening a gallery in Throdnall." Didn't listen. Thought I knew it all. At times I've felt so alone. So alone, Phyllis.'

'Nicola.'

'Absolutely. No mistake about it. Beautiful Nicola. Nicola?'

'Yes?'

'How about a little . . . er . . . to . . . er . . . to . . . er . . . welcome you to number eight?'

'A little what?'

'Let me ravish you, Nicola, because you are ravishing, as no man has ever ravished you before. Are you on for that?'

Oh God. Was she ready? She was still packing large pieces of plastic into her vagina every day to stop it from healing over and to stretch it to as great a size as possible. Was it ready for Lance? She swallowed a large mouthful of G and T. Still more G than T. She choked. He banged her on the back and with one opportunistic movement slid his hand round to the front and felt for her tits. It would be quite a search. Did she . . .? Oh God. Was she . . .? Down, Rex, this isn't a game for you.

'Down, Rex.' The dog obeyed Lance instantly. 'Silly boy. He needs a walk. He wants to do wee-wees.'

'Should we take him out?'

'Later. Later. Oh, Nicola, oh my gorgeous Nicola, oh I . . . I feel . . . I don't . . . I . . .'

He collapsed. He collapsed in her lap on the nicotine-coloured sofa. She was staring down at his bald head to which a few tufts of hair adhered like weeds in a patio. She thought for an awful moment that he had died. What could she do? Then he shuddered like a room that is too near a tube line, and snored once, very loudly. Rex barked. Lance twitched in his sleep and snored again. She lifted him off her very carefully and with great difficulty, he was heavy, and then she lowered his head gently on to a cushion.

She felt an overwhelming sense of relief, but it was tinged, yes it was, it was tinged with just a touch of disappointment. Would it have mattered how drunk they both were if that enormous hurdle had been jumped on her very first day on her own?

She couldn't find the key to the flat and she needed to take Rex for wee-wees. She jammed Lance's little pouffe in his door and led Rex into the street, and then he led her down Lane Road, up Crescent Rise, turned right into Avenue Crescent, past the cemetery, right again into Road Grove and right again into Lane Road. She felt as if she too was a dog, sniffing out the boundaries of her new little world. A fine drizzle began to fall. Rex ignored twelve lamp posts, but utilised seven. She could see no difference between the ones he ignored and the ones he utilised and she began to feel drunker and drunker as the cool evening air hit her.

Rex led her safely back through the chill sodium gloom into the brown fog of the flat, and he gave her an adoring look which seemed to say, 'Are you going to be my new mistress?' and she gave him a sad look which definitely said, 'Somehow, Rex, I don't think so.'

She stumbled upstairs, fumbled the door open, and tumbled into the least threadbare of her unlovely chairs. It felt like midnight, but her watch told her that it was only five to eight.

When she woke up, still in the chair, it was seventeen minutes past three. She had a stiff neck, a thick head, a dead leg, and an undilated vagina. She could hear Lance's regular, shuddering snores.

Sunday morning in Throdnall. People had been known to go to the crematorium for a bit of life.

Nicola felt beside herself. Not beside herself with anything, it was as if she was outside herself, beside herself, observing herself on her first full day on her own as a woman. It felt very strange.

Ms Nicola Divot (43), wearing blue jeans and a big white chunky mohair sweater, strolled to the newsagent's on Street Lane, where she purchased the *Sunday Times* and the *Mail on Sunday*. Then she entered the Kosy Korner Kafé, North Throdnall's sole attempt at café life, where she ordered a Danish and a cappuccino. With a supreme effort and a sigh, she lifted the *Sunday Times* out of her carrier bag. She took one look at it, cringed from its comprehensiveness, put it back, and got out the *Mail on Sunday*. She slid the Financial Section back into the carrier bag, because she had no money to invest, then read the rest with intense interest for twenty-seven minutes, before sighing, muttering, 'There's no news in it' and standing up.

She then strolled back to number eight by a different route.

As she approached her new home, she met Mr Lance Windlass (48), proprietor and owner of the Lafayette Gallery, who was walking in the opposite direction with his dog Rex (9). Ms Divot was clearly feeling much the worse for wear, but Mr Windlass seemed unimpaired by the previous evening's activities.

They stopped to speak. It would have been rude not to.

'We meet again,' said Ms Divot, who then cringed at the obviousness of her remark.

'We certainly do,' replied Mr Windlass, perhaps out of a natural kindness which did not want to show up the paucity of imagination in her opening remark.

'Thank you very much for the drinks,' she said rather dutifully.

'That's all right,' he replied wittily. 'It's not every day a new tenant arrives at number eight.'

Ms Divot did not particularly like the description 'new tenant'. She rather preferred some of the terms used the previous evening, which included 'extraordinarily lovely', 'the quintessence of femininity', 'absolute cracker' and 'corker'. She sensed that none of these words would be used about her by Mr Windlass again.

Ms Divot, standing beside Ms Divot, felt that Ms Divot should not have been upset by Mr Windlass's omissions, or by the absence of such phrases as 'We must arrange when I shall paint you', 'We must do it again some time' and 'How about a little dinner à deux at Le Flageolet?' After all, she did not say, 'I must return the hospitality', 'I make a mean cup of coffee' or 'You must come up and dilate my new vagina some time.'

The truth was, she deduced, that she did not think that this charming disaster of a man was the answer to a transsexual's prayer. The truth was, she also deduced, that she had herself deduced that in sobriety the bald gallery owner did not feel the overwhelming attraction for her charms that he had felt in drink the previous evening. Indeed, he almost admitted as much when he said, 'I think I must have had a bit of a skinful last night', to which she made the unspoken addition of 'to have thought you a corker'.

As she went into her little flat, she ceased to have that strange out-of-body experience. She had a little cry, actually. She missed Alan and Em and Gray and even Bernie. She was looking forward to Monday morning, and seeing Ferenc and Paulo and Emrys and Leonard Balby again.

How sad was that?

22 A Memorable Moussaka

Six weeks after she had left the home where she had once been the man of the house, Nicola returned as a dinner guest. She felt uneasy about this. It didn't seem right. She felt self-conscious.

In those six weeks, she had developed quite a comfortable routine.

Every weekend she would prepare a luscious casserole to see her through the week, and before she drove to the Cornucopia each weekday morning she would place a portion of the Casserole of the Week in her new slow cooker, and it would gently steam all day.

After work she would go, every evening, to the Trumpet in Biscuit Passage. Lance had suggested that she should, and had introduced her to 'the early evening crowd'. It was soon evident to her that her history was known, and, while one or two men flirted with her most pleasantly, they didn't mean it, and she knew that they didn't mean it, and they knew that she knew that they didn't mean it. It was a very masculine environment, the Trumpet. Women were welcome so long as they behaved like men. The paradox for Nicola was that she found it much easier to behave like a man now that she was a woman than she had when she'd been a man. She'd struggled with beer, felt self-conscious about drinking wine, and had dreaded dirty stories. Now she could enjoy her wine and even relish the occasional slightly risqué story in the safe knowledge that the really nasty ones wouldn't be tried on her.

There was no pressure on her to have more than two glasses of wine. Everyone knew that she couldn't afford to lose her licence.

When she got home she would prop a book on the table and read as she ate, very slowly, her Casserole of the Week. It simply was an enormous relief for her to be solitary, to be free to be herself, not to need to feel remotely guilty when she chose, in her very first week, to read . . . you've guessed it . . . *Tess of the D'Urbervilles*. What, again? Are you demented? There was nobody there to ask those questions. Now she no longer needed to be Tess. 'Oh, Tess, Tess,' she said one night. 'I am with you. I suffer with you. I am your sister.'

There was nobody to tell her that talking to yourself was the first sign of madness.

The loneliness that she had felt that first Saturday afternoon did not return. Instead, the delights of the solitary life were visited upon her.

Once a week, though, she did not go home to the flat. After her visit to the Trumpet she would go back to the hotel, dine in the Kenilworth Brasserie or the Warwick Bar, visit the brand new Health Club – Keep Fit The Cornucopia Way – and then she would sleep in the hotel, in a different room each time, to get a taste of 'The Cornucopia Experience' – usually an amalgam of insomnia and sciatica.

They were now third on the list for refurbishment – a process that had slowed down because of lack of funds because of low levels of occupancy because of delays in refurbishment – well, that was how Nicola saw it, but she wasn't on the Board, so what did she know?

As she walked up the path to the front door of number thirty-three, past the pathetically neat little lawns, clutching a bottle of Californian red and a bunch of the same spring flowers that were in such abundance in the tidy, well-groomed borders of the little front garden, she felt absurdly formal. Why had she not just walked in through the back door as usual?

She rang the bell. Nobody came.

Alan was also feeling self-conscious about the evening. He was in the grip of contradictory emotions. He hadn't yet begun his great new life. He was living the old one without the support of his partner, and that was very different. He was still missing Nicola very much. He was depressed by Bernie's descent into depression and decay. Although he couldn't pretend to be sorry that Em and Carl had broken up, he wished that it had not been Carl who had done it and that Em had not been so devastated. Gray was mooning around in a world of his own. He seemed even further away from their world. Alan longed for the family to behave with dignity and spirit that evening. He didn't want Nicola to think that he wasn't making as good a fist of being the man of the house as Nicola once had.

Yes, he was missing Nicola, but he also felt a real sense of grievance. Here was Nicola leading the bachelor life – what was he saying? – the spinster life. Why did that sound so much less attractive? Start again, Alan. Here was Nicola as free as air, a single woman, and here was he, laden with commitments, a single parent, and all because Nicola had got in first, and he couldn't even say, 'Typical man'!

He was running late. He'd chosen moussaka, one of his staple comfort foods, not wanting to do anything pretentious, but he wanted it to be a good moussaka, and he hadn't reckoned on bloody Beresford keeping him late because he was in a foul mood because they were being penalised for late deliveries of four car units to Mercury North Eastern.

He wanted the dining room to reflect the full glory of family life, to be overwhelmingly cosy, a riot of coal-effect fire and candles and soft wall lights and garden flowers and cut glass and all the things that Nicola wouldn't have in her rented flat.

Was that someone banging at the front door? Surely she wouldn't go to the front door?

I mustn't seem too content, Nicola reminded herself as Alan pulled back the double bolts on the front door and unlocked both locks with different keys.

They looked at each other hesitantly, and then kissed on both cheeks.

'What is this – Fort Knox?' asked Nicola.

'The Collinsons were burgled last week.'

'Why am I not utterly devastated?'

'And nobody ever comes to the front door except Jehovah's Witnesses. You know that. We don't have visitors. Our last visitor was Prentice.'

'Don't. No, I thought, "I'm a guest. I should go to the front door. I should do it properly." I brought these.'

Nicola pushed the flowers at Alan awkwardly.

'Thank you. They're very nice.'

'You've got a garden full of them. I needn't have bothered.'

'I was under the impression it was the thought that counted. Well, well, you look well.'

'I am well.' Slightly too late, she added, 'Oh, and so do you.'

Good old Nicola. Still the same old Nick. But Alan managed not to say this.

'This is strange, isn't it?'

'Yes. Yes, it is.'

'So . . . how are you really, Nicola?'

Nicola reminded herself that she mustn't sound too content.

'Oh, I'm all right. You know. Really.'

'Good.'

Noises. Meaningless noises in a suburban hall.

'I brought some wine. Californian.'

'Oh no. Wrong, Nicola.'

'Oh dear. Poor Em.'

The spicy parsnip soup went down a treat. Bernie slurped more than ever and had a spicy parsnip chin. He burped twice and didn't apologise or put his hand in front of his mouth. In the lounge his zip had been undone. Now it was done up, but a bit of shirt had got trapped in it.

Gray and Em were very silent. Em was sullen, sulky. Her jaw seemed very big when she sulked. Gray had a far-away smile, an old-fashioned soppy grin, on his immature, now only slightly spotty face. With his glasses and his dark hair he had all the appearance of intellectual brilliance, except for one thing – intellectual brilliance.

Nicola had to keep the conversation going. She talked about the residents of the flats at number eight. She described Lance in an amusing way which she felt was disloyal, but surely he would have understood that the party had to go with a swing. She talked of Mrs Milner in flat two, a deeply boring woman only interested in one thing – Mrs Milner of flat two. She talked of the young couple in flat five who weren't interested in anybody over the age of thirty. She couldn't wait for them to begin to get old. She described the ex army officer turned struggling financial consultant in flat six, who introduced himself, as he picked up a local election leaflet in the communal hall, with the words, 'Hello. I'm Captain Simon Bancroft. Straight in the bin, don't you think? The only good Liberal is a dead Liberal.'

She made them laugh, though perhaps not quite as much as she had hoped, and she made herself sound lonely without wallowing in it.

Alan couldn't believe how chatty Nicola had become now that she was a woman.

The moussaka went down well. They all liked Alan's moussaka. Cousin Freddy had once said, 'I've eaten moussaka in every corner of Greece, but none of them's the equal of yours, Alison', which was his way of telling them how much more travelled than them he was.

Alan watched Bernie packing the stuff into his hygienically challenged mouth – he didn't clean his teeth properly, his breath was bad these days – and he thought, 'I'll end up hating him.'

'Dad?' he said. 'Is it all right?'

'Very nice,' he said.

'It would help if occasionally you offered a compliment. It's a bit humiliating to have to force them out of you.'

Bernie looked at Alan in astonishment.

'So, Clinton got away with it, then,' said Nicola, breaking up a brief silence that she had found unbearable.

It sounded absurd, suddenly thrown into the melting pot like that apropos of absolutely nothing. It sounded even more absurd when nobody else commented on it. Well, Bernie belched, but you couldn't put that down as a political comment.

Alan saw Gray look at his watch, and it irritated him.

'Keeping you, are we, Gray?' he asked.

'What? No, but I do have to keep an eye on the time,' said Gray. 'Mustn't miss Choo Choo.'

'Choo Choo?' repeated Nicola.

'I know. It's a bloody stupid nickname,' said Gray, 'but it's what they call my girl friend from Chattanooga.'

'Don't you think it's about time you started meeting people in real life?'

Nicola was always brilliant at laying herself open to criticism when she was Nick, thought Alan, and it seems she still is.

'I've seen what a real life love affair has done to my parents,' said Gray bitterly. 'My career at Pricewaterhouse'll be knackered before it starts.' Then he remembered that bitterness wasn't cool. 'Actually it'll be quite a talking point at uni,' he said, 'telling people that my mum and dad are now my dad and mum. At least it isn't boring. Excuse me. Internet time. Sorry, Dad. Won't be long.'

He slid out of the room as if he hoped he was invisible. Em sent him on his way with 'Give our love to Choo Choo', which he greeted with the scorn it deserved.

There was another silence. Alan thought about his dad and began to wonder if he should have a confrontation with him; things couldn't go on the way they were. Then he had a very silly thought. It was seven minutes to nine. He would have it out with

Bernie if he burped without apologising before the clock struck the hour. If he didn't, he wouldn't. Absurd.

'Is the moussaka all right, Dad?' he prompted.

'Very nice, thank you.'

Well fucking well say so. The use of the swearword, even in the silence of his head, surprised Alan. His journey to manhood must be speeding up.

In the event, Bernie didn't burp before the clock struck nine, but he did fart, and again he didn't apologise.

And just after the clock had struck he said, 'Oh dearie me', and within two minutes of that he burped. All in all, Alan felt he had the moral right to read the riot act.

Nicola smiled bravely, and Alan knew that she just didn't want to be there, and he found this distressing. He'd always been the real strength in the house, he knew that, but now he felt impotent.

Gray returned with an even soppier smile on his face, said, 'Sorry about that. Nice chat,' and resumed his silent consumption of moussaka.

Em stood up.

'Sorry, Dad,' she said to Nicola. 'I don't want to be rude, but I can't bear seeing my brother mooning over some stupid virtual love affair with some virtual girl the other side of the virtual world.'

'Real love affairs haven't done *you* much good,' said Gray.

'Gray!' hissed Alan.

'You look great, Dad, like your hairstyle, but I have to go to my room,' said Em. 'Sorry, Mum. Great moussaka.'

She left with a certain dignity. Nicola felt quite proud of her.

Nicola and Alan smiled at each other and neither of them had the faintest idea what the other's smile meant.

'Oh dearie me,' said Bernie. Self-pity and sour burps emerged from his mouth in roughly equal quantities.

'I see travel agents are very worried about the low level of summer bookings,' said Nicola over the chocolate mousse. Her attempt to get a topical debate going thudded dismally into the buffers of silence.

As Alan began to clear away, Bernie said, 'Well, I think I'll be off to bed, then,' and Alan said, 'Yes, Dad, you've had a hard day. All that burping takes it out of a man.' The sarcasm escaped Bernie. He didn't listen properly any more, so he said, 'Good night, Nick,' and Nicola said, 'It's Nicola, Bernie,' and he said, 'Good night, Alison,' and Alan said, 'It's Alan, Dad,' and Bernie said, 'Is it any wonder I'm losing my . . .?' and he stopped dead and stood with vacant, frightened eyes and said, 'What are those round things called that you lose when you lose them?' and Alan said, 'Marbles, Dad, and you aren't losing yours, you really aren't,' and kissed him, and he said, 'Good night, Alison dear. Sorry I can't call you Alan, 'ti'n't in me,' and Alan thought, 'Maybe he still is capable of being saved. I'll have a real go at it.'

Nicola went to Em's room to say goodnight. Em came to the door and Nicola didn't like to go in: the room seemed very private and steamy with unrequited sex.

'Sorry about tonight, Dad,' she said.

'No, no, I understand,' said Nicola.

And then Em said something that went straight to her dad's heart.

'What is it about me and men, Dad?'

No longer, 'Men are such bastards.' No more bitterness. Just . . . incomprehension and sadness.

'Your time will come one day, Em. Your time will come.'

'Love you, Dad.'

'Love you.'

A long, deep, motionless hug, two women, father and daughter, in a cool corridor outside a hot bedroom.

'Sweet dreams, Em.'

'Unlikely.'

*

Then Nicola went shyly to Gray's room. Fair's fair. She made sure to knock on the door this time.

'Just a moment,' he called out.

What was he clearing up, hiding away, wiping away?

'All right. You can come in now.'

Nicola entered. The bed was unmade. The room seemed to her to be full of computer equipment and recording equipment and music centres and laptops and DVDs and screens. There was a large poster of Dennis Bergkamp over the bed.

Gray was seated at his computer. He smiled at Nicola but his eyes remained serious and his expression was strained.

'Are you sure you don't need new glasses?' she said.

'I wondered when the first bit of criticism would seep in.'

'It wasn't a criticism,' said Nicola through gritted teeth. 'Why do you assume everything's a criticism? It was a constructive comment designed to help. Everyone needs new glasses from time to time, for God's sake.'

She wished Gray didn't irritate her. She wished that she could feel as proud of him as she did that night of Em. She thought, Why can't I get closer to Gray? I gave birth to him, after all, and then she realised how absurd that was: of course she didn't give birth to him, Alan did. 'The product of my loins' was the rather coy expression that perhaps she was seeking, but it shocked her, and in a way pleased her, to realise that she had instinctively thought of herself as Gray's mother. It was a real sign of how much she was now thinking of herself as a woman. What she hadn't appreciated when she changed sex was that the process of adjustment would continue for years, perhaps for ever.

She thought of that solitary act of love that had brought Gray into the world, of how very nearly he had never been born, as millions of children are never born every day due to contraception, sterility, impotence and exhaustion. How many happenings and coincidences are needed to bring any of us into the world? How fragile, how extraordinary, how unbelievably fortunate is the existence of any of us, but especially of Graham Benson Divot, the product of two gender confused parents whose last real act together had led to his existence. She suddenly felt extraordinarily moved. She longed to say some of this to her son, her miraculous son.

She touched him on the shoulder, said, 'Love you, old thing,' in a hoarse voice and left him to whatever it was she was leaving him to.

Tears had sprung into her eyes. She needed a pee. (Those two things were not connected.) She went to the en suite and stood – stood at the loo before she remembered – oh my God – two minutes ago she'd forgotten that she hadn't given birth to Gray because she *hadn't* been a woman, and now she had forgotten that she had to sit to pee because she *was* a woman. She knew all about gender confusion, but this was ridiculous.

She had arrived at her old home as a happy single woman. She left as a lonely father. It dismayed her to realise that she could no longer live happily in the cocoon that she had woven.

It was only five past eleven when she left. She hadn't wanted to stay.

Alan watched her drive out, and then tip-toed to the granny flat. He couldn't hear any sound, but he could see, through the thin crack where the door didn't quite fit, that the light was still on. He knocked quite softly.

'Who is it?'

'It's me, Dad.'

'Oh, come in, Alison.'

There was an absolute fug in the granny flat, an airless aroma of human wind and mothballs. Both bars of the electric fire were on, despite which Bernie was wearing a cardigan and a jacket.

He was watching television with the sound turned down. Alan didn't make the mistake of commenting. He had once said, 'Don't you want the sound turned up?', and Bernie had found the devastating reply of 'No. It's rubbish.' On this occasion it was some kind of chat show, and Anne Robinson was speaking. Alan had to admit to himself that she was better with the sound turned down, but on the other hand he felt that she was better still switched off, so he switched her off.

'I were watching that,' said Bernie indignantly.

'And now you aren't,' said Alan. 'You never know what's round the corner in life, do you? Dad! Listen to me. I don't want to put you in a home, but I will if you go on like you are.'

Bernie looked at his daughter in astonishment.

'What have I done wrong now?' he asked, in his hurt little-boy voice, his self-pitying voice. 'I haven't done owt.'

'Exactly,' said Alan. 'The stonemason's working on it now.'

'You what?'

'Carving your tomb stone. "Here lies Bernard Kettlewell. He didn't do owt". I've told him to get it ready.'

Bernie gasped, belched, didn't apologise, stared at Alan.

'I don't think I'm going to like you as a man,' he said.

'That's got nothing to do with it,' said Alan. 'I love you, Dad, but you've become idle, boring, unhygienic, smelly, selfish, ungrateful and . . .' He paused dramatically. 'MISERABLE AS HELL.'

Bernie just stared, mouth open. He was shattered.

'There's no point in your living here as you are because you don't enjoy one single thing about it. It's an ultimatum, Dad. Start enjoying life or you go to Honeyfields.'

'Honeyfields? I hate Honeyfields.'

Alison had put him in Honeyfields Residential Care Home – the worst in the area, and that was saying something – deliberately, for a long weekend, so that he'd know what it was like. A couple of the staff had been excessively nice, overly caring, so she had been practically certain that they were cruel in private. She had hated every moment of that weekend, thinking of him in there, but she had felt that it had been worthwhile as a Dreadful Warning.

'What do I have to do?' he asked.

'Talk. Think. Listen. Wash. Bath. Clean your teeth. Do up your zip. Avoid self-pity. Put your hand in front of your mouth and apologise when you belch. Stop saying "Oh dearie me" when I'm doing my very best for you. Give praise without being prompted. Take an interest in Em and Gray. Take an interest in me. Go into the garden when you can't avoid farting. Take some exercise. Live.'

'Is that all?'

'For the moment. I'll think of some more when you've done all that.'

'I apologise for being born,' he said pompously. 'It were right inconsiderate of me.'

'Don't be stupid,' said Alan. 'Stop thinking about yourself all the time.'

'You're a hard woman, Alison. I can see why you want to become a man.'

'I'm saying all this for your sake, Dad.'

Alan didn't know whether Bernie believed him. He didn't know whether he believed himself.

'It's not very nice waiting to die,' said Bernie.

'*Exactly!*' Alan almost shouted. 'Exactly. Don't you see that you're bringing on the very thing you fear. Goodnight, Dad.'

Alan kissed him, and Bernie looked at Alan imploringly. Then he farted, but he did apologise.

'Sorry,' he said. 'Sometimes it comes up on me unexpected like.'

Next day he made no comment on what Alan had said, but Alan heard him running a bath.

23 A Bluffer's World

Nicola never felt the same about number eight, Lane Road, after that dinner. She realised that she needed to get away from Throdnall if she was truly to lead a new life.

There were two reasons for this. She couldn't start a true new life as a woman if everybody knew that she was a woman who had been a man; and she found it difficult to get away from her past role as the man of the house at number thirty-three.

Not that she wanted not to see her children. She loved them. She never ceased to be astounded that she met so many parents who didn't love their children. She found that one of the saddest things of all in a sad society.

But she would always be a visitor to her children now, and the best visitors don't live practically next door.

There was a difficulty, though, about moving. She had a safe, reasonably well-paid job at the Cornucopia. She couldn't see herself landing as good a job anywhere else unless she was able to conceal the fact of her sex change, and she couldn't face the idea of living a lie. She was a woman who had been a man, that was her history. If the subject didn't come up, so much the better, but to hide it would be to deny her history, to deny her true existence.

She wouldn't go through life saying, 'Hello. I used to be a man,' but she wouldn't deny it when asked. If people said, as they did, 'What big hands you've got,' she wouldn't say, 'Well, yes, I was a man, you see,' any more than she'd say, much as she might like to, 'Yes. All the better to throttle you with.' She'd say, 'I have rather, haven't I? Big feet too, I'm afraid,' and hope the subject would be so boring that it'd be dropped. But to actually hide her past, to live a lie, she had no taste for that.

Where could she live, within commuting distance of Throdnall, but where her past history wasn't likely to be known? There was only one possible answer. I'm sure you've guessed it. Cluffield.

Cluffield is a strange place. It's only twelve miles from Throdnall, yet it could be fifty miles away for all the impact Throdnall has on it. It isn't really a town, it's more like an overgrown village, a dormitory village for Birmingham, and it's to Birmingham that Cluffield people look for a night out. The arts are virtually unknown in Throdnall, there isn't a truly first rate restaurant, even the late night fighting's better in Birmingham. The odd Cluffieldian (and most Cluffieldians are odd) might pop into Throdnall very occasionally to eat at 'Le Flageolet' or the 'Trattoria Positano', but none would be likely to venture into the Cornucopia. She could almost certainly lead an anonymous life in this jewel in anonymity's crown, finding her feet (her large feet) as a woman.

She rented a little place called 'Sunny Cottage' on the very edge of Cluffield, in the direction of Clopthorpe, for those of you who know the area (well, still in the direction of Clopthorpe even if you don't). It was an old smelt-grinder's cottage and – you've guessed it – it was entirely surrounded by tall trees. Not sunny at all. It had small, latticed windows too, so it really was very dark inside.

The day she left number eight, as Old Bill lumbered her possessions into his smaller van (symptomatic somehow that she couldn't fill his bigger one), Lance and Rex came out to say goodbye. Rex's eyes were milky with regret for what might have been. Lance was less honest than his dog.

There was a bit of an awkward silence on the steps of number eight. They were both remembering the night of her arrival. Lance filled the silence with a question that might just have been a cover for his embarrassment or might perhaps have been genuine.

'You know Ferenc Gulyas, don't you?' he asked.

'Er . . . yes.'

'Can you do a little favour for me? Could you try to persuade him that he's a very talented painter?'

'Is he?'

'Oh yes. He could be the salvation of the Lafayette.'

'Ah. Well, of course I will, Lance.'

What a feast of insincerity that morning provided. Nicola had no intention of doing any such thing. The truth was, she just didn't like Ferenc. It was unfair, she didn't think the man had ever done anything to hurt her, but it was a fact.

Lance then came hurtling up on the inside in the Insincerity Stakes.

'I feel I hardly know you,' he said.

Nicola didn't bother to reply, 'Whose fault is that?'

Finally he surged past her in the finishing straight – left her flat-footed, he did.

'I shall miss you,' he said.

Cluffield is gloriously dull. It has three pubs, but they're all owned by chains.

One evening, feeling that she ought to make some attempt to get to know people, Nicola went into one of them, the Black Bull.

It took courage to go into a pub on her own as a woman, especially as it had taken her courage even when she'd been a man.

She strode, with a boldness she didn't feel, to the bar, uncomfortably aware that silence had fallen as she entered.

'Red wine, please,' she said.

'Large or small?'

'Oh, large, please.'

Ridiculous. Nobody knew her here, but she would have been ashamed to say 'small'.

The wine came from near the bottom of an unpromising bottle. It would not have been good even when it was first opened. Goodness knew how long ago that had been, not before 1997, anyway. Nicola had tasted vinegars that had more subtlety.

She sat at a table not too far from the bar, not wishing to look as if she was daunted by the ambience – all the customers were men, most of them were on their own, and they all stared at her. Was it because she was grotesque?

She took a second sip of the wine. There were subtle hints of old herrings and anthracite, just the faintest suggestion of mature dish-cloths, and a dry robust undertone of silage that lingered on the palate – how she regretted that single word 'Large' – yet she didn't feel that she could lose face by leaving it, and she certainly wasn't prepared to say to the uncomprehending landlord, 'This is undrinkable.'

She attempted to brazen it out, looking round as if she hadn't a care in the world. A man winked at her, and another said, 'Hello, darling,' and she realised, to her amazed delight and total horror, that they most definitely weren't looking at her because she was grotesque, they were undressing her because she was prettier than their wives. She heard a customer say, 'Nice arse on it, but not a lot in the tit department.' The biggest tit appeared to be over there!

She didn't know whether it was better to take tiny sips or to face taking large gulps and get through it quicker. She took a large gulp and thought she might die. Three sips followed, then another gulp. Sip sip sip gulp. It seemed to be the best way. Sip sip sip gulp. How large can a glass of wine be? Sip sip sip gulp. There, it was gone. She could hardly breathe.

She took the glass back to the bar. She knew that wasn't necessary, but having endured such agony she didn't want to be associated with even the faintest whiff of defeat.

'Same again?'

'Better not. Driving. Thank you. Goodnight.'

She beetled out as fast as her high heels would allow, and vowed never to go in a pub on her own again.

There were two small supermarkets in Cluffield, but they were badly stocked (Tahini? Forget it. Fennel? What's that?), so she soon started to get her meat and veg from the Farm Shop, which wasn't in Cluffield, it was halfway between Cluffield and Throdnall. In fact, you turned off by the Halfway Inn to get to it. Occasionally she was served by a rather slow but very good-looking man in early middle age, occasionally by a rather slow but very ugly woman in her seventies, who must surely be his mother. Their meetings were the nearest thing to human conversation that she found in the leisure part of her new life, yet she no longer felt tempted by the early evening crowd at the Trumpet. They pointed her towards the past, not the future.

Her remarks at the Farm Shop would be along the lines of 'Two pork chops, please. They are outdoor reared, aren't they?' (influence of Em) and they would say, 'Yes, madam, that pig was enjoying the spring sunshine only last week.' The mother never said anything unless spoken to first, but after a few weeks the son ventured the occasional pro-active sally, such as 'Another nice day, madam' or even 'That was a nasty accident on the main road yesterday, madam. The vet's got three cracked ribs,' to which she replied, 'Funny you should mention ribs. Have you any rib of beef?' at which he laughed and said, 'Yes, madam, how big?' and she said, 'Oh, just enough for two, please.'

Why for two? Did she have company? Had she an unusually large appetite for a woman, a relic of her apprenticeship as a man? No. In her new, uncertain life she couldn't bring herself to admit that she was on her own. If that wasn't pathetic, she didn't know what was.

One day in early summer, she was driving back from Throdnall. She'd had a bad day at the Cornucopia, well, perhaps difficult would be a better word, and she thought, I'll pop to the Farm Shop and get two sirloin steaks. She had to wait at the Halfway – it was a very awkward crossing, you had to nip across the other carriageway and sometimes you had to wait for quite a while, and this particular day she did have to – and she thought, Blow it. I'll go to the Spar in Cluffield, but then she thought, No.

I want to see the man in the Farm Shop. Yes, she admitted it to herself, she fancied him. She felt a slight warmth – yes, she really believed she did – in that hitherto inactive organ which she'd had for so long, and dilated for so long, that she no longer thought of it as her neo-vagina.

Suddenly she realised that she had not really enjoyed one evening of her solitary life since she'd moved to Cluffield. She found herself longing for the company of a man, and for more than the company of a man. She had begun to test her clitoris on her own, and had found it far from entirely unresponsive. Middle-aged masturbation in the Midlands! It seemed as sad as it was alliterative. She found herself longing for sexual fulfilment with a man. Longing for it – and dreading it.

She had endured a difficult day at the Cornucopia because the long-dreaded eruption in the kitchen between Emrys and Leonard Balby had finally happened. Emrys had attacked Leonard with a potato peeler.

Round about twelve o'clock, just at the beginning of preparations for lunch, Nicola was summoned into a kitchen smouldering with onions and resentment. At one side of the room, Mohammed and Gunter were holding Emrys firmly in an arm lock. Emrys had a potato peeler in his hand, and his eyes were bulging with fury. At the other side Leonard, clutching a bain-marie in both hands, was being held in an iron grip by Mrs Frost, the burly washer up.

Nicola hurriedly removed the onions from the gas before they burnt. Then she plonked herself in the middle of the kitchen and shouted, 'What the hell is going on?'

She could feel the hammering of her heart; she didn't know what to do – where was Ferenc when you needed him? She had no alternative but to attempt to exert her authority, ignoring her fear that she would turn out not to have any. A phrase spoken by someone in the Trumpet came to her: 'It's a bluffer's world.'

Right.

'Get a grip,' she shouted. 'All of you. Get a grip.' She lowered her voice, investing it with a calm she didn't remotely feel. 'Now, will somebody please tell me what happened?'

Gradually, a picture emerged. It was all caused by recriminations over the previous evening's Twinning Dinner. Emrys had taunted Leonard because his 'sodding soufflés' hadn't risen. Leonard had blamed Emrys for the fiasco of the parsnips. Suddenly Emrys had been jabbing at Leonard's face with the potato peeler, Leonard had been reaching for the bain-marie to scald Emrys with its contents. It had taken the combined efforts of Mohammed and Gunter to restrain Emrys, while Leonard, more slightly built, had been easily held by Mrs Frost.

Leonard had shouted that he'd resign unless Emrys was sacked. Emrys had shouted that he'd resign unless Leonard was sacked. Mrs Frost had said, quite calmly, that she'd resign unless they were both sacked.

'It's time to start serving lunch,' said Nicola. 'After lunch, I promise to deal with the matter fully, firmly and fairly. Let go your potato peeler, Emrys.'

She went up to Emrys, wondering what she would do if he refused.

It was a little miracle. He didn't refuse.

Nor did Leonard. He gave up the bain-marie without a struggle.

'Set them free,' commanded Nicola with a confidence that was entirely feigned.

Emrys and Leonard were released. For a moment, Nicola thought that they were going to tear into each other again, but they didn't.

'Three o'clock. Here. All of you.'

She strode out of the kitchens like a strong woman, then rushed to the toilets and sat there for several minutes, shaking.

She found it hard to believe, on her return, that they were actually cooking lunch. It was indeed a bluffer's world.

Luckily, lunch was reasonably busy, mainly in the bar but three restaurant tables were taken, one of them by Mr Beresford, who lunched with three railway people in an atmosphere of considerable tension. He had annoyed Nicola by asking for her personally when he'd phoned, as if the staff weren't competent, and saying, 'I'd like a table well away from anyone else. Shouldn't be difficult at the Cornucopia, should it?' Arrogant swine. She'd never liked him.

At another table, far from Mr Beresford as requested by Mr Beresford, there were two men who got drawings out and studied them at intervals throughout the meal. One of them, a tall man with receding brown hair and an intense gaze, fixed that gaze on Nicola for a moment, then looked away, then looked back to meet her eyes very briefly before looking away again. It had been the gaze of a man who found Nicola interesting physically. She didn't get many of those, so she would remember it.

At three o'clock, she entered the kitchens. She had butterflies, moths and mosquitoes in her stomach.

All the kitchen staff were there, standing, facing her. The atmosphere was expectant, cautious, tense, but not openly threatening.

'What happened this morning was inexcusable,' she began. 'Totally inexcusable. However, there clearly were reasons for it. Kitchens are places of great tension and intensity at busy times, I appreciate that, and last night was a supremely busy time. Our resources were stretched to the limit by the Twinning Dinner.

'Mistakes were made last night. Leonard taunted Emrys over the fiasco of the parsnips. I don't know whose fault the accident was, these things do happen, but I'm sure that Emrys accepts that it was an error to serve the surviving parsnips after they'd been scooped off the floor. It was an error, though, let us not forget, that was made in the heat of battle.

'Emrys in his turn taunted Leonard because his soufflés didn't rise. Let us not forget, now that we have time for reflection, that this was not Leonard's fault. The person who opened the oven door was on work experience, and the soufflés, though disappointingly flat, were still extremely tasty.

'Our hosts were upset by certain things in last night's dinner, but please don't think that it was a fiasco. Only one of our visitors, the journalist from *Verona Today*, actually complained about the food, and the bill has been paid almost in full.

'I am proud of you. Yes, proud of you all.

'Now, to this morning's little . . . incident. It was serious, but let's not get things out of proportion. Emrys, of course, should not have attacked Leonard with a potato peeler. That is disgraceful behaviour, but he clearly did so in temper rather than with a real intention to do harm. I can just imagine what Emrys might say.'

Now she gambled. She tried the South Wales accent she had been practising in her office.

' "If I'd wanted to hurt the bastard I'd have used a fucking carving knife, isn't it?" '

She'd hated using the f-word even as a tactical ploy, but if it convinced them that she had the common touch it was worth it. It's a bluffer's world.

They all looked at her in astonishment. Then Emrys smiled.

'Too bloody right,' he said.

'Leonard should not have gone for the bain-marie,' continued Nicola. 'He could have caused serious injury, but it was done on the spur of the moment in retaliation for a totally unexpected attack.

'I really don't want to call the police and have them plodding all over our kitchens. I want to resolve this among ourselves. Thank you, incidentally, Mohammed and Gunter and you, Mrs Frost. That martial arts course at night school came in handy, didn't it?'

Nicola saw Leonard relax slightly at that. She had guessed that he had been smarting in the knowledge that it had taken two men to restrain Emrys, and only one woman to restrain him. She knew perfectly well that Mrs Frost had never been near a martial arts

233

course in her life, but she gambled that she would be bright enough not to contradict her. It's a bluffer's world.

'Good work has been done in these kitchens over the last few months. I'm grateful to Emrys for his Welsh specialities, which have confounded the cynics among us, just as I'm grateful to Leonard for the brilliant way he has carried out Ferenc's Hungarian specialities, whose success has rocked the Euro-sceptics. This is a well-run kitchen. Today is but a blip in a success story.'

Nicola paused. She met and held Leonard's eye. She met and held Emrys's eye. She felt exhaustion creeping up on her, but she wouldn't give in. In fact, truth to tell, she got just a bit carried away. She had seen a programme about Churchill recently. He hadn't given in under a far greater threat than Emrys and Leonard combined. He was her inspiration.

'Leonard is an Anglo-Saxon,' she continued. 'He's from Goole. Emrys is a Celt. He's from Swansea. A clash of personalities is perhaps inevitable, but I would remind them – indeed I would remind you all – that they have more in common than divides them. Yes, they are both temperamental, but why are they temperamental?' She paused. You could have heard a chive drop in the still afternoon kitchen.

The pause continued. She had entirely forgotten what she was going to say next. She recalled – it's amazing what the mind brings to you in moments of panic – a comment somebody had made at the Collinsons' dinner table, somebody who made public speeches, and he'd mentioned a remark that you could drag into any speech on any subject. She fell back on it gratefully.

'I believe that the media have a lot to answer for.' Yes! She was off again. 'It's the media who have created the culture of tension in our kitchens. It's the media who have created the myth of the temperamental chef.'

People were staring at her in astonishment by now, but she didn't care, she was flying. And she had remembered what she was going to say.

'But, you know, behind every myth there is a reality. Why, I repeat, are Leonard and Emrys temperamental? Because they are artists. We are lucky to have such artists in our kitchen, and I say to them both, frankly, I will not dismiss either of you, but if one of you makes life intolerable for the other, then both will go. I will have no losers in my kitchen, and that means . . . that means, ladies and gentlemen, that I can have no winners either.'

The spoken word is very powerful. It can so easily carry audiences away, but what is sometimes forgotten is how easily it can carry the speaker away as well. Nicola was becoming very emotional. At that moment she felt that she loved the kitchen, adored Emrys, worshipped Leonard, fancied Mohammed and Gunter, wouldn't even have said 'no' to Mrs Frost.

'Let us all learn the lessons of this incident and work together in trust,' she said, 'and as an act of faith on my part, I'm awarding you all a two per cent rise as of today.'

She strode from the kitchen, strode back to her office, only sorry that Alan and Em and Gray and Lance and Prentice and the slow, incongruously handsome man in the Farm Shop couldn't have been there, to say, 'This was her finest hour.'

She collapsed zeugmatically into a jelly and her chair. Nobody can know how exhausting it is to spout a load of unmitigated cobblers unless they have done so, and nobody can know what a load of unmitigated cobblers Nicola's speech was if they haven't eaten in the Kenilworth Brasserie of the Cornucopia Hotel. Artists? Leonard and Emrys? They didn't know the meaning of the word.

But it worked. It's a bluffer's world.

She just hoped that they wouldn't have another row in order to wangle another two per cent. She regretted that offer, as sanity returned.

We have digressed. We left Nicola waiting patiently to cross the southbound carriageway of the main road from Throdnall to

Cluffield, in order to go to the Farm Shop, where she hoped to see the good-looking man, whose name, she had learnt, was Gordon.

She was served by his mother. It was that sort of day.

'Gordon not here?' she asked.

'It's a Thursday.'

'Ah!'

Why just 'ah!'? Why not, 'So what's the significance of Thursday, Gordon-wise?'

'Two sirloin steaks, please.'

She wanted to say, 'Mrs Fowler, will you tell him that I long to touch his beautiful, ordinary, exquisitely stubbly countryman's face?' She couldn't say that, of course, but she could have said, 'Will you tell him I called?'

She didn't say anything. She had used up her store of courage in the kitchen. She bought her two sirloin steaks and left.

24 A Strange Game of Scrabble

The first thing Alan saw when he came round was the smiling face of his husband Nick. He looked very odd. What on earth had he done to his hair, and why was he wearing . . .? Of course! He was a woman. And she . . . he . . . was a . . . woman without breasts. She . . . no, he . . . felt a stab of disappointment. He had lost his breasts and gained nothing. There was still such a long way to go.

Nicola reached out her hand to him. Alan almost refused to respond. It didn't seem appropriate somehow. Then he relented. He didn't have the strength to resist.

'I wanted to be here when you came round,' said Nicola. 'I remember how lonely I felt at first.'

'I let you down, you mean.'

'I didn't say that.'

'Have they said anything about how it's gone?'

'I've only spoken to Mrs Mussolini. You don't get much out of her.'

Alan tried, very cautiously, to move his body. There wasn't a great deal of pain, but then this was only the double mastectomy. The really invasive stuff was still to come.

Mrs Mussolini entered slowly, like a ship in full sail approaching its berth.

'Ah! Mrs Mussolini!' said Nicola. 'How have things gone?'

'"Mrs Mussolini"!' she gasped. 'That is not my name. My name is Mrs Pethers.'

'I'm sorry. I got confused.'

'It has been satisfactory. Mr McWhinnie's work is always satisfactory.'

She strode off angrily. They weren't surprised.

They shared a little horrified guilty smile when she had gone, and Alan thought, I find it hard to believe there is a *Mr* Pethers.

'Poor man,' said Nicola.

'Mr Pethers?'

'Yes.'

You can't live together for over twenty years without developing the ability to think the same thoughts at the same time, and for a moment or two Alan felt, in that white, starkly antiseptic private ward, that they were still a close married couple. Then he remembered that they hadn't been that close for years, and now they weren't close at all, and he didn't want to be that close, any more than Nicola did. He had a long, long journey to make, and he would need to put all his emotional strength into that. Oh Lord – Nicola had been talking and he'd missed it. He didn't want her to talk. He wanted to sleep.

'Sorry,' he said. 'I missed that.'

'No, I was just saying, you remember the Parkers who used to be at number thirty-eight. They're living in Cluffield now. I saw her in Spar. Nothing remotely expensive in her trolley. They've really come down in the world. Rumour has it that they're going to open a new shop in Plockwell using her sister's name because of the bankruptcy, so maybe they aren't as naïve as we thought.'

'Ah.'

'Don't try to reply, Alan. I'm telling you things you don't need to reply to, because I know how tired I felt after my op.'

'Meaning that I tired you out?'

'I didn't say that. Anyway, I had to endure Prentice. You've been spared that.'

'Thank God.'

'I'll be off in a moment. You won't want me staying too long.'

'I stayed too long, did I?'

'I didn't say that.'

She leant over and kissed him.

'I'll see you tomorrow.'

'There's no need to come every day. We aren't husband and wife any more.'

'Don't you want me to come?'

'It's up to you.'

'How are you today?'

'OK. OK.'

'How did you sleep?'

'Not well. I was upset with myself for what I said to you. "It's up to you." Awful. It's very kind of you to come and I appreciate it. It's just that . . .'

'I know. I know. I wasn't upset.'

Mrs Mussolini entered and Nicola infuriated Alan by apologising to her.

'I'm so sorry I called you Mrs Mussolini yesterday.'

What was the point of that, from new Nicola? It was so old Nick.

'It's quite all right,' said Mrs Mussolini frostily.

When Mrs Mussolini had gone, Alan couldn't resist criticising Nicola for it.

'I thought it was really silly apologising to Mrs Mussolini,' he said. 'All it did was remind her.'

When it was time to leave, Nicola said, 'Shall I come tomorrow, then?'

'I don't want to upset you,' said Alan, 'and I don't want to upset myself – I can do without another bad night – but it really is up to you.'

Gray was very uncomfortable. He would have been all right visiting a virtual ward in Patagonia or a hospital visitor chat line in Tokyo or sending grapes via www.intgrape.com, but seeing his actual breastless mother in bed in an actual hospital ward and depositing his unimaginative little gift on top of an actual bedside cabinet with its array of bottled waters, he was most uneasy – more uneasy, perhaps because he was older and more aware of sexual identity, than he had been with Nicola.

They talked about his homework and his looming A-Levels, but it was like drawing teeth.

'I suppose I'd better go,' he said after three-quarters of the longest hour in the history of time. 'I said I'd email my girl friend at eleven and it's over an hour home by train.'

'How *is* Choo Choo?'

'Oh, this isn't Choo Choo,' he said, with a touch of scorn, as if Alan should have known that. 'This is Juanita. She's Peruvian. She lives in Arequipa. That's a very beautiful city in the south of Peru. She's lovely.'

Alan didn't know if he was doing the right thing in asking further questions about Choo Choo, but he felt that he needed to try to improve his understanding of his son's mind – he felt this extra pressure because of knowing that Gray wasn't Nicola's, even though Gray would never know that – so he decided that he would ask.

'What happened to Choo Choo, then?'

'We all make mistakes, Mum, and Choo Choo was an adolescent blunder, I suppose. I mean I am only eighteen. I can't be expected to get everything right. Judgement of personality isn't easy.'

'True.'

When he left, he raised his arm in a gesture of cool farewell, and went to the door of the little white ward.

'Aren't you going to kiss me?' asked Alan. 'I'm still your mum, and kissing isn't childish except in Britain, and you're a citizen of the world, so you shouldn't be embarrassed by such things.'

'I'm not embarrassed at all,' said Gray, glaring at him. Then he smiled sheepishly and went over and leant down towards the bed rather awkwardly and kissed Alan very carefully, as if he thought that pressure on the cheek might kill him. 'Love you, Mum,' he said in a gruff voice.

That meant a lot to Alan.

'I wish I wasn't going off while you're still in hospital, Mum.'

Alan smiled to himself. Both his kids had decided that they'd call him Alan. Both of them still called him Mum. He liked that.

'Don't be silly, Em. You booked it before I got my dates. You go and have a lovely time. You never know, you . . .'

Alan realised that it would upset Em if he finished, so he stopped, but it was too late.

'. . . might meet some marvellous man?' Em snorted derisively. 'Are there any?'

'One or two.'

'I don't think they'll be in Paxos, somehow.'

Em clearly didn't want to talk about it any more, and it was obvious that she also didn't want to talk about her mum's sex change or the operation. In desperation she began to talk about food.

'What did you have for tea?'

'Fish pie. It wasn't bad, but it wasn't like mine.'

'Was the crust potato or pastry?'

'Oh, potato. Quite nicely browned. The food isn't bad. There were nice bits of white fish in it, and salmon. Farmed, of course.'

'Can you tell?'

'You must be joking.'

'What did you have with it?'

'Broccoli and carrots.'

'Yuk.'

'They weren't bad, though, Em.'

They discussed the pud, the breakfast, the lunch, the previous day's meals, then what she'd ordered for the next day. Then Em said, 'Well, I suppose I'd better be on my way. Sorry I . . .', and then she gave Alan a very brief kiss, said, 'Sorry I . . .' again and left, blowing a kiss from the door.

Alan finished her 'Sorry I . . .' for her. 'Sorry I can't talk about anything except food with you. Sorry I can't cope better with your defection. Sorry you had to betray your sex. Sorry I was born into such a dysfunctional family. Sorry I'm still living at home and still working for the *Advertiser*. Sorry I haven't got as much talent as I thought I had. Sorry I have such an appalling track record with men. Sorry I'm not a better daughter to you. Sorry I still love you. Sorry I came. Sorry I'm going. Sorry we aren't close any more. Sorry I keep having to say, "Sorry".'

Bernie sent a card. It read, 'Sorry I can't come. I can't handle this. I do love you, but you'll always be my little girl to me. But thank you for not doing it while Marge was alive.'

Nicola took to visiting every other day. Alan was making good progress. It was very peaceful to sit in the day room and play Scrabble.

Nicola took her first seven letters and looked at them and thought, Oh my God. What are the chances of that? This is a test of just how competitive I am. Should I do it or not? Would it upset Alan, anyway? Hardly, surely?

Mrs Mussolini walked in, eyes hungry for things she could tidy up.

'Oh, Mrs Pethers,' said Nicola. 'Do you play Scrabble?'

'I have been known to.'

'Well, look at my letters.'

Mrs Mussolini looked.

'Good Lord!' she said. 'That is astonishing. That's uncanny. What are the chances of that?'

'Well, should I do it?'

'I think so. Oh yes. I mean it's true you're wasting two esses, but the bee can go on a double square and you double the whole word and you get fifty for using all seven letters, so that's . . . six seven eight nine ten eleven twelve, doubled that's twenty-four, plus fifty that's seventy-four.'

'I was meaning from the point of view of tact, not tactics.'

Mrs Mussolini blushed, bristled, bridled and became even more starchy than usual.

'I wouldn't know about tact, would I?' she said. 'If I knew about tact, people would hardly refer to me as Mrs Mussolini behind my back, would they?'

Alan's heart sank as he realised that Nicola was going to apologise *again*.

'I'm sorry,' she said. 'I really can't tell you how sorry I am.'

But that won't stop you trying, thought Alan.

Mrs Mussolini spotted a dribble of orange jelly on the half-finished jigsaw of the Hanging Gardens of Babylon, so she brightened up and rushed off to gather it in.

'Well come on,' said Alan. 'What on earth is this word?'

Nicola put her word down on the board.

B R E A S T S.

'Why on earth should I be offended by that?' said Alan. 'I chose to have them removed.'

'I know, but nothing's as simple as that, is it?' said Nicola. 'I chose to have done everything I had done, but it's still mutilation, still traumatic.'

'You don't regret it, though?'

'I don't regret having it done. I regret that it was necessary. I regret the condition to which we were both born. You're pleased to lose your breasts, but you can't be pleased to be scarred. We are creatures of compromise, you and I.'

'This is too deep for me just yet,' said Alan. 'Let's play the game.'

'Well, it's your go.'

Alan studied his letters for quite some time.

'I feel very uneasy about this,' he said. 'I was hoping it wouldn't fit on to your word, but it does, and it scores me far more than any other word, so I suppose I'm going to have to do it.'

He laid six letters on the board to form a word with the first of Nicola's esses.

H Y B R I D S.

25 The Man From the Farm Shop

As she sped along the dual carriageway in the direction of
Cluffield, Nicola sang Ella Fitzgerald songs. She did not sing
them like Ella Fitzgerald.

She felt guilty about being so happy to be leaving the family,
but she didn't let the guilt spoil her joy.

She was a woman, she was free, she was speeding towards the
Farm Shop in the morning sunshine, it was good to be alive,
especially in view of the alternative.

She had looked after Alan well, cooked him his favourite meals
including a shepherd's pie at least as good as his, and seen him
make a rapid recovery from his operation.

She had listened to Em's excited chat about Paxos and above all
about Andropolos. 'All right, I know, you think I'm stupid, it's a
holiday romance, he's a waiter, but, believe me, Andropolos is
different.'

Dutifully, inevitably, she had made a moussaka. 'Not as good as
Mum's, but not half bad, Dad, just as good as on Paxos. Oh, Dad,
would you mind if I interviewed you for my series, "Women Who
Make Throdnall Tick"?'

'Not at all, sweetheart.'

She didn't really want the publicity, somebody from Cluffield
might read it, Gordon might read it, but what could she do? She
couldn't refuse Em.

Gray had said to Em, 'I'm really glad you're happy. It pisses me
off when you're miserable when I'm happy because it makes me
miserable that I'm happy and I like to be happy that I'm happy.'
Em had said the nicest thing that any of them could remember her
saying to Gray. She'd said, 'Piss off, idiot.' But she'd said it nicely.

And Bernie! He had apologised when he burped, he hadn't farted in public once in more than a fortnight, he'd started going to the Coach again, he'd started playing dominoes again. 'I thought I couldn't, 'cos me mind was going. It isn't. Sid Wheeler and I beat Tommy Hazledene and Dan Cosgrove six games end away. Couldn't do that with Alzheimer's.' He'd said, 'Nice moussaka. Thank you' without being asked. He'd also said, 'This wine tastes funny' about the retsina Em had brought back, but when he was told it was Greek he'd said, 'That explains it', and drunk it perfectly happily. Nicola just couldn't believe the change in him.

No, it had been a happy time and she hadn't slept too badly on the Zed-bed in the lounge. She smiled at the thought of the family and how much she loved them, she sang loudly and almost in tune, and she made such good progress that she missed the turning at the Halfway Inn completely. Imagine it, for weeks she had dreamt of seeing Gordon, she had a schoolgirl crush on him at the age of forty-three, and she missed the turning. She let out a great scream of laughter at the absurdity of life.

However, by the time she had reached the outskirts of Cluffield, gone round the big roundabout, and back down the dual carriageway to the Halfway Inn, she felt altogether more sober and more sombre. She might get Gordon's mother again. Gordon, even if she got him, might not feel about her as she did about him. He was a mother's boy. He might be gay. Oh God, she hadn't thought of that.

How pretty the shop looked, in its smart green and red livery. Could a shop have livery? How nice the old farm cart outside looked, stacked as it was with luscious vegetables in carefree profusion.

She got Gordon! He was there!

He served her with four lamb chops, two for her and two for her non-existent companion.

Her courage failed her and all she made was small talk.

Next time she was served by his mother, so summer was beginning to fade before she had the chance to pluck up her courage and say what she wanted to say to him.

'Two rump steaks, please.'

He got her two rump steaks.

'I don't suppose you'd like to come and eat one of them,' she mumbled. Yes, mumbled. Judge her not too harshly, sophisticated reader. It is very difficult for a woman to say something as forward as that, even for a woman who has been a man, in fact, perhaps, especially for a woman who has been a man.

He looked at her in astonishment.

'I beg your pardon?' he said.

'I . . . wondered if you'd like to come and eat one of them,' she repeated.

'That's what I thought you said.'

'Well?'

'Well . . . when?'

It seemed too forward to suggest that evening.

'Well . . . how about . . . tomorrow?'

'I can't really. It's Mother.'

'Yes, of course.' How craven! Why not ask why Fridays are impossible? 'Well . . . er . . . how are Mondays for you?'

'Mondays are difficult, with Mother.'

'Yes, of course. Tuesday?' she asked with diminishing hope and increasing embarrassment.

'Tuesday,' he said reflectively. 'Now then. Tuesdays *are* a little awkward.'

It wasn't an absolute, abject rejection. Did she dare continue? Yes, Nicola, Heroine of the Cornucopia Kitchen, Unflinching Victim of the Surgeon's Knife, you can do it.

'Wednesday?'

'Now then, the thing is . . . the thing is . . . I don't know that I'm entirely comfortable coming to a woman's house. Not when I don't know her. How about my taking you to the Red Lion next

Wednesday? They do a good grill, there's a lot on the plate, and it's very reasonable.'

That's how they started, her and the mother's boy.

An unlikely match? Have you not noticed how people of similar levels of attractiveness usually fall for each other? At one end of the scale there are couples of extraordinary beauty and glamour, at the other end you'll see two people who are both revoltingly ugly gazing with rapture into each other's bloodshot eyes. Well, you may think that Nicola's slow, shy, farm-shop mother's boy was no great catch, but she was a sex change woman who had never been to bed with a man, had no great confidence in her body, and was coming to courtship for the first time at least twenty-five years later than most women. On the whole, therefore, it was a meeting of equals. Besides, Gordon was kind, he never said anything nasty to her, his manners were impeccable, he really was good looking, and I won't have him mocked, do you hear?

Something had been worrying Nicola for quite some time, and that was the business of Ferenc's paintings. What did it matter whether she liked the man or not? Who was she to hold a creative artist back, especially in the imaginative desert that was Throdnall? It was on her conscience that she had never tried to encourage him about his paintings, as Lance had asked her to do.

It was strange, perhaps, but she wanted a clean conscience before she went out with Gordon. She wanted no unfinished business hanging over her.

She called Ferenc into her office. He looked slightly apprehensive.

'I don't expect you've any idea why I've called you in here, Ferenc,' she said.

'No. No, I did wonder.'

'Yes.' She paused, dangling him briefly on her line, she couldn't resist it. 'It's your painting. I'm not at all happy about it.'

'Which one?'

'No, no. No particular painting. Your painting in general. Your painting as an activity.'

'I never do it in working hours.'

'I know. It's a shame.'

'I beg your pardon?'

His expressive face was alive with incomprehension. She was enjoying this.

'Lance Windlass, who has the Lafayette Gallery in Biscuit Passage, tells me that you're a much better painter than you believe.'

'He does?'

'He thinks you have a real talent. Minor, perhaps.'

He frowned.

'Minor?'

'At present.' Nicola smiled. 'He believes it could become a major talent.'

'I have so little time. Work. Mrs Gulyas. Sally's a demanding woman.'

I bet she is, Nicola thought. And then there are your bits on the side, if rumour is to be believed. Several bits on several sides, if only half of it is true.

'The hotel needs paintings.'

'Too right, but with the refurbishment . . .'

They were reputed to have risen at last to second in the list of hotels to be refurbished.

'No, no, Ferenc. I didn't say "painting". I said "paintings". I think Mr Windlass would be prepared to give you a contract to produce paintings regularly – and so will I.'

'You?'

'Yes. The refurbishment, now. That's an idea. How about "before" and "after"? A record of the refurbishment. A record of an English hotel. Warts and all. Well, mainly warts, I suppose. A social document. In your style. I'm going to commission you.'

'Do you have the authority to do that?'

'No.'

'Well, thank you very much.'

'Please.'

She stood up. He stood up. They shook hands. She went to open the door for him, and tripped: tripped over one of his shoes, almost fell, lurched across the room, clutched the hat-stand, fell slowly against the wall with it.

'Sorry,' she said, disentangling herself, 'I tripped over your shoe.'

She looked down and noticed for the first time how large his feet were, for quite a small man.

'I hadn't noticed how large your feet are,' she said.

'Yes. Sorry.'

'Not at all. Er . . . Mrs Gulyas is a lucky woman.'

'I beg your pardon?'

'The size of feet and . . . er . . . maybe it's just an old wives' tale.' She couldn't resist a little dig. The opportunity had opened up for her irresistibly. 'Maybe, Ferenc, is it possible . . . not only Mrs Gulyas?'

He went white. He looked embarrassed. Nicola Divot, you idiot. You're a woman now. You can't make such man-to-man insinuations.

She was surprised that he was so embarrassed, though.

Gordon picked her up in his pick-up, which was more suitable linguistically than stylistically, smelling as it did of dog and fuel.

That Wednesday, in the Red Lion, she had rump steak, chips, peas, mushrooms, tomatoes and onion rings. Her partner, as they say in the food reviews, plumped for the mixed grill.

She couldn't remember, afterwards, what they talked about, for the simple reason that it wasn't memorable.

Yet she enjoyed it. That Wednesday evening was very ordinary indeed, but it was also one of the highlights of her life. She was the female partner on an evening out, and she felt comfortable with that.

Gordon drove her back to Sunny Cottage, went round to usher her out of the pick-up as if it was a Rolls-Royce, and solemnly shook her hand.

'Thank you for a nice evening, Gordon,' she said.

'That's all right,' he said. 'I've enjoyed it too. I can't manage every Wednesday – Mother, you know – but I can do Wednesday fortnight.'

A fortnight later they went out again. Gordon's choice of venue on this occasion was the Red Lion. Nicola had lamb cutlets, chips and peas, with a choice of mint sauce and redcurrant jelly on the side. Her companion, as they say in the food reviews, opted for the mixed grill.

As he saw her into the cottage he kissed her on the cheek.

The following Wednesday fortnight, Gordon suggested the Red Lion. 'It's very nice, isn't it?' he said. 'The Green Man isn't bad, but the food's more imaginative in the Red Lion, and I wouldn't take you, a lady like you, to the Black Bull. It's as rough as a bear's arse.'

He reddened most charmingly at his choice of words, but Nicola didn't mind. He'd paid her her first compliment: 'A lady like you.' Not exactly effusive, but Cluffield wasn't Seville.

She chose gammon, eggs, chips and peas. Gordon said, 'Oh, I'd have had you down for the pineapple. I've noticed that women usually have pineapple with gammon, whereas men usually go for the egg, but you've chosen egg.'

The waitress waited patiently, then asked Gordon for his choice. He puzzled over the many options for a moment, then said, 'I think I'll have the mixed grill.'

As he saw her into her cottage he kissed her on both cheeks.

The following Wednesday fortnight, Gordon's preferred entertainment was a meal in the Red Lion. Nicola chose breaded haddock, chips and mushy peas. Gordon said, 'Oh, I'd have had you down for the garden. I've noticed that men usually have mushy, but women prefer garden, but you've chosen mushy.'

The waitress waited stressfully, then asked Gordon for his choice. 'Do you know,' he said. 'I'm tempted by the mixed grill.'

Nicola teased him – her first bit of teasing.

'You always have the mixed grill.'

'I do, don't I? It's good here.'

She wasn't kidding herself that she was dining with Oscar Wilde. Witty conversation isn't everything, and Gordon was always pleasant to be with. Not a bad epitaph, that, in a turbulent world like ours. Always pleasant to be with.

She noticed the Parkers, who used to live opposite in Orchard View Close, two tables away, and they noticed her, but they pretended not to have seen her, so she pretended not to have seen them.

When he drove her back to Sunny Cottage, Gordon surprised her by kissing her on the lips and putting his tongue in her mouth.

'I hope you didn't mind my doing that?' he said.

'Not at all, Gordon,' she said. 'I liked it.'

'Goodnight, then, Nicola,' he said. 'Sleep well.'

The following Wednesday fortnight she couldn't make, there was a Round Table do at the hotel, Ferenc was on holiday, and the Duty Manager was Toby Marchmont: all of twenty-two, minor public school, plum in his mouth, nothing in his trousers, never had a woman, never would have, be no use in a crisis, where *did* Head Office find them?

She had a whole month, therefore, to think about Gordon's tongue. By this time it was cold and wet. The weather, not Gordon's tongue. Their relationship was so slow that the whole of the autumn had passed.

She could see that Gordon was nervous, and things weren't helped when he discovered that the menu had been changed and the mixed grill had been removed 'because there's no demand for it'. He ordered steak, lamb cutlets, bacon, sausage, liver, chips, peas, tomatoes, mushrooms and onion rings.

'Those are the exact ingredients of the mixed grill,' he said, 'so what's different?'

'Seven pounds fifty,' said the waitress. 'Cutting their own throats they are. Glenda's seen the writing on the wall. She's working at the Green Man now.'

Nicola was certain that the reason for Gordon's nervousness was that he had spent a month thinking about her mouth round his tongue, and he was hoping to go to bed with her. She was nervous too. She kept wondering how she would be in bed, whether her neo–vagina could really respond – well, you can imagine her anxiety, I should hope, it was awful, it was wonderful, it was the best and the worst evening of her brief life as a woman.

Her slow countryman, her mother's boy, her man of alternate Wednesdays, her mixed grill of a man was Adam incarnate that night to her in her position.

He drove her back to Sunny Cottage. He didn't speak. She didn't speak.

He lost his nerve and drove off.

The following Wednesday fortnight, Gordon had a very different evening in mind – a meal at the Green Man.

'It's not that I'm mean,' he said, 'but that Red Lion business was a racket.' He leant across and said, with a roguish tone, 'I did think of the Disappointed Lady, but there's a poor choice there.'

'The Disappointed Lady?'

'The Halfway Inn. Halfway Inn, Disappointed Lady, get it?'

Nicola got it. She was amazed at his boldness, actually. She was also determined not to be the Disappointed Lady again.

I need not detain you with their choice of meals at the Green Man. Let's get straight to Sunny Cottage.

'Would you like a nightcap?' Nicola asked, determined to take the initiative this time.

'A nightcap would slip down a treat.'

She had a calvados, he a Bailey's. (You want her to have a sophisticated lover? Sorry.)

'I want you,' he said simply, astonishingly, earthily, D.H. Lawrenceily.

'Good,' she said.

They went upstairs. Upstairs, Sunny Cottage smelt damp. Well, to be honest, downstairs smelt damp too.

She didn't think she could go through with it. She didn't think she dared show her body.

'Don't be shy,' he said.

'No,' she said. 'I . . . oh God, Gordon, there's something I have to tell you.' She couldn't go through with it unless she told him. She should have done, perhaps, but she couldn't. 'I . . . Gordon, I've had . . . the operation.'

'What do you mean – "the operation"?'

'I used not to be Nicola, Gordon. I used to be Nick.'

The penny still didn't seem to drop. Nicola would have been the first to admit that Gordon's pennies didn't always drop quite as swiftly as she would have wished.

But it did drop eventually.

'Sex change?' he gasped.

'Sex change. I used to be a man.'

He said nothing. Nothing!

'I had the operation several months ago. You're . . . you're my first, Gordon.'

He put his trousers back on again, in silence.

'Don't think I can handle this,' he said, when he was safely back in all his clothes. 'Sorry, Nicola.'

As he left he said, 'No hard feelings?' and she said, 'It looks that way.'

The following Wednesday fortnight, she cried. It was silly, she knew, but he was a nice man, Gordon, and she felt very flat in sunless Sunny Cottage. She found herself missing all the things about him that irritated her, so that she wished that they could have the chance to begin all over again and she could learn not to let them irritate her.

Besides, she would have liked to find out why he couldn't see her on Thursdays, Fridays, Mondays, Tuesdays and alternate Wednesdays. She thought he might have told her in a year or two.

It was another of life's unsolved mysteries. She didn't have the heart to go to the Farm Shop ever again.

26 The Long Silence

Alan became increasingly worried about Nicola's long silence. Was she all right?

Today he might find out. It was the day of the Midsummer Dinner at the Golf Club. The air was still and sweaty. Throdnall throbbed with humidity. There was no bird song. Even the thrushes were sweating.

'I hate the summer, me,' said Bernie at breakfast. Alan gave him a look. He didn't notice. 'You long for it all through the winter and spring and what happens? The bastard lets you down.' Now he did catch Alan's eye, and he grinned sheepishly. 'Well, take today,' he said. 'It's like a boil waiting to burst.' Then he gave a rueful little laugh. 'Aye, I know,' he said, 'but you must let me have a little moan now and again. An addict can't give up moaning overnight like.'

The Midsummer Dinner was a new event – pedants were already complaining because it wasn't actually being held at midsummer. It was the brainchild, if that isn't an exaggeration, of the PP, the Pompous Prat, Wing Commander Miles Forrester. He said that its purpose was to celebrate the short northern summer, but its purpose was to raise more money. At twenty-five pounds a ticket, even though that included a half bottle of house wine, it would be quite a profit-making event and a touch on the steep side for Throdnall.

Alan hadn't intended to go – until he discovered that Nicola was booked in 'with a party'.

He hadn't heard from Nicola since the day she left after caring for him – brilliantly once again – as he recovered from his hysterectomy and ovariectomy. It had involved a rather longer convalescence than the double mastectomy, being an altogether more invasive process.

The operation had gone well; Nicola had visited every other day; Mrs Mussolini had seemed a little softer, as if she'd thought about why people called her Mrs Mussolini; Pat (who had been on holiday during the mastectomy) had forgiven Nicola for letting their little secret slip and embarrassing her greatly with the aforesaid Mrs Mussolini; Em and Gray, a year older, had been just a bit more comfortable about hospital visiting; Bernie had sent his usual message of apology – it would all have been quite a routine affair if it hadn't been for Prentice.

Just before he went into hospital, Alan received a letter from him.

Dear Alan/Alison/Alan (you're on your way to Alanhood and are more Alan than Alison, but you aren't there yet!)

I was devastated to learn from a colleague of yours at the carriage works that you had been for your mastectomy and I hadn't known about it and hadn't visited to cheer you up with a few laughs. So now, if you go to Gaza and strip (Gaza Strip, get it? They didn't in Droitwich. Not a titter. O'oh. Titter! Sorry! Unintentional), you will not be 'Eyeless in Gaza' (Huxley novel – they hadn't heard of it in Droitwich!) but 'Breastless in Gaza'. And now it's time for the removal of your womb, which was once a 'womb with a view' (another floperoonie in Droitwich!) for the deliciously lovely Em and the not deliciously lovely Gray. I hope your recovery wasn't nippled in the bud (Oh dear! Who is this man?) by my absence.

Well this time I will be there in glorious person, in full Technicolor, to cheer you and speed your recovery.

Love and kisses

Prentice 'Fun with Flab' Prentice

The whole of Alan's time in hospital was blighted by his expectation of Prentice's visit, and he never went, just sent another letter a week afterwards.

Dear Alan/Alison/Alan/Alan (more Alan than ever now – nearly there)

So very sorry not to make it. Devastated in fact. Got invited for a free holiday in Crete, and you have to be selfish sometimes, don't you? Hope you weren't ovarily disappointed (they don't get any better, but I hope you have).

Love, hugs and wet kisses

Prentice 'Mirth with Girth' Prentice

Nicola had been rather quiet and self-contained as she went about the business of running number thirty-three while still coping at the Cornucopia. She had said that she was tired and Alan had allowed himself to believe that that was all it was, but now he was worried. Three weeks had gone by without a phone call, and all he got when he rang Cluffield was the answer machine and sometimes not even that. He'd only left two messages; he didn't want Nicola to know that he was anxious. It was for this reason that he hadn't rung the hotel. Nick had never liked being rung at work.

It had been getting to the stage when he thought he really would have to ring the Cornucopia, but then he had found out that she was going to the Midsummer Dinner, and he had decided to wait until then.

He'd still been ringing Cluffield almost every day, and for a week at least the answer machine hadn't been on, but now there was no need to ring, he would see her this evening – well, he hoped he would.

'With a party'? That didn't sound like Nicola.

It was all a bit worrying.

Usually, Bernie had breakfast on his own in the granny flat (making it helped him keep his hand in, and he'd even begun cooking the occasional meal for them, can you believe it? He had one recipe – Pork Normandy – which was truly excellent), but that Saturday Alan made him breakfast, two poached eggs on toast, because he suddenly felt that he would like his dad's company.

'Thanks, love, that were grand,' said his dear neo-dad. He thought about all the times he'd had to quarry the praise out of his stony face, and he marvelled.

'Good.'

'I think I'll pop into town on t'bus. Pop into travel agent's like.'

'Travel agent's? Why?'

'I thought I might book one of these Short City Breaks I've been reading about.'

Alan looked at him in astonishment.

'Aye,' said Bernie. 'Your old dad's turning into a bit of a goer in his old age.'

'It's a wonderful idea, Dad.'

Of course the thought of Bernie enjoying a few sunny days in Blackpool or Brighton filled Alan with pleasure, but he had to admit to himself that the thought of a few dadless days at number thirty-three filled him with even more. He loved his dad dearly, especially this new dad, but still . . . he was human . . . he would like to be able to open another bottle of red wine without somebody saying, 'Another bottle! Have we won the lottery or something?'

'Aye,' said Bernie. 'Get me out from under your feet for a few days.'

'No!' said Alan. 'The thought never crossed my mind.'

He offered to drive his dad in.

'No,' said Bernie. 'I've got me bus pass. Not much point in having a bus pass if you don't use it.'

Alan didn't insist. He didn't want to seem too eager.

At seventeen minutes to eleven, not long after Bernie had gone for the bus, Em rang from Kos.

'Hi, Mum. It's me.'

'Hello, darling. Are you having a nice time?'

'Very.'

He took the cordless out into the hall.

'Oh good. I am pleased.' He called out to Gray, 'It's Em,' and then he continued to Em, 'How's the weather?'

'Lovely. Too hot, though.'

'It's too hot here too. How's the villa?'

'It's fantastic. It's right by the sea.'

'Excellent.'

'We swim three times a day.'

'Excellent. Here's Gray.'

He put him on. Gray sat at the table and put his feet up on it – cool!

'Hi, Em . . . Yeah . . . Yeah? . . . Oh yeah! . . . Piss off . . . Yeah, bring some lettuces . . . Kos. Kos lettuces. Is Andropolos stuffing you as much as he did in Paxos? . . . And you! Do you want Mum any more? . . . OK. Bye, Em.' He put the phone back on its stand. 'I don't think that girl has any sense of humour.'

'Because she didn't laugh at your jokes about Kos and Paxos.'

'Not a titter.'

'Inadequate evidence, Gray, I'm afraid. So, it sounds good.'

'What does?'

'You know.'

Gray did. He might be lazy and inarticulate. He wasn't stupid.

'You mean that the Greek boy friend may not turn out to be as big a bastard as Giorgio, François and Carl.'

'Gray! Learn some compassion. At least her international relationships are real.'

'This is just a very old-fashioned way of thinking, Mum. My relationships aren't not real just because they're on the net.' He blushed. 'Juanita's real.'

'Gray?' There was something she wanted to ask him before he went back to his room.

'What?'

'On the phone just now you said, "Piss off."'

'Sorry.'

'No. I don't mind. I just wondered what Em said to make you say, "Piss off."'

'I can't remember. I . . . oh yeah. Yeah. I remember. She said . . .' – he twisted his face into a half-smile, half-grimace, very mobile, very Ferenc oh God!! – 'She said, "I love you, bruv."'

'I thought so.'

'Not cool. Well, I suppose Greece isn't cool. Laugh, Mum. That was a witty remark.'

'Ah.'

'That was self-mockery, Mum. "Ah! Maybe he's growing up at last."'

'What?'

'That's what you were thinking. Bye, Mum. See you later.'

If only he hadn't had to say, 'Piss off,' when Em said, 'I love you, bruv.' More importantly, however, if Em said, 'I love you, bruv,' things must be going really well with Andropolos. Thank God. Not that he hoped that Em would marry a Greek waiter, but he didn't want her to get hurt any more.

Bernie rang at twenty-eight minutes past twelve. 'I'm in the Coach. Don't make me lunch.'

He banged on Gray's door.

'Come.'

He entered the Temple of International Communications. All seemed calm.

'Fancy a pizza at the Positano?'

'OK. Cool.'

'See you in ten minutes. Get yourself untidied.'

'What?'

'Frayed jeans with holes in them. T-shirt that doesn't quite reach the frayed jeans, showing an area of young Divot stomach. Cool!'

He went in a jacket and neat open-neck shirt. He had an Americano. Alan had a Capricciosa.

They had a good time in the Trattoria Positano. A good time with Gray? What was the world coming to? They talked about uni and railway carriages and pizzas and Em and Andropolos and Peru. Gray didn't actually mention Juanita again, but suddenly he was an expert on Peruvian politics.

At forty-three minutes past two, Bernie returned, a bit flushed, weaving ever so slightly.

'I hope you didn't mind my popping into t'Coach,' he said, 'but I had to tell Clarrie and Edgar about me Short City Break.'

'Ah,' said Alan. 'You booked one. Where to? Brighton? Scarborough?'

'Krakov.'

'What?'

'It's in Poland. Paper reckons it's a grand city. It's got a cloth hall and such like and I don't know what. They said they could throw in Warsaw an' all and it'd only be a hundred and twenty-six quid more. Fly to Warsaw, train to Krakov, fly home from Krakov. I said to her . . . nice girl, stud in her nose, but quite well spoken . . . I said to her, "No. That might be a bit much for me, first time of asking like." She said, "How do you mean, first time of asking?" I said, "First time abroad, and on me own." Well, Marge always liked Eastbourne and such like and there didn't seem any point. I said, "I think Krakov on its own'll do very nicely, thank you." She said, "There's a supplementary tour of a salt mine, you're advised to book early." I said, "Aye, go on, then, let's go the whole hog while we're at it." She said, "How about Auschwitz?" I said, "What do you mean, 'How about Auschwitz?'?" She said, "There's a supplementary tour of Auschwitz and all. They ask us to warn you that it can be very distressing." I said, "Oh aye, it will be. Aye," I said. "I'm on for that. You're too young to remember, so who'll remember if I don't? Aye," I said, "be a pity to die wi'out paying my 'omage to 'istory." So that's whar I've booked.'

Alan went up to Bernie and kissed him. 'We leave at ten to seven,' he said.

Yes, neo-Dad was such a changed man that he was taking him as his guest to the Midsummer Dinner.

He sighed. He was so worried about Nicola. Oh, he did hope she was happy.

Time passed slowly. He had a hot bath, then a cold shower because the hot bath had made him sweat.

Then he got dressed. It was his first ever black tie do. Yes, it was black tie in that heat. 'Throdnall has to learn to be classy,' the PP had said. It was quite exciting, though, dressing up in his first penguin suit, and a whole lot easier than being a woman and having to agonise over what to wear.

He couldn't tie his bow tie. Gray did it for him. God, it was hot and tight.

'Great,' said Gray. 'Have to admit it, Mum. Cool.'

Alan thought that helping him in that way had made Gray feel rather grown up.

He was looking forward to seeing Nicola, provided she was all right, of course, but he wasn't looking forward to going to the Golf Club.

He'd booked his tickets almost at the last minute, after he'd learnt that Nicola was going, and the snotty-nosed Social Secretary had said, 'I think we can fit you in', even though everybody knew that tickets hadn't been selling too well. He'd been rather brusque, excessively brusque in fact, having been in the middle of a tense and tiring week at work. He'd had an extremely hectic time organising the guest list for the unveiling of the new tilting carriages, amid unsettling rumours that Northern Vision were going to cancel their contract and go to Bangladesh for their carriages. Mr Beresford had been like a bear with a migraine all week, and Alan had been contaminated by the fall-out.

He felt sure that the Social Secretary, who didn't like him any more than the PP did, would get his revenge by placing them on a table with all the people nobody else wanted to sit with – Major and Mrs Peskott, the 'abominable' Snowmans, Celia Pilkington-Wilks with her delusions of grandeur – and he wouldn't even be able to complain because he'd booked late.

Bernie's penguin suit was decidedly old-fashioned, and there was a distinct whiff of mothballs, but he looked good, he really did. He was a picture of elderly elegance.

The evening air was still and stale. It seemed impossible that there wouldn't be a storm. Alan set off too early, in his nervousness, so he had to drive slowly. The Ka behind him hooted impetuously in Owl Hoot Lane, as if it thought it was appropriate. Small men were tetchy, so were small cars.

There was very little traffic in the Kenilworth Road, so he had to drive right past the Golf Club, turn left into Frog Lane, turn round at the cattle grid at the entrance to Salter's Farm, go back down Frog Lane, turn right on to the Kenilworth Road, so as to arrive at the Golf Club at four minutes past eight.

Nicola was already there, standing near the entrance doors. She looked really quite glamorous and striking in a turquoise and black long dress and jacket, with black accessories and a diamanté necklace and earrings.

At her side was a fairly tall, very neat and by no means unprepossessing man in his late forties and a white tuxedo.

'Hello, Alan,' she said, with a hint of pride that she couldn't quite conceal, 'this is Eric.'

Alan felt a sudden, sharp stab. He hadn't wanted Nicola to be quite as happy as that.

27 Eric

The first time Nicola had seen Eric had been on the day of her Churchillian speech in the kitchen. Eric had been lunching with another man in the restaurant. They had been poring over plans.

He had looked at her twice, an occurrence rare enough to make her remember him. She'd seen him in the restaurant twice more in the following months, and each time he'd looked at her once. She had felt that there was something about those looks, that she had interested him, that if he had been on his own he might have stopped to speak.

And then she saw him alone. And he did stop to speak. It was towards the end of the winter, and not very long after the ending of her relationship (if it justified so definite a word) with Gordon. He was staying in the hotel, and was crossing the foyer towards the exit. He gave her a shy smile and said, 'Are you the manager?' and she made the stupid reply of 'Yes. For my sins. Why? I hope you don't have a complaint,' and he said, 'No, no. Everything's fine, thank you,' and then he looked a bit uneasy and said, 'I don't suppose you can recommend anywhere nice to eat. Oh dear. I don't suppose that's very diplomatic. I should be eating here, but I find hotel dining rooms a little cavernous on one's own,' and Nicola said, 'I know what you mean, sir. Well, I have to say Throdnall isn't Paris. There's the usual crop of ethnics . . .'

'I don't think so. I'm not very big on spices,' he said.

'I suppose the only two real possibilities, then, are Le Flageolet and the Trattoria Positano. I have to say . . . although I'm not exactly a disinterested party . . . that Le Flageolet has been described to me as probably the worst French restaurant in the world. The food at the Positano is at least edible, pretty reliable, and the place is very reasonable and always cheery.'

'Oh, I rather like the thought of somewhere cheery,' he said. 'I think I'll settle for the Positano,' and then, to her astonishment, he went a little pink and added, 'I don't suppose there's any chance of your accompanying me?' and, to her even greater astonishment, Nicola heard herself say, 'I have some paperwork to finish, but I could join you in half an hour.'

The paperwork was a fiction. She just didn't want to seem too eager – and she couldn't believe how eager she was. She had decided, after the Gordon fiasco, that she had to accept that to have become a woman would be the summit of her achievements, and to expect a sex life as well would be to ask too much of her transformation.

She liked the look of Eric. He was tall, with receding brown hair, a wide forehead and gentle, observant brown eyes. His manner seemed . . . what was the word? . . . yes, courteous.

The restaurant was all clattering floors and smiling waiters and buzzing customers, with quiet Eric sitting all alone in its midst, like the eye of a storm. He coloured slightly again as Nicola joined him, rose courteously from his chair, smiled, waited till she was seated before taking his seat again. She liked that.

Nicola ordered Parma ham and melon, followed by scallopine alla marsala. Eric asked if the veal had been humanely reared and, on being told that no definite assurance could be given, ordered lemon sole. He didn't have a starter. 'I'm not a big eater,' he explained.

Nicola felt guilty and insensitive about the veal, and called the waiter back and changed her order to spaghetti bolognese. This was stupid on several grounds: a) Spaghetti Bolognese is an English invention, the Bolognese eat the sauce only with tagliatelle, b) Bolognese sauce is a complicated affair and only good if made accurately and slowly. This was unlikely in the 'you wanna black pepper?' atmosphere of the Trattoria Positano, c)

She didn't like pasta as a main course. It was never meant to be a main course, and she was a bit of a food snob, and d) She was no good at eating spaghetti and should never eat it in 1) a restaurant 2) a restaurant with a companion 3) a restaurant with a companion of the opposite sex 4) a restaurant with a companion of the opposite sex with refined and immaculate table manners 5) a restaurant with a companion of the opposite sex with refined and immaculate table manners on their first date and 6) a restaurant with a companion of the opposite sex with refined and immaculate table manners on their first date when she was wearing her best business blouse and skirt.

While she ate her Parma ham and melon, Eric told her a bit about his life. He loved architecture. 'I first discovered I had architectural leanings when I was in Pisa,' he said. Nicola was on the point of laughing when she realised that he was absolutely serious, he'd seen nothing funny in the remark. 'That trio of duomo, battistero and torre pendente,' he continued, 'astonishing.' It struck Nicola that if most of the people she knew had used the Italian words in that way it would have sounded dreadfully snobbish and affected. With Eric it didn't. He used the words not to impress but unselfconsciously in genuine enthusiasm. 'Utterly inspiring. Bad, perhaps, to be inspired by something so beautiful. One is doomed from the start to be disappointed by one's own efforts.'

He studied in Hull. Anyone less suited to Hull Nicola couldn't imagine, and that might have been one of the reasons why he dropped out four days before his finals. 'Exams fill me with dread,' he said. 'That's why I became a furniture restorer. I could teach myself.'

He lived in North Norfolk in a small flint cottage. His business was successful enough, he told her, to finance his modest life style.

He ordered a bottle of Montepulciano, but only drank two glasses. 'I love wine,' he said, 'but I'm not a big drinker.'

Nicola drank the rest of the bottle. She hated waste. Also,

although she was not habitually a big drinker, she found herself drinking more as a woman than she ever had as a man.

What a lot of chance there is in life. Eric had never been to Throdnall before the day she first caught sight of him, but an old friend from his college days ('well, acquaintance more than friend, I'm not terribly big on friendship') had commissioned him to restore twelve Georgian dining chairs and had then got him interested in helping with a barn conversion west of Throdnall. Eric had thought about the plans and had made further visits to discuss them, deliver the chairs, see the half-completed barn and now to offer some ideas about furnishing it. He had decided to stay overnight . . . 'I don't drive big distances' . . . and had invited his friend out to dinner, but his friend had begun to go down with flu and had cried off. So here Nicola was.

She had come to the conclusion, after the disappointment with Gordon, that while she still wouldn't go around talking about her sex change in everyday life, she would have to do so in the context of personal sexual relationships, but she hadn't expected to talk of it on a first date. Now, with her tongue loosened by the wine, and her mood stimulated by the lively buzz of the restaurant, and her heart encouraged by a sudden feeling of confidence in this kindly and gentle man, she began to tell him.

'Eric,' she said, lowering her voice (they put the tables close together at the Positano, at those prices you had to expect it), 'I have something important to tell you.'

'Who's the spaghetti?' asked the waiter, with the usual immaculate timing of his calling.

Their conversation remained suspended while the waiter placed their main courses in front of them.

'Something important to tell me?'

'Yes. Er . . . something you ought to know right at the . . .' She couldn't finish the sentence. She had talked herself into a corner. She couldn't say, 'right at the beginning of our relationship'. It would have been presumptuous. Even 'right at the outset' would

have seemed presumptuous. An outset assumes a continuation. 'I
. . . er . . . a few years ago, Eric, I decided to have . . .'

'Black pepper, madam?'

'Er . . . yes, thank you. Yes. Just a bit. That's fine. Thank you.'

'You decided to have?'

'I decided to have . . . Eric, at that time I wasn't as I am now. I
was suffering from . . .'

'Parmesan cheese, madam?'

'Er . . . yes. Thanks. Yes . . . yes, that's fine. Thank you.'

This was not quite the dignified description of her great
journey that she had planned.

'Four years ago, Eric, that waiter would not have said,
"Parmesan cheese, madam?"'

'I'd be surprised if he was working here four years ago. There's
a tremendous rate of staff turnover in these places.'

'Oh, Eric, don't be so literal. Listen to me. He would not have
said, "Parmesan cheese, madam?" He would have said,
"Parmesan cheese, sir?"'

Eric raised his eyebrows. It was a minimalist's expression of
surprise.

'You've changed sex.'

'You're quick on the uptake.'

'It *was* a pretty broad hint. Well, well, well, Nicola. Fancy that.
Er . . . have you just called yourself a woman, or have you actually
had the operation?'

'I've actually had the operation.'

'Right. Well . . . good . . . that does make things . . . er . . . I say
"good". I'm assuming you're pleased.'

'I'm very pleased.'

'Good. That's good, then. Well thank you for telling me.
Would you like to . . . talk about it?'

So Nicola told him her story, interrupted by her attempts to eat
her spaghetti with dignity. If you have never embarked on a long,
important story about your personal life while wearing a smart

blouse and eating spaghetti bolognese, don't. She tried so carefully, avoided disaster so narrowly on more than one occasion. Then, right at the end, a long strand of sauce-drenched pasta snaked down her blouse.

'Blast and damn it,' she said.

'You need a man to look after you,' said Eric.

He invited her to Norfolk for a long weekend. Separate bedrooms. He made that clear from the start. 'I don't want to rush you,' he said. She liked that. It implied a future.

His cottage was in Blakeney, in a little backstreet relatively untouched by the tourist hordes. (Yes, there were hordes even in Blakeney, fairly up-market hordes, but still hordes.) The walls were entirely of flint, and the cottage was side-on to the road, and therefore very private.

At the back of the cottage was his workshop, where pieces of furniture sat in various stages of restoration.

Eric didn't restore any furniture that weekend. He restored Nicola instead. By the end of her visit she felt mended, smoothed and polished. She forgot entirely that she had ever been a man and she forgot entirely, therefore, that she was a woman. She was just herself.

They went out with binoculars. Eric had a spare pair. She wasn't surprised. He was the sort of man who would have a spare everything. They walked along paths across the marshes, and watched the tongues of the sea as they licked the deep, muddy creeks. They watched the tide sliding round dead boats, hulks listing in the mud. They watched it give them life. They watched the boats bob proudly, buoyantly, briefly. They watched the sea take away their lives again, and slip away from the glutinous creeks.

They watched a barn owl hunting in broad daylight, ghosting slowly over the rich marshes, silent, white, deadly. Eric told her that the great dark hawk gliding over the reed beds was a marsh harrier. They sat on a bench by the coastal path and scanned the marshes with their binoculars. An avocet flashed above them, a leggy streak of smart black and white with its spectacular upturned beak. And there, beneath the wide, wide sky, they chatted about their lives. Nicola would never forget their first morning on the salty marshes, with the sea invisible beyond the dunes in front of them, and the ancient villages of north Norfolk sheltering beneath the low hills behind them. The early days of a love affair are so sweet. There is so much to tell.

They didn't hold hands. They didn't gaze into each other's eyes. They didn't stop looking through their binoculars, yet Nicola felt already that they were lovers.

'Have you never married, then, Eric?' she asked gently.

'Never got that far, Nicola, no.'

'You've never wanted children?'

'Happen to believe – those are ringed plovers; brave, lively little things, aren't they? – I happen to believe that it's wrong to want children. They aren't a commodity, Nicola. I don't think you should be able to order them. "Two children, please. One of each, I think." So, not having them, I didn't want them. I can't see me with children, actually, can you? Bedtime stories and football and school plays. Can't see it. But, had I had them, I would have loved them, Nicola, of that you can be sure.'

'I'm sure you would. But you've –'

'Well, yes, of course.'

'How did you know what I was going to ask?'

'Conversations roll along in a certain way, Nicola. You were going to ask if I've had lovers. Redshank. Two redshank over to the left. Look. There. Did you see the flash of the sun on their red legs? Oh yes, I've had lovers. Not many. Among proper lovers, lovers who lasted, just one for each redshank. Felicity was a florist from Farnborough.'

Nicola felt a shiver of surprise at this remark. It echoed her own recent alliterative thoughts about her solitary sex life. Would all that soon be unnecessary?

Eric hesitated before continuing. She realised that what he was going to say wasn't easy for him.

'Sarah was a twitcher. Taught me most of what I know about birds. Taught me most of what I know about sex too.'

'What happened?'

He didn't answer at first. Nicola thought he hadn't heard, but he had.

'She died. Cancer. Very slowly.'

'I'm so sorry.'

'She wouldn't have wanted it to be quick. Every day was precious. Every day was a little triumph. She lived nineteen months longer than predicted. Just a herring gull.'

'What?'

'The bird on that old boat. Awful to say that: "*Just* a herring gull." It doesn't know it isn't rare. It isn't its fault its species is so successful.'

'If she'd lived . . .'

'I don't think so. I don't think so, Nicola. I think we'd have . . . had our own spaces, kept our own places, shared parts of each other, hidden others. But who knows?'

They didn't even touch as they walked back to Blakeney. They came across a young couple eating each other, dripping with each other's saliva. They didn't even touch. Not yet. Nicola felt sorry for people who came to sex too quickly and too easily. They missed all the tantalising excitement of gradual discovery.

They were hungry. Eric drove, slowly, very deliberately, to Burnham Market, a posh little place hidden from modern England by low hills. They ate in a long, strikingly yellow hotel called the Hoste Arms. The food was good. At the next table, in the window, a group of happy people were chatting about bridge. Their bridge seemed like fun. One of the men made a joke, and they all laughed. Nicola knew that she was with a man who would never make her laugh. She wanted to join these people and play bridge with them, but she also wanted to stay with Eric. She realised in that second that nobody gives you everything you want, and that at that moment she was actually truly happy. There aren't many such moments.

The owner came round, a big chap, quite jolly. She could see that Eric wanted to introduce her to him, but he didn't see Eric's diffident smile, he didn't see Eric at all, he moved on and said, 'Caroline!' to a lady at the window table, a striking lady, the sort of lady hoteliers notice. Nicola was with the sort of man hoteliers didn't notice, but she didn't mind at all. Eric was her treasure – her buried treasure.

As they left, Eric did meet somebody he knew, and Nicola was glad.

'Charles, this is Nicola,' he said. Nicola had the nice feeling, for the first time in her life, of being shown off by a proud man.

She shook hands with Charles.

'Has Joy had her baby?' Eric asked.

'Yes. Girl. Eight pounds. She's back home,' said Charles.

'Ah,' said Nicola. 'So Joy is unconfined.'

She found that she was drawn to jokes, in Eric's company, like moths to new sweaters.

The man called Charles smiled, a trifle wearily, but Eric said, 'Yes, it's horrible being in hospital.'

Lots of people don't see jokes, in the sense that they don't get them. Eric didn't see them in the sense that he didn't realise that there had been a joke. If you said to Eric, 'There was an Englishman, an Irishman and a Scotsman,' he'd be thinking, 'I wonder how they met.'

After a couple of these gentle long weekends in Norfolk, Nicola felt obliged to invite Eric to stay at Sunny Cottage. She dreaded this.

Again, they had separate bedrooms. Sharing a bedroom would be a massive step, and the dank gloom of Sunny Cottage was not the right venue for something so important. It seemed such a sad place with its rented furniture in comparison with the quiet elegance of Eric's cottage. She was beginning to dislike Sunny Cottage.

She wasn't ashamed of her shy, serious furniture restorer. She was delighted to invite him to the Midsummer Dinner at the Golf Club. It might not have been entirely worthy, but she had to admit to herself that she wanted to show off her capture to Alan. She knew that he would be pleased for her. Apart from anything else, it would show that her having changed sex had worked, and that couldn't but encourage Alan. She felt a bit odd, actually, saying, 'This is my ex-wife Alan', but she didn't know how else to put it.

Unfortunately the evening proved a bit of a disaster. She knew that Eric didn't know about golf, but she didn't know just how much he didn't know. How could anybody be so unworldly as to think that Tiger Woods was a safari park? Nicola felt such a fool, although it was Eric who was being foolish, not her, and Eric was blithely unaware of it.

They sat with a few golfing Rotarians who were customers at the Cornucopia. These people were polite to Eric, but didn't get very far, and the conversation just swirled around him. He didn't finish any of the courses, the food at the club was stronger on quantity than quality, and everyone assumed that he was drinking so sparingly because he was driving. But Nicola was driving. It's a bit galling when you drink carefully because you're driving, and the person whom you're driving doesn't have the decency to get over the limit. She could see that Eric was completely unaware of this consideration.

Mind you, the house wine at the club was pretty dismal. The comedian made a joke about it. 'I hear the tickets are twenty-five pounds with half a bottle of house wine, and thirty pounds without it.' That did *not* go down well with the PP.

Nicola thought that it was a mistake to have a comedian. What comedian worth his salt is going to be free to go to Throdnall Golf Club on a Saturday night? She didn't meet a single person who had ever heard of 'Bubbly Ben Broadhurst – the Champagne Comedian'. She laughed where she could, but Eric's face never cracked. Nicola wondered if he realised that there were any jokes. Perhaps he thought there really was an Irish salesman who tried to flog a Nomad a tow-bar for his caravan in the Sahara.

The thought crossed Nicola's mind that they couldn't have done much worse if they'd booked Prentice.

She saw Eric through the Golf Club's eyes that evening, and she saw the Golf Club through Eric's eyes. By the end of the evening she wanted to ditch Eric and resign from the Golf Club. She did neither.

Nicola and Alan had just a few moments' chat together right at the end of the evening.

'Long time no see,' said Alan.

'Is that meant to be a criticism?'

'Well, Em and Gray are your children – and I have phoned you more than once.'

'Ah. Well I've spent a couple of long weekends in Norfolk, and my phone's been out-of-order. I get so few phone calls that I didn't realise for several days. There's been this new development in my life.'

'So I see.'

'Eric and I could pop over tomorrow, perhaps.'

'I'm not sure the kids could cope with meeting your men friends just yet, Nicola.'

'I thought you might be pleased that I'm happy.'

'I am. I'm delirious. It's been the one bright spot in a simply awful evening.'

And Alan strode off. Nicola couldn't believe it. She didn't even have the chance to tell him how good he looked in evening dress, and how amazed she'd been to see Bernie holding court like a man of the world. Alan's jealousy shocked her. Her stomach, already shaken by being filled with sticky toffee pudding in the middle of a heatwave, lurched in dismay.

*

'I'm really looking forward to seeing you, darling.' And this on the phone! It would have been a pretty intimate remark from Eric face to face, but on the phone! The phone, for him, was a medium for conveying essential information only. 'I . . . er . . .' he continued. 'I . . . thought we might perhaps take things a little further if . . . if you . . . er . . . felt you were ready.'

Did she? Was she? Surely?

'Right. Right. Thank you for telling me.' She had to resist saying 'Warning me'.

'I mean I thought maybe, because you did say that you hadn't much room in your small case and you didn't want to bring your big case, I thought maybe . . .' he lowered his voice, as if he feared that telephone engineers, working up poles, might hear his intimate confidences, '. . . you might feel you didn't need to pack pyjamas.' He gave a nervous little cough.

There's boldness, thought Nicola.

She arrived at about three. They went for a rather brisker walk than usual. Already she loved these coastal marshes, the flint villages hugging the low hills, the Dutch gables and windmills, the wide skies, the cruelly beautiful sunsets.

They went to the Hoste Arms for dinner. Nicola's choice. Her treat.

Before the meal they had a drink in the front bar. It was a lively, buzzing place, a sexy place. Nicola could see that this quiet man of hers liked to lose himself in the froth of humanity, where London girls bronzed and smoothed by sun lamps mingled with salty men bronzed and roughened by briny winds, and financial consultants down for the weekend wore yachting caps to drink their pints of bitter. Eric had a half, she had a sherry, they tried to relax.

The meal was good; neither of them chose anything with raw onions or garlic. They lingered nervously, drove back to Blakeney slowly in a mauve dusk, Eric offered her a nightcap, she refused:

she felt it might burn her throat and give her indigestion. Supposing she belched in Eric's bedroom. What a solecism.

'Well, I'm for bed,' said Eric.

'Me too.'

They walked up the narrow stairs to the tiny, immaculate, pale pink bedroom. An owl hooted and Nicola thought, They don't change sex, they don't have pre-coital nerves, I wish I was an owl. That was a silly thing for her to think, because she was no good at late nights and would have been very unsuccessful as an owl.

We should perhaps spare Nicola the embarrassing details of that first experience of sexual intercourse as a woman. You can imagine, can you not, how little natural confidence she would have had in her unnatural, medically created genitalia?

Can you imagine how difficult her first attempt at dancing was, as a woman, learning to be led? Would it not have been at least as challenging, after half a lifetime as a man, to learn to find lying under a man and opening your legs for him a natural expression of that great and wonderful thing – sexual love?

It was difficult to be unselfconscious about one's vagina when one had spent several months sticking pieces of plastic into it at regular intervals. Most virgins hadn't had to do that.

Virgin? Could a woman who had experienced intercourse as a man be described as a virgin?

To be thinking of such linguistic niceties at a time like this! But Nicola just couldn't find it in herself to respond to Eric in a more appropriate fashion.

We have discovered that Eric was not a big drinker, he didn't have a big appetite, he wasn't big on spices or on friendship, he didn't drive big distances. It perhaps needs to be said, in fairness to our dear furniture restorer, that, if Nicola had made a certain deduction from these facts, she would have found out that she was wrong, on that star-studded, owl-rich night in Norfolk. It should perhaps be no surprise that such a private man proved to be good at what is, or should be, among the most private of all activities.

Nicola felt that she had blown her great chance of fulfilment as a woman, and hoped that her dramatic performances were good enough to conceal her failure from Eric.

On later weekends she learnt to relax, learnt to think of Eric's pleasure more than of her own fears, and finally found fulfilment beyond the reach of owls.

28 Dropping Off

What was it about Nicola's smiling, reassuring face that made him feel so uneasy?

Was it the sense of déjà vu? It was the third time he had awoken in a hospital room, after a major operation, to see his ex-husband smiling at him. Silly thoughts, like: We can't go on meeting like this, flashed through his mind.

No, it was more than the sense of déjà vu. It was a feeling of guilt.

'Congratulations, Alan,' said Nicola fervently. 'You've made it! You're a man.'

Of course! Alan tried to clear the fog from his head, but he was still in the grip of the anaesthetic. Yes, that was it, he was a man.

'The operation's gone well,' said Nicola. 'They're very pleased.'

He remembered that he had cheated on Nicola, that Nicola was not Gray's father. Was that the cause of this unease? No. He had come to terms with that long ago.

'Eric sends his very best wishes,' said Nicola, slightly defiantly.

Eric! That was it.

Nothing had appalled Alan more about himself than his outbreak of jealousy at the Golf Club.

They said that jealousy was a woman's thing. Alan was a man now. Did that mean that he would no longer feel jealous?

'How do you feel?'

'It's hard to tell. I haven't dared move yet.'

The spoken words needed to engage only a tiny piece of Alan's brain. The greater part continued to debate this jealousy thing. He didn't want to debate it, he was far too tired, but you can't switch worry off. You have to defeat it first.

No, he didn't believe that jealousy was a woman's thing. It was a human being's thing. It was the Siamese twin of love. He had loved Nick and so it was natural that he should not wish Nick to take another lover, even though Nick was now Nicola.

But it was absurd. He was no longer married to either Nick or Nicola.

'Do you need the nurse for anything?'

'No, I . . . I think I'm fine.'

He remembered that he had fought against the jealousy – been out to dinner at the Positano with Nicola and Eric – managed gradually to be able to see them without feeling wretched. Well, now he was a man. Well, as much of a man as he would ever be. Soon he would be leading his own independent life . . .

'Can I get you anything?'

'No. No. Nothing.'

Please don't interrupt with these trite remarks, Nicola. I'm busy. I'm thinking deep thoughts about you.

Soon he would have his own adventures. It was absurd to envy Nicola her adventure.

He didn't, anyway. He had overcome those feelings before he went into hospital.

He sniffed.

'I'll get you a tissue.'

'Thank you.'

He blew his nose very gently, as if even that degree of activity might send pain coursing through his body.

That was why he felt guilty. He'd remembered. He had never truly apologised to Nicola. Never truly given her relationship with Eric his blessing.

Absurd to do it now, exhausted, fragile, half-anaesthetised. Absurd.

Must. Had to.

'Nicola?'

'Yes.'

'I hope you and Eric will be very happy. Truly happy.'

'Thank you.'

Nicola went over and gave him a quick little kiss.

'Thank you,' she repeated.

'I felt jealous at first.'

'Did you? Good Lord.'

Ha ha!

'You know I did.'

'Don't worry. You're tired. Relax.'

'Yes.'

'I hope you meet somebody wonderful.'

'Thank you. I have a funny feeling that I will.'

'I'm sure you will. You'll make a great man, Alan.'

'Thank you.'

Alan was beginning to feel excruciatingly uncomfortable physically.

'I need . . . I can't bear lying in this one position any longer,' he said. 'I need to move.'

The need was overwhelming, it was like a severe attack of claustrophobia, but how difficult would a move be?

'Do you need help?'

'No. No.'

He began to turn on to his side, very slowly, very carefully, so carefully. Beads of sweat formed on his forehead. He felt an indescribably piercing pain around his crutch, and he gasped.

'Nicola,' he squealed. 'I think it's come off.'

'What?'

'My new penis. It's dropped off.'

'Don't be silly.'

'I can feel it flopping around in my bandages. Ring the bell!'

Nicola rang the bell.

'It can't have,' she said.

'It has. It has. Oh God.'

'They'd stitch it on absolutely securely.'

'Well, I'd have thought so.'

'It's a trick of the nerves.'

'Oh God, I hope so. Oh God, it's terrible.'

It was Mrs Mussolini. It had to be. Life was like that.

She assured them, back to her starchiest in defence of Mr McWhinnie, that things put on by him did not drop off.

'He's a surgeon,' she assured them frostily, 'not a builder.'

She thought he might be in the building. Grudgingly, she went to hunt him down.

He wafted in on a tide of self-importance.

'Now then,' he said with jovial contempt, 'what's all this nonsense?'

Alan felt a bit of a fool, talking to Mr McWhinnie about his new penis, especially in front of Nicola, but he couldn't expect her to leave till the crisis was over.

'It's my penis,' he said.

Mrs Mussolini went even redder than usual.

'I do have one, do I?'

'A small one.'

The sky, uniformly dull and grey though it was, seemed to have become extremely interesting to Nicola.

'It . . . couldn't have dropped off, could it?'

Mr McWhinnie smiled. It was the lofty, superior smile of a great surgeon. Then he saw the depth of anxiety and revulsion on Alan's face, and his own face suddenly became human, warm, concerned. He began to speak to Alan as to an equal.

'No, Alan, honestly, it is utterly impossible for it to drop off. I haven't just sewn it on. I've made it integral. It's your clitoris transformed. Your fear is perfectly natural; having been a woman you have no built-in defence against castration anxiety, and the nerves play terrible tricks after operations.' He looked at Nicola and Mrs Mussolini and then back at Alan. 'While we're on the subject, Alan, a word of warning. Don't expect too much from this penis of yours. It's very young.'

Mr McWhinnie swept out. Mrs Mussolini was dragged along in his slipstream. As she got to the door, Nicola spoke and Alan realised, to his horror, that she was going to apologise *again*.

'Mrs Prothers?'

'Pethers.'

'Sorry. I just wanted to say how sorry I am for what I said last year.'

Nicola!!!

That night, still considerably under the influence of the anaesthetic, Alan had extremely vivid dreams. He was Mussolini's right-hand man, only Mussolini wasn't Mussolini, he was Eric, except that he wasn't nearly as tall as Eric, and he was known as Il Erico to his friends, and 'The Little Furniture Restorer' to his enemies.

He awoke feeling very uneasy. He didn't want to have Eric in his dreams. He had settled his emotional worries about him. The man had no business to be lurking in his subconscious.

He fell asleep, and Il Erico was there again, but this time Alan was nothing as important as his right-hand man. He was a foot soldier in the Italian army. Many platoons were lined up in St Peter's Square under a broiling sun. Il Erico, 'The Little Furniture Restorer', stood on the balcony and gave the order, in Italian, which Alan understood in his dream, 'Parts private inspection for the purpose of, trousers . . . wait for it . . . trousers . . . drop.'

All the men dropped their trousers in unison.

'Underpants . . . drop.'

All the men dropped their underpants in unison. Teams of nurses marched on to the vast square, led by Mrs Mussolini. The Pope, extremely frail, struggled on to the balcony and stood beside Il Erico.

Mrs Mussolini pointed to Alan's tiny young prick and laughed. Everybody laughed. St Peter's Square was rocked by a great rumbling, growing, spreading roar of laughter. Terrified pigeons took wing. Mothers clutched their babies to their breasts. Il Erico roared with laughter. Beside him, the Pope jumped up and down with glee and hugged himself.

Alan awoke bathed in sweat, stinking, and steeped in anxiety.

Luckily it was Pat's turn to bathe him.

Gray made teasing small talk but Alan knew that he had something important to tell him. He waited patiently.

'Mum,' Gray said at last, 'I've something to tell you.'

'Oh?'

'Yes. I'm . . . I'm engaged.'

'What??'

'Don't sound so surprised, Mum. Not everybody thinks I'm a hopeless case.'

'I didn't mean that.'

'Yes you did.'

'No, what I meant was . . . well . . . who to?'

'Oh, Mum. That's hurtful.'

'What?'

'I'll assume that you're still befuddled by the anaesthetic, even though it has been four days. Surely you must realise, Mum. Juanita. Who else?'

'Oh I see.'

'Oh for God's sake, Mum . . . sorry, you've had a major op, you're in pain, I mustn't upset you, but . . . I'm disappointed in you. We live in a multi-cultural world. What does it matter that she's Peruvian?'

'Of course that doesn't matter. What disturbs me is that you've never met.'

'Mum, we have. We've met in our minds. Isn't that the most important place? That's what you don't understand. There's no difference between virtual and real any more.'

'So, is it going to be a virtual marriage?'

Gray looked a little sheepish.

'Well, no, actually. I suppose it ought to be, but . . . no . . . we want to be together.' He smiled – still sheepishly, but it was still a smile: 'We're just old-fashioned softies at heart – and I'm not sure virtual sex has a great deal going for it, to be honest.'

'Good. Good. Well, congratulations.'

'We've both been saving up for her fare. Why do you think I chose to go to uni at Warwick?'

Because you didn't have the bottle to go away?

'I suppose you thought it was because I didn't have the bottle to go away. It was so that we could save.'

'If you'd told us . . .'

'If I'd told you, you'd have mocked me. You'd have called it my internet romance. You wouldn't have taken it seriously. She's coming over in about a month, Mum. Oh, Mum, you look great. You really do. Honestly.'

Alan was surprised and touched to hear such a compliment from Gray, but then he spoilt it in a manner so typical of Nick that just for a moment she forgot that he wasn't Nick's son.

'But then I'm so excited that everything looks great to me at the moment,' he said.

'It's good about Gray, isn't it?'

'Well, yes, it is, Em. Well, scary, risky, I'd have thought, but, yes, if it works, great.'

There was something different about Em, Alan thought. She seemed more at peace with herself. He didn't like to comment on it in case his comment destroyed that sense of peace.

'So, how's things, then?' he asked, hoping it would come out as 'And how are things going in your personal life? How do you really feel about Andropolos?'

'Things are all right. Things are going all right.'

Hardly an answer. Evasive.

He tried to move. Em saw his pain and said, 'Are you all right?'

'Fine. I just get very irritated and tense lying here in one position, but it's still agony moving. So, what are you doing with yourself?'

'Oh, this and that.'

Very evasive.

'I went to an Indian restaurant with a friend last night.'

'Oh. Which one?'

'The Taj Mahal.'

'I meant "which friend?" actually.'

'Oh, Mum, you're being so inquisitive.'

'You're being so evasive.'

'Mum, I admire what you've done. It's EFT.'

'EFT?'

'Extraordinary For Throdnall. You've gone for what you want and I admire that, but it's made life difficult for me. I can't have heart to heart chats with you now you're a man. I'm sorry, it may be stupid, but it's changed things.'

'All right, no heart to heart, but I have a long time to think about things here, and I'd like a simple answer to a simple question. Are you happy, darling?'

'Yes, I'd say I am, Mum. Yes.' She smiled. 'I know what you're thinking. You're thinking, "Is she envious of Gray? Is she very upset about Andropolos?" '

'Well I haven't liked to ask about that.'

'Oh, Mum. No, I'm not upset about Andropolos. I broke it off with him, not he with me.'

'That was important to you, was it?'

'Well, yes, it was. I still like him. He's a good guy.'

'I never thought I'd hear you say that about anyone.'

'Oh, Mum!'

'So why did you break it off?'

'I came to chat to you, not to be grilled.'

'Sorry.'

Silence. Alan moved again, very very carefully. A stab of pain down there. God, he felt raw.

'I don't really have an answer, Mum, except . . . it just wasn't right. You're probably relieved. Hardly a great catch for your beloved daughter, a Greek waiter. But he won't stay a waiter. He'll be a successful restaurateur. Food's in his blood. I'm glad I still respect and like him, though. It's done wonders for my faith in . . .'

She hesitated, as if she wasn't quite sure what she had faith in.

'Men?' prompted Alan.

She shook her head.

'Human nature,' she said.

A very fat African lady with a smile as wide as the Sahara wheeled in the late drinks trolley, which had a very annoying squeak. It was half past eight. Almost time for sleep. Alan dreaded the nights.

He had an uncomfortable feeling that, although he had enjoyed a rare moment of intimacy with his daughter, she had left unsaid as much as she had revealed.

'Well hello!!'

The little ward suddenly seemed very small when it had twenty-two stone of blubber in the middle of it.

'Prentice!'

'Well I had to come and see you. Must do my bit. I was so upset about not coming last time.'

'A very important holiday.'

'Well it was free, Alan. I could never resist anything free.'

'Have a grape.'

'Thank you. I'll have several. So, how's our new man?'

'All right. Coming on.'

'Fantastic. Hey, listen, this'll amuse you . . .'

'Why do I doubt it?'

'Alan! No, on the bus coming over, because I don't drive and I can't afford taxis . . .'

Alan did a violin mime, slightly too flamboyantly, and winced as the pain struck him.

'It's true. M'm. Nice grapes. Mind if I take a tangerine?'

'Be my guest.'

'No. I'm not exactly flush. People see a financial consultant with shabby shoes and no car, they think, if his advice is that good, why isn't he rich?'

'What about the comedy?'

'Bookings have dried to a trickle. A trickle, Alan. I rang the manager at Droitwich, asked him why he wouldn't have me back, he said, "You're obscene." I said, "Excuse me. I don't do obscene." He said, "Not your act. You!"'

'Oh, Prentice, that's cruel.'

'Quite. M'm. Delicious tangerine. Mind if I have one of those peaches? They look luscious. Thanks. So, in the bus, I suddenly thought, "I am not only obscene, I am obese. And the word 'obese' can be made from the word 'obscene'." So I started amusing myself by making other words out of "obscene" and, do you know, they all fitted me. All of them. Isn't that uncanny?'

'Such as?'

'"Cobs", which is what I sweat. "BO". Not actually a word, I know, but highly applicable.'

'I don't like this.'

'No. Listen. "Scone". What I have too much of with jam and cream. "Cones", as in icecream, see above. "Been". What I am if you put "has" in front of it. "Snob". All my pseudo-intellectual guff about comedy. "Cons". What I do to my audience.'

'Stop it.'

'"Scene". What people make when I try to fuck them.'

'Prentice! Why are you saying all this?'

'To cheer you up.'

'I'm finding it extremely sad and depressing.'

'Well there you go.'

What a double whammy. It was the king of double whammies. Prentice and Mr Beresford in one evening.

He couldn't believe that Mr Beresford came. He had never spoken to the man or even seen him out of the context of work, unless you counted those dreadful Christmas parties, but they were work really. Horrid things. Mr Beresford looking absurd in a paper hat, bellowing out a joke from a cracker, 'What worker drives his customers away?' and being childishly disappointed when Connie hadn't the sense not to blurt out, triumphantly, 'A taxi driver', thus ruining Mr Beresford's moment of glory and her prospects of promotion.

Now, there he was with his bag of grapes, with only three minutes of recovery time between him and Prentice.

Mr Beresford didn't even like him! Since the announcement of his sex change he had virtually been ostracised. After all the work he had put in towards organising the reception for the launch of the tilting carriages, he hadn't even been invited. Anyone who was anybody in railways had been there – 'arrivistes from Virgin, virgins from Arriva, con artists from Connex', as he'd put it in his usual forthright biased way – but no Alan Divot, née Alison Kettlewell.

An unworthy but splendid picture crossed Alan's mind. He imagined Mr Beresford on his way up meeting Prentice on his way down. He imagined Prentice saying 'It's love at first sight. Those eyebrows. Irresistible', and throwing himself on Mr Beresford by the lift doors. His heart hammered with the hatred that he felt for these two men. He was having a heart attack! He forced himself to calm down, he wasn't having a heart attack, the hammering slowed down, sweat poured off him, he hadn't heard a word of what Mr Beresford was saying, and Mr Beresford hadn't even noticed that anything was wrong.

'Sorry,' he said. 'I rather missed all that.'

'What?' Mr Beresford noticed him properly for the first time. 'I say, are you all right?'

'Hot. Very hot. Couldn't dampen a cloth and run it over my forehead, could you?'

Mustn't hate. Hatred was self-destructive. Be a man, Alan. You almost are, after all. Try to see the funny side.

It wasn't too hard to see the funny side of Mr Beresford returning with a damp flannel and solicitously wiping his forehead for him. He looked so awkward and out of place. It quite restored Alan's heart and humour.

'Thank you, Florence,' he said.

'What? Ah! Florence Nightingale. Me as Florence Nightingale. Very droll,' said Mr Beresford. 'Glad to see you haven't lost your sense of humour. I see you're a bit over-stocked with grapes. Sorry.' For a moment Alan thought that Mr Beresford was going to take home the ones he'd brought. He did have a mean streak. 'No, I was just bringing you up to speed with developments at base. Things are looking up.' That seemed unlikely, in view of the disastrous news that Bangladesh had got the contract for the Northern Vision Three-Car Units. 'Everything is hunky-dory.'

He pulled his chair close to Alan's bed. Alan thought that his transformation must be difficult for Mr Beresford. He had always suspected that the man held a bit of a torch for him as Alison, and the awful thought occurred to him that maybe he still did! Maybe he was bisexual. Maybe he wouldn't have been too displeased if Prentice had thrown himself on him.

'Alan,' he said. Alan was amazed. He had only once used his first name before, in the old Alison days. 'You don't mind my calling you Alan in this context, do you?'

'Not at all, Mr –'

'Call me Clive.'

'Oh. Well . . . Thank you . . .' Gulp. '. . . Clive.'

'I have an apology to make, Alan.'

'Oh? . . . Clive.'

'Yes, Alan. I have not responded to your sex change in as sympathetic a way as I should have done. Since you've been away I've spoken to the Almighty and He has told me that I have been small-minded.'

'Oh. Well . . . thank you . . . Clive.'

'Don't thank me, Alan. Thank Him.'

'Right. I . . . er . . .' Alan was going to say that he wasn't actually a believer, but it was too weighty a subject to touch upon at this early stage in his recuperation. 'Right. I will.'

'Good. He'll be pleased. Don't look so sceptical. God has time for everybody. What God has shown me is that you and . . . er . . . your ex-husband . . . your divorce is complete, isn't it? . . . have done no harm to anyone but yourselves.'

'Exactly, Mr . . . Clive.'

'The world is full of people doing the most dreadful harm to other people – sex offenders, paedophiles – and things not connected with sex, hardly even worth a mention. The grinding everyday cruelty of humanity, almost always towards those weaker than themselves.'

'I could let such thoughts get to me if I didn't have a stream of visitors to cheer me up and take my mind off things.'

'Precisely. Our job precisely.'

There was silence then, deep and loud as only a hospital silence can be.

Suddenly Mr Beresford brightened. He had thought of something else to say.

'Had your supper?'

'Yes.'

'What did you have?'

Well, it passed the time. He spun it out as best he could, even made him smile as he described their attempts at crème brulée. He wasn't sure he'd ever seen Mr Beresford smile before, and he wasn't sure that he ever wanted to see him smile again, there was something unconscionably mirthless about his smile. Alan had the absurd thought that he looked like the Old Testament. He longed for him to leave.

'Yes, well,' said Mr Beresford at last, 'beastly old tempus has done his rotten old fugiting again.' He stood up. 'Alan, take as much time as you need to get well, but come back soon. With Mrs Walsh, it isn't the same, it just isn't.'

Mrs Walsh. It took Alan a moment to realise that this was Connie. He didn't think he'd ever heard her called Mrs Walsh before.

'Perhaps I shouldn't have said that, Alan, and I'd not like it repeated. I wouldn't want you to think she isn't doing her best, and really she's not doing too badly at all but . . . well . . . there just isn't any substitute for quality.'

That was easily the nicest thing Mr Beresford had ever said to him. In fact it was the only nice thing he had ever said to him.

Or ever would say to him, come to that.

29 A Hungarian Masterpiece

Alan was discharged from hospital two days before Bernie went off on his cruise.

His cruise! He had booked a fortnight on the *Oriana*, on his own.

Nicola slept on the Zed-bed in the lounge for those two nights, and their time was spent almost entirely in getting Bernie ready. Alan sat in an armchair in his bedroom and shouted instructions – 'Don't forget his cufflinks' etcetera.

'Leave it to me,' Nicola called out. 'You are no longer the woman of the house.'

'Nor are you,' shouted Alan.

Two things disturbed the calm of Alan's convalescence, one involving Em, one Gray. Both were important. One was serious.

The one that was only important first. Em.

She said to them early one evening (a Thursday), 'I won't be in this evening. I should have told you earlier. I'm going out with my lover.'

Alan thought that she looked quite slim that night, almost ethereal, certainly beautiful, paradoxically feminine, his . . . their . . . chameleon of a daughter.

'Ah!' he said. 'A shame to miss Nicola's curry, but . . . I'm glad you have a lover. I guessed that you had, but you've been unusually quiet about it.'

'I had cold feet. About telling you.'

'Good heavens. What's wrong with him?'

'Nothing. She's a chiropractor. That's how we met.'

This shouldn't have been a surprise at all, it was utterly logical.

Of course it would just about ring their death knell in Throdnall society, but from their perspective as transsexuals it could hardly be described as shocking.

Nevertheless, it has to be said that neither Alan nor Nicola welcomed Em's news wholeheartedly. It's difficult even for loving parents, perhaps especially for loving parents, to accept that a child of theirs is gay.

Some of the reasons for this are creditable. They know that life will be at least a bit more difficult for the child in question. They know that the child in question will never have children of his or her own. This could, and often did, lead to a lonely old age, and the fact that they would be dead didn't stop Nicola or Alan from worrying about Em and Gray in old age.

Some of the reasons are less creditable. There will be remarks in the pubs, comment in the shops, sympathy from the complacent, explanations to the neighbours. There will not be the patter of grandchildren's tiny feet.

Nicola and Alan's disappointment did not run deep and, once they had met Clare, was less than they would have felt had Em married her Greek waiter, or her American control freak, or her oversexed French egotist, or her Italian overburdened with charm and style at the expense of content.

Clare was slim, quietly elegant, always immaculate, and seemed rather cool towards all the world except Em. Some men found it disturbing that it was so impossible to deduce that she was a lesbian. They felt that it was an affront to their sex that somebody so pretty and so well-balanced should prefer her own sex.

Two foolish remarks were made, however, about Em's relationship with Clare – one of them merely foolish, the other foolish but rather more fundamental.

The merely foolish remark was made by Gray. No surprise there, then. 'I've always hated lesbianism,' he said to Em. 'I like homosexuality, but hate lesbianism.'

'How on earth can you justify that attitude?' asked Em indignantly, rising to the bait like a suicidal salmon.

'Because two gay men are rivals I don't have to bother about, while two lesbian girls are two opportunities I'll never have the chance to have.'

'I might have guessed your comment would be trite, trivial, stupid and self-centred,' snorted Em, and she stormed out, slamming the door violently behind her.

The more fundamental error, sadly, was Alan's, and it came two days later, over Nicola's lasagne – creditable, but not a patch on Alan's.

'I hope you don't think it's our fault,' he said to Em.

'I suppose I should have anticipated that as you become a man you'll start to become utterly and totally crass,' Em retorted. 'The word "fault" is deeply offensive to me. Since there is absolutely nothing "wrong" with lesbianism the use of the word "fault" is intolerably narrow-minded and falsely judgemental.'

'You're talking like a debating society, not a human being,' said Gray.

'Oh, fuck off,' said Em.

'That's better!' said Gray.

'I apologise,' said Alan. 'I apologise utterly and totally. But you must realise that your moth . . . your father and I . . . God, *I'm* getting muddled now! . . . are quite naturally extremely sensitive to the possibility that our sexual confusion and subsequent unusual though not confused behaviour may not have been a great example to you.'

'You're talking like a pamphlet,' said Gray. 'What's got into everybody?'

'Arrogance,' said Em. 'Patronising arrogance. I make up my own mind. I deeply resent the suggestion that you're responsible for my actions, not me.'

'Ted Jackson,' said Gray.

He flinched and held his hands over his ears as the door crashed shut behind Em.

'Ted Jackson?' echoed Nicola.

'He makes doors,' said Gray with a grin, luxuriating in the rare experience of being the better behaved of the siblings.

And the other thing to disturb the calm? The one that was serious? Gray.

Well, the fault was Ferenc's. Alan thought that a grown, mature man, even if he was Hungarian, would have had more sense. Later he understood.

Nicola's encouragement of Ferenc had borne fruit. He had begun to take his painting more seriously. He had had seven pictures exhibited at the Lafayette, and five of them had already been sold, and for good prices, by the Windlass man, whom Alan thought to be as nutty as a fruitcake, not to mention as fruity as a nutcake. So Ferenc had given Nicola a present as thanks, and Nicola had brought it home from the hotel and unwrapped it, and there it was, a portrait of the family, with Alan and Nicola in their sex change roles, and a wonderfully vivid portrait of Em, and there beside her, Gray.

It was good. It went beyond the surface of their characters. It captured them. And Gray was Ferenc's son. It leapt from the picture, as it didn't in life.

They stared at it in silence – a terrible silence. A family struck dumb. Thank goodness Bernie wasn't there to blow their reticence out of the window.

Oh Ferenc, you prick, you great prick, thought Alan with accuracy on two counts. How could you have done this?

The next morning, after Nicola had left for work, Gray went into Alan's bedroom, where he was still accepting breakfast in bed. Alan didn't think he'd ever seen their . . . his . . . son so ashen. A very grey Gray indeed.

'That picture, Mum,' he said.

'Yes.'

'Ferenc's my father, isn't he?'

'I'm afraid so, yes.'

'Oh my God.'

'Oh, Gray, I'm so sorry.'

'I mean, I knew it the moment I saw the picture, but, I don't know, hearing you say it . . . it's . . . it's hit home.'

Alan patted the duvet, inviting Gray to sit. He became his mother's little boy again. It made no difference now that he was grown up and his mother was a man.

Alan wrapped his dressing gown firmly round his chest. He'd grown used to the scars after two years, but he was still uneasy about his children seeing them. He told Gray all about Nick and his troubles, and the isolated affair, and how he'd felt pregnant and had known instinctively, and how he'd had to make love to Nick, so that Nick would never suspect. He told him how he'd always seen little bits of Ferenc in him, and had always been amazed that Nick hadn't seen them too.

'Did Dad ever know you'd slept with Ferenc?'

'I'm sure he didn't.'

'Then the possibility of my being Ferenc's simply wouldn't have occurred to him, because the impossible can't happen.'

Alan thought that very perceptive of Gray. He wondered if he had been underestimating him.

'But he'll see it now,' he said.

'He may not, Mum. Not if it's still an impossibility.'

'But won't he see the resemblance?'

'Who knows? We can never be exactly sure that what other people see is the same as what we see. I mean it's still me, and she may just see me as he's so used to seeing me. I mean she was never exactly observant, was he?'

Alan couldn't believe what he was hearing. Gray sounded so level-headed about it, so analytical.

'How can you be so analytical about it?' he asked. 'Doesn't it . . . I don't know . . . devastate you? I'd have been devastated if I'd found out something like that about my father.'

'It was a terrible shock last night, Mum. My blood ran icy. Luckily it was such a shock that it struck me dumb. I've hardly slept. But I'm used to being on my own and thinking things through on my own, and I've decided . . . I'm not saying it was easy, Mum, and I'm not saying I'm not disturbed by it . . . but I mean, in the end, it doesn't really make all that much difference, does it? To me, I mean. It would to Dad. I mean, to Nicola.'

'You really mean that?'

'Well, I haven't got much choice, have I? It happened, and a long time ago. No point in resenting you now.'

'Thank you.'

'May as well try to be cool about it.'

'Being cool's fine. Burying traumas isn't.'

'And I've talked to Juanita.'

'Talked?'

'Well emailed, but to my generation that's like talking, we think of it as talking, that's what you don't seem to understand when you think I'm a freak. Juanita's very mature for her age.'

'How old is she?'

He blushed.

'Eighteen. Well, almost. She says it makes no great difference, because I'm still exactly the same person as I was yesterday, and a better person because I have one less delusion.'

'Phew!'

'Exactly. She's very bright, Mum. Actually . . .' he looked a little embarrassed, '. . . she and I quite like the idea of my being Anglo-Hungarian. One more blow for multi-culturalism. Quite cool, really. And let's face it, Mum, it does help that Dad's a woman. I mean I have sort of lost him as a father already.'

'Oh, dear – and do you feel you've lost me?'

'As a mum, obviously, but not as a person. You're still here for me. She isn't. I still love you, Mum, and I'm still yours.'

Alan hugged him. There, in Throdnall, an Englishman hugged his son!

It would have been more extraordinary still if it had been an Englishman who hadn't previously been an Englishwoman.

'Can we go for a walk?' said Nicola that evening, having returned early from the hotel.

'Of course.'

There wasn't any need to ask why.

'Are you sure you're up to it?'

'Well, I'm supposed to have gentle exercise.'

They went down Orchard View Close and turned right into Badger Glade Rise, retracing the route Alison had taken on the night on which Nick had told her of his intention to change sex.

At the end of Badger Glade Rise they turned left into Spinney View.

At the end of Spinney View stood the Coach, weighed down by hanging baskets. There were only four cars in the car park, and at least two of those would belong to staff.

'Pub?' said Alan.

'People will speculate,' said Nicola.

They retraced their steps down Spinney View, continued into Elm Copse Crescent, and went down the ginnel to the back end of the golf course, which was almost deserted as evening took hold.

At last Nicola spoke.

'Gray's not mine, is he? He's Ferenc's.'

'Yes.'

'You worked on me that night, that night you were so very affectionate, that night I've remembered through all this as the most genuine moment of passion between us. It wasn't genuine at all.'

'No.' Alan's reply was hardly even a whisper, more like a rustle in the undergrowth.

'It seems absurd to worry, now that I'll be leaving for good in a few days' time, but it hurts, Alan. It hurts a lot.'

'Yes. I suppose it's absurd to defend myself now that I'm a man about my unfaithfulness as a woman when you were a man but it was the only time, Nicola.'

'The only time? Just one time and Gray was created. What virility. What sperm. What eggs.'

'I mean, Ferenc was the only man.'

'Why?'

'Because I hated being unfaithful.'

'You know what I mean. I meant, "Why did you do it?"'

'Does it matter now?'

'Yes it . . . the Fergusons. Smile. Look casual.'

They smiled at the couple drifting in the opposite direction, hand in hand, normal, happy (as far as they knew).

'Evening.'

'Evening.'

'Nice night.'

'Very.'

'We're lucky.'

'We are.'

The Fergusons moved on.

'Yes, it does matter. I'd like to leave not hating you.'

'We were young and our marriage wasn't working for reasons we were too ignorant and inexperienced to understand. I was unhappy. I did something I regret. Except.'

'Except?'

'I can't really be angry with Ferenc and I can't really regret that it happened because if it hadn't happened Gray wouldn't exist.'

'That's a very rational view. It leaves the emotional side out altogether.'

'It *was* twenty years ago. I can rationalise it now. And it's a fact which must perhaps help to define our emotional response. Are you happy that Gray exists?'

'Well of course I am. That's a very unfair argument.'

'Happy even though you know you aren't the father?'

'Well . . . well, yes, of course I am. I'm not a monster.'

'Well then. Beside that, does it all matter now? After all these years?'

A skylark began to sing, high above the par three eleventh. They hadn't had skylarks on the golf course for some years. They looked up, trying to see it in the fading light. Nicola slid her hand very briefly into Alan's and straight out again so quickly that Alan was never absolutely sure that he hadn't imagined it.

Juanita arrived two days before Alan was considered fit enough to be left by Nicola.

Gray went to Gatwick to meet her. It was a tense day for them all, but for him most of all. It was the beginning of *his* real life test. 'I'm terrified,' he admitted and he added, in that way of his that made them wonder if he had inherited any of Ferenc's artistic talent, 'I'm bloody shitting myself.'

Alan hugged him, and Nicola kissed him.

'Good luck, darling,' Alan said.

'Good luck, son,' Nicola exaggerated.

Later that day the text messages began to arrive. 'Plane landed. Shitting myself.' 'She's lovely.' 'On the Gatwick Express. Ha ha. At a standstill. I lied about her being lovely. She isn't. She's gorgeous.' 'Limping towards Throdnall. She's a queen.' 'Due Throdnall 19.15 hours. ETA 19.59.'

Juanita was short, barely five foot, her complexion was sallow, and there was an Indian look to her broad, somewhat squashed nose. Her hair and her eyes were dark and Spanish. She was slim and moved with a natural grace that few girls in Throdnall could match. What made her lovely was that her face shone with goodness.

She spoke English well, with a strong accent, and shyly. Gray was unbelievably considerate. Can this really be my son? thought Alan. Can this really be . . . the person I wish was my son? thought Nicola.

They went off to Throdnall's little Latin American Club to sleep.

'I thought it would be more tactful,' said Gray. He grinned sheepishly. 'What? Tactful? Moi?'

'I'm happy for you to sleep together in my house,' said Alan, 'just as I am happy for Em and Clare to sleep here.'

Nothing was to be gained by forcing them out.

'Thank you,' said Gray, 'but Juanita would be embarrassed.'

Juanita raised her eyebrows in mock astonishment.

'Oh all right,' admitted Gray. 'I'd be embarrassed.'

'I intend to have a word with Ferenc,' said Nicola on the morning of her departure back to Cluffield. 'I hope you don't mind.'

'Why should I mind?' said Alan, 'but I would like to have a word with him first. He helped me betray you many years ago. He has betrayed me this month. That painting is a betrayal of our secret and of our . . .'

'And of your what? Love?'

'Trust.'

Alan did confront Ferenc first. He hadn't seen him alone since she'd left his bed for the last time twenty years ago.

Although there was no desperate need for secrecy, Alan didn't want anyone in Throdnall to see them together. Nor did Ferenc. So they arranged to meet at twelve-thirty on the following Saturday at the Smelters' Arms in Plockwell.

It was a grey morning. Mist brushed the fields and hung around the hedgerows. Some mornings there seem to be rooks everywhere.

Alan was a little nervous, so he got there early. He waited in the car in the pot-holed, puddled car park. In the sad row of shops opposite there was one called '2001 – A Spice Odyssey'. So it was true. The Parkers had opened up again. In the ten minutes during which he watched, nobody went in or out. Their little dream didn't stand a chance.

Then he remembered that he didn't need to wait in the car. He was a man now. He could walk into pubs and not be raped by several pairs of eyes.

He strode in boldly, to the manner born. He ordered himself a pint. His first ever pint in a pub. It felt odd to be standing there, in a dark, cavernous town pub, with a pint of bitter in a straight glass, discussing the rival merits of Aston Villa and Tottenham Hotspur with mine host, in the deepest voice he could manage, while waiting to talk to the man who had fathered his second child.

Ferenc was ten minutes late. Alan began to think he wasn't coming. Maybe his 'There's something we need to talk about' hadn't been strongly enough expressed. And then there he was, her brief lover of two decades ago.

They sat in a far and obscure corner, and talked in low voices.

'Why did you do it?' he asked.

'Do what?' Ferenc seemed genuinely puzzled.

'Paint Gray like that?'

'Like what?'

'Like you, Ferenc.'

'Like me?'

'Oh come on. You know he's your son.'

'What???'

Ferenc's question was like a rifle shot. Several of the shoppers and gamblers who made up the Saturday lunchtime crowd turned to look.

'S'ssh! People will notice us.'

'Are you serious? I'm Graham's father?'

'Yes. I can't believe you didn't know.'

'I had no idea. Are you sure?'

'Absolutely.'

'My God. My God!'

'Didn't the possibility even occur to you? I mean with the dates . . .'

'I had no idea when he was born, Alis . . . Alan. I stayed here in Plocknell when you moved to Throdnall. Graham must have been nine or ten before I moved to Throdnall too, before I even knew he existed. I had no idea. Oh, Alison . . . sorry, I just can't call you Alan . . . this is some shock.'

'But how could you paint him like that and not see?'

'I paint a truth, Alison. I paint an essence. I painted mainly from photographs. I've only met the boy once. I see only what I see. I'm objective. There's no subjectivity. There is no context. I met Em and she gave me the idea. She introduced me to Gray. He didn't know why he was meeting me. I studied him and he thought it was just a casual drink. I never saw. I never dreamt . . . well, because I never dreamt.'

'Gray said much the same, funnily enough.'

'Well there you are. And why "funnily enough"? Like father, like son. Does Nicola know?'

'Yes. It's the past with her. It's over. She's not pleased, of course, but it's no longer important to her.'

'We should never have done it, of course,' he said. 'We have a saying in Hungary, "Don't piss in your brother's goulash." I am so sorry.'

He reached out to clasp Alan's hand, remembered that Alan was a man now, withdrew his hand hurriedly, glanced round the pub furtively, smiled at him uneasily: he was having a very adverbial moment.

'Alison, nothing can take away the memory of a very happy little episode.'

Alan smiled coquettishly. He couldn't help it.

'But why,' said Ferenc, 'do you want to tell me now, since you have known for so long and said nothing?'

'Vanity.'

'Vanity?'

'I couldn't bear to think your painting was spitefully intended. You were the only lover I ever took. I didn't want to think you didn't like me.'

'Oh, I liked you.'

'Perhaps I shouldn't have told you.'

He shrugged.

'I'm glad to know. I won't disturb the applecart. We have a saying in Hungary, "If the clock ticks, don't chop it up for firewood." Another pint?'

'Better not. Goodbye, Ferenc.'

It was like putting the very last full stop on his sentence as a woman.

He needed to pee. He went to his first urinal. Sadly, nobody else was in there. He would have liked to have stood there, and flowed there, beside his fellow men.

It wasn't a great, imposing stream, but it was urine, and it was his, and he was standing up. Jane Austen and Tolstoy never once mentioned peeing, but I have to. It was a massive moment in Alan's life. Massive.

'I think you know why I've called you in here.'

'Yes.'

Ferenc looked annoyingly composed. Nicola would have so liked to make him uncomfortable.

'You don't deny that you had an affair with my . . . ex-wife?'

'Not at all. It was a very long time ago, when she wasn't entirely happy. I brought a little happiness. I did nothing that she didn't want me to do.'

So Hungarians use double negatives as well, thought Nicola with absurd irrelevance. All Ferenc said was true, but, damn it, the man might have the manners to look at least a trifle discomfited.

'Did you truly have no idea that Gray was yours?'

'Of course not. I hardly saw him. By the time I did see him, the affair was buried in the past. When I had the idea of painting your family, I thought it a lovely gift to mark your brave achievement and to thank you for the support you have given to my painting. I am devastated that it has had this unintentional effect, Nicola.'

Well have the common decency to look devastated, then.

'I painted from photographs given me by your lovely daughter, apart from meeting Gray once. I never saw. Why should I? You didn't.'

'Then how did it come out in the painting?'

'Art reaches deeper, Nicola. Art reaches deeper than the artist knows.'

'How did you know Em?'

'I met her in a pub. Her and another girl. They were attractive. I talked to them.' He smiled, slightly complacently and with irritating urbanity. 'I talk to every attractive girl I see in Throdnall. The number is not so overwhelming. Oh, Nicola, nothing happened. In any case I soon discovered that your daughter keeps goal for the opposing team, as we say in Hungary.'

'We say "bats for the other side".'

'Yes. Nicola, if you want me to say I'm sorry, of course I will, it's only polite, but don't expect me to mean it. There. That's honest, isn't it?'

Nicola abandoned her attempt to disconcert Ferenc. It had been an unworthy aim. She must be more generous than that. She must put Gray's interests before her own. She had discussed this with Alan, and they were agreed.

'Ferenc,' she said, 'Alan and I both want you to know that we will be very happy for you to see as much of Gray as you want, and to be as much of a father to him as you want to.'

The blood drained from Ferenc's face. He shifted uneasily in his chair. He was discomfited, disconcerted and devastated.

'Good God, no!' he said. 'None of this must ever come out. My wife would kill me.'

30 A Man About Town

It took a couple of months more, after Nicola had left, before Alan really felt ready to burst upon the world in all his manhood. It's unusual for a young buck to reach manhood at the age of forty-six, but that was what happened to Alan, and it happened at a time when he was free of responsibilities, and suddenly all alone in the house. Perhaps we can forgive him for letting it go to his head just a little bit?

He enjoyed feeling that he was a man about town. He could have wished that the town that he was about had been more glamorous than Throdnall, but he didn't let it dampen his spirits.

It was such a relief, after all those years combining the roles of PA to Mr Beresford and housewife, to find that number thirty-three was transformed almost overnight into a bachelor pad. It all happened so quickly. It wasn't entirely a pleasant phenomenon, of course. He could feel quite lonely in the evenings, in the suffocating quiet of Orchard View Close. He was not a man to kneel on a pad and weed his little garden, as dusk laid her velvet counterpane upon the world, and the first dew formed on his tiny lawns.

He wasn't too surprised that Em had left home and bought a little flat with Clare. He'd expected her to move in with somebody sometime, even though he hadn't expected it to be a woman.

He was rather more surprised to find Gray moving out, but, once he had dipped his toes into the real world, Gray had decided that it was a wonderful place and had whipped off his clothes and jumped in – figuratively and literally. He and Juanita lived with a bunch of students in a large, crumbling house at the wrong end of Leamington Spa.

And then Bernie too had gone, as you will have deduced.

Had he died on his cruise? Please please don't tell us that he had died on his cruise.

No. He hadn't.

Had he died after his cruise?

Nope.

Was he then still alive?

Very much so.

So had he moved into a home?

Yes.

Was it Honeyfields? Please don't tell us that it was Honeyfields.

Relax. It wasn't Honeyfields. It was his own home! Well, his and Peggy's.

Peggy's???

Yes. Peggy's. Peggy had money. Peggy was a wealthy widow. Bernie had found himself a sugar mummy. Well, that was what he called it, and Peggy just smiled and didn't spoil the story by saying that she was only three years older than he was. When you're aged five and two, a gap of three years is vast. When you get to eighty-seven and eighty-four it isn't of much significance, but she played along with Bernie, and called him her toy boy.

Wonderful things can happen to old people if they don't give up, and the whole idea of cruising is a bit of a romantic fantasy anyway. They were introduced to each other in the Crow's Nest Bar on the *Oriana*. They soon became inseparable. They sat together in the Pacific Lounge listening to a man called Mike Craig, who brought the old comedians wonderfully to life. They discovered that they both liked laughter. They lunched together in the Peninsular Restaurant, took coach trips together, played Scrabble together in the games room, went to the shows together, took a nightcap (or two) together. After the cruise they decided to live together. Peggy had no family left, except a son in New Zealand, so she came to Throdnall. They decided not to get married, 'for tax reasons'. Her son in New Zealand disapproved.

'Then sod the little prig,' she said. The little prig was fifty-eight.

So there was Alan on his own, as much of a man as he would ever be, and definitely 'up for it'. His only problems were that he wasn't sure what 'it' was or where it could be found.

He began his voyage of pleasure in a safe port, the Coach, but the joys of drinking pints and peeing standing up were not sufficient for him. His aim was to meet women, and women on their own did not wander into the Coach, as he knew all too well.

Occasionally he propped up the bar at the Golf Club, which had its share of divorcees and lonely women, but none of them (except for Jennifer Griffin, who would go out with almost anybody) would even consider going out with this man who had formerly been a lady member at this very club. He thought of approaching Jennifer Griffin and attempting to go bravely where two hundred and seventy-eight men had bravely gone before, but he couldn't face the barely concealed ridicule and contempt that would follow.

He visited the pubs of down-town Throdnall, which were heaving with young people. He felt very out of place.

His children came to his rescue, leading him on pub crawls and club crawls in Throdnall and Warwick and Birmingham. When he'd last been to a club a DJ had meant a dinner jacket. He was unprepared for the frenzy of the modern world.

Gray and Juanita took him on a tour of Throdnall's night spots: to Danny's and Pemberton's and Ricky's Raver and the back bar of the Metropolitan. It was the beginning of winter now, but often he was the only person with a jacket. On the streets it was freezing. He found himself looking at unattainable young women whose tempting goose-pimpled legs seemed to extend all the way to their waists. He found himself avoiding looking at attainable young women with untempting goose-pimpled thighs that made Prentice seem almost dapper by comparison. He realised why nobody wore coats when he got very hot in Pemberton's and discovered how difficult it was to find anywhere to hang your jacket, especially if you wanted to be reunited with it later in the evening.

He moved among young people drinking beer out of bottles and Red Bull and exotically flavoured vodkas. He saw much popping of pills, and very little ecstasy except in drug form. Calling a drug Ecstasy was like calling his street Orchard View Close and calling Nicola's hotel the Cornucopia. Modern English replaced reality instead of illuminating it.

Juanita commented that people here had so much compared to Peruvians, why did they seem so desperate? Alan said that the British in the mass had never had a natural talent for enjoying themselves.

Desperation and violence never seemed far away, Alan thought, but he didn't feel disposed to condemn these people. Many of them worked in jobs of mind-numbing boredom in call centres and banks and building societies and insurance companies, jobs where all the interest was in the balance sheet and none in the job. It was a society whose main activity was moving money around so that as many people as possible could get their hands on some of it. It was a society without any real foundation, and one day it might implode.

If you spent your mornings saying, 'Good morning, my name is Donna, how can I help you?' and your afternoons saying, 'Good afternoon, my name is Donna, how can I help you?' it would be a very harsh moralist who condemned you for spending your Friday and Saturday evenings saying, 'Good evening, my name is Donna, how can I fuck you?'

Alan didn't condemn this new world that he was discovering. He even found it exciting at first. His attitude was, 'I'd like a slice of the action before I decide that I disapprove of it all.'

However, there was no slice of the action for Alan. He was too old. He wouldn't have stood a chance even if he hadn't formerly been a woman. He was surrounded by female flesh, and none of it was for him.

The only person who spared him a second glance during those lonely evenings in crowded rooms was a gay young man who thought *he* was gay. Unlike Nicola, he had never been spotted as a transsexual by members of the public. Small hands and feet don't stand out like large ones. But he had been the object of occasional homophobia from men who noticed something unusual about him. When he'd asked for best minced beef in Frogmore's, a customer had said, 'Oh! Mince. Not surprised. She minces beautifully, doesn't she?' and it had taken resolve to continue to use the butcher's and not go to the supermarket for meat. Now he found himself being horrified, and that horrified him. Surely he of all people couldn't be homophobic? He rationalised it afterwards, ascribing his revulsion to the thought of what a waste it would all have been if he'd gone through three painful operations and ended up fancying men. But it made him feel uneasy.

He found it quite restful, if the truth be told, when Em and Clare took him to a lesbian club, and he knew from the start that there would be nothing doing for him. He noticed a lot of charming and gentle young lesbian couples, and others with spiky hair and even spikier manners who moved through the crowds with the relentlessness of frigates on manoeuvres. Clare's thesis was that the nice ones were motivated by love of women, and the nasty ones by hatred of men.

'I grieve when I see young people full of hate,' said Alan. 'I long to tell them that hate always hurts the hater more than it hurts the hated. I realised that when I was visited by Prentice and Mr Beresford on the same evening in hospital.'

'Sorry, what did you say?' shouted Em.

That was another problem about this world. The noise level was so high that conversation was exhausting, if not impossible. That was the whole point of this world: that you couldn't hear yourself speak and you couldn't hear yourself think. Alan, who couldn't stop thinking, who longed to communicate, felt as out of place as a diva on a karaoke night.

He thanked his children for their efforts on his behalf, and abandoned his attempts to be a man about town. He did something far more suitable for his age: he went to the Cornucopia Hotel for a quiet drink in the Warwick Bar. You never knew. He might meet a beautiful female executive on a business course far, far from home.

Oh, the ageless moaning of the rain-flecked wind. Oh, the rippling glory of the curlew's cry. Oh, the flapping of the halyards against the masts. Oh, the bobbing of the tiny boats. Oh, the startled whistle of the oystercatcher. Oh, the silence of the setting sun. Oh, the loving of a peaceful man.

Nicola couldn't have imagined what it was like to be a man about town. She was so very happy to be a woman about marsh.

Alan met her on the steps of the Cornucopia. He didn't even need to go in.

She moved to her left to avoid him just as he moved to his right to avoid her, so they blocked each other's passages – as it were. They had a little laugh about that, and he could see that she had lovely teeth. She had full lips, a long but shapely nose, and warm, grey eyes.

'I was just going in there for a drink,' he said. 'Would you think it awfully bold if I asked you to have a drink with me?'

'*Awfully* bold,' she teased. 'I don't know that I could face such boldness. Not in Throdnall.' She smiled. 'I'd love a drink,' she said, 'but not in there.'

He suggested the Norfolk, and it proved an eminently suitable watering hole.

She told him that her name was Sally Garfield, and she was forty-two. She was wearing a blouse and skirt, and he could see that she had delicious, shapely, slightly fleshy legs and not inconsiderable breasts. He decided that he liked Sally Garfield. He enjoyed listening to her tales of her youth in Devon, her unsuccessful marriage to a boat builder, her career as a designer for a furniture maker in Bristol, her trip to Throdnall to see a client.

He was more than happy to tell her the details of his life too. He told her that his name was Alan Hargreaves, and he was Professor of History at Warwick University. The next day he would wonder what possessed him to tell these lies. Was it a juvenile desire to impress a lady, or a sudden loss of faith in his own credentials, or did it run deeper? Had he begun to realise that his new role as a bachelor hunter was untenable?

He took her to dinner at the Positano. She asked if the veal was humanely reared and, when told that no assurance could be given, chose melanzana parmigiana instead. He liked that.

She asked him awkward questions about history, and he told her that he had enough of that at work, and he wanted to talk not about the past but about the future – their future.

They had a second bottle of wine, which was unwise. He offered her a sambuca and she accepted, but astonished him by saying, 'Are you sure you'll be able to perform after all this alcohol?'

It pierced his heart, that night at the Positano, that he was not a complete man.

He ordered a taxi. She expressed surprise that he lived in Throdnall and not in beautiful Warwick. He explained that it was cheaper and he needed to save money for his very expensive research trips, which weren't as exciting as they sounded because he often ended up sitting in very exotic places feeling lonely. She stroked his leg at that point.

He didn't usually approve of sexy behaviour in taxis. It was so unfair on the driver, but that night he couldn't resist. Her mouth was so lovely and her left breast fitted so beautifully into the palm of his hand.

It pierced his heart, that night in the taxi, that he was not a complete man.

He led her upstairs through the silent house to the master bedroom. They sat on the bed and he ran his hand up her thigh under her skirt and what he felt was very beautiful. He was very excited and felt very sick indeed.

'There's something I have to tell you, Sally,' he said.

'That's intriguing,' she replied. Her words were more than slightly slurred.

'I'm . . . er . . . I've had a sex change,' he said. 'I used to be called Alison.'

She gawped at him and removed his hand from her thigh. He sniffed it to see if it had any scent from her, but it didn't.

'I think you've been telling porkies,' she said. 'I think you've been a very naughty man.'

'What makes you think that?' he said.

'You're Alan Divot,' she said. 'There can't be two Alisons who became Alans in Throdnall. You're a very very naughty man. Such porky pies!'

'I'm sorry.'

'Oh don't worry,' she said sadly, with a touch of bitterness. 'I've been telling porkies too.'

This revelation did not entirely surprise Alan. He was fairly drunk, but not so drunk that he couldn't realise that it was unlikely that Sally Garfield from Bristol would know of his change from Alison Divot to Alan Divot.

'Shall I tell you why I was coming out of the Cornucopia?' She was even drunker than he was.

'Well yes,' he said. 'Tell me.'

'I'd gone in to leave a little note on my husband's desk, because he was supposed to be on late duty. "Don't bother to come home tonight, you bastard. You'll be locked out."'

Now Alan *was* surprised.

'Sally Gulyas!' he gasped. 'I don't believe this. I . . .'

Don't tell her!

'He's started not to bother to hide his affairs from me. That shows . . . lack of respect. Don't you think it shows lack of respect, Alan?'

313

'I certainly do. It shows lack of respect, Sally.'

'Exactly. That's what I think. It shows lack of respect. He deserves to have his wife having an affair with . . . with his . . . with his boss's ex-wife.'

'Sally, I have to tell you, they're good doctors but they aren't miracle workers. I can't . . . I mean it's just not possible. I would love, however, to give you as much pleasure as I can . . . in other ways.'

'Sounds reasonable to me.'

She gave a shout of laughter and kicked her feet high in the air on the bed.

'Alan Divot!' she shrieked. 'Wonderful! He deserves it.'

They undressed. She had a stretch mark or two and the very faintest hint of cellulite, but her breasts were high and her legs were seriously lovely and her stomach was surprisingly flat, and he felt that he had never seen anything as beautiful in his life. She knew what he had been, and what he was and what he wasn't, and what he could do and what he couldn't do, and he knew that she wouldn't blame him for any shortcomings or indeed any longgoings that he might display.

He gave her as much pleasure as he could, and she gave him as much pleasure as she could, and he thought himself a lucky man, and then they fell asleep in each other's arms.

In the morning he felt proud, ashamed, happy, disgusted, knackered, hungover, raffish and weedy, all at the same time.

He made them breakfast, and as she ate her toast and marmalade, wearing his dressing gown, she said, 'I'm not sorry for what I've done. He's had or tried to have every good-looking woman in Throdnall, and one or two who aren't good-looking as well.'

Has he indeed?

He longed to say to her – and of course he couldn't – that he had only had two flings since he first got married, and they were with Mr and Mrs Gulyas. What could possibly be more appropriate for a transsexual?

31 Los Altiplanos

The Latin American Club was small and intimate and very unimposing, and Juanita would feel at home there, and it seemed the obvious choice.

It consisted of a ground floor room, which had recently been licensed for weddings as well as alcohol, an upstairs room where they would hold the reception, a kitchen at the back of the ground floor, two small guest bedrooms in the cellar and two more in the attic. The building had formerly been the premises of Piccalilli Circus.

It was frequented by a smattering of people from South and Central America who had moved into the Throdnall area. There was the only truly untalented Brazilian footballer ever to come to Britain. He played left back for Throdnall Athletic. There was a Guatemalan priest who was on a year's exchange with a priest from Solihull. There were students and an Argentinian chef and his family, and there was a Chilean on a three-month contract to investigate the feasibility of creating a vineyard between Throdnall and Cluffield, near the Farm Shop. (Nicola sometimes wondered what had happened to Gordon, though she could guess. Alan went once to the Farm Shop and found that Nicola's guess had been correct – nothing had happened to Gordon.)

It was all very informal. Gray wore a lightweight suit with very broad lapels and no tie. His bride wore a long, flowing yellow dress and had yellow ribbons in her long, black Spanish hair. Alan wore his brightest and least formal suit, with a rather daring Paul Smith tie. Nicola looked almost excessively feminine in pink. Em and Clare wore carefully orchestrated trouser suits in green and purple. They might as well have carried placards stating, 'We are an item'. Bernie wore his smartest suit, which was also his least smart suit, being his only suit. Peggy looked somewhat overdressed in a long red Max Mara number, with a gold necklace, but at eighty-seven nobody was going to object. The registrar wore quite well for her years. You wouldn't have guessed she was fifty-three if she hadn't kept telling you.

There were only a few other guests – university friends of Gray, Peruvian contacts of Juanita, and the manageress of the club.

After the ceremony there was Chilean wine, being nearest, since very little Peruvian wine is exported, and a rather strange Anglo-Peruvian buffet, with ceviche nestling alongside coronation chicken, but it worked.

In an imaginative touch, well suited to the Divots of Throdnall, Gray chose Em as his best man.

At the end of the buffet, Em rose to speak. She was very nervous, and shaking slightly, but when her voice trembled it was from emotion and not from nerves.

'Welcome to this so so happy occasion,' she said. 'I am so proud to be my dear brother's best man, not that this is to be taken as any reflection on any role I might play in my relationship with Clare.' She blew an unaffected, unembarrassed little kiss towards Clare. 'Rather I think Gray sees it as a gesture symbolic of the unusual sexual history of my own immediate family.

Gray has always fully understood the traditional role of a brother in a British family, which is to be a pain in the arse. He fulfilled it splendidly for many years, but then something happened. He grew into a lovely young man.'

Her voice trembled. Alan, awash with pride and love, but trying to hide it because now he was a man, looked across and caught Nicola's eye and knew that she was also awash with love and pride, and wasn't attempting to hide it, because she was now a woman. Neither of them heard Em for a few moments as they held each other's looks. Then there was a laugh, and Nicola averted her eyes suddenly, and they both began to listen to Em again, although Alan could hardly concentrate. Something had happened.

'Gray always seemed odd. Now here he is, the only straight heterosexual in two generations of our little family. You've always wanted to be so modern, and it turns out you're thoroughly old-fashioned.

'Gray met Juanita on the Internet. I think it was very brave of him, but it was even braver of Juanita. She came all the way from her lovely Spanish southern Peruvian city of Arequipa to live in Throdnall. You can't be much braver than that. Juanita, we are so glad you did. We love you.

'You all know the story of Gray's and my mum and dad, who are now our dad and mum. It's been written up so brilliantly by that superb newspaper, the *Throdnall Advertiser*, by their ace female reporter. I know that they are both very proud today.'

Alan looked across at Nicola again, but this time she didn't return his gaze.

'In a moment we'd like you all to go downstairs while the room is rearranged. We have a lovely Peruvian group here tonight, from the town of Puno on Lake Titicaca. They are touring Britain and have given their services tonight for expenses only, though there will be a plate for contributions. They are called Los Altiplanos and I know you will give them a warm Throdnall welcome.

'Well, that's enough of me, but now I want you to listen to a very special recording. Juanita's parents can't be here today, but they are with us in spirit. Thank you.'

Em returned to her seat. Clare ran her hand swiftly over Em's crutch and hoped that nobody noticed.

The manageress switched on the recording. A man's voice crackled out to them from far away, in stilted English.

'Hello, everybody. Hello, Juanita. Hello, Gray-ham. I am Alfredo. I am Juanita's father. I wish you happy day.'

A female voice came on, even slower and more stilted.

'I wish you happy day. I am Maria. I am Juanita's mother.'

The male voice resumed.

'We welcoming you soon, Gray-ham and Gray-ham's ma and pa in Arequipa? Yes? We hope. Many many thank you to listen from us, and very many happinesses.'

While the room was being set up, Alan found it difficult to engineer a private word with Nicola. There were so many people downstairs, some of them drinking Peruvian beer from the bottle, a few venturing on to Peruvian pisco sours, and Cuban mehitos, full of mint and sugar and white rum.

When it was announced that the band was ready, people began to move upstairs again, but Alan managed to get himself beside Nicola and stopped her moving by engaging her in conversation.

'Thank you for not bringing Eric. It was considerate.'

'Of him. I wanted him to come. He felt it . . . inappropriate.'

'I see.'

'He's a very sensitive man.'

'Clearly.'

This was not at all the conversation that Alan had planned. How foolish, he told himself. He should have known at his age that you can't plan conversations. Other people can't be relied upon to say what you expect. Other people are notoriously awkward.

Em came into the room from upstairs, and said, 'I hope I'm not interrupting anything.'

'Definitely not,' said Alan.

'Oh.' She sounded disappointed. 'Well it's just . . . we're all needed upstairs. Gray and Juanita are going to do a little dance.'

'What??'

'I know. Where's our awkward, gawky little Gray?'

She led them up to where Los Altiplanos, four short stocky young men with wild faces and even wilder haircuts, or absences of haircuts, were poised. At their side stood Juanita and Gray. Em took Alan and Nicola to seats that had been saved for them.

Gray stepped forward. Both Alan and Nicola thought how handsome he looked, hardly gawky at all, though he should get more flattering glasses.

'Ladies and gentlemen,' he began, with an assurance that astounded them, 'before we let you all dance as we know you're longing to, there will be a special presentation of a Peruvian handkerchief dance by Juanita and I . . . what am I saying? My mum will kill me . . . by Juanita and me. Allow yourselves to be transported to the bare, bleak, haunting lands of the Andean altiplano, where the condors roam and the pan pipes moan. Ladies and gentlemen, the dance of the virgins.'

The music began, rich with melancholy, sodden with wistfulness. Alan and Nicola felt the hairs on their necks stiffen. Juanita was expert, graceful, unselfconscious, beautiful to behold, and Gray . . . well, he was adequate. They couldn't believe it. Their own son, adequate!

Alan's eyes were full of tears. He turned to look at Nicola just as she turned to look at him, and he saw that her eyes were full of tears too. He felt a huge love for Nicola at that moment – a revelatory love. It was Marks and Spencer's all over again, a revelation not on the road to Damascus but in the former premises of Piccalilli Circus.

He was a man. Nicola was a woman. There was no obstacle to their loving each other. They had been so obsessed with making new lives that the thought had never crossed their minds. Sally was beautiful. Her body gave him great pleasure on their occasional meetings, but each meeting ended with a feeling of faint disgust and a desire to end the affair, which would be followed, after about a week, by a desire to meet again. He didn't love Sally, and she accepted his unfulfilled and unfulfilling cavortings only to get her own back, in private, on Ferenc. He was manking about. But Nicola – he had loved her for more than a quarter of a century.

All that takes longer to express than to think. The thoughts came not in neat sentences but all at once in a flash, with the dance so riveting and beautiful in the background.

Alan hoped that all this was in his look, but what was in Nicola's?

She held his look for quite a while, but then she turned away. Alan knew that something had happened, but he wasn't sure what.

At the end of the dance the applause shook the rafters. Juanita accepted it with delight. Gray returned to gawkiness at the last. Nicola saw Em jumping up and down with joy. What a generous young woman she had become.

Alan turned to Nicola and invited her to dance. She couldn't refuse.

It wasn't ballroom dancing, of course. You couldn't waltz to the music of Los Altiplanos. The band grinned. The young cavorted. Alan wanted to say so much, but he couldn't get near enough to the frenzied, inelegant dervish that Nicola had become.

Los Altiplanos played a slow, more mournful piece, and Alan clutched Nicola and held her almost motionless as they moved very slowly around the minuscule floor.

'Were you proud of Gray?' he asked into her ear.

'Of course I was.'

'As proud as you would have been if he'd been your son?'

'Of course I was. What kind of love would it be that was dependent on that?'

Alan squeezed Nicola's hand. There was no answering squeeze.

Between numbers the musicians would briefly confer over what to play next. Then they would change some of their instruments. They had brought so many. In the course of the evening they played three kinds of pan pipe: the huge zampona, the flute-like quena made of cane, and the little antara. They played the twelve-stringed charango made of armadillo shell. They played mandolins, guitars, drums, tambourines and a comb stroked against the side of a gourd. Throdnall became exotic that night.

It was exciting, emotional stuff, with dramatic changes of

tempo that sent surges of adrenalin into the bloodstream of the listener.

But to Alan this was not the time for music. Only one thing could have sent a surge into his bloodstream.

'I must have a word, Nicola,' he mouthed to the music.

He led her over to a far corner of the little room, and there they sat, so unobtrusively that their unobtrusiveness might have been blazoned in lights. Em and Clare, Gray and Juanita, Bernie and Peggy, even in this emotional and lively gathering all of them were so aware that there in the corner were Alan and Nicola, trying to conceal the fact that they were holding a meaningful conversation.

This conversation occurred in little bursts while the musicians conferred after each tune. It was impossible to talk during the music.

'I have to tell you this,' said Alan. 'I am a man. You are a woman. There is no obstacle to our loving each other.'

Nicola made no reply.

'I know it's ridiculous, but it's only just occurred to me, so it occurred to me that it might not have occurred to you. Nicola, I love you.'

The music stopped them before Nicola could reply. Maybe she would not have replied.

'I love you far more than I did when we were our original sex,' resumed Alan as soon as the next tune had stopped. 'We were a couple of fumbling freaks, for God's sake, and now we're both truly ourselves. We did all right, on the whole, for half a lifetime. Think what we could do together now. I love you. I don't want you to go. There! That's pretty straight and up-front for Throdnall, isn't it? Why do you have to go?'

'I . . .'

'Don't tell me you love Eric.'

'Please don't start running Eric down. I know you don't like him, but he's a dear dear kind loving lovely man.'

The music began again. Alan pretended to be listening intently.

He didn't know whether Nicola was listening intently or also pretending to. He didn't know what she was thinking.

This was perhaps as important a discussion as Alan had ever had in his life, and it was being conducted as if it was the conversational equivalent of a game of musical chairs. The moment the music stopped he resumed his impassioned pleas as if he had never been interrupted.

'I know he is,' he said. 'I'm not jealous of him any more. I just don't believe you love him. Do you love him?'

Nicola looked at him like a cornered rat. She wasn't prepared to say that she did and she wasn't prepared to say that she didn't. She thought of saying, 'What is love?' or 'Does anybody know what love really is?', but managed to avoid such pathetic cop-outs.

She gave a helpless little shrug.

'We've learnt a lot from all we've . . .' began Alan, and again the music stopped him. Em glanced anxiously in their direction.

'We've learnt a lot from all we've been through,' continued Alan when the musicians conferred once more, 'and if at the end of all that we haven't learnt that true love should be an unselfish emotion we've learnt nothing. If you truly love Eric, then go, be with him, be happy, I want you to be happy, Nicola. If you truly love him, you go with my blessing. You really do. But I don't believe that you do. You don't live with him. I think you're very fond of him, but I don't think you love him. That's all. You don't need to say anything now.'

Nicola didn't look as if she had any intention of saying anything.

'Perhaps we'd better move,' said Alan, 'or people will start looking at us.'

32 Reflections on the Validity of the Turner Prize

The tide was coming in, sliding sexily up the creeks, lifting the boats off the mud, sending the birds packing. An oystercatcher piped noisily overhead.

Nicola had arrived the previous evening. It had been a long drive; traffic had been heavy. She had crawled through the flat lands of the Fens, where the fields were like carpets of sticky toffee pudding. She had felt extremely tense. She hadn't known that she was going to feel extremely tense.

'I've made a real Norfolk fish stew,' he had said.

'Good-oh,' she had said.

'So, how was the wedding?' he had asked.

'It went all right. No, it was very good actually.'

'Good.'

'Actually it was extremely moving and I was very proud of Gray and Em.'

'I'm so glad.'

Was he?

The fish stew was subtle but just a little thin, Nicola had thought. Rather like Eric. She'd felt ashamed of herself for having that thought.

She hadn't wanted to make love. She hadn't known that she wouldn't want to make love. She had feigned extreme tiredness and he had suggested that she went up early while he cleared up. He could never leave anything less than immaculate. He might be awash with desire, but he'd still lay out the breakfast things ready for the next morning.

When he had come up to bed, Nicola had feigned sleep in the

pale, pink bedroom. She hadn't needed to do that for a long while, but it was like riding a bicycle, once learnt never forgotten.

In the morning Eric had driven the car to Thornham, painfully slowly, and now they were walking along the coastal path to Hunstanton.

'It's good to have you back,' he said.

'It's good to be back,' she said.

It was and it wasn't.

They walked steadily, trying to keep themselves warm. There was a cruel, snidey breeze from the north, and the air was as raw as herrings. If the sad sky had begun to weep it would have lost control and deluged.

The path plunged into a melancholy wood. Nicola felt that she would die of gloom among the dark trees if she didn't say something cheerful.

'I felt that old feeling as I left Kings Lynn behind and turned north for Hunstanton,' she said. 'That feeling of coming home.'

She had and she hadn't.

'Good,' he said.

She wished she hadn't said it.

Now the path was in the open again. It rose and fell across the dunes like a miniature Alpine pass. To the seaward side there were salt lagoons, where shelduck swam serenely. A cormorant flew low over the water, late for an appointment as always.

'Birds live and die and leave no individual mark, and neither will I,' said Eric.

'Eric! Don't be so depressing,' said Nicola.

'Oh, it doesn't depress me in the least,' he said. 'I think it's a relief.'

Yes, his mood was strange, and she wondered how much he knew of her mood.

They walked along the side of the golf course. Only one hardy couple had braved the winds on that early spring day.

A tiny wren scolded them valiantly.

'See what I mean?' said Eric.

She did and she didn't.

They caught a bus back to Thornham from Hunstanton. They sat in the front seat upstairs, as if that could bring back the spirit of childhood. They lunched on smoked salmon and chardonnay in the Lifeboat Inn, and then Eric drove, painfully slowly, to Wells-Next-The-Sea. Eric told her that Wells had once been a raffish place. People from Burnham Market had only gone there in disguise. Now it was Chelsea-Next-The-Sea.

Easter was coming, and the tourist attractions had just begun to creak into gear for the season. They went to an exhibition of marine paintings in a tiny gallery, and then to a little tea shop in a sweet old cottagey street. It would all have been twee, had it not been beautiful.

They discussed the works that they had just seen, which had been pleasant, safe, a million miles from the world of the Turner Prize.

'What do you think of the Turner Prize?' Nicola asked.

'I can't comment on its recent decisions,' said Eric, 'because I haven't seen the works in question except in the papers and on television, but I hate the whole award. I hate it because I hate all prizes, and I hate it particularly among prizes because Turner would have hated it, because Turner hated all prizes.'

She gazed at Eric, and she drank of his passion among the toasted tea cakes, and she knew that she loved him at that moment as much as she ever could.

'Art is about truth, not glory,' he continued. 'It's about beauty, not rank.'

She wished that she could listen solely to Eric's words, and not have to listen at the same time to her emotional reaction to those words.

'Nothing in the world of creative art is as contemptible, in my opinion, as to shock for the sake of shocking, and if that is what these Turner artists are doing they are traitors to art,' said her furniture restorer.

She felt privileged to listen, she felt proud and moved that she agreed, but she had nothing to contribute.

'Nothing in the world of art is as craven as not daring to shock when necessary,' Eric continued. 'Shock is the most precious of all the weapons in art's armoury, and that is why to abuse it is the most serious crime in the world of art.'

Yes, at that moment she loved Eric as much as she ever could, and she knew that it was not enough.

She lay back as he clambered on to her. She made all the right noises and all the right movements, and she didn't think there was any way in which he could have deduced that she was playing a bridge hand in her head, for fear that she would be unable to go through with it if she thought about it too closely. She bid two hearts and her partner went three spades and she felt that a small slam might be on, and by the time that they'd bid it and she had played the hand and made the small slam Eric had come inside her with *such* energy and with *such* a cry: Oh yes! He wasn't only passionate among the toasted tea cakes.

Quite soon after that they were asleep, oh blessed sleep, far far from owls and lies.

In the morning, after their immaculate breakfast, laid the night before and served on the best Worcester, with not a milk bottle to be seen and the evenly browned toast wrapped in an Irish linen cloth, Eric said, 'You still love him, don't you?'

33 Up the Wooden Stairs to Bedfordshire

The sun beamed with pleasure on Alan and Nicola's wedding day. It shone on the fourteenth-century church of St James. It shone on the bird shit on the roof of the Cornucopia Hotel. It shone on the unlovely lift-shaft tops that disfigured the unlovely roofs and the unlovely sixties blocks that dwarfed the fine old church.

It shone on Mr Beresford, but he didn't notice.

They had spent their wedding eve in traditional separation, but not for them the excesses of stag fortnights in Prague and hen weeks in Dublin. Alan had taken Bernie and Peggy to the Positano, and Nicola had been given a Peruvian dinner cooked by Juanita.

They had remained in separate beds until after the wedding, even though Nicola had gone back to number thirty-three after she had confirmed Eric's suspicion that it was over. Alan had slept in the master bedroom, Nicola in the granny flat. This was less a moral gesture, fatuous in today's climate, than an attempt to make their second wedding day something special. They felt that something should be denied them before the marriage, so that the day itself might seem, and indeed be, special.

Neither of them slept well on the wedding eve, Nicola at number thirty-three, where Gray and Juanita were spending the night, so that Juanita could help Nicola get ready in the morning, and Alan at Bernie and Peggy's flat.

Mr Beresford did not sleep well either.

By eight o'clock Peggy was cooking Alan a man's breakfast in their flat, Juanita was cooking Nicola a Peruvian breakfast in number thirty-three, and Mr Beresford was in all probability walking across his dewy lawn towards his garden shed. It must have been about that time, according to the pathologist.

They had wondered whether to invite Mr Beresford and his wife. In the end, reluctantly, they did. However, they didn't turn up. They couldn't. They were both dead.

Round about half past eight Alan finished his breakfast with a slice of toast and marmalade – the sweetness of the marmalade was luscious after all the fat – a nervous Nicola gave up the struggle to do justice to Juanita's splendid bacon and eggs – yes, they have those in Peru too – and a loud scream from the jobbing gardener in the grounds of Helvellyn, home of the Beresfords, awoke their neighbours in Gairloch and froze the blood in their veins.

The police called first at number thirty-three, whence Nicola directed them to the flat.

Bernie answered the door, and came to Alan with a pale, stricken face.

'It's the police,' he said. 'They want you, Alan. I told them it were your wedding day. "It's his bloody nuptials like," I said.'

'Bernie! Talking to the police like that!' said Peggy.

'Aye, but it's his wedding day. It's not right. I were resentful. I were being protective.'

Alan hadn't stayed to hear Bernie's justifications. He hurtled to the door, heart pounding.

'It's a Mr Clive Beresford,' said the police officer, and a wave of the most enormous relief churned through Alan and made him go all weak at the knees. Oh, thank goodness. Oh, thank God. It was nothing to do with Nicola.

'What's happened?'

'He's been found dead in his garden shed. First indications are that he's hanged himself.'

It was a shock – a terrible shock. Of course it was. On that emotional morning Alan felt a great swirl of conflicting sensations: compassion for the misery Mr Beresford must have endured to bring him to that; compassion as he saw, more vividly in his mind than he had ever seen it in the flesh, the sadness in Mr Beresford's face; but also, he had to admit, he felt relief, overwhelming relief that this was not something that affected his family, that it was not something which anybody could reasonably suggest was a cause for postponing the wedding. Also, he had to admit this too, he felt spasms of irritation (Oh God, we'll have to rearrange the table plan) and even of hatred (I bet the bastard chose this day deliberately – he never liked me).

'I appreciate that this is serious,' said Alan, 'but it's my wedding day. Can't it wait?'

'I'm sorry, sir. We need you to take us to his office, show us a few things. We don't want to break in. We'll drive you there, drive you back. We'll get you to the church on time, don't you worry.'

So Alan whipped on a few clothes, didn't shave – he still didn't quite need to every day though obviously he would today – and was driven across Throdnall, up Sir Nigel Gresley Boulevard (longing to make an illegal U-turn) and into the office block, deserted on a Saturday morning. Suddenly his office, and Mr Beresford's, seemed utterly dead, defunct. The great sheds stood silent too, now that there was no weekend working due to slackness of business. He began to wonder about his job, and then an even more pressing worry struck him.

'I'm off on my honeymoon tomorrow. I hope you won't need me for questioning.'

'No need for that, sir. We will question you, but on your return. The inquest will be adjourned. In any case, you are not a material witness.'

'That surprises me,' said Alan. 'I should have thought I knew about the difficulties at the works as well as anybody.'

'We can't say too much, sir, but I think I can inform you that Mr Beresford's presumed suicide is not considered to be a direct result of trading difficulties.'

They took away one whole filing cabinet, for which only Mr

Beresford had a key, and all the books relating to financial matters.

One of the officers rushed Alan back while the other officer continued to search the office and move stuff downstairs. As they drove (and even at that awful time he felt a certain thrill at being sped across the town with the aid of a police siren, traffic at a standstill on and around the Colton roundabout and all because of him!) he thought that it might be worth asking a few more questions. Maybe this officer would be less discreet when not accompanied by his colleague.

'Can't you tell me anything about what kind of thing you're investigating? If you leave me in the dark, I may imagine things that are worse than the truth. That's how damaging rumours start.'

'Let's just say that the company accountant has discovered a huge black hole in the company accounts. We're talking millions.'

'My God! Do we have any idea where it's gone?'

'None whatsoever, sir. A prostitute in Peckham has purchased a Porsche.' The officer frowned, perhaps at the severity of his attack of alliteration, perhaps in recognition that he was being excessively indiscreet. 'That may be nothing to do with it, of course. However, the same lady of the street has been seen recently in Throdnall and Mauritius with Mr Beresford. It would be indiscreet of me to say more than that, sir.'

'But what about Mrs Beresford?'

'What indeed, sir? That is the question.'

'And what's the answer?'

'I think it would be very foolish of me to speculate on that before we've dug up his new patio on Monday morning.'

'Good God.'

'Indeed, sir.'

They drove the rest of the way in silence. The officer was worried that he had said too much, and Alan was absolutely shaken. He knew that such things happened, of course, but one didn't expect them to happen to people one knew.

*

As Alan bedecked himself in his hired morning suit, and as he saw Peggy and Bernie give each other's hands a quick little stroke, he strove to put the morning's dramatic events behind him. He began to emerge from the dark tunnel into which Mr Beresford had (deliberately?) plunged him.

The sky was blue, the sun was shining, he would not let any more shadows spoil his great day.

The reason for their marrying in church, incidentally, was that the vicar of Throdnall, the Reverend Simon Phillips, got in touch with them to tell them that they would be most welcome.

'We aren't believers,' Alan had told him.

'God understands,' he had said. 'He gave you free will. He hopes that by marrying in church you may be helped to *become* believers. I must come clean. I am a passionately liberal Christian. I would welcome not only women priests, but gay priests and lesbian priests, so long as they are good people. I believe that the battle between human good and human evil will be decided for ever – I was going to say "for good" but I can't be that confident! – during the twenty-first century. Weapons are now so terrible that man must be destroyed if he doesn't destroy the evil in him. You will be pawns in my political game, sending a message of tolerance to the world.'

Alan and Nicola had thought that it might be better to be loved than tolerated, but they hadn't quibbled. It amused them, after the simplicity of their first wedding, to hold their second in the Perpendicular splendour of St James's.

Entry to the church was by invitation only, due to security fears, not so much political as that some self-righteous freak would take a pot shot at one or both of them, or object when invited to do so and cause a scene.

As he walked solemnly towards the door of the church Alan became aware that it would not be easy for him to avoid letting more shadows spoil his great day – a huge shadow loomed across

331

the path, and he realised that it was being cast by twenty-four stone of blubber.

'They won't let me in,' said Prentice. 'I keep telling them that I'm the bride's best friend. They don't believe me. They say, "If you're the bride's best friend, why aren't you invited?" I must say it's a good question.'

'I'm sorry, Prentice. It's me really,' admitted Alan. 'How can I put this tactfully? I can't stand you.'

'I'm not surprised,' said Prentice, not in the least upset. 'I can't either, but I do think I could at least be allowed in the church now I'm here.'

Alan instructed the ushers to allow Prentice in.

Nicola arrived at the church late. The wedding car had been delayed by road works. They were removing the speed bumps from all the roads around Orchard View Close. The humps had caused problems for ambulances.

Alan thought that Nicola looked quite wonderful that day. She was wearing a lovely full-length ivory silk dress and a long-sleeved jacket with a stand-up collar. The jacket was most beautifully beaded. On her head she had a little beaded tiara with a short veil. She had lovely, specially made ivory shoes, which managed to look delicate even on her large feet, and she carried a simple spray of three cream lilies. She embodied elegance with simplicity.

It was a huge church and far from full, but the Reverend Simon Phillips ensured that it all went with a swing. Nicola and Alan both admitted afterwards that when it came to the moment for anyone who objected to speak up, they dreaded some ghastly joke from Prentice. None came.

After the service, as the happy couple and their family posed for photographs, Prentice hovered.

'We've got to invite him now. He *is* my oldest friend,' said Nicola.

'But he's awful.'

'He is now.'

'He always was from what you've told me.'

'I suppose that's true, but he's still my oldest friend, and he's not a happy bunny.'

'Oh God,' sighed Alan. He gave a swift cheesy smile as the cameraman clicked into action. 'Oh Lord. I concede with deepest foreboding.'

The reception was held in the Cornucopia – where else? The refurbishment had happened at last. They started with champagne and canapés in the splendidly refurbished Aston Suite, still watched over by Charlie Athersmith, Pongo Waring, Ron Saunders, Charlie Aitken and Peter McParland. Alan said, 'I don't at all mind these photos of Aston Villa heroes. Historically, Spurs have always done quite well against Villa.' One of the great minor pleasures of becoming a man, for Alan, was that he didn't have to face constant surprise when he revealed that he loved football.

The champagne was good, and the canapés were GFT (Good For Throdnall). Over the champagne Alan and Nicola talked to as many guests as possible, including Sir Terence and Lady Manningham (good employment move to invite the chairman), who were graciousness personified, and Lance Windlass, who said to Nicola, 'Missed the boat as per bloody usual, didn't I? Trust old Lance.'

There was a strong medical representation. It was a pleasure to see Mr and Mrs McWhinnie, Doctor and Mrs Langridge, and Doctor and Miss Rodgerson (his wife had died, so he took his daughter). They put them all on a table together for the wedding breakfast, and they told tales of medical disasters to each other till they dropped.

There were Gray's best friends from uni, and a couple of Peruvians who had become good friends of Juanita, and there was Connie from the carriage works with her husband Tony. Work wouldn't have been bearable for Alan if he hadn't invited Connie. (Work! Would there be any work now?) Connie commented, 'You didn't invite Mr Beresford then?' and they had to tell her what had happened, so that for a few moments at least, not exactly perhaps a shadow, more a shadow of a shadow, if a shadow can have a shadow, passed across their sunny day. 'It's awful,' said Connie, 'but I can't find any tears for Mr Beresford. He wasn't a man who inspired affection.' What an epitaph. Then she said, 'And he was always so religious. Sometimes I feel quite sorry for God. He has such awful friends.' Alan thought that was surprisingly well put, for Connie.

Nicola was pleased and relieved that Eric came. She hadn't been able to get her last sight of him out of her mind. He had been standing at the door of his cottage, waving goodbye. A herring gull had been shrieking angrily from his chimney, and on his face there had been one of the saddest smiles that she had ever seen. It was a relief to see him now, looking so dapper and neat. They had a nice little chat over the champagne . . . 'No more, thank you, I'm not a big champagne man.' Alan was very friendly to him in victory, and was a little ashamed of his earlier jealousy. Eric smiled a lot, and hoped that they'd be very happy, and that they could remain friends. He invited them to north Norfolk if they ever wanted to go, though it was one of those vague invitations, with no date attached, the sort you don't take up – but still, he did it. Alan asked Nicola later in the day how sad she thought Eric really was – he'd made a great play of being a confirmed bachelor, liking his own company etcetera – did she think he protested too much? She felt that she didn't know him quite well enough to know. Eric was the sort of person you could never quite know, which was why you could never quite fall in love with him.

Ferenc was supervising the whole food and drink side of things, while Sally was there as a guest, at his request. Their joint presence verged on being a shadow for Alan, and Ferenc wished that he hadn't had to invite Sally when Gray went up to him for his very first meeting with his real father, right in the middle of the Aston Suite, just beneath Pongo Waring.

'Hello, Dad,' he said. 'How are you diddling?'

Ferenc looked round anxiously towards Sally.

'Oh, don't worry,' said Gray. 'I won't spill the beans. I don't regard myself as your son. You mean nothing to me. I've got a wonderful dad. She looks great, don't you think?'

'Lovely. Fantastic. And I'm sorry, Gray.'

'I don't accept your apology, sorry,' said Gray. 'I think it's awful that you haven't even spoken to me, and I'm only speaking to you to scare you in front of your wife.' He moved off, back towards Juanita, who was looking lovely in traditional Peruvian costume.

After the Champagne reception they moved for the wedding breakfast to the equally splendidly refurbished St Andrew's Suite, where they were overlooked by such Birmingham City luminaries as Joe Bradford, Harry Hibs, Bob Latchford, Jeff Hill and Frank Womack. Alan said, 'I don't object to all these either. There's no way Birmingham could be described as one of our bogey teams.'

The meal of Welsh cawl (is there any other kind?), duck goulash (what else?) and crêpe Goole (like crêpe suzette but with Bailey's – the invention of Leonard Balby, who refused to participate in a meal of Welsh and Hungarian specialities unless he laid his own stamp on the proceedings. 'It's my new signature dish, is crêpe Goole,' he averred) was 'better than it sounds', which was the restaurant equivalent of 'as comfortable as can be expected'. It was all 'washed down', as they say so inelegantly in the restaurant reviews, with 2002 New Zealand Marlborough cabernet sauvignon, 1998 Mercurey and Niepoort Fine Tawny Port – non-vintage, in other words decanted, so the guests didn't see the bottles.

After the meal there were the usual speeches, and then, at the end of the speeches, the great shadow that was Prentice loomed over the proceedings.

'I would like to say a few words,' he shouted. 'I am Nick's oldest friend.'

Unease flowed across the room like lava. Maybe the guests saw the tension in the faces of Nicola and Alan and Em and Gray and even Bernie.

'My name's Prentice Prentice,' said Prentice. 'I was actually born John Prentice, but that was too ordinary for me. I'm a part-time comedian. I've done a stand-up spot at comedy clubs up and down the country. Don't worry. It only lasts an hour.'

Nicola thought that she might faint. She caught Em's appalled eye.

'Nicola and Alan have been extremely brave,' said Prentice. 'I just want to wish them luck and raise our glasses to them one more time. To Nicola and Alan.'

Everyone stood up and said, 'To Nicola and Alan' and drank and sat down.

Prentice sat down too. Nicola and Alan and Em and Gray and Bernie couldn't believe it.

After the speeches they were all invited to go back to the Aston Suite for the dancing, and as they filed towards the door, Nicola and Alan found themselves alongside Prentice.

'Thank you for that,' said Nicola.

'That's all right,' said Prentice. 'I looked round and I realised that I had you in my power. You couldn't have shat yourselves any more, whatever I said, so I didn't need to say anything. It was brilliant. It was the culmination of my career.'

They manoeuvred Prentice out of the doorway, so that the other guests could filter through.

'Why do you feel obliged to be so unpleasant?' asked Alan.

'Because nobody has ever made love to me except for money, and never will.'

'Why do you think that is?'

'I'm so fat.'

'Prentice! There are fat people who are loved. Fat people can be happy. Fat people can be beautiful,' said Nicola.

'I know,' wailed Prentice. 'Don't you think I know that? But

I'm not. That's what makes me so angry. I'm not beautiful, and I'm not likeable.'

'Then change,' said Nicola. 'I have. Alan has. Bernie has. You can.'

'I can't. I'm a slob.'

'Stay a slob if you're happy, but you obviously aren't, so take yourself in hand.'

'I do, regularly. I have to. Nobody else will.'

'Don't be silly. I'm serious.'

'Can't cope with that.'

'Yes you can.' Nicola was fervent. Suddenly she was on a mission. 'Lose weight. Give up comedy. You know it doesn't suit you. Try being nice. You might find you take to it.'

'Do you really think I could do it?'

Nicola hesitated, chose her words carefully.

'I think it's not utterly impossible.'

Prentice rested his podgy hand briefly on Nicola's shoulder.

'I suppose that's something,' he said.

He could only get through the door sideways. They followed him as he waddled painfully to the Aston Suite.

The dancing was to the music of Throdnall's very best jazz band, which also just happened to be . . . you've guessed it . . . Throdnall's only jazz band. They hadn't wanted a disco, it wasn't that sort of wedding.

There's something a bit sad about most ageing jazz bands – it's sad that they're ageing, for a start – but it's impossible to believe that Sid Sargasso and the Doldrums weren't sad even when young: three tall men with a short percussionist, all four with white, nicotine-stained beards, two of them with red boozers' conks, and Sid himself with watery eyes and a microphone technique which managed to give the impression that he had always forgotten the next word but one.

'Drink as much beer as you like, smoke as much as you like, but play for us, not for each other,' Alan instructed them. 'We've booked you,' he added, lying through his teeth, 'for your pzazz.'

It's wonderful what a compliment will do, even an insincere one. Sid Sargasso and the Doldrums obliged them beyond their wildest dreams. Sid said afterwards, 'That's the best night we've had for ten years.'

Everyone wanted the happy couple to begin the dancing, and they had no alternative but to oblige. It was appropriate that they should perform what could well have been called The Dance Of The Double Negatives. Nicola found it hard not to forget not to lead, and Alan found it hard not to forget not to allow himself to be led – but they did all right, they tried, and people do make allowances, and certainly the applause was whole-hearted.

Bernie led Peggy on to the floor, and they tripped the light fantastic, and the years rolled away from them, but not entirely. They were as arthritic as they were ecstatic.

Eric took Nicola on to the floor just once, danced very correctly but rather stiffly, escorted her to her table, said, 'I'll be making tracks. I'm not big on dancing,' and walked out of the hotel and, they suspected, out of their lives.

Em danced, only slightly defiantly, with Clare whose dancing was cool and controlled. Em no longer harboured media ambitions. She understood her destiny and didn't rebel against it. She would become a local institution, the eccentric lesbian stalwart of the *Advertiser*, present at every Throdnall event, a legend in her Throdnall lunchtime. Clare would indulge her eccentricities, and be the rock around which she danced.

Alan took Juanita on to the floor and danced like the tomboy he once was. Gray danced with Nicola and said, 'I haven't half given bloody Ferenc a shock, *Dad*,' and winked. He no longer had any idea what he wanted to do for a living or even which continent he wanted to do it in, and he felt intoxicated by the uncertainty.

Lance fell over and had to be put in a taxi. Sir Terence Manningham danced with Nicola and said, 'To think I wanted to sack you!' and added, 'I shall be coming to stay in a few weeks' time, *without* Lady Manningham, if you get my drift.' Nicola got his drift, was thrilled by the compliment and horrified by the implications.

Ferenc felt obliged to dance with Sally. Her lovely face was disfigured by anger.

'I hadn't seen him before,' she said, as they moved slowly round the crowded floor.

'What? Who?'

'Your son.'

Ferenc stopped dead in his shock. It caused quite a traffic jam. Then they moved on.

'How did you find out?' asked Ferenc.

'I have eyes to see, and I wormed the truth out of Alan.'

'Alan? I didn't know you knew him.'

'Oh, yes, I know him. How many times did you sleep with her?'

'I don't . . . oh . . . about three, I suppose.'

'Beat you!'

'What?'

'I've slept with him six times.'

Ferenc's second shock was perhaps even greater than his first. Certainly the traffic jam on the dance floor was greater. People piled into each other. It was like being on the dodgems, but without any cars.

Nicola would always recall one image above all others from her second wedding day, and that was of the huge, grotesque Prentice gently moving around the dance floor on his own, arms held round a non-existent companion, and with a beatific smile on his face. He looked almost beautiful. Was it the smile of a man who is about to begin to change his life?

Only time will tell.

What Alan would recall most vividly was a moment of deep shock, when a huge shadow darkened his great day. He looked across the room and there was Bernie, with his head slumped forward on to a table. He was certain straightaway that he was dead. The shock sent convulsions through him. He thought for a moment that *his* heart had stopped.

Oh no! he thought. Tonight of all nights. It was a beautiful way to go, for him, happy with his Peggy on a happy day, but still . . . to have to remember your wedding day for that. And he didn't want to lose his dad. He realised just how much he loved his dad. Had he told him? Even if he had told him, had he told him enough? Too late now.

Then Bernie stirred, looked up, smiled sheepishly, and said, 'I must have nodded off.' His smile changed from sheepish to coy. 'Peggy's wearing me out.'

All too soon for some, and all too late for others, it was time for 'Auld Lang Syne', in the rather individual rendition by Sid Sargasso and the Doldrums.

So ended their second wedding. So ended the most glamorous night, perhaps, that the Cornucopia Hotel in Brindley Street had ever seen (that isn't saying much).

It was time to go 'up the wooden stairs to Bedfordshire', as Marge used to call it.

Alan and Nicola walked slowly up the recently recarpeted main staircase of the old hotel, arm in arm. They crossed the corridor and reached the door of their suite. They opened the door and went in. Alan returned to put a 'Do not disturb' notice on it.

Can it really be that they will defy medical predictions and overcome the artificial nature of their reconstituted genitalia? Or will their loving be a matter of kissing and touching? Do we really need to know? It wasn't ever about sex. It was about gender.

They have so much in common – sense of humour, love of golf and bridge, of travel and food and wine. They will exchange smiles across the log-effect fire, vie to make the best moussaka, enjoy snubbing the Collinsons, gasp politely at Bernie and Peggy's photos of their cruises, take the children of Gray and Juanita to the pantomime, with Auntie Em and Auntie Clare, to laugh at a man dressed as a woman, and to cry for a girl dressed as a man.

It's time to take our leave of them. Our age is far too interested in other people's sex lives, perhaps because it has made sex so easy that it is no longer sufficiently interested in its own. Let us, though, not regard sex as a spectator sport.

Alan closes the door. It squeaks, despite the renovations. Surely, after all they have undergone, they deserve to have their wishes respected?

Let us disturb them no more.

I Didn't Get Where I Am Today

David Nobbs' acclaimed autobiography . . .

As a small boy David Nobbs survived the Second World War unscathed, until his bedroom ceiling fell on him when the last bomb to be dropped on Britain by the Germans landed near his home. It was the nearest he came to the war, but National Service would later make him one of Britain's most reluctant soldiers. It was an unforgettable and often unpleasant experience.

As a struggling writer, David was catapulted into the thrilling world of satire at the BBC when he rang *That Was The Week That Was* with a joke and got through to David Frost, who sent a taxi for the joke. He never looked back. His greatness as a modern comic writer was confirmed by the publication of *The Fall and Rise of Reginald Perrin*, which he adapted into the immensely successful television series that has entered the fabric of British cultural life, through phrases, images and brilliant humour.

A mesmerising, beautifully told tale of a life in writing and comedy, *I Didn't Get Where I Am Today* is the hilarious, poignant and very personal story of David Nobbs' life, which also describes some of the most famous comedians of the last century and captures a golden age of British television.

'*I Didn't Get Where I Am Today* . . . is anecdotal, angry, heartfelt and laugh out loud funny' *Time Out*

'Genius got him where he is today . . . breezy, funny and often touching account of his life . . . Like all the best comic writers, he spins a healthy line in self-deprecation. . . . This book is more than just a collection of memories of life in television' *Daily Mail*

arrow books